Prince
of
Time

Bantam Books

New York
Toronto
London
Sydney
Auckland

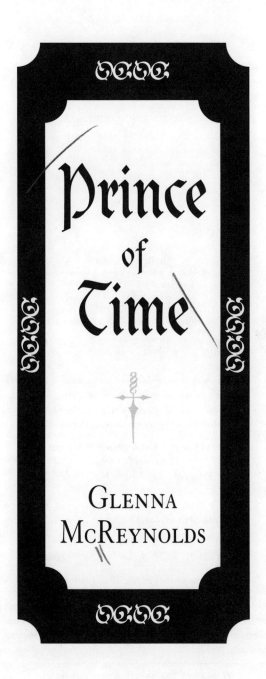

Prince of Time

Glenna McReynolds

Prince of Time

A Bantam Book / December 2000

All rights reserved.
Copyright © 2000 by Glenna McReynolds

Maps by Jackie Aher

Library of Congress Cataloging-in-Publication Data
McReynolds, Glenna.
Prince of time / Glenna McReynolds.
p. cm.
ISBN 0-553-10394-6
1. Wales—History—1063-1284—Fiction. I. Title.

PS3563.C75 P7 2000
813'.54—dc21   00-056472

Published simultaneously in the United States and Canada

Bantam Books are published by Bantam Books, a division of Random House, Inc. Its trademark, consisting of the words "Bantam Books" and the portrayal of a rooster, is Registered in U.S. Patent and Trademark Office and in other countries. Marca Registrada. Bantam Books, 1540 Broadway, New York, New York 10036.

PRINTED IN THE UNITED STATES OF AMERICA

BVG   10 9 8 7 6 5 4 3 2 1

To Katie and Chase

Of all the millions of words to be
put into place, my thanks go to you for
giving me the very best one—Mom.
You fill my life with love.

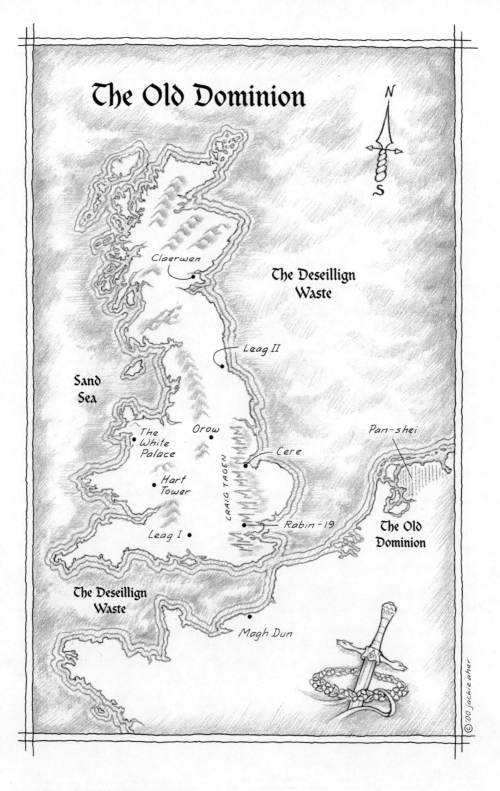

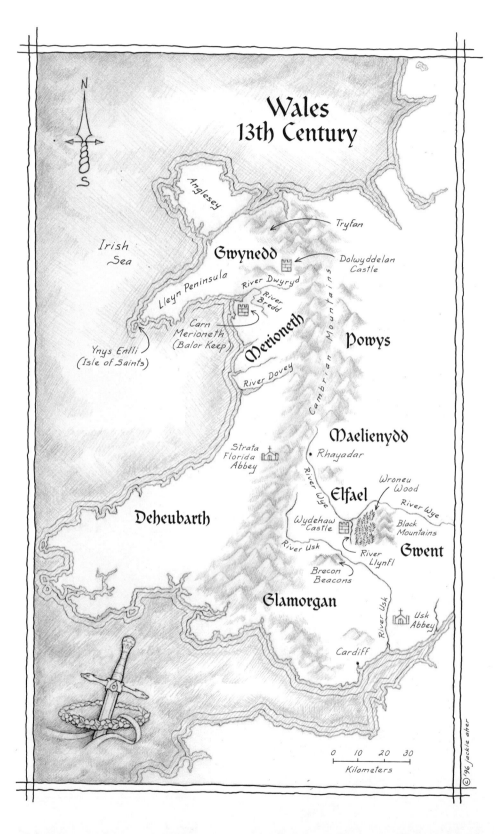

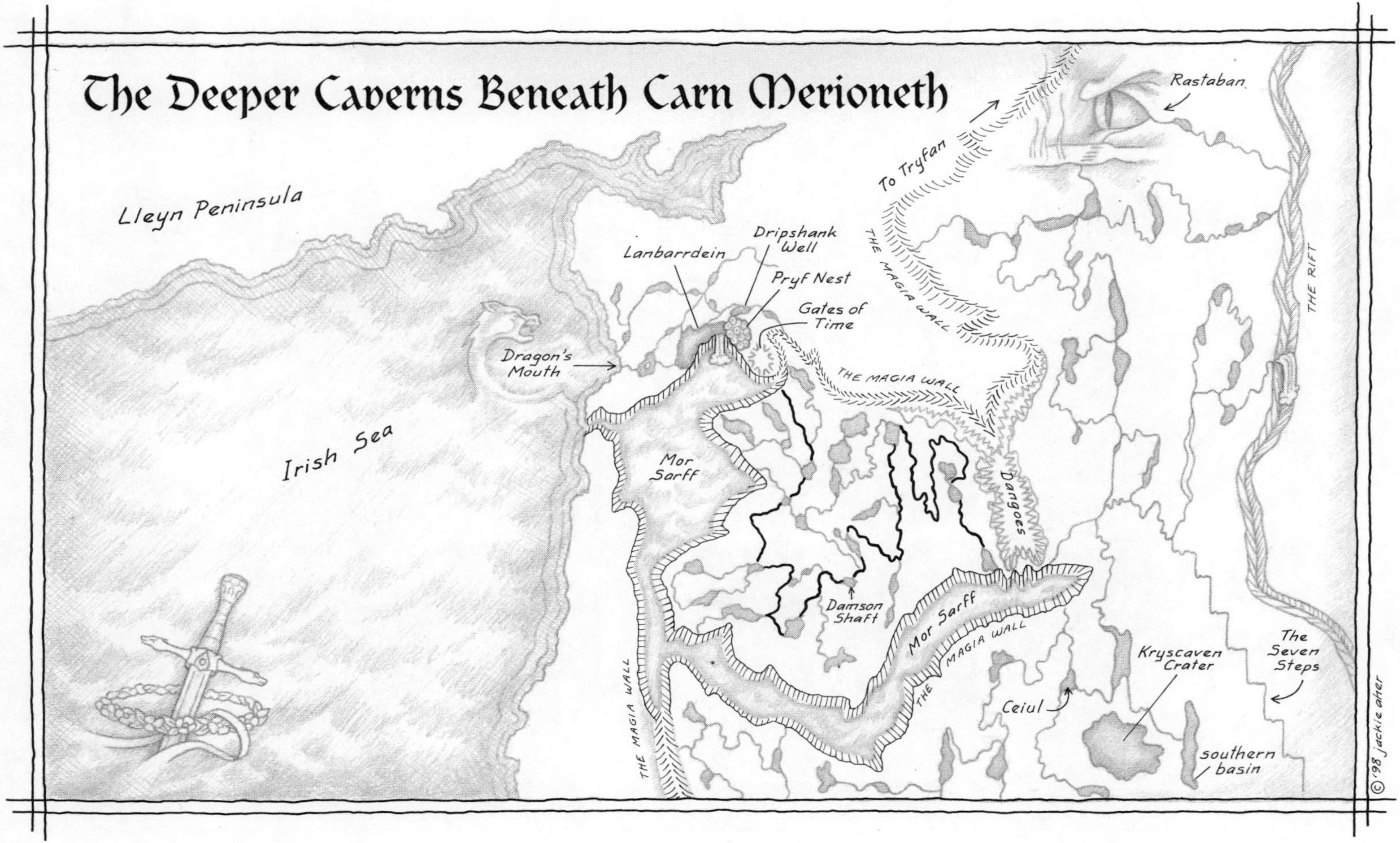

The Deeper Caverns Beneath Carn Derioneth

© '98 Jackie after

The Rift

Rastaban

To Trygan

THE MAGIA WALL

THE MAGIA WALL

Dangoes

Mor Sarff

THE MAGIA WALL

Damson Shaft

The Seven Steps

Kryscaven Crater

Southern basin

Ceiul

Dripshank Well

Pryf Nest

Gates of Time

Lanbardein

Mor Sarff

Dragon's Mouth

Lleyn Peninsula

Irish Sea

Cast of Characters

THE OLD DOMINION

MORGAN AB KYNAN—*a thief*

HIS BAND OF MEN
AJA—*the captain*
YORK
WILS
ROBBI
JIANG

FERRAR
JONS
CORVUS GEI—*the Warmonger*
VISHAB—*a witch*

CLAERWEN, TEMPLE OF THE WHITE LADIES OF DEATH

AVALLYN LE SEVERN—*Priestess of the Bones*
PALINOR—*Priestess of the Bones*
HIGH PRIESTESS OF CLAERWEN
DRAY—*captain of the Sha-shakrieg Night Watchers*

THE WHITE PALACE

AU CADE—*Queen of Deseillign and the Sha-shakrieg*
TAMISK—*an Ilmarryn mage*

❦

FROM THE PAST

CERIDWEN AB ARAWN
DAIN LAVRANS
MYCHAEL AB ARAWN
LLYNYA—*a Liosalfar*
MADRON—*a Druid priestess*
NAAS
MOIRA
TRIG
NIA
MATH
SHAY

THE LOST FIVE

AILFINN MAPP—*Prydion Mage*
RHUDDLAN—*King of the Quicken-tree*
OWAIN—*a Welshman*
WEI—*a Liosalfar*
VARGA—*a Sha-shakrieg*

SEVEN BOOKS OF LORE

SJARN VA LE—*Violet Book of Stars*
ELHION BHAAS LE—*Indigo Book of Elfin Lore*
PRYDION CAL LE—*Blue Book of the Magi*
TREO VEILL LE—*Green Book of Trees*
CHANDRA YEULL LE—*Yellow Book of Chandra*
GRATTE BRON LE—*Orange Book of Stone*
FATA RANC LE—*Red Book of Doom*

Prince

of

Time

Not my kind of story —

Stacia M. Holland

2005

Prologue

SONNPUR-DZON MONASTERY
MOUNTAINS OF THE MIDDLE KINGDOM

In the failing light of a midwinter's eve, high in the mountains of the Dhaun Himal, the monks of Sonnpur-Dzon trudged across a frozen courtyard filled with ice and snow. A fierce wind howling down from the mountain peaks whipped at the hems of their robes and made the nightly devotional a prize to be won. Behind the monks, a half-dozen novitiates cloaked in gray wool plodded through the worsening storm, following their masters to the assembly hall. A black-cowled mendicant brought up the rear.

From beneath the hood draped low over his face, he squinted into the wind. Dark clouds raced across the horizon, leading the night into the west across a barren, sharp-edged landscape of gray rock and steep slopes. Drawing his gaze closer, he scanned the castellated wall connecting the monastery buildings one to the other. Torchbearers walked the ramparts of the wall, heading toward the braziers flanking Sonnpur-Dzon's only gate.

On either side of the gate, stone towers rose from the braziers, each one crowned with a fearsome dragon head chiseled from stone.

Every night of the two weeks that he'd been at the monastery, the fires had been lit at sunset, sending flames shooting out of the dragons' mouths. Smoke would then curl from the beasts' nostrils and the night watch would sound the Dragon Hearts. The resonant vibrations from the great bronze gongs would echo the length of the valley below, calling anyone within hearing distance to prayer—though from what he'd seen, it was a rare occurrence for anyone to be within a hundred miles of the place, let alone within hearing distance.

He shifted his gaze to the west again, noting the last sinking rays of the sun. The men outside the monastery this night were unlikely to drop to their knees when the gongs were struck, for they were his, and the sounding of the Dragon Hearts was their signal to breach the wall. He'd used his time between the daily prayer assemblies and meditations to search for Sonnpur-Dzon's weakest point, and he'd finally found it in the grates of an ancient, unused hypocaust. He'd then spent the last two nights unsealing those grates, working his way from one level of monks' cells to the next until he'd reached the last round of bars set into the north wall. With the breaking of the final seal, he'd opened a path from the outside world into the heart of Sonnpur-Dzon, defeating the monastery's last defense.

Sonnpur-Dzon's remoteness had been its first line of defense against him. Even after being assured of its existence, he had needed over three months to narrow down its possible location, and then another six weeks of hard travel to reach the area. In the highest mountain range on Earth, he'd finally found Sonnpur-Dzon clinging to the sheer sides and craggy peaks of the Dhaun Himal. No pilgrim came there except through hardship and design. The nearest outpost was five hundred miles to the southeast, on the coast.

Poverty had been the monastery's second protection. Sonnpur-Dzon's only treasure had been bliss achieved through devotion, until seven months past, when the monks had come into possession of a small gold statue highly prized and eagerly sought by a trader in the west.

On the basis of a whispered rumor, the trader had come to him for help. He, in turn, had come to Sonnpur-Dzon for a considerable amount of money, more than he'd believed any small gold statue could be worth, except possibly in the western markets of the Old Dominion, the greatest den of vice and iniquity in the Orion arm of the galaxy.

Despite the initial difficulties in finding the place, it was the kind of job he liked—straightforward and paid in advance—even if the seals on the hypocaust had been cheap and messy Carillion knock-offs and the bars had been surprisingly tough alloy digitals. He'd been prepared for worse. There would be some softwork in the courtyard shrine, but softwork was his captain's specialty.

Ahead of him, the saffron-robed monks and the novitiates halted and turned to face the dragon towers. Snow began falling, mixing with the flurries the wind swept off the snowcap. The torchbearers on the wall touched their flames to the braziers and fire roiled across the pans. Against the night sky, the dragons breathed smoke and flames. The heart gongs were struck, and as one the monks and novitiates prostrated themselves on the ice-riven stones, intoning praise for the gods and divine defenders.

He prostrated with them, the picture of piety, his voice joined with theirs in the chant, utterly guiltless though he would steal their statue that night. Whether the gold figure was a sacred relic or not, the dragon gods of Sonnpur-Dzon were not his gods. He'd lost his God in the past.

The reminder elicited a softly spoken curse, interrupting the words of praise. He'd lost his God, but not his skills. He was still light of finger if not of heart, and still quick of mind, assets that had served him well in the past, and that had saved his life in the strange and dangerous time he'd been thrown into by the friggin' weirworms. He was still a leader of men, though none knew his lineage; still a prince, though his country no longer existed.

He'd lost his family and his friends, the mountain streams and valleys of his youth, every woman he'd ever loved, and nearly his mind, but he'd not lost his name. He was still Morgan ab Kynan, and he was still the Thief of Cardiff. Before the next rising of the sun, the monks of Sonnpur-Dzon would know he had been among them.

The last echo of the Dragon Hearts was swept away on the wind, and the votaries rose. As the line neared the main assembly hall, Morgan slowed his steps, falling behind and slipping into the shadows of a grain storehouse. The novitiates' dormitory, empty at this hour, was to his left, its doors covered with heavy striped curtains. A ladder leading up from the storehouse to the kitchen rested against the wall to his right. Other monks were converging on the hall, crossing the central courtyard from wherever they'd prostrated themselves for the nightly devotional.

He waited, out of sight, his back against the dormitory's stone wall, until the monks passed. When they'd all entered the hall, he climbed the ladder. At the top, he skirted a wooden porch and posted himself on the south side of the nearest building. The smell of roasted barley coming from a hide-covered window confirmed his position by the kitchen. He'd marked every turn in the hypocaust, laying a trail for his captain, Aja, to follow. The boy had the burrowing instincts of a rat dog and would not lead the rest of the men astray. With Aja pushing them, even the clumsiest of the lot should make the kitchen in ten minutes. The monks would be well into their prayers by then.

He checked his comwatch, then cut his gaze to the shrine in the center of the courtyard. A curtain flapped in the doorway of the temple supporting the monument. Fierce demons were carved on the lintel above the door. The statue was inside the temple room, a dragon wrought in reddish gold, sleeping on a bed of snakes, about fifteen centimeters in length, no gemstones. He and Aja would make the snatch together. Even a place as remote and backward as Sonnpur-Dzon had a security system rigged up to protect their new treasure. From what Morgan had seen of it, Aja shouldn't have any trouble neutralizing the power field. The trick would be dismantling the alarm.

Snake-beds and dragons, firegods and demons, the future had proven to be a place rife with religions and idolatry. A pervasive trade in divine artifacts kept a good portion of the populace, including the religious houses, in and out of each other's pockets. With rightful ownership being proved more by possession than provenance, 'twas a lucrative climate for a thief. When politics and the benefactions of patronage were added in, few in the Old Dominion were left uninvolved. As for the vast backwater of the Middle Kingdom, he hadn't seen a living soul whose life didn't revolve around one religion or another, with the dragon sect of Sonnpur-Dzon being one of the more obscure. Other than the couple of hundred monks in the monastery and the Dominion trader who'd hired him, few people had ever heard of the place. Luckily, he'd found those few.

Dragon gods. *Christe.* He shook his head.

In his world there had been only one God, the God he'd fought for, the God he'd nearly died for, the God who had ultimately abandoned him in the shifting lair of the worms that had taken him far from his home—far from his time.

Waiting in the frigid darkness, the temperature dropping toward zero, he resisted the temptation of his memories. Richly colored in his mind's eye and ever-beckoning, they were a siren's call into the past, into the life that had been his until a fateful battle had sent him falling into the time weir.

Wales, his mind whispered. *Land of the Cymry, of wild, clear-water rivers and woodland idylls a thousand shades of green, land of mountain sunrises streaking gold across the horizon, land of harps, song, and war.*

Always war.

He swore again and pulled his cloak tighter about himself. There was no salvation in his memories. Naught but pain and longing awaited him there. He checked his comwatch again. Five more minutes. With luck, he and his men would be back in the hypocaust before any of the monks knew their treasure was missing. If not, and a warning was sounded, it was over the wall with all of them. Jiang and Robbi would be carrying grappling hooks, ropes, and zip lines. York and Wils were bringing in the diversionary firepower, a few blastpaks guaranteed to throw enough smoke and sparks into the air to cover their escape. Morgan had ordered all lasguns and carbines trigger-locked. He didn't mind thievery. It was what had kept him alive in the beginning, when he'd first come through the weir. Ten years later, it was still what kept him alive, but he drew the line at massacre, and the monks were unarmed. A fortnight in the place had given him plenty of time to find any weapons hidden in the monastery, and there were none—except for the longsword concealed beneath his cloak, a cool length of steel resting in the scabbard laid along his spine, its rune-engraved cross-guard shadowing the curve of his shoulders, the one piece of his past he was never without. Ivory-gripped, its hilt chased in gold and silver, its blade engraved with a runic spell, the sword was named for an ancient king of a land that, like his, no longer existed—Scyld, King of the Danes.

A flicker of light drew his gaze to the kitchen window in time to see Wils slip through the opening. Aja was already out, no more than a shadow sliding along the wall, closing in on him through the wind-driven snow.

Morgan smiled. The boy was a cat.

Robbi came next, followed by Jiang and York.

Wils was literally a one-armed bandit, having lost his left arm in an Old Dominion bar one night. Morgan had taken the man on despite his handicap, partially because Wils was faster with a lasgun with one arm than most people were with two, and partially because the first time they'd met, Wils had nearly conned him with a scam so skillfully contrived, Morgan had decided he'd rather have the man working with him than against him. Robbi, Wils's younger brother and a fair thief in his own right, went wherever his older brother chose to go.

The third member of the group, Jiang, was a self-professed wastrel, sometimes in Morgan's band and sometimes not, depending on whose bed he was in or who was buying the drinks, and how big a prize Morgan was going after. Too small, and Jiang wasn't interested. Too big, and he figured the risks were too high. Their current job had been the exception. A hefty price had been agreed upon and half paid before they'd left Old Dominion for the mountains of the Middle Kingdom, and Sonnpur-Dzon was no fortress. Easy in, easy out, and easy money had been Jiang's cheerful summation of the undertaking. Despite the weather, so far he hadn't been too far off the mark.

The last man came through the window and started down the wall. Huge and hulking, York was a brigand to the core, hard-faced and harder-hearted. He was marked for death in half the solar system with a bounty on his head posted by Van the Wretched, a lunar warlord of vile reputation—enough reason for Morgan to take him on. He'd had a few run-ins with Van's skraelpacks, troops of beastmen as brutish as they were fierce, and he'd figured anybody who had dared to cross Van would be an asset in his own line of work.

Morgan looked over his assembled band. To a man they were as loyal to him as they could be, which ofttimes wasn't much, except for Aja. If Morgan had sired the boy himself, he could be no more stalwart a companion. A shock of red hair, usually standing on end, framed an impish face kept from innocence by a wickedly mischievous grin and a pair of green eyes that saw far more than they missed. There was little of a child about Aja except for his damnable curiosity and his seventeen years. He was more than a boy, for certs, but far from fully grown. A refugee from Earth's great deserts, he'd been with Morgan the day he'd arrived in Pan-shei.

The boy materialized next to him from out of the shadows, a slender form dressed in black, his face camouflaged with broad, dark stripes of paint. "Bitchin' weather, milord," he said, and blew on his hands.

"Aye," Morgan agreed, watching his captain size up the courtyard, the shrine, and the great wall, the boy's eyes flicking from one potential lo-

cation to the next. Aja was the only one who ever called him *milord,* a title
the boy could have gotten out of him only on a night when he'd been deep
in his cups. For the most part, Morgan tried to forget the past. He didn't
allow himself to dwell on it, for therein was the definition of hopelessness.
He couldn't go back. He didn't talk about the past, ever, to anyone.

Regardless, the past wouldn't let him go. He was tied to it with
every breath he took. It crept up on him in the no-man's-land between
sleep and dreams. It came upon him with the scents and sounds of the
marketplace. Some nights he awoke in a cold sweat, once more falling
through the weir, freezing to death with terror clenching his gut. Worm
nights, he called them. 'Twas then he would drink, looking for oblivion
and a remnant of home in the illusions of Carillion wine. Aja could have
gotten anything out of him, if he'd asked on a worm night.

"Robbi over there on the wall with the ropes," the boy said, pointing to a crenellation south of the dragons. "Wils by the temple door. Jiang
standing guard with Wils. York stays here to cover us."

"Agreed," Morgan said, having reconnoitered the positions as
soon as he'd discovered that the hypocaust emptied out under the
kitchen.

"What have they got inside the shrine?"

"Some ancient Lectron trip wires, field security on a board—"

"Good," the boy interrupted, a quick smile curving his mouth.
"And the alarm?"

"A series of color-synchronized lights on the column holding the
statue."

A moment's silence met that particular answer, then Aja asked,
"Like what we saw on Mercury Island?"

"Aye, much the same," Morgan said, his tone of voice noncommittal. He thought he heard a soft curse, or mayhap it was only the wind.

They'd pulled off the Mercury Island job four months earlier, and
despite Aja's nimble fingers and quick mind, the alarm had gone off and
damn near gotten them caught. It was the closest call they'd ever had,
with he and Aja both sustaining minor injuries. With all else that could
go wrong on a heist, the softwork specialist was supposed to keep the obvious disasters from happening.

"The seals in the hypocaust were Carillion knockoffs. The alarm
might be too," the boy suggested, his tone equally noncommittal.

"Maybe," Morgan said.

"Well, I don't want another friggin' Mercury Island catastrophe," York said, shoving himself forward from the rear and giving them each a tech-jaw to bite down on. Morgan put the marble-size piece of soft plastic on his back teeth and closed his mouth for a count of four.

"Friggin' catastrophes are your stock-in-trade, York," Aja countered before biting down on his own tech-jaw. With his teeth closed, he flashed York one of his trademark grins, unperturbed by the older man's complaint. York always expected the worst, and Aja never did. Morgan figured the two made a good pair.

"Are we going to do this thing or not?" Jiang asked, and Morgan heard him half through the storm and half through the tech-jaw.

He looked again at the deserted courtyard. They were going to do it, aright. Two weeks of living shrouded in a monk's habit was pretty much his limit, and two weeks of listening to himself think was about seven days past it. The monastery was getting to him. Too much praying was part of the problem. He'd long since given up prayer. As to what else about the place discomfited him, he wasn't sure, but something did, niggling at him, stirring up things best left forgotten, and he would as soon be away. With hand signals and a succinct set of commands, he deployed his men, directing York to stay behind.

One by one, the bandits disappeared down the ladder, melting into the night and the storm. As the five split up, the tech-jaws kept them in communication. Like so much of the hardware they used, the tech-jaws didn't come cheap, but Morgan had gotten past the point where he and Aja had to spend their downtime trying to cobble together bulkier and less reliable alternatives.

The snowstorm was working in their favor, keeping any stray monks inside. The temperature had finally sunk below zero, and the windchill was well into negative double digits.

The future, Morgan had discovered, afforded a few luxuries, especially in footwear. His boots were supple and warm, with two-inch soles that cushioned his every step while giving him better traction than he'd ever gotten in a leather shoe. But it was a long way to have come for a good pair of boots. A friggin' long way.

He and Aja made one last check of the other men's positions before lifting the curtain on the temple door and slipping inside. They both came to an immediate stop. The room was cast in pitch darkness, except for the blue sheen of the power field around the statue and the low bar of lights illuminating the alarm.

Aja slipped a night visor on over his eyes—and froze into perfect stillness.

"*Crikey* . . ." he breathed through the tech-jaw, his hand absently touching the small yellow wallet on his belt. Morgan put on his own night visor.

Large gilded statues of demon guardians loomed up on either side of the temple, revealed in the gloom by the visor's green light. Great beasts of all types lined the walls, reaching fifteen feet from ceiling to floor: tiger-devils and lions silently roaring, bull-headed men and leopard-ghouls. He'd first seen the sentinels in daylight, their long fangs glinting with the rays of the sun, their chatoyant gilt eyes shining, looking alive. The cover of darkness did naught to mitigate either the demons' frightful countenances or their eerie watchfulness. The altar was between two great dragons, one cast in green stone, the other in red, the whole of it fronted with a metal latticework grille.

He looked to Aja, signaling him to begin, and after the briefest of hesitations his captain bent to his task.

"Don't move left," the boy said, crouching to disable the first trip wire. "Okay, go."

Aja disabled two more trip wires before they reached the field security board. It was set into the floor, part of the circle incised around the column holding the dragon statue. The field itself projected from the numerous ports drilled into the circle, creating a translucent blue cylinder of protection. Even from a distance, Morgan could feel the power pulsing through the blue light. The boy stood close to the board and pulled a pliant metallic glove from his belt. When he was ready, he reached out with his gloved hand and touched the field. Light streaked up his arm, limning half his body. Sparks skittered from his fingertips. Wind gusted through the door, lifting and fluttering the boy's hair, and for a moment he was held there, captain of the elements.

'Twas as close to magic as Morgan ever hoped to get again, what Aja could do with binary code and a wavelength-sensitized glove. The boy knelt to the board, being careful not to break his charged contact with the power field, his fingers trailing lines of blue fire down the length of the cylinder. Digits flashed on the board, lines of zeros and ones reflecting red on the green lens of the boy's night visor. He worked the keys with his left hand, while reading the code through the gloved fingertips of his right.

Any hack could read code, make code, and even break code given enough time, but no hack could do it through an active field. More than a few had been fried trying. Aja's touch was immeasurably light, nearly psychic. That he could skim the surface of a field while reading a board made him rare even among those with similar talents.

Aye, Morgan thought, the boy was a rare one, gifted mayhap with a bit of sight. More than his captain's softwork skills made Morgan think so; the boy showed other signs. Morgan had oft thought about Aja's parents—one of whom must have bequeathed the boy his blazing red hair—and what had happened to them.

A cracking bolt of energy streaked the length of the cylinder, signaling Aja's breaking of his connection. The boy stepped back, his glove smoking. A smile spread across his face as the power field faltered, the blue light flickering and then failing altogether, leaving nothing between them and the twenty-four-karat dragon except the alarm system. Aja moved in close and knelt in front of the color-synchronized lights on the column.

Morgan watched him run his hands along the alarm's frame, searching for the telltale signs of Carillion manufacturing. They were always there: joints that didn't meld, burrs that hadn't been filed off, keys that stuck, fluids that leaked.

A snick of sound broke the silence, and Aja turned, holding up a small lever that had all but fallen off the alarm.

"Carillion," he said.

Morgan nodded, pleased. He would as soon avoid another fight, even though he doubted the monks could put up much of one.

Aja took a few extra minutes with the alarm, double-checking himself twice before cutting it off. When nothing happened, Morgan sounded the okay to the other men, letting them know he and Aja would be coming out. Stepping forward, he pulled a padded leather bag from his belt and reached for the dragon, only to stop suddenly, immobilized by a strange scent drifting out of the darkness.

His nose knew what it was before his mind could acknowledge the truth, and his blood instantly ran cold. Aja was sniffing the air himself, his brow furrowed.

"What in the h—" The boy got no further. A soft keening followed the scent, echoing around the temple, sounding as if from a great distance. The smell intensified, warm and rich, redolent of the deep earth.

Morgan stared into the dark, washed through with dread and disbelief, unable to move. Demons, dragons . . . and *worms*. The memory of them coiled around his heart and lungs, sinuous and winding, reclaiming their place—the very breath and pulse of him.

"Milord?" Aja questioned when he didn't pick up the dragon, but only stood there, sweat breaking out on his brow, his fingers outstretched, his whole arm trembling. "Morgan?" the boy repeated uncertainly.

Morgan cursed under his breath. He should have known. They were time worms. No passing of years would ever see their demise. Now they had a cult of monks worshiping them. He wondered if the buggers knew what they were messing with, and in the next second knew that of course they did.

Friggin' worms. They'd not get him a second time.

Gritting his teeth, he grabbed the gold statue and turned to run, wanting nothing more than to be anyplace else in the world other than Sonnpur-Dzon Monastery.

Another curse lodged in his throat. He and Aja were no longer alone. A dozen monks had emerged from the gaping belly of a tiger-devil, arisen from God knew what wormish rites, and were staring at him and his captain in horror. Behind them were more monks, some carrying torches.

"Rush them," Morgan commanded, pushing his hood off his head and dragging his longsword up out of its scabbard.

"Rush who?" Jiang asked through the tech-jaw from outside by the door.

"Move!" Wils roared, making Morgan's ears ring. In the next instant, the one-armed bandit ran into the temple, his lasgun drawn. A monk stepped out of the shadows and caught him from behind, knocking him out cold with an iron key he swung from a strap. Wils splayed on the floor, his lasgun sliding over the stone into darkness.

Jiang got off a shot, and the monks went wild. More of them poured out of the tiger-devil's belly, filling the temple and creating chaos.

"On my way," Morgan heard York say, the older man's voice crackling through the tech-jaw.

Two monks pulled metal staffs off the latticework grille of the altar and rushed Morgan, looking like they planned to knock his head off.

"Damn," he whispered. So much for his idea of placid monks.

"Zips fixed, ropes over. On my way," Robbi reported.

Aja was holding off four monks with his lasgun, but Morgan could see it was still trigger-locked and knew it was likely to remain that way. Aja had never shot a man in his life. Skraelings, yes, for the boy had a morbid fear of the beasts, but never a man. Monks swinging keys at him were unlikely to push him into murder. The boy had too many other options.

"Away, Aja," he ordered.

"Milord," the boy protested, backing toward the column.

"Away, *Captain,*" he repeated, emphasizing the boy's rank and responsibilities. He threw the leather bag, and nearly quicker than the eye could see, Aja caught it and was gone. The four monks searched around one another, dumbfounded, trying to find him.

Morgan knew they wouldn't, then he had no more time to think. The staff-wielders were upon him. The clash of metal striking metal rang out in the temple. The taller monk was also the faster, getting in two attacks to the other monk's one. Morgan parried all of them, swinging Scyld with a two-handed grip. The tall monk switched tactics, bringing his staff around in a swipe meant to break ribs. Morgan jumped back, and instead of hitting him, the tip of the staff grazed his chest and sliced his shirt open. A second swipe left a trail of blood on his skin and reduced the front of his shirt to nothing but a rag hanging from his shoulders.

"Son of a bitch," he swore. The staffs were razor sharp on the ends.

Wils was down, maybe dead. Jiang was surrounded. They were outnumbered five to one, and the monks were loaded with deadly weapons. Shooting their way out might be their only chance. He started to give the order to unlock triggers, knowing York would come in with carbines blazing, but was stopped short when his attackers suddenly backed away.

"Bo si wong gi," the tall monk whispered, staring at his chest.

Morgan knew it was a mess. He had scars from wounds that should have killed him. In the beginning, he'd wondered if they had and he'd woken up in hell. Sometimes he still wasn't sure.

The monk's gaze shifted from his chest to his hair, and his eyes widened. From what Morgan had seen of the strange and varied beings that inhabited the future, he didn't know how a white stripe in his hair could cause such a shocked expression. Half the inhabitants of the Old

Dominion had something weirder than a stripe going on with their hair. After a second of stunned staring, the monk lowered his gaze and fell to his knees, leaving himself to Morgan's mercy—or the lack thereof.

"Bo si wong gi," he repeated in a voice full of wonder. The words were quickly taken up by the other monks, the sound rushing around the temple and leaving a hush in its wake. By twos and threes, monks knelt on the floor, all of them facing him.

Morgan didn't like their reaction. He didn't like it at all, but neither was he going to second-guess it.

"Morgan check," he muttered into the tech-jaw, still holding his sword in a defensive position. "Aja away. Wils down. Jiang check. Bail. Bail."

Warily, he began making his way toward Wils. York and Robbi burst through the curtained doorway at the same time, their guns at the ready, expecting the order he hadn't yet given.

"Bo si wong gi . . . Bo si wong gi." The words were becoming a chant, rising up from a floor littered with the saffron-colored robes of supplicating monks.

York took one look and gestured for Robbi and Jiang to get out, while he went for Wils.

Morgan reached the one-armed bandit at the same time as York and helped heft him onto the older man's shoulders. With Robbi covering them, they backed their way to the door.

Once outside, they raced for the wall, with Morgan taking Robbi's place as rear guard. By the time they reached the ramparts, Wils was coming around. Aja was waiting for them, a breach of orders, but one Morgan would deal with later. With a quick, underhanded throw, the boy tossed him the leather bag. Morgan caught it and looped it onto his belt.

Unbelievably, no monks were following them. The courtyard was deserted, filled with nothing but falling snow and the muffled sound of the chant coming out of the temple.

Bo si wong gi. Morgan didn't even want to know what it meant.

York went over the wall first, taking Wils with him in a harness down the zip line. Robbi and Aja went down a parallel line. Morgan clipped onto a rope, and he and Jiang went over the wall with descenders, dropping in near free falls to the valley floor.

The snowstorm had heightened into a blizzard while they'd been in the temple. No moon had risen, and the wind and the cold cut through Morgan as he slid down the rope, freezing his gloved fingers around the descender. Somewhere below them in the night, their camp awaited with hot food, warm tents, and a GS rover to take them into the canyons of the Middle Kingdom. From the canyons, they would make their way into the lower valleys and head toward the eastern shore of the Sand Sea.

Falling through the darkness, his life hanging by the thin line of rope, Morgan felt the weight of the gold dragon pulling him down. It was a bitter victory. The smell of the worms was in his nose, churning in his gut, lapping at his mind.

Dragons, snakes, and worms . . . his nightmares resurrected. *Christ have mercy.*

Inside the monastery, in the assembly hall, the tall monk knelt before the High Lama of Sonnpur-Dzon. The old man's white hair streamed down his robes. Blue tattoos swirled up the left side of his face, the archaic symbols nearly lost in the wrinkles of his dark skin. Incense rose from the burning censers flanking the yellow pillow on which he sat.

"You are sure it was he?" The old man's voice wavered in the thin, cold air.

"There is no doubt, Most Holy One. I saw the signs for myself. The white stripe in his hair and the mark of the rowan tree gracing the skin over his heart."

"Others have had the stripe of the time weir in their hair," the old man said, lifting a hand to the pale blond streak running through his own.

"Yes, master, but none other has ever had the sacred leaf emblazoned on his chest. It is he, *Bo si wong gi,* the Prince of Time we have so long awaited. He is come, master."

The old man's eyes drifted closed, and in the long moments that followed, the younger monk feared his master had fallen asleep.

But such was not so. Without opening his eyes, the High Lama lifted a silken cord from around his neck and draped it over the younger man's shaved head. A silver disk hung from the cord, incised with a square rimmed in gold and inset with a triangle of carnelian.

"Take this to Deseillign, to the White Palace on the edge of the Waste. Take it to the desert daughters and tell them their talisman has arrived. Tell the Lady Avallyn her traveler has finally come."

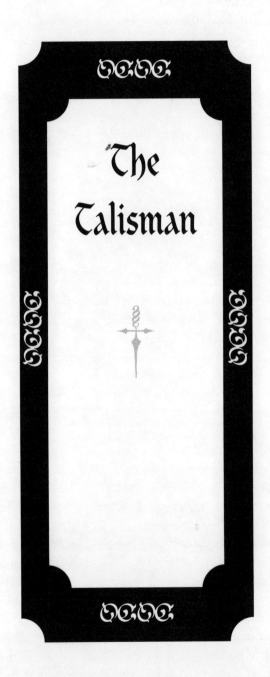

The Talisman

From the mage's cauldron came the beasts and
the blade—and the binding love of the thief for
the desert-born maid.

Chapter 1

THE WHITE PALACE
DESEILLIGN WASTE

Avallyn Le Severn walked the length of the palace corridor alone, her strides smooth and sure, her boots silent on the marble floor—the tread of a desert walker. A faint flush warmed her cheeks beneath her vision visor, a damnable inconvenience she needed to remedy before facing the tribune. All other signs of her inner turmoil were hidden beneath a layer of carefully contrived calm that two days of travel over the trackless Waste had not shaken.

She had been summoned.

She had come.

And now it would begin.

A sere wind blew through the open windows on each side of the hall, bringing with it the withering heat of the day. Sand moved with every breath of air, drifting over the sills and spilling onto the floor, a fallow flow from the endless Sand Sea. Someday the dunes would engulf the White Palace and there would be nothing but sand from the Dragon's Mouth to the Old Dominion. But for now, the sweepers would come. For now, her concerns lay elsewhere.

The color in her cheeks deepened, yet her stride did not falter.

He was here, as sworn by the monk from Sonnpur-Dzon.

He had been found, in this time, on this world.

Her prince.

The years of waiting were over. The destiny for which she'd been born would now begin to unfold in all its terror and glory with him by her side, the one for whom she had waited—the prince of the *Fata Ranc Le,* the Red Book of Doom. In another life he had written his fate upon the pages of the scarlet-bound book with the touch of his hand, and so had bound himself to her.

Sweet Mother, she had waited. Waited in despair that he would never come, and in fear that he would. She'd scarce believed it when the monk had confessed to letting him walk out of the Sonnpur-Dzon monastery three months ago without so much as a by-your-leave. Ten thousand years he had been in the coming, and the monks had lost him in a matter of minutes.

A mendicant, the monk had called him, a wandering brother who had come to the monastery to pray and meditate. He had revealed himself on a new moon night in the Sanctuary of Demons, a golden dragon grasped in his right hand and a blazing sword in his left, a warrior as the Book had foretold. He'd disappeared in a whirl of blue fire, walking off the monastery's great wall into the night sky—and the monks had let him. The next morning no body had been found, only the prince's tracks in the snow where he had landed with celestial grace.

The powers of a mage, the heart of a warrior, and the courage of a saint. So it had been written of the prince, and so it was. Thank the gods, she thought. They would need all three to survive their fated journey.

The Prince of Time.

A thrill of excitement edged with fear sliced through her, threatening the thin veneer of her composure. He'd traveled far, a time-rider from a primitive, barbaric age. Would he be a danger, she wondered, this warrior-saint from out of the past? History was littered with destruction wrought in the name of saviors. Would the prince of the *Fata* be such a peril? And if he was, would her course be changed?

No, she vowed. The fiercer and more barbaric, the better. Only the Prince of Doom, as some called him, would have a chance of surviving their destination, and only the mightiest warrior would have even half a chance of bringing her out alive with him.

Shadana, she sent up a fervent prayer. *Let him be all that is written and more.* No matter how fierce, her will would tame him to the deed. The duty they shared would bring him to his destiny, and in their moment of triumph, she would grace him with a kiss.

Her blush deepened, the damnable thing, but the prince was hers, and it was right that she should kiss him.

The entrance to the Court of the Ilmarryn loomed in front of her, white marble columns rising up out of the shadows on either side of a towering stone door, and for the first time since reaching the palace, Avallyn tempered her steps with caution, slowing her pace. Fey creatures of the *tylwyth teg,* the Ilmarryn were not to be trifled with, not even by a priestess of the old line.

At the door made from two great slabs of stone quarried from the caverns beneath the White Palace, she stopped and lifted her gaze. Names flowed down the granite panels, delicately chiseled letters run through with an arborescent crackling of rose quartz, the ancient lineage of the sylvan Ilmarryn traced back through the Prydion Age. Near the middle were names echoed in her own ancestry, Llynya of the Yr Is-ddwfn and Mychael ab Arawn, a lord of Merioneth.

Standing quietly, she used a novice's trick to school her breath and cool the blush from her cheeks. There was no advantage to her in allowing the tribune to see her excitement, and a distinct disadvantage to her if they sensed her unease. The tribune and their force of Sha-shakrieg Night Watchers were a means to an end, her end, and she would not have her desires or her weaknesses turned against her.

She moved her gaze over the gray doors once more. Beaded steel bars circled round with bands of iron had been fashioned into massive handles that ran the length of the granite panels, a testament to all who would enter: Those inside feared naught on earth.

Neither did she, now that the prince had come. Barbarian or not, whatever dangers lay ahead, they would face them together.

She stepped forward, onto the tile directly in front of the doors, and they swung inward. A rich scent rushed out to meet her, cutting through the barren dryness of the desert and enveloping her in the smells of fresh leaves and bitter tannins, in the sweet redolence of the flowers and plants thriving in the glass-domed forest, the Lost Forest of the

Waste. 'Twas here where her heart was, in the woodland glades and meadows, not in the desert where she'd been born.

Lushly overgrown, the Court of the Ilmarryn lay at the heart of the White Palace, the last bastion of power overlooking the Sand Sea. Sweeping up from the palace walls, the dome arced high over the trees, a winding curve of pale green glass seven miles wide and fourteen miles long, a marvel of twisted steel struts and sun-struck expanses of glazing held aloft by Ilmarryn magic. Catwalks hung suspended from the internal scaffolding, and around and through the structures, both above and below, the flora flourished, ivy covering the walls and twining upward into the canopy, beech trees dappling the forest paths with shadows, oaks with over a thousand years of growth standing guard in groves throughout the wood. Coppices of alder, birch, and pine met and blended with hawthorn, elm, yew, and hazel within the confines of the great dome, the terrain that held them as varied as the species it harbored. Ferns abounded, unfurling over rocky streams and freshets and gracing the waterfalls whose music filled the Court.

Avallyn chose a dirt path along the River Alduin, whose waters rippled over a rocky streambed, following a miles-long course before cascading into the caverns below the Court and joining the River Bredd in a place called Dripshank Well. Avallyn had dared the rapids of the Alduin's falls more than once in her youth whenever she'd visited the White Palace. The river still beckoned, for far beneath the rivers' confluence in Dripshank lay the remnant pools of a primordial sea, Mor Sarff. And in the deepest, darkest pool lay the nest of the Merioneth dragons, Dragonmere, with the mighty serpents themselves held captive there through the millennia by the advance of the desert and the freezing of the polar seas. Their power flowed through the White Palace as surely as the sands and Ilmarryn magic, warming it against Deseillign's frigid nights and holding it against the tides of war.

But still war came, war and pestilence. The Old Dominion seethed with it. The Middle Kingdom had been decimated by it, leaving large tracts of the mountains as empty as the Waste that lay just outside the palace doors. And the ice advanced, encroaching on its daughter the desert with each passing year. But hope was nigh. By the grace of the gods, the prince had come.

At the end of the trail, the castle ruins of Merioneth rose into view, the gray stones burnished by the sun to a silvery sheen, the grassy meadows abloom with mountain lilies. When last she'd been home, in winter when the monk had come, the Court had been bound in Ilmarryn ice and covered in snow. A season had passed since then, and the prince had been found.

Heart of a warrior, courage of a saint, powers of a mage . . .

"Sticks," she swore softly. She was no saint, and no Ilmarryn to have magical powers. She was a good fighter, but not the best. That designation went to the Night Watchers. Yet she and the prince were bound by duty. There was no room for doubt on her part, especially self-doubt.

An increase in activity near the Queen's Quarters heralded Au Cade's arrival, and as Avallyn watched, the ebony-skinned queen of the White Palace appeared, a regal form in a flaming orange gown trailing retainers across the sward.

The queen joined the priestess Palinor on the dais, and taking a fortifying breath, Avallyn stepped out of the woods.

Palinor sighted her daughter immediately, the desert-worn figure coming out of the trees, and felt a familiar pride laced with resignation replace her fears of the last days. The girl had dirt on her face. Palinor could see it even from a distance, the band of sand and dust across her nose, between where her vision visor had protected her eyes and her turban had been wrapped across her mouth and chin.

Avallyn had been partially raised at the Court and knew the subtleties of custom and etiquette as well as any, and had typically chosen to ignore them. But for her daughter's appearance this day, perhaps Palinor had only herself to blame. She'd sent a message for haste, not protocol.

She gestured to the younger of the two novices serving her, directing the girl's attention to Avallyn. The novice bowed slightly before slipping away, and soon enough Palinor saw her making her way across the bailey toward Avallyn, carrying a basket of lavender-scented towels. Palinor would prefer Avallyn to stand before the tribune with at least a clean face.

"She's a lovely mess, as usual," a silky voice said at her side. "Are you so certain that the sight of her won't send the prince running?"

Palinor turned to Tamisk, the Ilmarryn mage, her gaze taking in the indigo runes tattooed in curving swirls up the side of his face, the deep blue lines a stark contrast to his fair skin, the letters marking him as an adept of the Books of Lore. A silver disk incised with a square rimmed in gold and inset with a triangle of carnelian hung from a cord around his neck, matching the medallion she wore. He was dressed in rich browns and forest greens, the colors of his world. Bracelets in the guise of snakes coiled around each of his wrists, their tongues and eyes and scales intricately wrought in silver, the color of his magic.

"She is a Priestess of the Bones, Tamisk, a White Lady of Death. If the prince is not sent running by those truths, no doubt he can brave the rest," Palinor said, refusing to rise to his baited comment.

"No doubt." Tamisk smiled in return, his eyes a green so deep and pure as to appear unnatural, even for an Ilmarryn. His hair was dark brown streaked with gray, with the *fif* braid plaited down one side proclaiming him *tylwyth teg.* "Yet I would ease her way."

"Ease her way?" Palinor questioned with an arched eyebrow. "Or set another upon her course?"

An elegant shrug was her reply.

"Your daughter is stronger than you think," Palinor said.

"And the Prince of Time is not what you expected. He's not worth risking Avallyn in a journey to the Old Dominion," Tamisk countered, the subtle censure in his voice daring her to prove him wrong. "Let me send another in her place."

Palinor returned her attention to Avallyn, dismissing the mage with her silence. 'Twas an old argument she refused to lose. Ilmarryn, she thought with concealed pique. The fairest of all the gods' creatures, they were lovely beyond compare, yet Tamisk underestimated Avallyn's art if he thought the prince would be more easily led by an Ilmarryn maid. And Tamisk did think such, had dared to go so far as to suggest to Au Cade that mayhaps an Ilmarryn could better bend the prince to their will. Au Cade had told Palinor so.

Half mad, his mind twisted by Carillion wine, Tamisk had whispered in the queen's ear, repeating the dire words of the Night Watcher captain who had found the man named Morgan. The prince was half mad and beyond Avallyn's ability to control, his thieving band of miscreants no less than the vilest of the Old Dominion's tech-trash. Magic, Tamisk had insisted, was the only reliable way of bringing him to heel. Ilmarryn magic.

Palinor would have none of it. If Avallyn couldn't bring him in, she couldn't hold him, and she had to hold him. The Prince of the *Fata Ranc Le* had been sent to do the White Ladies' bidding. An Ilmarryn's fragile beauty might draw his notice, especially if Tamisk so chose, but it was to Avallyn he was bound, and it was to Avallyn he would heel, or she was lost. As for the risk of sending Avallyn to the Old Dominion where the Warmonger might find her, craven though he be, the Warmonger was as naught compared to the doom she and the prince must face. Too long had the priestesses waited for the future for it not to come to pass as it had been written.

Too long, and yet in the gravest manner possible the words of prophecy had already proved false. *Heart of a warrior, courage of a saint, powers of a mage* . . .

Lies.

Palinor's hand closed on the sheath hanging from her jeweled girdle, her fingers tightening around the soft leather and the dagger hilt within.

All lies.

Countless years they had waited, and the gods had sent them not a bold warrior, nor a saint, but a madman enslaved by off-world wine and the debaucheries of the Old Dominion. Drunken sot, mercenary, thief, cripple. Raving. Such were the words Dray, captain of the Sha-shakrieg Night Watchers, had used to describe Morgan ab Kynan, and yet in the next breath he had confirmed that the man was indeed the Prince of Doom. The marks were on him. There had been no mistake.

Palinor followed Avallyn's progress across the yard and felt her fears rise anew. The girl was a lovely, beautiful mess indeed, her cloak nearly in shreds, her boots and tunic stained red with northern sand, her hair an urchin's mop of pale blonds and honey golds. Elflocks tangled her silvermost strands. A *fif* braid tamed a silken swath on the left side of her face. If not for the fairness of her features, she could easily be mistaken for one of the wild boys who roamed the Waste.

Yet she was fair, a miracle of delicacy and strength—and she had been meant for so much better than the company she faced.

A thousand regrets rose in Palinor's breast, but she would hold her course. In the end she would bind her daughter to a lunatic, if need be, to insure that the dread journey was made. The White Palace would not hold forever, not even with Ilmarryn magic as its bulwark. The time weir had long since broken free of its terrestrial bounds, becoming a whiplash of destruction across the cosmos, and the dragons were locked in their watery hole, powerless in their misery.

She tightened her grip another degree on the sheath, and her fingers warmed with the kindling light of dreamstone. The enchantment was an ancient one, and simple enough for a priestess of Avallyn's skill. She could cast the prince into sleep and bring him to the northern temple in chains, if he proved too unyielding or too mad. For this, at least, Palinor need not indebt herself to Tamisk. Time enough later for the mage's conjuring if the prince proved too brutish to bear or too fainthearted for his fate.

Tamisk would want blood from Avallyn before she left for the Old Dominion. Ten thousand years in the making, the lifestream running through Avallyn's veins was the key to the future. It had been no happenstance that had mated Palinor to the mage. She'd been bred to give the world a child, and 'twas the blood of that child that would save them all.

Seven measures of blood were needed, each dose meant to seal one of the Books of Lore in their chamber. Three had been given. Tamisk would want three more this day. Avallyn would deliver the seventh measure herself. Such was the bargain that ruled their days.

Avallyn stepped up on the dais, coming first to Palinor. Despite the girl's calm demeanor, excitement lit her eyes, and Palinor detected the faintest trace of a blush on her cheeks. Avallyn knelt, and Palinor extended a graceful hand for her kiss. 'Twas a lingering touch of soft lips on her skin, a silent recognition of the bond they shared, though in truth Palinor had always been more the priestess than the mother. Now, as the time drew nigh for Avallyn to leave, Palinor felt more keenly than ever before the price she had paid to hold on to her measure of power.

The girl rose and stepped forward to greet Tamisk.

"Magia Lord." She touched her fingers to her chest in a gesture of respect.

"Fair daughter of Palinor, receive my blessing on this auspicious day," the mage murmured with a benevolent smile. If there was a slightly cynical edge to that smile, it did not reveal itself in his voice, and Palinor refrained from taking too great an offense. In the end, the prince would be hers.

"Accept my gift," Tamisk continued, giving Avallyn a vial of green potion. "Should the prince's longings prove more potent than prophecy, the potion will effect a cure."

Avallyn sent Palinor a glance, complete with raised eyebrow, as she pocketed the vial. Palinor responded with a hand signal for patience. Her daughter's confusion wouldn't last long. Au Cade would tell her all.

Tamisk could have been a little more discreet though, she thought, piqued anew. The truth was bad enough without his cryptic mutterings.

At the last, Avallyn took her place before the queen and made her obeisance on bended knee beneath the green bower of the Court. As Dragonmere was the heart of the White Palace, so the hilltop carn was the heart of the Court. Merioneth had been its name since the First Age, and though all else changed with the turning of the Wheel, Merioneth it remained, the island fortress of the Starlight-born, resurrected from out of the sand by the Ilmarryn.

Thousands of years before the Trelawney Rebellion, great sand-storms had arisen in the south of the world and swept northward, a ceaseless tempest turning all the land into the Waste and driving the *tyl-wyth teg* from their ancient home into the mountains of the Middle King-dom. Over the following millennia, the wars of men had driven them back, bringing them together as the Ilmarryn, a people returned. The de-scendents of the Quicken-tree, Daur, and Ebiurrane, of the Wydden, Red-leaf, Kings Wood, and all the northern tribes, they had set forth from their mountain fastnesses in search of the lost fortress, finally find-ing it on the coast of the Sand Sea, buried beneath the dunes—and there, waiting for them, had been the Sha-shakrieg and their Desert Queen, the true masters of the Deseillign Waste.

The sinking of the sun cast light into the shadows beneath the canopy, gilding Avallyn's hair and limning the high curves of her cheek-bones, her upturned nose, and the indelible trace of her Ilmarryn her-itage—her delicately pointed ears. Her ragged cloak fell from a bloodred garnet brooch on each of her shoulders, the pale, stained cloth pooling about her on the granite dais.

She was stronger than she looked, thank the gods, for she looked as fragile as any Ilmarryn beauty. Strength or nay, though, Palinor would countenance no physical union with the tech-trash prince Dray had un-earthed. Those plans had died with the Night Watcher captain's words. The priestesses of Claerwen would bind the pair another way. If Morgan ab Kynan could fight, she would consider the day's needs well met.

"Blessed daughter," Au Cade began, addressing Avallyn in her richly resonant voice. "The captain of my guard has brought the news for which you have so long awaited. The prince has been found."

Thus was the first and the last of the queen's good tidings. Palinor held her tongue as Au Cade unwound the tale, with no sordid detail of the man's existence left unrevealed. Whatever comfort she might have offered was withheld, no matter the growing paleness of Avallyn's face, for any comfort was hollow in light of the truth—the prince had come, and he was no more than the least of men—a drunken thief from the Old Dominion.

Chapter 2

THE OLD DOMINION

The woodland below Dolwyddelan Castle lay still in the morning light, the ground untrammeled beneath Morgan's feet, the grasses laden with dew. Nary a breath of wind stirred the leaves on the trees. Nary a bird's song sounded in the cool air of the rising dawn.

Above him on the hill, the walls of the keep faded in and out of the mists, Llywelyn's keep. He had not forgotten. He had not forgotten anything.

He breathed deep, filling his lungs, and pleasure rushed through him, intense and sweet, making his head spin. Reaching out to steady himself, he laid his hand on the trunk of a tall beech tree. All was as it should be, the smooth, gray bark damp beneath his palm, the forest alive with the smell of old leaves, the fainter scents of flowers. A horse snorted close behind him—so close he felt the soft breath move through his hair—and he stilled.

The Cypriot? he wondered. Dain's shadow mare?

For certes he'd seen no horse on his walk up the hill,

and who other than she could stand so near yet remain unseen? And if the Cypriot was here, could Dain be far?

"Du Kommer sent," *an unmistakable voice, wry and gently chiding, said. You're late.*

Hope took hold of Morgan's heart, daring him to turn around and once more see the face of his friend. He started to pivot, but stopped, his attention diverted to the west by the stray melody of a song. Softer than an angel's kiss it wound down through the mist, seeming near and then far.

"Pwr wa ladth . . . pwr wa ladth . . . fai quall a'lomarian, es sholei par es cant." *The strange words, sung in a fair voice, bound him with longing. 'Twas a woman's voice—or rather, a sprite's voice. Llynya.*

She was here, the elfin maid.

"I expected you before St. Winnal," *Dain spoke again from behind him.*

Smiling, Morgan turned—and stumbled back, a groan of horror torn from his throat. All around him was darkness, malevolent, frigid darkness. The abyss. Screams came at him from every direction. Dain's voice deep and agonized: "Morgan! Morrrgannn!" *Llynya crying his name in a plaintive wail,* "Morgannn!"

He leaped, dragging his sword out of its scabbard.

"Son of a bitch!" a man shouted.

A table crashed to the floor, hewn in two by his blade, shards flying everywhere. A lantern rolled off into the gloom. Men and women scrambled in all directions, trying to get away. His next lunging strike shattered glasses and bottles, and a cry of pain echoed through the cavernous building called Racht Square.

"Somebody stun him!"

"Or shoot the bastard!"

"No!" A more familiar voice intruded on Morgan's haze of darkness.

He struck again, and a chair splintered.

"Morgan! Milord!" The familiar voice grew louder, closer, and a hand reached out to take hold of him.

Morgan roared, swinging his sword up over his head and bringing it down to within a hairbreadth of Aja's brow. Eyes wide and near colorless with terror stared up at him from beneath a shock of red hair.

"Morgan," the boy whispered, his voice a rasp of fear. "Milord, 'tis me, faithful captain good and true."

Trembling, Morgan stared down the length of his blade, the edge so sharp and fine, and so close to cleaving Aja's skull.

"Morgan, we are here in Racht Square, the hour is late. You fell asleep, milord, and dreamed. Only dreamed."

It had been no dream. Aja knew the truth as well as he.

Morgan looked around him at the destruction he had wrought and the people who had backed away, some cowering, others with their lasguns drawn, silently daring him to strike again, to give them an excuse for murder.

It had been no dream. Carillion wine had the potency to take a man beyond the delusions of dreams. The fermentation seeped into the cerebrum, some said changing it, rewiring synapses, delving deep into the cells and enticing memories to the fore, sliding them into the conscious mind on a trail of Carillion ooze. Eyes, nose, tongue, ears, skin— all believed what the wine told them was real.

But as with all things Carillion, the method was not foolproof. Mistakes were made, memories were tangled, and in the end, he was never truly back in Wales with the people he loved. He never really saw Dain's cynical smile, nor ever really gazed into the green eyes of the warrior sprite, Llynya.

Slowly, Morgan lifted his blade away from Aja's head. He heard the boy take a breath.

"More wine," he ordered, stumbling back and clearing off the closest table with a broad sweep of the sword. Glasses broke on the stone floor and mugs clattered in their wake. "Bring me more wine."

He lurched into a chair and slammed his sword down hard on the table, his knuckles white around the hilt. The wine would take him back to Wales, to Dolwyddelan Castle, and this time he would not make the mistake of looking behind him.

"Milord, it's late," Aja said. "We are better off going home."

The last word no sooner left the boy's mouth than Morgan whirled and grabbed him around the throat.

"Home?" he snarled, dragging the boy in close. "That friggin' hole where I sleep isn't home. Only one thing takes me *home,* boy. Fetch it." He shoved Aja away, heard him fall, and heard the curse that left the boy's mouth.

He dropped his head into his hand, dragging his fingers back through his hair, and swore even more vilely than Aja. Lights danced all around him, streaming in from beyond his peripheral vision and glittering in front of his eyes, messing with what little was left of his mind. A cold wind blew into the square through Racht's cracked roof. The chill of it seeped into his bones, adding to his misery.

"God's blood," he muttered. He was half blind on wine, and his skull felt like it was cracking open, the fracture raw and jagged. He hurt everywhere, inside and out, and in places too deep to delve. The rotting Carillions couldn't even get a good drunk right.

Jiang had been the first to leave him. Wils and Robbi had soon followed. York was no doubt lurking somewhere in the Square's many shadows, waiting for God knew what. There would be no more money, no more jobs. Morgan hadn't paid them for the last one, the heist in Sonnpur-Dzon, the friggin' hole.

He was broke, the gold dragon still in the bag looped around his belt, smelling of worms, and his, by God, until the end.

Rotting prize. He was doomed. The Dominion trader had been backed by the Warmonger of Magh Dun, and the Warmonger wanted the cursed dragon. Already he had hired Van the Wretched's skraelpacks to sniff it out. They'd caught the trader three weeks past and dealt him a brutal death. Morgan figured he'd be dead himself inside of a month, unless the wine killed him first.

His money was on the wine. The streets of the Pathian Quarter were littered with the bodies of Carillion wine junkies, some breathing, many not. Aja was the only thing keeping him out of the gutter, but even Aja had to give up soon and let him go.

Aye, that's what he wanted, to be let go. Let go by whatever force had brought him to the future. For as surely as he breathed, he should have died in the weir. He had only to look at the scar that ran from his chest across his abdomen to his hip to know he'd been nearly cut in half by Caradoc's last blow. He should have died from such a grievous wound.

Death was what he wanted, and there were many about who were willing to deal it to him. If not for Aja, he most assuredly would have been dead five minutes past. The price on his head was large enough to lure even the fainthearted into violence; the fear of Aja's wrath was enough to stay their hands—for now.

Friggin' wine, he swore to himself, shaking his head. He needed more wine.

.   .   .

"Have you seen enough, lady?"

From high on a balcony in the southeast sector of Racht Square, Avallyn nodded to Dray, not trusting herself to speak. Her sense of loss was a hard, painful knot in her chest, her disappointment skirting the borders of despair. Au Cade had not been wrong as she had prayed. The supposed Prince of Time that Dray had found was no more than a man, a tech-trash thief who was cruder even than Tamisk had warned, abusive, violent, and most assuredly insane, his mind eaten away by the Carillion wine he kept demanding.

Palinor wanted him brought to Claerwen. So be it. Avallyn would take him there—and leave him there. The wretch below was of no use to her. There would be no shared kiss of triumph.

"Take him," she ordered—and ten thousand years be damned. She was better off alone.

"And the boy?" the Night Watcher captain asked. He and the other Sha-shakrieg guards were shrouded head to toe in their tattered black robes, as was she, all of them no more than shadows against the wall. They all had tech-jaws in their mouths.

Avallyn shifted her gaze to the wild boy. He, at least, appeared to have his wits about him. Racht Square, the remains of a spaceport hangar bombed out in the Second Rising, was at all times a place for caution, something the boy's master was sorely lacking. Thousands of people milled about the multilevel square, and Avallyn doubted if many in the southeast sector had not been noted by the boy or the hulking mercenary working with him. The man changed positions every half hour like clockwork, his last move taking him halfway up the side of the building to Racht's third tier.

Great steel beams encased the square's inner structure of balconies and platforms, holding up what was left of the main building. The hangar doors above had been blown off, exposing all and sundry to the night sky and the elements, and giving Racht the look of a giant, cracked-open egg. Rain had fallen earlier in the day, and water yet dripped off the beams and pooled on the floor, much of it finding its way into the canals that had once held cables and fuel lines for the bays to the east, where Dray had left their rovers. The wind that had begun shortly after sunset was picking up strength, bringing with it a peculiar tension and the musty scent of impending rain. The storm was returning in force, and Avallyn would as soon be done with the job at hand and headed back into the desert, away from the Old Dominion. The rotting city was even worse than she'd been told, its streets choked with the refuse of civilization, its rancid quarters full of religions and bereft of truth.

Picking up the prince posed no problem. He was nearly catatonic, staring at his table, one hand gripping his sword, the other holding his head, a travesty. She had no need of her mother's dreamstone. Dray could take him alone.

The boy did pose a problem, though, one the people around him seemed to appreciate. Tiny glints of silver ran the length of his left arm, throwing stars poisoned with the sap of the bia tree, the weapon of the Waste. He had a dagger in each boot, a carbine strapped to his back, a shortsword hanging from his belt, and a lasgun holstered on his hip. Almost everyone in Racht Square was armed in a like manner, but they had not the boy's deadly speed. No one drew on a wild boy and lived to tell the tale.

"I will speak to him," Avallyn said.

Dray shot her a questioning glance, his eyes shadowed by the folds of his hood. A thin purple scar marked the Night Watcher's weathered face, running from his ear across the rise of his cheek. Similar scars, but shallower and webbed in a fine tracery, covered the back of his right hand, mementos of a life lived in desert battles.

Avallyn shrugged away his doubts. "Given the man's condition, the boy might welcome the chance to be rid of him."

"His loyalty runs deeper than that, I think."

"And I am a White Lady of Death." Avallyn's natural arrogance rose to the fore. "The boy will think twice before gainsaying my wishes." Only two tribes dared the northern deserts of Earth, the White Ladies and the wild boys. For hundreds of years they had fought together against the never-ending stream of Warlords who wanted to conquer the Waste and control its vast supply of chrystaalt, the most precious mineral on Earth. When in trouble, the boys knew a place awaited them in the White Ladies' temples. Although never completely dependable, they were good fighters who more than once had helped stem the tide of the Warmongers' armies, fierce battalions of men, beasts, and every configuration in between, the dregs of creation recruited from the nethermost reaches of the galaxy.

"As you wish, my lady," Dray conceded. "I'll leave the boy to—"

Avallyn tensed in the same instant as Dray fell silent, both of them seeing the skraelpack enter the square three floors below. The crowd parted for the pack, with people shoving and pushing to get out of the way. Avallyn knew 'twas as much because of the pack's stench as because of their bristling weapons. Beastmen all, skraelings were the offal of the galaxy, clawed and fanged more like animals than men, with overlarge jaws to accommodate their rapacious eating habits. *Sweet Mother,* they even ate each other.

Seconds later, across the square, an armed troop marched onto the main floor, their presence announced by sudden shouts and a bulging swell of bodies being pushed aside.

"Van's beasts," Dray said, identifying the skraelpack.

Avallyn nodded in acknowledgment. She'd recognized the captain, a sallow-faced, hunchbacked ogre with a morning star welded to his wrist. Then she swore when she saw the armed troop's insignia. It was the Warmonger's Third Guard, with a Lyran mark-tracker in the lead. Capable of discerning her prey's scent at a remarkable one part per million, the female Lyran loped into the square and scanned the crowd with a slow swing of her head. Back and forth she sniffed, quartering the hangar, her mane of fine orange-gold hair lifting into the wind and flowing across her face in gossamer strands. In shape she was nearly human, her skin cast in shades of green. A black hauberk protected her torso. Leather leggings covered her powerful legs. When her nose passed in the prince's direction, she halted, her feral, verdured features frozen in the stillness of a carefully indrawn breath.

A cold shiver coursed down Avallyn's spine.

"We're too far outnumbered to fight for him," Dray said, voicing her sudden fear. The Lyran's golden eyes had narrowed in concentration, her gaze fixing along a line of sight that undeniably led to the wild boy and his drunken master.

Two troops against their handful of guards? Not even Night Watchers could overcome such odds. Yet as dearly as Avallyn was tempted, she couldn't leave the thief to the doom preparing to descend on him and his cohorts.

Until proven otherwise, he belonged to the White Ladies.

Carillion wine and a Lyran mark-tracker—Shadana, she thought in disgust. No half measures for Morgan ab Kynan, whether in vice or enemies.

"Then we'd best keep it from becoming a fight," she said, closing her hand around the dreamstone dagger sheathed on her hip. "Move out."

Aja heard York's warning through his tech-jaw and released the trigger lock on his lasgun, cursing under his breath. He knew they should have gone home. They should have gone home hours ago.

"Skraelings," he muttered, loosening a row of iron stars.

Moving with all possible speed, York contacted him again from his new position on the lowest balcony. Aja felt himself blanch at the mercenary's words: The Third Guard—led by a Lyran—had entered the main floor of the square and was closing in, the master's right hand come to spur on the beasts.

They were doomed.

"Morgan, make ready for a fight," he said, reaching over his shoulder and switching his carbine to automatic. "Milord. Please."

His lord didn't move, not so much as a muscle, not so much as the twitch of an eye, and frustration tightened Aja's jaw, frustration aggravated in no small measure by guilt.

It was his fault. All of it. He'd been the one to give Morgan his first taste of Carillion wine years ago. He'd thought it would help ease Morgan's loneliness if he could see his friends. He'd thought Morgan would be less inclined to bouts of melancholy if he went home for a bit now and again. He'd thought Morgan, a survivor of the weir, was too strong to fall prey to the grapish stuff.

And truly, he'd asked himself, what harm could there be in a few judicious drams?

Enough and then some had been his answer, for the price of Morgan's ease had become unbearable since Sonnpur-Dzon. The other times Morgan had escaped to the strange and enchanting world from whence he'd come, Aja had gone with him, reading him through his own taste of wine and a delicate touch, reliving the laughter of Owain and Rhys, Drew and Rhodri and Dafydd. Over the years, Aja had ridden the length and breadth of the land called Wales with Morgan's band of men, taking surefooted horses through the snowcapped peaks of Eryri and fording the quicksands of the Neath. They'd swum naked in cool, clean rivers and hunted deer in the king's forests—lush, wild greenwoods unlike anything left on Earth. Some of the wild boys told tales of a lost forest in the Waste, but Aja had been born and bred in the desert and never seen more than a scrub of grass growing anywhere.

Yet he liked to dream about forests, and think such a place might exist, somewhere, rising out of the sand.

He released the ties on the dagger sheaths in his boots, readying the knives for a quick throw. Aye, he knew Morgan well, for the thief he was and for the prince he had once been. But not even he could follow his lord through such dark corridors of memory as Morgan now chose to tread.

Aja touched the larger sheath on his belt, checking its position, and his fingers absently brushed across the yellow wallet always secured at his side. The short sword inside the sheath was rimed in bia sap, a sure death for any who felt the blade, though the storm brewing above Racht might do as much to save them as any of his weapons, if it broke soon enough. A fierce electrical charge was building in the clouds. He could feel the energy skittering across his skin, heralding deadly bolts of lightning. The Old Dominion had once been powered by such bolts, the lightning captured and channeled by a grid of spiraling towers that reached thousands of meters into the atmosphere, but no more. Most of the towers had been shattered in the wars. Huge pieces of the open-metalwork structures lay scattered throughout the quarters. One good cracking blast close to the square would shake up the skraelings for sure, and mayhap even throw the Lyran off her scent. The Third Guard was less easily startled, but any delay worked to his and Morgan's advantage. York he counted on to take care of himself, if things took an inescapable turn for the worst.

Bones, what an end after all their glory.

He'd oft thought he should get Morgan a greenwood tree, a reminder of his home, but he'd left it too late. They were rare things, trees, hard to come by, but available to a man with enough gold. The dragon statue would buy a tree, but he dared not touch it. Morgan's bane he called it under his breath. Since the night in the monastery, the golden beast had not left his lord's side—and neither had flask after flask of Carillion wine.

Morgan was killing himself. The truth could be no plainer—and Aja had handed him the death weapon.

He checked the crowd and saw that York was nearly halfway to them, running when he could, muscling his way through the milling throng when he had to, but he wasn't going to reach them in time. The skraelpack was closer, and the Warmonger's guard not far behind. For himself, Aja could have disappeared, eluding even the Lyran, but he needed York to get Morgan out.

He pulled his lasgun free of its holster and knelt by his prince's side, working quickly to untie the leather bag holding the gold statue. He'd seen the trader's body, or what had been left of it, and the friggin' skraelings weren't going to take him or Morgan alive. If they wanted the dragon, he was going to give it to them right down their mange-infested throats. If they wanted Morgan, they were going to have to blast their way through him first.

Aye, by the bones he held so dearly, he'd rather be dead when they ate him.

Three hundred miles to the south, where the last outposts of the Old Dominion gave way to the Deseillign Waste, a lone messenger hurried along a dark corridor in Magh Dun, the Warmonger's stronghold. The smoothly rounded fortress squatted amidst the dunes and rocks, a windowless iron keep streaked with soot from the fires kept burning in its oily moat.

"Doomed," the nameless minion muttered, looking down every hall he passed in hopes of finding someone else to deliver the encrypted message crumpled in his fist. "I'm doomed."

Any dispatch from the captain of the Third Guard was bound to have consequences. Good news meant a possible promotion for the messenger. Bad news inevitably meant death.

A bad death. Swift and sure and agonizing, and unbearably strange.

Sweat broke out on the minion's brow. Better to be eaten by skraelings than to suffer at the left hand of the Warmonger, or even worse, to be given to the witch Vishab for her dreadful experiments. How in the world, after so many years of unremarked existence, had he allowed himself to be passing Magh Dun's command center at the exact moment when a message had come through from the Third Guard?

He reached the last corridor before the entrance of the Hall of Tombs, an arched vault of black glass in the heart of the fortress. His eyes darted one way then the other. No one. There was no one to save him.

He looked down again at the missive. Mayhap he could avoid the hazards of delivery by placing the message in his helmet and sliding it across the floor while running madly in the other direction.

Yes. That was it. Relief flooded through him—until the unmistakable voice of the Warmonger reached out of the darkness and ensnared him with a single word.

"Enter."

It was the voice of doom.

From where he sat on his great stone throne, Corvus Gei, Lord of Magh Dun and Warmonger of the Waste, saw the man hesitate and thereby prove himself more intelligent than the average slave, but no one in the realm would dare disobey a direct order from the Warmonger. There was no future in such an action. Not so much as an instant.

His left hand twitched, and Corvus looked down at the blackened thing that lay on the arm of the throne.

Smoke and darkness, he thought, gazing upon his strange limb. In certain light, his fingers seemed to disappear altogether. Sometimes his whole arm. Sometimes his mind.

And there was the rub.

He'd gone mad.

"He delays, my lord," a raspy voice said to him from beside the throne. "Shall I draw him near?"

Corvus glanced at the ancient crone standing to his right. Her long gray hair wisped about her heavily lined face and stooped shoulders in a nimbus of sparse strands. Her body was no more than a small bag of bones contained within a thin, leathery casing of skin, ninety pounds of usable terror covered in shabby dark robes—but he did not need her to control the messenger.

"Stay yourself, Vishab. If the news is bad, you'll have him quick enough."

Twice he'd breached the wormhole. Twice he'd slipped into the maelstrom of the time weir. Twice, it seemed, was once too much—yet he would go again. Thousands of years in the past, he had still been whole, and undoubtedly the most brilliant mind of the age. He alone had deciphered the secrets of the great worms and found his way back to the time of the Old Dominion. He alone had followed in the footsteps of the Druid savant, Nemeton, compiling a library to make even the most erudite of scholars weep with envy.

Knowledge. He had drenched himself in it, devoted himself to it, murdered for it, yet he'd still not had enough to save himself. Something had gone wrong in the wormhole, a minute change in a regrettably acquired substance that he could not have foreseen.

He willed his black hand to move toward his chest, demanded that the smokelike fingers grasp the pendant he wore as an added reminder of the cost of ignorance.

Nemeton. The name whispered through his mind. Nemeton had known. Perhaps he'd even set the trap through his daughter. For it had been she who had burned the earth next to the River Bredd, leaving the traces of chrystaalt that had opened the way for him into Merioneth and the wormhole. The bait had been irresistible. Chrystaalt was a vital ingredient for traveling through time. Any time-rider would have scooped up the rare crystals from the scorched dirt and secreted them in a pocket.

But he'd scooped up a bit more than chrystaalt, hadn't he.

He opened his fingers, cradling the pendant in his palm. A small piece of parchment lay frozen within the brilliantly faceted crystal, a few grains of chrystaalt embedded in its surface, its edges blackened by the eldritch rot that had shifted its domicile to his arm.

Strange stuff, he brooded. When he'd been spat out on the desert ten years ago, he'd taken a careful inventory of his belongings. One of the two ancient books he'd brought from the past had still been with him, and with it he'd found his ally, Vishab. He'd also still had three small packages of twisted parchment he'd placed in a pouch on his belt. Two of the packages had been pure chrystaalt and worth enough to supply his needs and begin the process of reclaiming his lost empire. The third had changed the course of all his plans. One touch, and the strange rot he'd tried to scrape off had begun blackening his fingertips. The pestilence had claimed his left arm over the years, and it would not stop there. The fresh marks on his chest were proof of the danger.

Time, he thought. Time was working against him in this. If he found no way to stop it, his whole body would become nothing but a blackened shadow with an awesome power he would not be able to control.

His fingers twitched again, but he held them in check with a surfeit of will—for now.

He needed to go back. He needed to find the damned witch who had sent him into the future, and the even more damned witch who had trapped him with the chrystaalt. Naas and Madron were their names.

They had cursed him. They could heal him. No death-witch he'd ever captured in his own time had been able to stem the tide of his destruction. He'd bled priestesses dry, literally, to no avail. He'd called on them to wield their power against the rot, and every White Lady had failed. They ruled the time weir from their northern temple of Claerwen, but they did not rule the scourge of the Dark Age he'd read about in a book on Ynys Enlli, a scourge that he feared was the same all-devouring Dharkkum spoken of in the book he'd brought through the weir, the Yellow Book of Chandra. It was an everlasting night, like the strange and frightening substance that now comprised his arm. Only dragons could destroy it, according to the books.

Dragons, and maybe Vishab. No White Lady she, but a very dark woman, a desert sept outcast who a century past had set herself against the Priestesses of the Bones. He had bought her loyalty with the Yellow Book, a farrago of ancient history and priestess bloodspells she spent her time combing through, searching for her enemy's weaknesses and his salvation.

Witches, he thought with a grimace. Women had always brought him to ruin, especially the White Ladies, Claerwen's Priestesses of the Bones. They'd been the ones to stake him out for the worms on a pile of chrystaalt the first time he'd traveled through the weir. They had destroyed him to protect one of their own, a royal bit of baggage he had once loved. Now the favor was his, and he was eager to return it in full measure.

Love, he silently scoffed. His one experience with the emotion had been his downfall. No act of murdering vengeance or criminal intent had ever done him as much damage as love.

A soft noise brought his head up. The messenger had finally minced his way across the hall to the throne.

Corvus held out his right hand and accepted the hesitantly offered dispatch. The captain of the Third Guard's mark was on the digitally encoded seal. His eyes narrowed. He'd set the Guard to finding the most daring fool in the Old Dominion, the one who had dared to steal from him. The man was a tech-trash thief contracted by a trader in religious artifacts to retrieve a statue Vishab believed might prove of value as a cure for his grave malady.

"Worms," he muttered, breaking the seal on the dispatch. The great time worms that had brought him to this pass were the dragon larvae of the past. Vishab had traced a dragon cult to a Middle Kingdom monastery called Sonnpur-Dzon. The trader had double-crossed him with the statue and paid with his life. The thief would be next.

He skimmed the brief message and felt a surge of satisfaction. The Third Guard had found the tech-trash sot in Racht Square. The Lyran mark-tracker he'd paid so dearly for had proven to be worth the price. The thief and the golden dragon would soon be his.

Chapter 3

The Old Dominion

The Sha-shakrieg Night Watchers moved with swift assurance along the edge of Racht's balcony. While the boy below made ready to sacrifice himself, and the mercenary was proving too slow to be of help, Avallyn and Dray acted to save the drunken thief, covering the distance to a place above Morgan in seconds.

"Take the skraeling captain *en chrysalii dea,*" Dray ordered, reaching under his sleeve for one of the thin coils of thread adhered to his arm. The coil came free, and with a flick of his wrist, Dray sent thread sailing out into the gloom of Racht Square. Slickly wet and glinting with bits of reflected light, the purplish-brown thread snaked through the air to find its mark. Dozens more of the puce filaments followed, all thrown with the same unerring accuracy.

"Night Watchers!"

The cry went up even as the skraeling captain grunted with pain at the first touch of the thread. Within a minute, the beastman was down, his body wrapped in a tangled skein of bia-steeped *pryf* silk. The stench of burning hair and flesh drifted up to the balcony amidst the captain's death squeals.

"Drop a web and come with me," Avallyn said to the Night Watchers closest to her, peeling a silver thread from the inside of her forearm.

The skraelings fell on their downed leader in a feeding frenzy, their advance halted by the insatiable hunger of their breed. The Third Guard was yet twenty meters away from the prince, their passage blocked by the uproar caused more by the manner of the skraeling's death than the death itself. None in Racht Square—or in truth, in the whole of the Old Dominion—relished the company of the Sha-shakrieg.

A half-dozen threads uncoiled in quick succession from the skilled hands of the Sha-shakrieg guards, crisscrossing to the main floor. Avallyn secured her length of silk and swung over the balcony rail with three of the guards close behind.

She knew what they looked like, four death-shadows dropping out of the darkness, harbingers of doom for hapless souls—and so it would be for the sake of the wretched man below. A cry went up from the Third Guard, a cry for the death of the desert wraiths, and Avallyn speeded her descent.

The death squeals woke Morgan from his stupor, the trilling terror in the high, elongated notes cutting through the fog of wine and exhaustion and sparking him back to life. Once he was conscious, the blood-scent accompanying the swinish screams hit him like a wave, clearing his brain as nothing else could.

"*Christe,*" he swore, staggering to his feet, sword in hand. Racht had erupted into chaos. More than the dying beast were screaming. People were shouting and running in every direction. The wind was strengthening, lifting debris off the floor and flying it in the air. The square's few hanging lamps were swaying on their cords, casting long arcs of light through the gloom.

He barely had time to register the slathering pile of skraelings feeding on the floor, before the crush of the crowd took them from view. Someone bumped into him, and he swore again, the words as slurred as his brain. Skraelings. He tightened his grip on the sword. They weren't ones to savor a meal. Time was short.

"Aja," he called, turning his head—and paying the price for the deed. Pain rocketed around his skull, but not enough to blind him to his captain's folly. The boy was at his side, readying to throw the Sonnpur-Dzon statue into the battling throng. Morgan watched in dismay as the dragon left Aja's hand and arced into the air, all gold and glittering and moving inexorably toward the phalanx of hairy fists reaching up to grab it . . . *over his dead body.* The bloody dragon was his.

With a roar, he leaped for the statue, and in brief triumph, his fingers closed around solid metal.

"Milord!" Aja yelled—too late.

Morgan was hit in the side and knocked facedown on the floor. His breath left him in a pained gasp. His ears rang with the force of the blow. In a trice, his attacker was on him, a growling creature with arms and legs like iron, every limb wrapping around him and squeezing. The gold dragon was beneath him, digging into his ribs. He tried to twist his body free and failed, outmatched by the beast on his back.

The fierce hands threatening to break him were merciless in their grip, the fingers gouging into his muscles in search of bone to crack. He gasped for a breath and then groaned in agony as the creature wrenched his shoulder as if to pull his arm from its socket. When the limb didn't give way, his attacker let out a roar of its own and slammed him against the floor. His sword was still in his hand, but he was too stunned to use it. The beast closed its jaws around his throat and a great orange mane of hair fell over his face, forming an all-too-clear picture in his mind.

Merde, he swore, in the tongue of his old Norman enemies. Double rows of teeth, two sets each for the top and bottom jaws, with radical canines pressing into his skin and a cloud of sickly sweet breath billowing up around him—a smell too unique to ever forget—confirmed the rotting truth. 'Twas a sodding exotic Lyran on his back, and she had him by the throat.

Groaning, he tried to angle his blade upward for a cutting strike and couldn't. Her teeth pressed harder, and she gave him a shake, playing with her food. Switching tactics, he went for the lasgun on his hip and found himself blocked by a quick, upward move of her knee, her huge, knobby, hip-crushing knee.

There was only one chance, and fighting every instinct he had, he forced his body to go limp within her grasp. Lyrans liked live prey, the livelier the better, especially for the female mark-trackers, who were known never to eat anything they hadn't fought to the death.

The pressure of her jaws lightened faintly. Then the thing let out a screeching howl, releasing him. The smell of burning flesh assaulted his nostrils, hot and rank. The Lyran bounded off him, and he rolled to his feet, the freed lasgun in one hand and Scyld in the other, swinging out to cut the beast.

Blood gushed where the blade sliced into her thigh, and she stumbled backward, roaring in rage and pain, her orange mane flying, her green face marked with a smoking purple scar.

A dozen screams rent the air as whiplike threads streamed down from above, burning whomever they struck and clearing a place around him and the Lyran, cordoning them off. Outside the weblike structure, the skraelings were regrouping from their feast. To the right, an armed troop was breaking through the crowd—the Third Guard.

Worse and worse, he thought. He was bent half double in pain, his gun arm nearly numb from the Lyran's wrenching, his body aching from her crushing weight. He took a deep breath, trying to straighten himself, and the Lyran snarled, her lips curling up to reveal the extra-long canines curving down from her upper jaw. She crouched low to pounce, her arms flexed at her sides. In the next instant, her gaze shifted, her golden eyes fixing on something behind him.

Morgan whirled around, his finger on the lasgun's trigger—and came to a dead halt.

Llynya.

The sight of her hit him like another blow. His hand tightened on Scyld's hilt, threatening to break it with the force of his grip.

Llynya . . . dressed in black, the wind wrapping her cloak about her. *Llynya . . . here?*

Confusion flooded through him. Had she fallen into the weir during the battle? Spent a frozen eternity in the hell of the wormhole?

Had she spent the last ten years lost in this godforsaken time?

He started to take a step toward her, drawn by the face that haunted his dreams, the last face he'd seen from his time—so wild and pretty, so determined, her eyes as green as a thousand trees in deep summer. Except the eyes that shot him a brief glance were gray, not green, a lucid, piercing gray as clear as mountain water and just as cold.

He stopped short, suddenly unsure of what he was seeing.

Her hair was a tumble of braids and knots—but shorter, much shorter than he remembered, and the wrong color, a whole array of the wrong colors, all blonds and silvers, not the rich darkness of a velvety night. 'Twas much worsely knotted, too, less skillfully braided, and without a single twig, without a single leaf to adorn the silken strands.

He thought of his chest and the mark of the leaf permanently traced on his skin, the leaf he'd stolen from the elf maid in Lanbarrdein.

So not the fair and wondrous Llynya, not without leaves in her hair. Cold truth replaced his confusion.

"Friggin' wine," he growled, shaking his head. He didn't have time for its illusions.

He hazarded a glance at the Lyran, holding steady in an attack position under the threat of his lasgun, all eight feet of her, then looked back to the woman.

The illusion hadn't evaporated as Carillion illusions were wont to do.

He narrowed his gaze and took another step forward, willing her to be gone, to go the path of all the drunken, self-indulgent images he conjured with the wine. To his surprise, she lashed out with a fighting thread, the end of it snaking by him and finding its target behind his back.

The Lyran roared her rage and rushed forward, only to be brought up short by a firm command.

"*Creassa, Ly-ray! Creassa!*" the woman shouted, threatening with another thread. "*Chak ga, bey bey Rhayne. Bonse bey bey.*"

To Morgan's astonishment, the Lyran fell back, snarling and snapping, and when the woman advanced on her, the beast turned and ran, retreating through an opening in the hastily strung web, heading toward the armed troop.

Llynya had fought with a sword and a bow, and none better, Morgan remembered. No one in his time had known fighting threads. They were weapons of the Waste, weapons of the Sha-shakrieg Night Watchers, like the men forming up behind the woman—desert wraiths all, her included, judging by her outfit. No elfin maid.

But the resemblance—*Sweet Jesu.* 'Twas enough to hurt, as everything had hurt since Sonnpur-Dzon.

"*Har maukte! Har!*" The skraelings sent up their war cry.

"*Corvus! Corvus!*" came the answer from the right. "*Har maukte, har maukte! Har!*"

Time had run out. From beyond the Sha-shakrieg's web, York

burst through the crowd and threw him a tech-jaw. The small silver ball flew through the air, breaching the threads. Morgan caught it with the hand holding the lasgun and dropped it in his mouth. The web, no matter how poisonous, wouldn't hold the beasts off forever.

"Tri-opt Four," York said, giving a location outside the square.

"Aye. Aja, point," Morgan said, taking command. "And pick up the damned dragon." Forget the Carillions. He couldn't get a damned drunk right anymore, either.

"Aye." For once, the boy did as he was told, scooping the statue up off the floor as he did a lightning-quick reconnaissance to find the fastest way out of the web and out of Racht.

Morgan swung back to the woman. Whoever she was, she obviously hadn't been sent by Van or the Warmonger. That made her less than an enemy, if not exactly an ally.

Yet she and her guards had saved him from the Lyran and, with their deadly web of threads, had bought him time to escape—or they'd captured him for themselves. He'd been carrying a hell of a bounty lately.

Her face. He still wasn't sure that she wasn't an illusion. Everything about her was too familiar, too perfect, even her less-than-perfect hair.

A commotion behind him jerked his attention back to the crisis—which, for all its fascination, wasn't about some woman's face. Three skraelings had dared the threads. More brute force than grace, they brought the smell of burning hair and scorched skin with them—and the sound of lasguns winding up for a showdown.

Morgan dove for the floor as the skraelings let loose with a round of fire. Sliding across the slick, wet stone, he rolled onto his back, his lasgun pulsing. He took out one of the skraelings before a Night Watcher retaliated with a blastpak and pitched the area into an impenetrable fog of smoke and flame bursts.

"Tri-opt Four, Captain," Morgan ordered, sheathing his sword. "Relay! Go!"

He twisted around, squinting against the smoke, searching for the woman. She'd been less than three meters from him.

"Seven points west." Aja's voice came over the tech-jaw. "Stay low and watch for the cable canal."

Morgan glanced at the locator on his comwatch, marking the direction. From somewhere east of him, he heard the captain of the Third

Guard shout orders to surround him, and he knew he had to make a break for it or lose his chance. Yet he hesitated. She was out there. Close. He could feel her, some sense telling him she was just out of reach.

Suddenly, a hand appeared out of the smoke, small but strong, and wrapped around his wrist.

"I've got him, Dray," the woman said breathlessly, sliding to a stop next to him. She quickly rose to a crouch, a modified lasgun gripped in her other hand. "Disburse. I'll meet you at the rover." She slapped a tracking bracelet on Morgan's arm. "Come on."

Morgan scrambled to his feet, all hesitancy gone. He'd obey her— up to a point. It was time to get the hell out of Racht, and she was going with him. He grabbed her hand and took off, following Aja's directions. He didn't know what the woman's plan was and he didn't care. He'd trust his captain over a bounty hunter any day.

And she was a bounty hunter. That question had been answered beyond a doubt. No one else carried around tracking bracelets, pairs of locking metal bands tuned to a single frequency. He glanced down at her wrist and saw a bracelet that matched his, the lights in both cycling synchronously. They had an odd glow about them that he hadn't seen before on tracking bracelets, but tech-trash innovations were Aja's specialty, not his.

She'd banded him, though. He had to give her that. He'd outmaneuvered Van's beasts and the Third Guard for three months, and been drunk most of the time. The Lyran had been a close call, a real close call, but hell, he was still in one piece—except for his head, which felt even more like someone had cracked it open with a jagged pike.

I've got him, she'd said to one of the Night Watchers.

Not for long, he could have told her. As soon as they were out of Racht, he would get the bracelet's lock sequence from her and be on his way to Tri-opt Four.

Another skraeling went down in front of them, his blood spilling onto the floor like a red tide, the neatness of his slit throat and the throwing star sticking out of his chest proclaiming him a piece of Aja's work.

Good, Morgan thought. The boy was only seconds ahead of him.

They dodged tables and overturned chairs. Broken glass littered the floor. Black cloaks swept by them in the smoke as they ran—her Night Watchers taking up the fight behind them, guarding their backs instead of stopping him cold as he made off with one of their own.

It didn't make sense, and that bothered him. Not enough to slow him down, but it bothered him.

Something else bothered him too. He didn't know how in the hell she thought she could hold him with just a tracking bracelet. The bounty hunters he knew, and there were quite a few, always backed up their bracelets with something a little more deterring, something with a lethal component. Maiming devices were popular, something triggered by a break in the frequency connection.

His bracelet was completely smooth, without any devices attached, the only oddity being the glow that seemed to emanate from the metal itself. 'Twas strange, but apparently not deadly or drugging, or he'd probably know it by now. He felt nothing—nothing except the warmth of her hand in his, holding him at least as tightly as he was holding her.

Stranger yet, he thought, bemused. He ran, and she kept up with him, offering no resistance.

"Take the canal southeast under the threads, then due east at the first intersection. I left a zip line," Aja said, and Morgan knew the boy had made it beyond the web and was running through the canal. His captain would relay directions to him all the way to Tri-opt Four. From there they could circle around and pick up their transport.

"York," he said, expecting the mercenary to report.

"Four points east of the intersection. I've got the boy marked, and if he'd quit pingin' off the friggin' walls, I could keep up with him when he flies by," the older man muttered. "Unless you want me to wait for you."

"Nay. I'll meet you there." He was deliberately vague. He'd heard the woman giving orders through a tech-jaw and didn't want her relaying their destination to the Night Watchers, not until after he, Aja, and York were gone.

The web loomed ahead of them through the smoke, a drape of silvery threads interspersed with darker ones. Sheathing his lasgun, Morgan tightened his hand around the woman's, wanting to make damn sure he didn't lose her.

"Hold on," he warned.

A shadow beyond the web heralded the canal. Morgan unhooked a descender from his belt and snapped it open in readiness. When he saw the opening in the threads, he looked for the zip line. It was there, thicker and duller than the threads, looped around a hunk of Racht junk no bigger than a table.

He swore under his breath. The piece of twisted metal had held Aja's weight, and it might hold his own, but unless it was bolted to the floor it sure as hell wouldn't hold his and the woman's. Somewhere in the last thirty seconds, he should have told Aja that he'd taken a hostage.

Another blast of skraeling fire exploded behind them. He was out of options and out of time. Three more running strides and he dropped to the floor, pulling her down with him and reaching out to snag the zip line. He thought he heard the descender click closed and hoped he felt the line catch before they slid under the threads and over the edge into the canal—and into darkness.

Chapter 4

She was smart. Morgan had to give her that. They'd no
sooner hit the floor than she'd wrapped her arm around
him, angling her lasgun across his chest and holding on
like he'd told her, like her life depended on it. And even
as they'd gone over the edge, she'd managed to release a
descender of her own and snap onto the line.

Quick. She was damn quick, almost as fast as Aja,
and obviously used to being in tight places. He knew a
few female bounty hunters, all good, but none quite so
slick as the woman who had caught him. Under other
circumstances, he'd be tempted to take her on for a job
or two. He sure as hell would like to know what she'd
said to the Lyran to scare the beast off.

Damn, they were falling fast.

The zip line hummed through his descender, the
speed of their descent increasing with each passing second, which could only mean the piece of Racht junk was
not bolted down and was giving way above them, scrap-

ing across the floor, pulled by their weight. Any moment it was going to come tumbling down right on top of them.

With luck, they would reach the bottom and have time to get out of the way before they were crushed.

With the desert woman wrapped around him, feeling so alive, Morgan hoped he still had some luck to call on.

So did Avallyn, but she had her doubts and plenty of them. The man was insane. No one in his right mind would have jumped into one of Racht's canals on the off chance that awash in Carillion wine he could snag a zip line anchored to a piece of scrap metal—a small piece that by her calculations was sliding across the floor above them at roughly the same speed as their descent, effectively negating any advantage the zip line had given them over simply throwing themselves off the edge.

Her heart racing, she swore under her breath. They were moving too fast, and she'd used her last thread in the attempt to save him, a futile endeavor. The only way the situation could be worse would be if the zip line ran short of reaching the bottom of the canal—which it promptly did. They jerked to a halt, their descent slowed to the rate of the pile of metal moving across the floor.

"Hold on," he shouted, his arm tightening around her.

Shadana. What was he going to do next? She twisted her head around, trying to find a way to save herself.

"Dray—" she started, but the thief didn't give her a chance. Kicking off from the canal wall, he lofted them out into space, the two of them hanging from their descenders off the end of the zip line.

"Mother," she prayed. He was mad, mad beyond reckoning, as Au Cade had foretold. Then she saw it, the opposite canal wall coming into view, the face of it encrusted with cables and pipes. They had a chance, if they weren't impaled on contact.

He took the brunt of the impact, but the jolt still shuddered through her, jarring her bones. She grabbed for the nearest cable and scrambled for a foothold on the pipes bolted to the wall.

"Release your descender," he ordered, unhooking his from the line with a flick of his wrist.

Knowing the danger, she did the same, then watched as the line swung away from them, back into darkness. No sooner had it disap-

peared than it returned into view, followed by the twisted hunk of metal
it had been tied to above. She felt the wind of the metal's passing, heard
the tinny whoosh as the air set some part of it vibrating, and for an awful
second she feared it would scrape both of them off the canal wall. So
much then for the future of the White Ladies and everything else she
held dear, the whole of their planned destiny wiped out by the damned
time-rider they had awaited for thousands of years.

The piece of metal hit the canal floor with a resounding crash,
sending dust and chunks of debris flying into the air. The thief's reaction
was too fast to be anything other than instinctive. He covered her body
with his own and pressed her hard against the wall, protecting her from
the fallout. Avallyn had one hand clenched around a cable and the other
fisted in his shirt. He said something into her ear, but she couldn't hear
him over the echoes of the crash. She could feel him though, everywhere.

He was bigger than he'd looked in Racht, a wall of tensed, active
muscle between her and the emptiness beyond, hard and lean, and over-
whelmingly male. Her senses were twitching with information overload:
the length of the legs flanking hers, the breadth of the shoulders blocking
her view, the sleekly muscled torso pressed against her chest, and the
strength of the arms holding her to the wall of the canal. She'd shackled
herself to a man more physically powerful than she'd thought. It was a
disturbing realization, especially since she now found herself alone with
the mad thief.

The scent of wine was thick in the air around him, richly overripe,
lushly drenched with the fruits of half a dozen planets: grapes and plums
from the Eastern Dominion; ashoki and haesa from the Friina Group;
shampberries and blood oranges from Russ II. The fumes alone were
said to be enough to intoxicate a person, and Avallyn feared she was suc-
cumbing. The thief's head was angled toward hers, his chin grazing her
cheek, the unprecedented intimacy of their position enough to steal her
breath.

His hand came up and gripped her shoulder, a silent gesture for
her to be still, and she realized she'd been tensing her muscles in readiness to flee. She forced herself to relax, squelching her fight-or-flight response. She could do neither while hanging off a wall.

The last pieces of junk and debris settled, plunging the canal into
silence. He immediately swore, a softly muted word, barely audible.

"Are you hit?" she asked, her voice carefully neutral, belying the effect his nearness was having on her. She wanted nothing more than to squirm out from under him and run.

"No," came his curt reply, followed by another whispered curse that sent a blush across her cheeks.

They were tangled so closely together, it was as if he'd spoken the words directly to her, and the curse's distinction was its crude sexual connotation.

He hadn't been speaking to her, of course. The words were common, and commonly used by tech-trash and their ilk. Regardless, her mother had assured her there would be none of the physical intimacies normally expected between a priestess and her consort. In fact, she'd expressly forbidden such activity with the thief.

Not that Avallyn needed such prohibitions. One look at him in Racht had sunk him lower than beast fodder in her opinion. He couldn't possibly be the Prince of Time. In all the history of the world no priestess had been bound below her rank, and certainly not to a tech-trash denizen of the Old Dominion. Nor would they be, ever. So Palinor had vowed, and Avallyn had heartily concurred. There must have been a mistake, and the priestesses would find it. Until then, the drunken time-rider was as close as they'd come, and he was to be taken north, to Claerwen. That was her job, and by the gods she would see it done.

His curse had been only an expression of dissatisfaction, but it made her even more uncomfortably aware of him and the length of their bodies pressed together. She'd never been crushed up so close to anyone in her life, let alone a man who smelled like a Carillion wine vat.

Her nose twitched, and she was tempted to try to deep-scent him, but caution and common sense overruled. Deep-scenting through so many layers of off-world wine was nigh impossible.

No, she would wait until he was sober and they were in a safer place before she searched his mind.

"Did the Lyran hurt you?" she asked. It was possible he had broken a rib, if not suffered worse injuries from his grappling with the beast, not that every square inch of him didn't feel perfectly hale and hearty. She could actually feel his muscles contract and extend with every move he made. She could feel him breathing, his chest rising and falling against hers. Both were extraordinary and novel sensations.

He gave a negative shake of his head, and a silken swath of midnight black hair slipped over his shoulder and brushed her cheek, so soft and fragrant, she instinctively turned her face into it. Lavender. The Carillions put lavender in their wine, and tangerines. The fresh citrus smell mingled with the flowery redolence and wrapped around the dark strands of his hair, utterly delicious, luring her closer with pleasant memories. She nearly nuzzled him before the scent faded and she caught herself. She pulled back, mortified at her reaction.

It had been a week since she'd washed her face with the lavender-scented towels at the White Palace, but the fleeting memory had been startlingly clear in her mind—the heat of the desert suffusing her bones, the shade of the Lost Forest cooling her skin, Au Cade's orange gown, her mother's serene smile, and the warm towels offered by a child.

Shadana. The wine was everything she'd heard and then some. If the scent alone could make her mother's smile seem as close as this morn, what did the time-rider feel after a full night of drinking? What did he see and feel? Where, of all the places in his past, did the wine take him?

Somewhere violent, she thought, remembering how he'd drawn his sword in Racht and slashed through the table, scattering people in every direction. The poor wretch, to long for wine that gave him naught but access to his nightmares.

She shrugged off her moment of pity. He had made his own choices, most of them bad by her standards. Having Van's skraelpacks and the Third Guard after him made her job a lot more difficult, but she was a Priestess of the Bones and would prevail. If he wasn't hurt, they didn't have time to waste hanging on the wall.

"I estimate a seven-meter drop to the floor," she said in a clipped, impersonal tone, ignoring the fact that they were practically laminated to each other. "We can be down in two minutes and still hold our lead."

Having summed up the situation, she started to slide out from under him, but he shifted his weight, stopping her.

"Don't move," he murmured, and she thought she detected an unusual accent in his voice.

Nonetheless, her brows rose. The wine hadn't gone so far to her head that she was ready to concede her authority. She was in charge, despite his success with the zip line.

"You're wearing my tracking bracelet, time-rider," she reminded him. "That means I give the—"

"Shhh." He cut her off with the soft sound, moving his mouth closer to her ear. A fresh wave of lavender and tangerines washed over her, flooding her senses and sounding warnings in her brain.

Mother. What in the galaxy did the Carillions put in the stuff? The off-world wine was outlawed in two solar systems, and now she knew why. The potion rivaled any of Tamisk's for danger to a sane mind.

"You're not the squeamish type, are you?" he went on, breaking into the muddle of her thoughts.

The question was little more than the feel of his jaw moving against her cheek, the warmth of his breath on her skin, but she heard him and the surprising lilt that ran through his words. The thief did have an accent, a most unexpected one. He spoke with the cadence of an ancient tongue heard nowhere on Earth beyond the walls of the White Palace—Ilmarryn. One of the more rustic, dialectical voices, to be sure, but elfin all the same.

"No," she assured him, disconcerted by the wine, the question, and his accent, and even more impatient to be away before something dreadful happened. The Third Guard could come down the canal at any moment, skraelings in tow. The storm could break above them, sending a few hundred thousand megawatts of energy streaking down into the canal to fry them. Or, nearly worst of all, she could give in to temptation and turn her face into the curve of his neck.

"No," she said more strongly, forcing her attention off his hair and skin and the marvelous smells swirling around him. "I am not the squeamish type."

"Good. Then we'll just stay put until they pass."

Alerted, she softened her voice to match his. "Until who passes?"

The answer slid into view before he could reply, their serpentine forms winding a sinuous path through the rusted pipes and shredded cables connected to the wall above her right shoulder. Sewer snakes—hundreds of them—roused from their den by the crash, poisoned skin glowing with a toxic phosphorescence, razor-sharp scales fanning out along the finger-width length of their long, undulating spines.

She shrank back, an involuntary gasp escaping her.

The snake closest to her slowed and lifted its needle-nosed head in her direction. Eyes like red-rimmed seed beads held hers with a hot, steady stare as its tongue flicked out to smell the source of the sound.

"Shh, *geneth*. Easy now," the thief murmured.

She hazarded a glance to her left, where he had been looking, and saw hundreds more of the snakes flowing down the wall, enough to make anyone swear—or pray.

Sweet Mother. A shudder coursed through her body. The slightest touch of a sewer snake was enough to paralyze a limb and rot the flesh from the bone. The bite of the reptile ensured a torturous death—and a full score of them were mere inches from her arm. Her instinct was to throw herself off the wall and take her chances with landing on the floor of the canal, anything to get away from them, but the thief held her firmly to their perch.

"You're not afraid of snakes, are you?" he asked with a calmness she scarce could conceive.

She shook her head, too frightened to speak.

"Ah, then it must be me you find so alarming," he said, turning toward her with a slight movement of his head. She instinctively lifted her gaze—and her breath slid to a slow, stunned stop.

Shadana.

Up close, the thief was far more alarming than he had appeared in Racht. His eyes glittered beneath thick, black lashes, the irises a strange indigo color, a richly saturated blue of startling darkness and clarity. Layers of jet black hair swept back off his face in a silken fall past his shoulders, with the time-rider streak stair-stepping the whole length in blocks of purest white. A day's growth of beard shadowed the lean curve of his jaw. In truth, he looked an utter reprobate. He was unkempt, dangerously feral, and possibly the most beautiful man she had ever seen.

"What's your name, *geneth*?" he asked, his gaze holding hers with a directness she found unnerving.

"Avallyn," she managed to reply, wondering if the wine was coming over her again. She suddenly felt flushed everywhere they touched.

He cast a quick glance at the sewer snakes and returned his attention to her.

"Avallyn," he repeated, a faint smile teasing the corner of his mouth. "Is that all?"

"Avallyn Le Severn," she filled in, knowing for certain that Dray had made an error. The dark angel she faced could not possibly be the savior promised by the Red Book of Doom.

"Well, you've had a good night's work, Avallyn Le Severn," he said. "How much bounty are you getting for me?"

"Nothing." Of course he would think the worst. She hadn't had time to explain.

His smile broadened, revealing a flash of white teeth. One winged eyebrow lifted in amusement. "Keeping me for yourself, then? I'll try not to disappoint, but I've had a bit of wine, and I'm never at my best in my cups."

Her cheeks flamed at his insinuation. In the Old Dominion, only bounty hunters and the flesh peddlers of Pan-shei used tracking bracelets, or brothel bracelets as they were sometimes called. "You're drunk."

"Aye, but not nearly drunk enough, *geneth,*" he told her, then turned his attention back to the snakes, leaving her to stare at him in confused dismay.

They had made a mistake, a terrible mistake, she and Dray. The thief did have the time-rider blaze in his hair, but though rare, there were others who could claim the same deed, and one of them might turn out to be the true prince.

But not this man.

His crudeness aside, he could not possibly be the one for whom she had waited.

The Prince of Time was scarred by the battles he had fought. So it had been written. Duty alone charted his course, not drunkenness. Nowhere had it been said that he would speak with the voice of a Kings Wood clf and possess the face of an Orion slave boy.

The thief turned to her again, and a single truth hit home with a vengeance. Despite the artistry of his features, Morgan ab Kynan was no boy. Beneath his sable brows, his eyes gleamed with the unholy radiance of the wine and a shrewd intelligence that she felt taking her measure clear through to her bones.

"Forty thousand marks," he said clearly. "That's the bounty the Warmonger has put on my head."

"I'm not after you for the bounty, or . . . or—"

"Sex?" he filled in, his smile turning languid. "The only people who use tracking bracelets are pimps and bounty hunters. Which do you claim to be?"

"Neither," she said.

His smile called her a liar.

She called herself a fool. Once she'd seen the sort he was, she should have left him for the Lyran. Instead, she'd bound him to her with the bracelets.

And she was twice a fool for the way his smile made her pulse race. He was supposed to have been her doughty consort, or Tamisk's dismissable sot, not a recalcitrant, unpredictable tech-trash hybrid she had no prayer of controlling.

She dared his gaze again and immediately felt the heat of another blush steal up her cheeks. She'd chained herself to a thief, a dangerous renegade, and until she reached Claerwen and had the bracelets removed, she couldn't get more than thirty feet away from him.

She hoped it would be enough.

Morgan stared at his captor, utterly beguiled. If a more innocent sight than her blush existed in all the Old Dominion, he had not seen it. Despite his resolve to be done with her as quickly as possible, he was intrigued—and more than a little chagrined. He'd been captured by a child, or someone who was very nearly so, despite the soft, decidedly feminine curves pressed up against his body.

Had he grown so unwary?

Upon closer inspection, the girl's resemblance to Llynya was not so perfect as he'd thought. 'Twas there, true, in the shape of her face, the slant of her cheekbones, and the curve of her mouth, but more than just her hair and the color of her eyes was awry. It had taken a rage-filled boar to unnerve the sprite, whereas his bounty hunter had faced down the Lyran with more courage than she was able to muster in facing him. Whatever defiance had been behind the icy look she'd given him in the square, it had been lost. Getting the tracking bracelet lock sequence out of her would be as naught, unless they were both poisoned by sewer snakes.

He gave the reptiles another glance, but only a glance. To look at them too closely made his skin crawl. The scaly buggers were practically radioactive with toxic waste. He'd once seen a man who'd stumbled into a clew of sewer snakes and lived out a sennight, his skin rotting and draping off his body, his internal organs consigned to the fires of hell.

Aja had been right. They should have left Racht hours ago, before the night had deteriorated into a series of catastrophes and too-close calls, and bounty hunters barely come into their own. 'Twas the wine that had stayed him, and the hope of another hour in the past, though why he would wish for another hour of his own private nightmare was a question he preferred to ignore.

He looked at his captor again, taking note of the soft color still staining her cheeks and the wariness clouding her silvery gray eyes. His gaze drifted to her mouth, and he felt a stirring of desire. Aye, she had lips he would dearly love to taste, but she was far too dangerous for him to indulge himself in fantasy. No bounty hunter, however lovely, was to be trusted. Not with forty thousand marks on the line.

A snake hissed close by, and her eyes widened in fear. A distraction was in order. The last thing he needed was for her to make any sudden moves.

He lifted his tracking bracelet to where she could see it. "What are they made of, *geneth*?"

Her gaze slowly came back to his. *"Thullein,"* she answered.

He'd never heard of it.

"And is it the *thullein* that makes them glow?" All the colors of the rainbow flashed and flickered from the lightbars on the bracelets, but it was the strange luminescence of the metal that intrigued him.

"The changing nature of the metal causes it to give light once it has been conjured into a shape," she said as if by rote.

A frisson of unease coursed down Morgan's spine. No tech-trash bounty hunter worth her weight in blastpaks would have talked about a metal's changing nature or a conjured transformation. Metal was forged, tempered, ionized, magnetized, and subjected to at least a dozen other processes that Aja knew by heart and could perform when necessary. It was not conjured. Nothing was conjured except in the hearts and minds of the followers of any of the hundreds of religions the future had to offer. As far as Morgan had been able to piece recent history together, religion had been the most pervasive fallout of the wars that had nearly destroyed Earth. Zealotry abounded, except in the Old Dominion, the last bastion of science and technology, even if those disciplines had been reduced to rusty shadows of their former glory. The wars had turned people from the failure of science to the mystery of God, or gods, or demons. Anything went in the mystical marketplace.

Which brought him back to his current situation. Worse even than a bounty hunter, he'd been captured by a religious fanatic. He bit back an oath and with effort put more warmth in his smile, hoping to ease her fear and thereby draw her out.

"Is the nature of the lock sequence in the metal then, or is it in the lightbars?"

"There is no nature for that which is not," she told him, "unless it be in the hands of a mage."

His smile faded.

"Are you telling me there isn't a lock sequence for this damn thing?" He lifted his wrist.

"Are you a mage?" she asked with what looked, unbelievably, like a measure of hope in her eyes.

"No," he said, feeling his bloody headache tighten another notch.

"Then there is nothing. Nothing." She shook her head, sending her odd concoction of twists and braids moving about her face. The action revealed another startling fact about her, one he thought at first was an illusion, but which closer notice bore out.

Her ears were pointed—which made her a religious fanatic of unknown origin. Aja's ears had a bit more angle to them on top than pure curve, but the girl's ears were out-and-out pointed, delicately, like everything else about her. He tried to think if he'd ever seen the like, and if so, where. Except for a few unavoidable off-world trips, he had kept pretty much to Earth and the Lunar settlements, but neither here nor out in the galaxy had he seen pointed ears on anyone who looked otherwise as purely human as she did.

His unease was increasing exponentially with every new fact. If she'd planned on turning him in to the Third Guard for the bounty, she could have done it in Racht and saved herself a whole lot of trouble. She obviously had someone else in mind, and Morgan was definitely not interested in finding out who. He didn't for a minute believe she wasn't intending to sell him to somebody. Nobody passed up forty thousand marks. *Christe.* He hated to think who else might want his hide tacked to their wall.

"Then how do we release them?" he asked through his teeth.

"We don't," she said, lifting her chin and sounding admirably stoic about the situation.

Morgan stared at her for a moment, then squeezed his eyes shut and began swearing in three languages he hoped she understood and at least two she probably didn't. A child, to be sure—to have locked herself to him with no way to get out.

What had she done? Forgotten to memorize the damn sequence? Or had she simply failed from the beginning to understand the nature of the equipment?

Friggin' nature, bah. He had to tighten his hold on the cables to keep from shaking her.

"Milord? Are you there, milord?" Aja's voice came over the tech-jaw.

"Aye," he barked, opening his eyes.

"York and I are four points east of the first intersection." There was a short pause, then, "Where are you?"

"On the canal wall, chained to a bounty hunter and surrounded by sewer snakes."

Aja seemed to consider his situation for a moment before asking, "Do you need any help?"

"No," he snapped. What he needed was a lock sequence, and by God he was going to get one. Nobody made tracking bracelets without a lock sequence.

"Who—"

"Avallyn Le Severn," he interrupted Aja's question. "Ever hear of her?"

A longer pause this time. "No, milord."

"No," York added, "and I know 'em all, Morgan."

"Dray, Captain—" the girl began.

Morgan cut her off with a hand over her mouth. "Spit it out," he said, not having to work at a menacing tone. He wasn't going to have her giving their position away to the desert wraiths.

He uncovered her mouth, and when she hesitated, he grabbed her wrist and held her hand out toward the last of the snakes sliding down the wall. Her eyes grew wider.

"Spit what out, milord?" Aja's voice came over the tech-jaw again.

"It's a particularly nasty way to die, *geneth*." Morgan's words were a promise.

She gave him a mutinous look, then spat the tech-jaw into the canal.

Great, he thought. At least one thing was going his way.

"She came in with the Night Watchers up in Racht," he said to his men. "The captain's name is Dray. Ever hear of him?"

"Aye."

"Yes."

Aja and York both spoke at once.

"A Sha-shakrieg legend—" York continued.

"A hero of the Deseillign Waste, milord," Aja added.

And he'd passed the boundary into the Old Dominion with a girl, to take a bounty. Mayhap the Night Watcher captain had the lock sequence. Morgan's spirits lifted at the thought. The girl should prove adequate bait. All they needed was a setup. Once they reached Tri-opt Four, he would give her another tech-jaw and let her talk all she wanted. For now, they needed to get down into the canal.

"Can you crawl a wall?" he asked, releasing her wrist and unhitching a small hook and line from his belt.

"I could if I had the right equipment," she said, pulling her arm back close to her body, a flash of fury in her eyes.

Forgiveness would be a while coming for his threat with the snake. He didn't plan on being around long enough for her to give it, or long enough for her to realize his hand had been closer to the poisonous reptile than hers.

Hell, he was the one with the friggin' death wish.

"Then I guess you'll have to come with me." He leaned away from her, swinging the hook in a gentle arc before lofting it sideways at the wall. It hit and stuck about three meters away from them, enough space to get them over the snake trail. The serpents were all past, but the route they'd taken through the cables would be "hot" for a sennight or more. The rats, ratlings, and kudges scared out of their holes by the crash would keep the snakes busy eating, giving him and the girl a clean getaway to the north.

"We'll have to take her with us," he said to Aja, giving the line a good pull. It held, and he locked it into place.

"Aye, milord."

"Hold on," he said, slipping his arm around Avallyn's waist and drawing her close. Her jaw tightened, and he had to fight a grin. She'd started this mess, but she could damn well be sure he was going to finish it.

He looked over his shoulder, trying to guess the distance to the floor through the gloom. She'd estimated it at seven meters, and he could tell nothing more.

Knowing he had six meters of line to feed out, he bent his knees and pushed them off. Again they landed with a jolting degree of force, but he wasn't able to take the brunt of it. The breath was knocked out of her along with a gasp of pain.

Ridiculously, he felt a pang of regret.

When she'd recovered, they made their descent, reaching the floor without further mishap. To the south, erratic flashes of blue light lit up the piece of junk, each one the strike of a sewer snake. A kudge screamed, the sound cutting through the stagnant air like a knife. Rats were running in every direction.

"Wait here," he commanded, and started toward the pile of wrecked metal.

Twenty feet away from her, he felt a tug on his wrist and the tracking bracelet grew warm against his skin. Its lights began to cycle faster. At twenty-five feet, the tugging became a constant pressure and the lights shone brighter. At thirty feet, he was stopped cold. He tried to go forward, but the bracelet held him back. He turned to find her right where he'd left her, one hand on her hip, the other on her lasgun, her bracelet flashing as wildly as his.

"Move up," he ordered. "I want to retrieve the zip line."

"The way is clearer before us than behind us," she said, holding her ground.

A daring chit, he thought, but no match for him. If he had to, he could drag her to the pile of metal. He started to do just that when she called out again.

"Palinor will give you a thousand ropes to replace the ones you've lost, dread lord."

He froze where he stood. Dread lord, she'd called him, and in the same breath his memories of Sonnpur-Dzon came clearly to mind. What was it they'd called him? *Bo si wong gi?*

"Palinor?" He phrased the name as a question.

"My mother. The Northern Waste is her Order's to rule, and they will give you all that you desire; I swear it. But we must be away."

Another flash of electric blue light skittered a path up the piece of junk. Another kudge screamed, but the snakes weren't what kept him from retrieving Aja's zip line, nor was it the tracking bracelet. It was her, Avallyn Le Severn, and her "dread lord" plea.

He knew who ruled the Northern Waste, and no tracking bracelet on Earth was strong enough to drag him into those desolate dunes, into the lair of the White Ladies of Death, the Priestesses of the Bones.

He looked at their acolyte, her angel face and tattered black robe, her wild hair and desert wraith clothes, and he felt his blood run cold. 'Twas no bounty hunter who had captured him, but a messenger of Death itself.

Chapter 5

"Aye. Let's be away," Morgan said, ignoring the tightness in his gut and striding past her, more anxious than ever to be rid of the girl. Aja was a wizard with metal. Mayhap he could break the tracking seal between the two bracelets, and they could forgo meeting with the desert wraiths.

Night Watchers were a sure sign of impending doom. Every tech-trash denizen of the Old Dominion knew as much. He was a fool to have considered dealing with them. They had saved him from the Third Guard only to deal him a more grievous blow. The Warmonger, for all his innumerable sadistic inclinations and moral faults, could be bought, and Morgan had his price—the Sonnpur-Dzon dragon.

The White Ladies were known only for dealing in death. Their temples were said to be built out of bones, the sun-bleached bones of every man who had ever gone against them.

Sweet Jesu. What had he done to gain their notice? He couldn't re-member offending any women of late, let alone any woman of priestess persuasion.

If Aja could break the lock sequence, they would leave the girl at Tri-opt Four. She would be safe enough there. He didn't want any death-witch mother of the northern dunes after him for the demise of one of her daughters. Aja could tune one of his tech-jaws to her frequency. Avallyn Le Severn could then call her Night Watchers to her, and they could all go back to the desert where they belonged, and leave him where he belonged.

The thought soured his mood even more. Aye, that would be a good trick, if they could leave him where he belonged, a half-dozen or more millennia in the past.

He lengthened his strides, not worrying if she kept up or not. If she didn't, he'd be the first to know. The bracelet would see to that.

He looked down at the band of metal she'd put on his arm. *Thullein.* Conjured shape, indeed. When he'd first emerged from his strange, timeless daze ten years ago, he'd looked the length and breadth of the earth for an explanation of what had happened to him. Unversed in science, he had searched for magic and found naught. To this day, the only two instances of magic he had ever seen had taken place thousands of years ago. One had been on a blank page in a red book, the other in a cave of the Canolbarth beneath Carn Merioneth. In the cave there had been a sorceress named Ceridwen ab Arawn, and her mage had been Dain Lavrans. Brave Ceri had traversed to the otherworld in a dazzling display of enchantments, working magic to right the wrongs of the past, and Dain had held the doorways open for her. Between the two of them, they had made the land tremble and had opened up the very ground be-fore them, unleashing the great worms that had unexpectedly brought him to this sorry pass—running for his life down a junk-strewn canal with a chorus of screaming kudges in the background and a desert priestess in tow.

There had been one other bit of magic in all those years long past. The sprite, Llynya, and everyone of her kind had possessed daggers with crystal hilts that gave off light, mostly in varying shades of blue, white, green, and violet. He'd seen a cave called Lanbarrdein come alive with a trailing web of the crystal lights, and at the time had thought himself in the presence of magic.

Since then, he'd seen far more remarkable sights, though with far less effect; since then, he'd learned about the energy inherent in crystalline structures. He'd seen that energy used and exploited in ways no one of his time could have imagined. Just as no one of his time could have imagined what had happened to him.

Of late, since Sonnpur-Dzon, he'd thought of little else but Dain and Ceri, Llynya, Owain, Drew and Rhys, all of the family he'd held so dear, and his companions, all dead these many years, the very land where they'd lived long buried under the sand. It was a heartache to him—and so he drank.

And so he'd come to this.

The way opened up before them, and Morgan realized they were at the first intersection. The girl was still with him, barely a step behind.

"Turning east, Aja. How does it look up ahead?"

"Clear, milord. I'm picking up some disturbance, but it seems to be coming from above. You won't be out from under the main dome until you pass the second point. From there it's a straight shot to the east bays and—whoa, wait a—" Aja's voice disappeared in a wave of static.

Morgan halted. The hairs on the nape of his neck rose. His skin tingled. Whirling, he reached for the girl and pulled her into his arms just as a roaring crack of lightning rent the sky with an explosion of light, sending hot spikes of energy into the square above and electrifying half the place in search of a grounding point.

A split second of pure terror froze them in place as the canal flashed white with the surge of power. Racht's open ceiling lit up in stark relief against the night, then all the lights went out and only the faint illumination of table lanterns remained. Screams and the smell of burnt flesh and hot metal filled the air.

With any luck, the Third Guard had been at ground zero, but Morgan wasn't going to count on it. The Warmonger's troops were noted for their resiliency.

"That was close," the girl whispered, her voice hoarse from fear.

"Aye." He nodded, his own heart pounding. "Damn close."

The first drops of rain fell into the square and sizzled, raising a cloud of steam that tumbled and rolled against the dome. The rain quickly turned into an ice-cold downpour, flooding the floor of the canal. It was enough to remind Morgan of what they were about. Ignoring a damn stupid reluctance to do so, he set her aside. There weren't any overhangs to protect them, and even if there had been, he wouldn't have wasted time trying to stay dry. They'd survived one of the sky's mighty firebolts, fiercer and more deadly than any storm-born lightning of the past, but they were still in danger.

He put his hand on a Luma swatch adhered to his jacket and pressed, igniting the phosphorescent glow gel inside. Aja would have an h-beam to better light their way, but the Luma swatch was enough to keep them from falling into a hole or tripping over a cable.

"Come on," he shouted over the growing deluge, pulling her along, not yet choosing to let go of her.

"I have a rover waiting in the east bays," she shouted back, no doubt supposing herself to be helpful.

Morgan swore under his breath. Aja and the Night Watchers had obviously come to the same conclusion about the quickest way out of Racht. He wondered who else might be heading for the east bays and Tri-opt Four.

"Aja. We've got a problem. The Night Watchers left their rovers in the east bays. Find us an alternate route to Tri-opt Four."

"Alternate route?" She balked, pulling him to a stop. "We're going to the east bays, not Tri-opt Four."

"No, we're not."

She jerked her hand free and drew her lasgun. "I'm giving the orders here. We're going to the east bays."

She made a fetching sight, standing in the pouring rain and brandishing her weapon, but Morgan wasn't buying her threat.

"You didn't band me and follow me down here just to shoot me."

"Don't count on it." She pumped a charge into the lasgun's barrel.

An interesting move, but Morgan remained unconvinced.

"Aja, report," he said when no confirmation of his last message was forthcoming. He kept his eye on the woman, which was no hardship. Even soaking wet, she looked good. He wondered if she was a priestess yet, and the thought gave him a chill. A fullblown priestess just might shoot him.

The continued silence from his captain didn't portend well.

"Aja," he repeated. "York?"

"M—gan . . . we . . ."

"Aja, repeat." Now was not the time to lose contact with the boy.

"—cut off . . . skraelpack in the east bays . . . retreat to—"

Morgan's brow furrowed. "Retreat? Aja, come in."

Static was his only answer.

Uttering a vile oath, he grabbed the woman and moved to the nearest wall, dragging her with him. Looking to either side, he was able to see little more than sheets of dark rain, but the enemy was out there.

"We've been cut off," he told her, releasing his lasgun and slipping in a fresh charge pack. Water ran down the wall behind them and pooled around their boots.

"You're lucky I didn't shoot you."

"If you wanted to shoot me, I'd be dead. I saw how you moved in Racht, and I couldn't beat you on a draw." He looked up and caught her gaze, and saw as much truth as he needed. "You want me for something, and until you get it, I figure I'm safe."

Her mouth tightened. "Actually, I think there's been a mistake. I don't think you're at all what I want." She seemed very sure of it, which for some reason annoyed Morgan.

"So?" He lifted the bracelet in question.

She gave an abrupt shake of her head. "No. I can't release the locks."

Or won't, he thought, the maddening chit.

"Then we're stuck with each other, and my priority is getting out of these canals in one piece. How about you?"

"The rovers in the east bays are the quickest way out."

He locked in the charge. "The east bays are full of skraelings."

"Skraelings?" she repeated. "Sticks!"

Morgan slanted her a bemused glance. Sticks?

"What about the wild boy?" she demanded. "I assume he's the one giving you information."

"Retreating, but I don't know where. Too much static."

She made a soft sound of disgust. "We could have used him. They are wily to a fault and good fighters."

"Aye, well, it's not like we lost a whole troop. There is just the one boy."

"One is ofttimes enough," she said, wiping the rain from her face. "In the north, we use them for scouts, like you do. They invariably pull the tide in our favor."

Aja had done the same for him more times than Morgan could re-member, but it irked him to have her refer to his captain as if he were interchangeable with some scout she'd used in the north, as if she knew more about him than Morgan did.

"The boy's name is Aja, and there is only one like him in all the galaxy," he said, clearly correcting her. He checked his comwatch and turned on its finder function to see if he could get a bead on Aja's position. If the boy was retreating, Morgan wanted to know where he was going.

"One?" she scoffed. "There are thousands of wild boys in the desert and out on the Sand Sea. They come to the temples to trade chrystaalt, great packs of them from every tribe."

His headache, which the lightning strike must have scared out of him, returned with sudden intensity, a fierce throbbing in his forehead.

"Aja is an orphan, and not part of any tribal pack." He forced himself to look in her direction without wincing, his voice taking a firmer tone. "I found him on the streets of the Old Dominion when he was but a child."

The look she leveled at him called him a fool more plainly than if she'd used the word.

"More likely he found you, dread lord . . . or someone from his desert sept did."

Morgan held her gaze for as long as he could, which was an embarrassingly brief moment, then looked back at his comwatch and tried a new setting. Her allegation discomfited him in a way he didn't like to admit even to himself, in a way it wouldn't have before Sonnpur-Dzon. It hadn't exactly been the streets of the Old Dominion where Morgan had found Aja, but in Pan-shei, the west-side market, where the city ended and the desert began. The boy and he had both been covered in sand. The market talk had been about the great storm that had raged out on the dunes weeks earlier, the likes of which had not been seen for twenty years. That had been ten years ago, and Morgan had only the most fleeting memories of anything before that day, except for the memories of his deep past. Those were always painfully clear.

The finder screen red-lined, and he said something foul.

"What's wrong?" she asked.

"The storm has screwed up the finder."

"Then let's make for the rover," she advised with an edge to her voice. "Even with skraelings in the bays, we have a better chance in a rover than on foot. We left them north of the fuel tanks. The skraelpack might not have even found them yet."

He ignored her, and would swear he could hear her grinding her teeth in frustration.

"You did well to survive in the desert," she said, taking a different tack, "but whoever found you did you no service. The priestesses could have saved you much pain."

Aye, Morgan agreed. Having his bones bleaching on a temple door would have been far less painful than the "derangement" he'd suffered, but what in the hell could she know about it?

"What makes you think I was ever in the desert?"

Her gaze went to the stripe in his hair. "All rogue time-riders come out of the desert. It's the only place on Earth with enough natural chrystaalt to lure the weirworms in from deep space."

Weirworms.

Sweet Jesu.

Morgan forced himself to take a steadying breath and bent down to check the knives he kept on his boots—and he did his damnedest to ignore the trembling of his hands.

"It's no wonder you drink to wretchedness," she continued, and mayhap would have gone on to list more of his faults, if not for the sound of marching feet coming from the east.

Absurdly, Morgan was relieved. In the very few minutes since he'd met Avallyn Le Severn, he'd felt his whole life start to unravel. If he could have left her, he would have without a backward glance, but he couldn't, and he couldn't reach Aja with the tech-jaws down and the finder blown and who knew which group of slags hoofing it down the canal between them. Aja would do his best for York. Morgan didn't doubt it, any more than he doubted that York would tell the boy to get lost if escape began to look unlikely.

Damn. He should be with them.

"Do you want some tea?" he asked, squinting at the desert woman through the rain. He sure as hell could use a cup, and it was well past time to go home. His head was killing him, and any mellow afterglow the wine might have given him had been annihilated by the turn of events.

"Tea?" She looked at him like he was crazed, which no doubt he was for even offering.

"Aye." He rose and pulled his carbine over his shoulder to check the load. "There's a *chai wallah* at Thirty-aught-two near the East-West

Ninety: Ferrar's, home of the best *chai* to be had this side of the Middle Kingdom."

"You're so sure we're going to get out of this canal?" She sounded skeptical at best.

"Aye." He nodded, releasing a strip of throwing stars and casting her a hard glance. "This isn't where I die, princess." He didn't know what prompted him to call her "princess," but it seemed to fit her a hell of a lot better than priestess or death-witch.

Her face paled. "You've seen your death?"

"Nay," he replied, surprised by her reaction. "I've lived it. Come on. It's back to the west with us."

In the deepest part of the night, Corvus suddenly awoke. The throne room was dark except for a lone streak of light coming from a doorway at the end of the hall, the doorway leading to Vishab's tower.

The witch never slept.

An odd, scorched scent was on the air, and though he wondered what she was burning, he knew it wasn't the smell of Vishab's latest cremation that had awakened him. It was the smell of fear.

Someone else was in the hall.

"Abase yourself," he commanded, and was rewarded with the sound of nervous footsteps. A helmed, corpulent figure approached the throne and prostrated itself on the floor.

By the faint light, Corvus saw the offered dispatch and the trembling hand that held it. He was in no mood for failure, but the very fact that another dispatch had been sent did not bode well. If the Third Guard had been successful, the thief and the dragon statue, not more messages, would be en route to Magh Dun.

He took the missive and broke the seal. A quick scan of the top few lines revealed the unfortunate news: The thief had escaped, but not without help.

Corvus read on, straightening in his great chair. His brows furrowed. Sha-shakrieg Night Watchers had come to the wretched sot's rescue. Even more interesting, the desert wraiths had been led by their most notorious captain, Dray.

He paused in his reading and pressed a sequence of light keys recessed into the arm of his throne, calling the captain of Magh Dun's

Home Guard. His spies should have known Dray was in the Old Dominion. A raid should have been launched against Claerwen. The death-witches knew far more than he or Vishab had ever been able to torture out of them. It was their damn book that had told him about dragons destroying the darkness. Yet there was nary a dragon or dragon image in all of Claerwen, at least none that he or his troops had ever found, and they had scanned Claerwen innumerable times. Maybe without Dray to lead the defense, Corvus's troops could have finally broken the priestess's resistance. Then he would have had the run of their temple and the power to call the golden worms, the dragon larvae, out of the sky. He would be Lord of the Time Weir, and the desert septs would bow to him.

His blackened hand clenched into a fist. There was untapped power in the septs, those scraggly bands of desert nomads who seemed to do naught but survive and breed their damn wild boys. Something kept them alive in the Waste, some life force, and as with all other forms of power, he would have it to use for his own ends.

An answering sequence of lights flashed on the screen: The captain was on his way. Corvus keyed in another sequence to summon Vishab. Let the captain explain himself to her, Corvus thought, and returned his attention to the dispatch.

His gaze dropped quickly to the bottom of the page, and as he read, his entire body tightened with rage. He scanned the final lines again, disbelief warring with his anger.

Avallyn Le Severn had been in Racht Square. His most loathed nemesis, the woman who had turned her back on him and left him to his doom, had overcome the Lyran and saved the thief.

The dispatch crumpled in his hand, crushed within the vengeful grip of his fist. Sacred bitch, she had finally put herself within his grasp, and for that she would die.

"Vishab!" he roared.

The messenger at his feet let out a strangled cry of terror, expecting the worst—and the worst it would have been if the news had been any less grim. But with Avallyn's involvement, the whole problem of the thief took on unprecedented proportions. Now more than ever, Corvus was convinced of the statue's virtues. Torture would have to wait until he returned from the Old Dominion. Where the Lyran had failed, Vishab would triumph. The dragon statue would finally be his, and so would vengeance. The useless thief would be killed outright, fed to a skraelpack as a warning to anyone who would steal from the Warmonger.

But for the Lady Avallyn, death would not be so swift. No, it would not be swift at all, but night after night of endless suffering. Youngest of all the ordained priestesses, she was the one Vishab would break. She was the one who would betray her sisters and give him Claerwen.

Aye, Corvus would take his revenge not only in her death, but in her shame.

Chapter 6

Morgan slogged through the last canal leading out of the Old Dominion, keeping a north-northwest heading, making toward Pan-shei Market, toward home. Three times he and Avallyn had been forced to deviate from the course he'd set because of the sound of troops on the march, weapons clattering, voices shouting, and twice because the desert woman had smelled skraelings up ahead. By the time they pulled themselves up out of the maze, the rain had stopped and dawn was breaking across the sky.

Morgan stood at the edge of the canal where it crossed the East-West Ninety, his gaze scanning the marketplace coming to life in the streets below. Light from the rising sun spilled into the grim alleyways and over the rickety storefronts and stalls of Pan-shei, cutting through the ever-present haze that hung above the Old Dominion.

West of the market the desert began, low undulating dunes of endless sand stretching the length of the horizon. To the east the city lay quiet, a jagged skyline of broken buildings and lightning towers backlit by the coming day.

Wincing, he pressed his hand to his rib cage. It had been a hell of a night. He felt like he'd been hit by a truck, and not one of the small scant-ton chassis that roamed the quarters, but a full-size rover. His own transport had most likely been confiscated by now, meaning he'd have to deal with the cretins at the City Guard impound lot.

A soft curse sounded behind him, and he turned around.

"Buggers," the woman said again, her tousled blond head rising out of the canal.

"We're clear," he said, bending down and offering her his hand. Her fingers gripped his and he pulled her up to stand by his side, an act of chivalry that damn near killed him. He gritted his teeth and tried not to groan.

"Rotting kudges," she muttered, dusting herself off. She shook the sides of her cloak and half a dozen of the tiny, furry animals dropped to the street, just a few of the hundreds that had been dogging her steps and clinging to her on and off for the last three hours, turning her—she feared—into a prime piece of sewer snake bait. He hadn't told her that the reason there were so many kudges in the northern canals was because there weren't any sewer snakes.

No, he hadn't told her. He'd just walked on and listened as her stoic arrogance had turned into bitchy whining, and he'd grinned, his own mood lightening as hers had deteriorated.

He wasn't grinning now, with the sunlight stabbing into his eyes and his head pounding. He watched the animals scurry back into the darkness of the canal and almost wished he could go with them. He wasn't ready to face the day or the bounty-hunting priestess with her damned tracking bracelets.

The last kudge went over the edge, and with a weary sigh Morgan turned his attention back to the woman, making yet one more mistake in a long line of mistakes.

She stood looking out over Pan-shei, her slight form cast in profile against the rising sun, her face into the wind. Though her tattered black cloak swirled around her, the shadow raiment of a Night Watcher, she was luminous, and the sight of her sent a strange and unexpected ache right down through the center of him.

He couldn't remember the last time he'd seen anything so beautiful, any creature so radiant—except in his memories. Her hair was bright and shining, the gold and silver strands framing a delicately curved face whose sun-warmed skin brought to mind nothing so much as a kiss, his kiss; the chance to feel her soft cheek, to inhale the green scent that had driven him crazy half the night with trying to figure out where it was coming from, and after realizing 'twas hers, with wondering how a desert woman could smell like crushed grass in a birkland glade.

A soft curse escaped him, deriding the wanderings of his mind, and he turned his attention back to the market. He felt like warmed-over hell and she looked good enough to eat—another typical encounter of his with the opposite sex of the future. In his other life, he'd been as quick as the next man to sing the praises of a maid, but the maids of old hadn't been as dangerous as the women of the Old Dominion and its environs. There had been some deserving caution—Madron, the witch of Wydehaw, being one, and the predatory Lady D'Arbois of Wydehaw Castle being another. On the whole, though, the women he'd known in the past hadn't made a habit of killing their mates during climax, as Lyrans were known to do, or of selling them into slavery, as York's wife had done. Nor had they gone around armed to the teeth and hunting bounty in low-life bars as Avallyn Le Severn had been doing in Racht.

Which brought him back to the question of why. She hadn't denied that she wanted something, only doubted that she'd banded the right man. He wasn't so sure, after listening to her talk about desert septs and Desert Law and friggin' weirworms.

He hazarded another glance at her. She was beautiful, aright, but in truth no less tired than he. Blue smudges marred the skin beneath her eyes, a sure sign of weariness. Her mouth was tight, her shoulders stiff, as if she was holding herself together by pure will.

She stood so very still, her attention so intensely focused on the market, he could almost feel her gaze searching the streets below, more a hunter than the prey they'd been all night. For certes she had the look of a hunter, with her lasgun holstered next to a dagger sheath on her belt and the top edge of another knife glinting out of a sheath on her left boot. Her knee-length tunic was pure camouflage, patterned in black and gray swirls like her leggings, the whole costume meant to disguise her in darkness. A pair of garnet brooches secured her cloak. Dulled by shadows in the canals, they shone bloodred in the sunlight.

Her ears twitched as he stood gazing at her, and he wondered again what to make of them—so oddly pointed, like some wild creature's.

Aye, and she was, he conceded. Wild. No tame priestess from the desert, but a hunter who had come seeking him with her Night Watchers—yet no more a hunter than he, mayhap.

A shiver of warning ran down his spine, for all the good a warning would do. 'Twas more than a kiss he would have from her, and a more dangerous turn he could hardly imagine, but like so much of what he wanted or desired, he wasn't likely to get her. No doubt, that was a saving grace in this instance. The wine must have finally rotted away his last shred of common sense for him to feel such a sweetly damning lust.

He looked down at his wrist and the tracking bracelet, and a slight smile twisted a corner of his mouth. He still couldn't believe she'd banded him. Just how drunk had he been last night?

Her Night Watcher captain must be going crazy trying to find her. An acolyte of the White Ladies of Death was probably worth a small fortune on the open market, and Pan-shei was as open as they came. Slaves could be bought and sold on at least ten street corners that he knew about. Her ears alone would class her as an exotic. Given the jaded appetites of the wealthier Old Dominionites, he could probably get more for her than he could for the Sonnpur-Dzon dragon. Not that he'd be selling her off while he was still attached to her, or—hell—that he'd be selling her off at all. If he could just get rid of her before the Night Watchers found them, he'd count himself lucky.

But even as the thought crossed his mind, Morgan doubted if getting rid of her was going to be as simple as breaking the frequency code on the tracking bracelet. Her resemblance to Llynya was no coincidence. He felt that truth in his gut.

A church bell sounded in the distance, ringing clear in the rain-freshened air, calling the pious to prayer. He poured the water out of the empty slots on the munitions belt he wore diagonally across his chest, like a baldric, and checked his lasgun. He still had half a charge left.

"Come on." He gestured toward the market, moving out. If they didn't want to get picked up on the East-West Ninety, 'twas best not to delay. He would as soon have her tucked into his lodgings at the back of Ferrar's *chai* shop before the City Guards started their patrols. With luck, Aja and York would already be home. News of the fight in Racht was bound to have reached an official ear. If his name was attached to the report, it might be best for them to leave the city for a while—and it would be best if they didn't have to take the desert woman with them. He was counting on Aja to get him free, lock sequence or no lock sequence.

He got no farther than thirty feet before his bracelet tugged him to a stop.

God's blood, but she tried his patience.

He turned around and found she hadn't moved so much as an inch. "What's the matter now? I thought we had an agreement."

"An agreement to get out of the canals, not to go in there,"—she pointed to the market—"the biggest cesspool in the galaxy."

Cesspool? It might not be the priestess temple complex she lived in, but he wouldn't call Pan-shei a cesspool.

Hell, no, he called it home.

"I guess you don't get out of the desert very much," he said, giving her a long-suffering look as he massaged his temple. "The biggest cesspool in the galaxy is way out on Europa." The pain in his skull had gone past headache to full-blown hangover. He needed a drink, preferably Carillion.

And the woman, damn her, was looking at him as if she had expected better of him, though he'd be damned if he thought she had the right to expect anything from him.

"And just where do you think we should go?" he asked. They had two choices, Pan-shei or the Old Dominion, and going back into the Old Dominion was out of the question. Even she must realize that.

"The desert."

Fine, he thought. They could walk into the desert and die, and when their bones were all nicely bleached out, some priestess could come and tack them up on a temple wall.

"We don't have a rover," he said.

"No thanks to you."

Honestly, he hadn't thought she had the energy to argue. God knew he didn't.

He looked up at her through what he knew were two very bloodshot eyes and agreed to her suicidal plan. "Aye, then. First tea, and then the desert."

If his head had hurt any less and they had truly been companions, he might have been concerned at how easily the lie came to his lips. In an odd way, she reminded him of Aja, and he'd never lied to the boy. As it was, he didn't give a damn. All he wanted was to get her to Ferrar's, where she could have tea and he could get a wine boost, not enough to take him anywhere, just enough to take the edge off. The last thing he needed was to slip into a detox wine fever, and that was exactly where he was headed. His temperature had been rising over the last hour, and he'd suffered a couple of reality shifts in the canals, brief moments when the walls and rubble had slid off their bearings in a hallucinatory meltdown. That was the problem with drinking Carillion wine. You couldn't stop without facing some dire consequences.

She gave him a slight nod, and he considered the deal done. Ignoring his aches and pains, he started walking. Ferrar's wasn't far.

Hardly mollified but too exhausted to argue the point any further, Avallyn fell in behind the thief. She was amazed that he was still on his feet. He'd been falling down drunk when she'd first seen him in Racht, and the Lyran had worked him over pretty well, yet he hadn't faltered. For herself, she was weary beyond measure from their night-long trek. Her feet ached from scrambling over endless piles of junked metal. She'd cut herself twice, and worst of all, she smelled like a kudge.

But by the Bones, she wouldn't stop until he dropped, which didn't seem likely anytime soon. Her gaze flicked over him again, and she had to stifle a surge of annoyance.

In the desert, people wore loose-fitting tunics and robes. The thief's pants hugged the lower half of his body like a second skin. Black with a thin gold stripe up each side, the supple cloth moved with every one of his loose-hipped strides, revealing far more of his body and its musculature than it concealed.

Out of fairness, she had to admit that he wasn't clothed any more indecently than the Ilmarryn, who were prone to all manner of dishabille, but he was a man, and there was far more to him than there was to any Ilmarryn sprite—more breadth, more muscle, more length, more everything. She hadn't forgotten what his legs had felt like pressed on either side of hers, the strength of his arms holding them both to the wall. No other man would have dared to be so bold with Palinor's daughter, not even to save her life—not if he valued his.

All kinds of men came to the desert, adventurers and mercenaries, soldiers and the Warmonger's spies, but she'd never seen anyone quite like Morgan ab Kynan, except one: an Orion slave boy whose caravan had gotten lost in the Northern Waste. She'd been allowed only a glimpse, but a glimpse had been enough to stun her into silent adoration. He'd been beautiful, but refined, not like the thief. Yet there was a noticeable similarity, and she wondered if, even worse than a tech-trash thief, Morgan ab Kynan had once been one of the highest-paid whores in the galaxy.

She should be thanking the gods he wasn't the prince—but she wasn't, and as the night had worn on she'd wondered if she had been too hasty in dismissing him.

She turned her attention back to the market, and her already low spirits sank another notch. Every horror story she'd ever heard about the Old Dominion had its origins in Pan-shei, the market of chaos and decay. Slaves were sold there, along with souls and all manner of vice. A rousing trade in religious artifacts had left few of the world's temples untouched. Nothing was sacred in Pan-shei, and everything was for sale.

The thief couldn't have chosen a more corrupt destination, which only further discredited him and made her position that much more untenable.

"Rotting Prince of Time," she grumbled under her breath. If he was the Prince of Time, she was the Princess of Fools. They were supposed to have been the match of ten millennia, bound by fate for a glorious destiny, not two rats running through a maze.

The scents from the market reached her as they descended from the East-West Ninety, heavy with spice and dust and the smells of a thousand years of human and not-so-human habitation. Surprisingly, it wasn't a bad smell, just far more complex than the desert. She was glad to note that at least on its southern border Pan-shei didn't have the reek of Racht.

The first stalls they passed were sturdy, made of sun-dried bricks with sun-bleached canopies, but as they continued north, each successive layer of the marketplace looked shabbier than the last. Morning fires were being lit and goods carted out as the shopkeepers and grain-sellers readied themselves for the day. There were very few fruits or vegetables to be seen, and when an old man set out a box of apples, the thief surprised her by stopping and buying the whole thing. He tossed her two.

"Better hide the extra one in your pouch, if you don't want it pinched," he advised, then took a big bite out of one of his own.

"Hey, Morgan!" a chipper voice rang out. "Whatcha got there?"

Avallyn turned toward the voice and saw a girl of no more than twelve standing with her hands on her hips at the entrance to an alley strung with laundry. Her face was winsome and dirty, her hair a wild tangle of black curls. Half a dozen other children were clustered around her, the smaller ones peeking out from behind her, the bigger boys standing by her side. All of them were dressed in a hodgepodge of rags and eyeing Morgan's box of apples.

"Hey, Klary," Morgan replied. Hefting the box to his shoulder, he took another bite of apple and resumed walking with a nonchalant air. Avallyn fell in beside him. The sound of pounding feet followed, and soon they were surrounded by a gaggle of street urchins.

"Whatcha got there, Morgan?" Klary asked again. Her red paisley pants were two sizes too big and cinched around her waist with a green scarf. Her once white shirt sported eight different shades of ground-in dirt.

"Yeah, Morgan. Whatcha got there?" a bigger boy with straight brown hair and freckles chimed in. Avallyn could count every one of his ribs through the opening in his blue plaid vest.

"Where you been, Morgan? We been hungry," a little round-faced girl with freckles and frizzy red hair said.

Klary shushed her with a hand on her shoulder and a meaningful glare. "Ain't nobody been hungry, Baba."

"Jus' me," Baba disagreed with a pouty lower lip.

"I'll toss you for those apples, Morgan," Klary suggested, lengthening her strides to keep up with him. Two of the bigger boys were skipping along backward ahead of the pack, neatly trapping them inside the circle of diminutive thieves.

Morgan must feel right at home, Avallyn thought.

"Nay, Klary," Morgan answered, shaking his head. "The last time we tossed, I lost four marks and my kit."

A whisper of sighed memories ran through the pack of children.

"They was cheese in the kit. Remember, Klary?"

"And raspberry candies."

"And corned kudge in a can. Oooh, I like corned kudge."

"They was peaches."

"And milk, real milk."

"And chocolate drops." Klary added her own reminiscence. "Betcha forgot about them chocolate drops, Morgan."

Morgan stopped and looked down at the girl, one eyebrow lifted to a skeptical degree. "Aye," he said slowly. "I had forgotten about those chocolate drops."

"Well, they could still be yours, Morgan. We been eating on the kit for a full week, but we ain't ate all them chocolate drops." The gleam in the girl's eye was pure larceny. "I'll toss you double, chocolate drops for apples."

Morgan's mouth curved into a smile that made Avallyn distinctly uneasy. He was going to steal the child's candy.

"Double?" he repeated.

"Aye." Klary nodded and pulled a pair of dice out of a voluminous pocket in her pants. She tossed them lightly into the air and caught them as they fell.

"No." Avallyn stepped forward. This was Pan-shei at its worst, and she'd be damned if she stood by while he robbed children. She pulled a handful of marks out of her pouch. "I'll buy the—"

The hand on her wrist stopped her in mid-speech. Morgan wasn't holding her hard enough to hurt, but he was definitely holding her hard enough to make her think twice.

She blinked up at him.

"Don't worry, love," he said in an easy lilt that reminded her once more of Kings Wood elves. "I can win you a bit of chocolate. My luck's been runnin' like a river in spate today." There was definite sarcasm in his last words, thick enough to make his point.

He gestured subtly and Avallyn followed his gaze to Klary's hand, where the girl was still tossing the dice and catching them. Every time they landed in her open palm, a pair of winning diamonds showed faceup.

They were loaded.

Avallyn shoved the marks back into her pouch, still not certain what game he was playing, only certain she was best left out of it—a fact he proved as one by one the apples were lost and eagerly snatched away by little hands.

At one point, he did win some chocolate drops, but for the most part he lost, and he kept losing until all the fruit was gone and he was down another four marks.

"Enough," he growled, rising from his knees where they'd played in the dirt. A grimace flickered across his face, and she nearly reached for him, but he made it to his feet in one piece without her help.

He paid up amidst the children's hoots of laughter, and as soon as the money changed hands, they were off and running down the street, shouting, "Klar—ee! Klar—ee!"

"You let her win," Avallyn said.

"Not really," he answered, brushing the dust off his pants.

"Then how come the dice only came up diamonds once for you? They were weighted to come up diamonds."

"Only the pair she was using." He handed her the chocolate drops. "The pair she kept slipping to me were loaded to lose."

"But how?" Avallyn had watched every roll and every time the dice had been picked up—or rather she'd watched nearly every roll and pick-up. Sometimes she'd been distracted by one of the other children.

Oh, she thought.

"They're all in on the scam," he said, "but Klary's the oldest with the fastest sleight of hand."

"Then how did you win the chocolate?"

He grinned. "I may not be as fast as you, or a wild boy, or a Pan-shei street snipper, but I manage to get by. Come on, now. We've dallied long enough." He started walking again.

"You could have just given them the apples," she said, catching up with a couple of quick strides.

"No, it's better that Klary wins them off me. It makes the other ones feel safer if they know they're living off their wits and Klary's speed and not off charity. Charity can be damned inconsistent."

Avallyn glanced up at him and hazarded a guess. "I'd say you've been fairly consistent, and good for four marks a week plus oddments."

"Aye," he admitted, "but what if I'm not here next week, or the week after that? Then what does Klary do to feed her brood?"

Avallyn felt a moment's guilt. He wasn't going to be there next week, nor the week after, and if he turned out to be the true Prince of Time, he would never return to Pan-shei.

She was still mulling that over when he turned the corner on an alley and abruptly stopped.

"What's wrong?" she asked.

"Nothing," he said, wrapping his arm around his rib cage and leaning back against a crumbling brick wall.

"Then why do you look like that?" His face was suddenly pale, the lines around his mouth tight.

"Like what?"

"Like I'm going to have to carry you the rest of the way to the tea shop," she said curtly, trying to conceal her concern. If he did drop in Pan-shei, she didn't dare stop. There was no safety for them until they reached the desert.

"Don't worry. You won't." He took a breath, then shook his head and pushed off the wall. "Come on. It's not far now. I promise."

She followed closely behind, not sure who he was trying to convince, her or himself, but she wished more than ever that she had the rover and its fully equipped sick bay.

"Do you have another tech-jaw?" she asked. "If I can contact my captain, we can get some help."

The look he gave her told her she was going for a long shot in that quarter. He'd already made it clear that he didn't want anything to do with her Night Watchers, and they were the only people she trusted in the whole of the Old Dominion.

Biting back a smart retort, she let him lead her through one alley after another, each more litter-strewn and disreputable than the last, until they reached a dead end. She had kept her eye out for a public comcell to try calling Dray, knowing her captain capable of outwitting a dozen skraelpacks, but Pan-shei was devoid of any amenities. Survival of the fittest seemed to rule the market streets, with more than just Klary's band of little thieves running through the alleys.

No trade was taking place in the stalls lining the dead-end street. In fact, it was eerily deserted given the shabby but abundant life scurrying around elsewhere in the market. A few ratty streamers flew over a squat open shop at the end with a yellow neon sign proclaiming "Ferrar's."

He'd said they would be safe in Pan-shei, safe at the tea shop, and she'd doubted every word, not ever having heard of a particularly well-fortified tea shop. The looks of Ferrar's did nothing to change her mind. Crammed between a windowless high-rise and a dilapidated metal Quonset, it was little more than a few planks of wood hammered together and bolstered up with cinder blocks. She wouldn't feel safe until she was well out into the desert.

An old man and an even older woman sat on the ground in the shade of the shop's ragged canopy, playing *choppes,* a game of sticks and tiles. A small brazier flanked by low stools stood unattended off to the side. Morgan sat down on one of the stools. Avallyn gratefully lowered herself onto another and looked around to see if there was a comcell booth in the vicinity.

There wasn't.

She stretched her hands out over the glowing coals and felt warmth seep into her fingertips. The morning was chill, and she was still wet from the rains, her hair still damp.

"I don't see any *wallah*," she said, referring to the person who would make the tea in a tea shop. She didn't see any tea either, or a cup or a pot.

"The important thing is that she sees us," the thief said, his gaze lifting to a shadowy corner beneath the canopy.

Avallyn glanced up and saw the flicker of a scanning camera. They were being observed.

A quiet rumbling drew her attention to the Quonset, where a door slowly swung open, its wheels churning up plumes of dust, its hinges creaking. The metal panel looked to be solid steel beneath its rusted tin casing.

"Morgan, love," a woman said, stepping out into the cool sunshine. "Welcome home." She was short, with a mop of graying tawny hair, her soft curves swathed in a pair of loose ivory-colored pants and a matching over-tunic, but it was her eyes that captured Avallyn's attention. Sea green and ageless, they were warm and lively with genuine delight at seeing the thief.

"Ferrar." He stood and crossed to the woman in two long, limping strides.

Avallyn witnessed their lengthy embrace with a growing sense of pique. Not only was the woman's delight genuine, but so was her affection, genuine and generous, right down to the kiss she offered with a tilt of her head, a kiss he readily accepted by lowering his mouth to hers.

Their lips no sooner touched than Avallyn's pique took a turn for the worse. By the time the kiss ended a moment later, her mood had gone beyond pique to immeasurably foul.

Chapter 7

The inside of the Quonset was no more a tea shop than the boards on the fence in the alley were, yet there was tea, hundreds of kilos of it. Bales and crates of all sizes, marked with the symbols of foreign lands and off-world colonies, were stacked next to the walls and in untidy rows down the center of the long room. At the end of the rows, a stone courtyard cluttered with chairs and plants lay bathed in amber light beneath a partially glassed-in ceiling.

A rectangular brazier running through the middle of a low table held a half-dozen odd-sized pots on its grate, all of them steaming. Dishes and cups were stacked nearby.

"The morning meal is ready, if you want food brought to your quarters," Ferrar said, her voice soothing, her arm draped around Morgan's waist.

"Do you have any guests?" he asked.

"One or two, a rumrunner on his circuit," the

woman replied with a slight shrug. "Overnights only. No one new in the private quarters."

Avallyn peered into the pots, doing her best to ignore the affectionate embrace and the surge of jealousy she'd felt when they kissed. Schooling her features, she cast a questioning glance over her shoulder at the thief. Everything in the cooking pots looked good and smelled wonderful—rice, noodles, spiced legumes, hot fruit soup.

"Eat in peace, princess. Ferrar only serves the best," he told her, then lowered his head to the woman's and whispered something in her ear.

Avallyn's jaw tightened. Damn him. If he turned out to be the prince, the woman would have to go. There wasn't *supposed* to have been another woman, anyhow. How could a prophecy be such a mess and last for ten thousand years?

Only one way that she could think of: He really wasn't the Prince of Time. But the thought didn't bring her nearly the relief it should have.

"Of course, Morgan," the tea trader replied, her expression growing concerned. "Let me get my kit and I'll be right over. Your friend can eat here while I see what you've done to yourself."

In answer, the thief lifted his wrist, showing the woman his bracelet. A knowing expression passed over her face and she glanced at Avallyn. Ferrar's gaze was assessing, but not lacking in warmth.

"Then your friend will have to join us. Jons," Ferrar called as she walked into the courtyard.

A faint sound coming from the far end of the tea stacks drew Avallyn's head around. A man stood up from where he'd been working on an electronic slate. He was a giant, as tall as a Lyran, his bald head shinning in the amber light, his boldly carved features reminding Avallyn of some ancient warrior from Earth's past. A scar ran the length of his face, creasing the corner of one eye in a perpetual squint. Powerful muscles bulged and rolled down his arms. His legs were like tree trunks.

He looked like a Prince of Time, and she couldn't stop staring— until her tracking bracelet lit up and nearly pulled her off her feet.

She threw the thief a scowl, which he was returning in full measure. He beckoned for her to come, and her lips thinned. It was past time for her to explain to him who she was, for her to recite her lineage and watch him squirm, for her to tell him the fate for which the prince had been born. No man in the Old Dominion did not fear the Priestesses of the Bones and their prophecies.

Ferrar met Jons next to the brazier, and as the two of them conferred, Avallyn stalked across the courtyard to the thief.

"You'd best not let Ferrar catch you mooning over Jons," he said before she could speak, "or we'll both end up back on the street."

"Mooning? Me?" She halted, taken aback by the sheer audacity of the man. She had to clench her hands by her sides to keep from poking him in the chest. "*You're* the one kissing everyone in sight."

She was overreacting. She knew it as surely as she was standing there wondering why. Hunger and exhaustion had never done this to her before, and neither had a man.

"Not quite everyone," he assured her tersely, his eyes glittering.

She went very still, though her pulse was racing. Was he daring to offer her a kiss? This low-down, low-life, tech-trash thief who would probably be chained in the hold of one of the Warmonger's desert ships by now if she hadn't saved him?

Her gaze slipped to his mouth, and in an instant she realized her mistake.

His lips curved into a dangerous smile, revealing a flash of white teeth. She didn't dare look up, didn't dare move.

"So you would be kissed," she heard him say.

He covered the short distance between them with a limping stride and caught her chin in his hand. He tilted her face toward his, and when their eyes met, an undeniable thrill coursed through her body, burning away every ounce of common sense she had.

"Do you know my name, *geneth*?" His voice was silky, the question barely audible.

"Morgan," she said, hating the breathlessness she heard in her own voice. "Morgan ab Kynan."

"Aye." His smile faded and his eyes darkened to a fathomless shade of blue. "I am Morgan."

With his name still in the air between them, he lowered his mouth to hers, and she was flooded with a new and wondrous awareness. Scents and tastes flowed and melded together, giving her a glimpse of the essence that was uniquely his.

Shadana. No wonder the woman had wanted to kiss him within seconds of his arrival. He was delicious. Intoxicating. Exotically animal. She could feel his breath and the heat of his skin, the strength of the body standing so close to hers. A faint taste of the wine was still on his lips, but the more intense flavor was purely his.

He lifted his head, his eyes meeting hers with a look of confused wonder. Then he lowered his lashes and kissed her again. With his second touch, she wanted more, and he obliged, one soft caress following another, each more daring than the last, until she felt as if she were being gently devoured by the grazing of his teeth across her lips and the lazy stroking of his tongue. Time ceased to exist, and when he whispered, "Open your mouth for me," she eagerly complied, wanting nothing more than to lose herself in the heated enchantment.

Morgan was reeling, holding himself in check by the thinnest of threads and the knowledge that he was in no condition to do more than kiss her. His bad leg was near to giving out, and halfway through Panshei a fierce ache had started in his chest. He'd sprained or torn something under the Lyran's handling, and the night's trek had finally shaken it loose.

But the chit, *sweet Jesu,* she'd asked for a kiss with her bold look and he hadn't had the self-control not to give her one, not when indulging her gave him an excuse to indulge himself.

He tunneled his hand through her hair, turning her deeper into his kiss and plundering her mouth. The taste of her swirled through his senses, so richly verdant, unlike anything he'd ever tasted before. She was sweet like flowers, sweeter than Carillion wine, her tiny braids and twists of hair softer against his fingers than the finest silk, the feel of her body against his an exquisite pleasure he could drown in.

It had been a long time since he'd held a woman in his arms, a long time since he'd felt desire for anything beyond getting drunk, but one kiss from her had him hard and wanting to claim her for his own— this stranger who had already claimed him with her bracelets.

The realization washed over him like a bucket of cold water.

God's blood—was he out of his mind?

He dragged his mouth from hers, ignoring his arousal with an iron will, his mood going from passion to suspicion in one fell leap of logic. She had breached something in him he had not wanted breached, and she'd done it with just a kiss. He'd be a fool to take something that powerful at face value. The women of the future had a thousand tricks to employ for any one of a thousand different ends—and very few of them were to a man's advantage.

He captured her face with his hands and forced her to meet his gaze. "What do you want from me, death-witch?"

Her lashes were brown, tipped in gold, the gray of her eyes edged in forest green. Her mouth was wet and softly swollen, and it was all he could do not to soothe her lips with a gentler kiss than the one they'd already shared.

"Only the Warmonger calls us death-witches," she said, not even trying to escape his hold.

"The Warmonger and half of the Old Dominion," he begged to differ. "So you are a priestess then, and not just a messenger."

"A priestess, yes, of Claerwen in the northern dunes, and princess of the White Palace."

Morgan's grip tightened for a second before he stepped back, releasing her. He'd known it. So help him God, he'd known it.

"Ferrar!" he called out, taking another step away. His headache had never left, his chest was killing him, and he'd just kissed a White Lady of Death, who was also a princess of something called the White Palace, whatever the hell that was. If things were going to get any worse, he was definitely going to need more wine.

Avallyn watched him back away, too stunned to follow.

He'd kissed her.

The thief had kissed her and she knew to the depths of her bones that her life was never going to be the same again. Indeed, the Prince of Time had come.

An hour later, Avallyn still felt the impact of Morgan's kiss. Ferrar had settled him in his bedroom, in a palatial bed draped with hand-blocked cerulean curtains. Unlike the bunks she was used to sleeping in, his bed looked big enough for three people. Ferrar had left the door partially ajar, and from all his muttering and the woman's placating, Avallyn had determined that though hurt, he would live.

He had a small galley kitchen in his quarters and a profusion of plants growing in pots in the living area. The furniture was comfortable but worn, a divan strewn with orange and gold pillows and all manner of chairs and stools scattered over intricately patterned rugs. There were no windows, only the same amber-glassed skylights as in the courtyard—an upscale den for a thief.

She sipped her *chai,* an ancient drink made from spices, tea, milk, and honey. Ferrar had sworn its recuperative powers were powerful enough to raise the dead, and Avallyn agreed. With her belly full of soup and the tea warming her insides, she felt renewed enough to face the journey into the desert. They could not delay. She had indulged the prince long enough. The Third Guard would not give up the search, and she couldn't take a chance on their being captured.

She thought longingly of the rover in Racht's east bays. Skraelings or nay, she doubted if Dray had abandoned it. Ferrar had to have a com-cell she could use to contact her captain, but short of dragging Morgan off his bed and out into the tearoom, she didn't have much chance of finding it. Her search of his quarters had yielded nothing beyond the virtu and curios of a vagabond's life.

The scent of burning incense wafted out from behind the bedroom door. Myrrh, she thought, lifting the cup of *chai* to her mouth, with a hint of rose. Ferrar was a woman of varied talents, to use a healing incense along with her bottles of pills, salves, and elixirs.

Avallyn had enough marks on her to buy some sort of small transport, a scant-ton chassis or a double-wing sandtrekker. Neither would provide the protection and comfort of a rover, especially the fully armed rover they'd left in Racht, but both were capable of getting them to one of the caravanserai—scantly populated outposts that marked the trade routes into the desert. Beyond the last caravanserai, her skills more than any transport would be needed to keep them alive, but she was undaunted by the challenge. She would face the desert on foot before she would face the Third Guard. The Warmonger had no love for her, not after what the Claerwen priestess had done to him. However much Corvus wanted Morgan ab Kynan, he would want her more—and the two of them were together, one neat package sitting in a tea shop in Pan-shei with the Third Guard on their trail.

"Sticks." Frustration brought her to her feet in one supple move. The thief couldn't have picked a worse enemy. With the Sha-shakrieg Night Watchers lost to them, she dared not wait any longer for Ferrar to finish. They had to get out of there.

She started for the bedroom just as the door to the courtyard opened behind her. Spinning around, she dropped to a crouch, her lasgun drawn, cocked, and aimed—straight at the heart of the wild boy from Racht.

He'd drawn even faster than she, and she found herself staring down the barrel of a lasgun modified much in the same manner as hers, with an extra charge pack rigged for superfast reload. Everything inside her tensed for the shock of his first pulsing shot.

The door behind her opened wider, but she didn't dare take her attention off the boy. His green-eyed gaze swept over her in a flash, and in that same flash came a recognition she hadn't expected. His fierce expression melted into one of awe, and he dropped to his knees before her, his lasgun scraping the floor, his head bowed.

"By the Bones, milady."

It was only then that she noticed his lasgun was trigger-locked.

Morgan stood in his bedroom doorway, staring at the strange and thoroughly unwelcome sight of his captain kowtowing to his captor.

"Aja," he barked, then winced as a sharp pain lanced through his chest. Nothing was broken, according to Ferrar. He'd only sprained the muscles holding his ribs in place. Ferrar had given him what wine she had, a small bottle he'd slipped into his munitions belt. One swig had done as much to revive him as all the rest of the *wallah*'s potions and ministrations.

The boy looked up and grinned. "Morgan, milord."

The desert woman glanced at him as she rose from her crouched position, but she wasn't smiling. Her face was pale, understandably so. She was fast, but not as fast as Aja, and she wouldn't have known his lasgun was trigger-locked. It was always trigger-locked. She'd been in far more danger of being impaled by a throwing star, and Morgan trusted Aja to know better than to impale anyone in Ferrar's.

But this business of his captain on the floor, bowing to the death-witch, was taking things a bit too far.

"Where's York?" he asked.

"In the alley with our transport, milord."

"Transport?"

Aja's grin broadened. "Aye. When you mentioned a rover in the east bays, it struck me that we might be needing one."

Morgan felt a layer of his tension dissipate. *Thank you, sweet Mary.* They weren't trapped at Ferrar's.

"Good work, Captain." The boy deserved a reward. Mayhap 'twas time to give the Warmonger his friggin' dragon and collect the final payment. It would be a nice change to have Van and the Third Guard off his back.

"You have my rover?" The desert woman stepped forward, her face showing the same relief he felt.

"Begging your pardon, milady," Aja said, "but the rover is Morgan's now."

Morgan saw her stiffen at the boy's words.

Slowly, she turned to him. "You're stealing my rover?"

"Aye." He gestured to Aja. Ferrar had poked and pushed and taped on him for nearly an hour, which was half an hour longer than Morgan had planned on staying at home. He and the woman had been fed and gotten as much rest as they dared. More could be had later. He'd decided to take her to a place he knew on the eastern fringes of the Old Dominion. She could sleep all she wanted once he had them safely hidden.

The boy started to leave, but got no farther than two steps before the desert woman spun around and issued an imperious command.

"Hold."

Much to Morgan's consternation, Aja did just that, stopping and turning to her, his face wiped clean of any smile.

"Do you know who I am, boy?" she asked in a tone that implied she damn well knew he did, though Morgan found it ludicrous that someone of her few years would call Aja a boy.

"Not who, milady," his captain confessed, "but I know what you are."

"And are you not sworn to the Priestesses of the Bones along with the others of your sept?"

Aja slanted Morgan an odd, nearly guilty glance, his hand going to the yellow wallet on his belt.

The warning hairs rose on the nape of Morgan's neck, and he knew the day had just taken another turn for the worse.

Chapter 8

"Aye," Aja said, averting his gaze.

"Friggin' hell," Morgan muttered. He reached for Avallyn and pulled her close, disarming her with the ease of long practice. Locking his arm around her, he pinned her to his side and held her off the floor while she squirmed like a madwoman. "Well, she's mine now, Captain. So you'd best do as I say, and I say we're getting in the friggin' rover and getting the hell out of here."

With that, he headed for the door.

He had to work to keep Avallyn from elbowing him in the ribs, which would pretty much put him out of commission. It was a risk he was willing to take. He'd be damned if he would let her have the rover and take him to the death-witches.

"Oh, aye, milord." Aja's smile returned in full bloom as he caught up with them.

The boy was ever one to recognize an opportunity, and Morgan had just handed him one. Desert septs and priestesses aside, Morgan knew where his captain's loyalties lay, just as he understood the occasional necessity of swearing allegiance to save one's skin. The boy, though, had rarely been out of his sight for the last ten years, so Morgan had to assume the priestess-swearing had been done when Aja was a small child at most, which by his code made the oath invalid. He had not taken Aja's oath to him until the boy had been old enough to understand exactly what such an oath meant.

Aye, he knew where his captain's loyalties lay. He'd known from the day Aja had allowed Van the Wretched to capture him rather than have Morgan taken alone to the warlord's lunar colony. A miserable time that had been, with the boy—only ten years old—frightened to a near witless state by the skraelings, and Morgan wondering if there was any possible chance for escape. That night, chained in the filthiest of Van's orbital dungeons, Aja had shown him the contents of the yellow wallet he kept on his belt. Bones, they were, small bones, divining bones, the boy's mother's finger bones nested in a bit of sand.

In retrospect, mayhap Aja had been trying to tell him something then about the Priestesses of the Bones and his connection to them. If so, he'd been too damn subtle. All Morgan remembered from that night was the stark fear in the boy's eyes and how tightly he'd held on to those small bones, praying for protection.

Avallyn suddenly went still in his arms.

Too still. Every muscle in her body was tense and thrumming with alertness.

He stopped, only partway across the courtyard, and looked at her. Her chin was lifted. Her ears twitched once. He glanced in the direction she was staring and saw nothing beyond the crates and bags of tea cluttering the storeroom, but he didn't doubt for an instant that she saw something more. He looked to the boy and found Aja in the same state of hyperawareness.

"Captain?"

Aja turned his head. The boy's mouth was thin with worry. "The Third Guard, milord, coming up the alley."

"And a skraelpack," Avallyn added. "I can smell them."

Morgan loosened his hold on her. She retrieved her lasgun as she regained her footing, lifting the weapon out of his hand. He let her have it without so much as a glance in her direction. Concentrating on the Quonset wall, the one fronting the alley, he could hear the faint sound of marching feet and, after a moment, thought he could hear faint echoes of the skraeling war cry in the distance—*"Har maukte har"*—but he'd be damned if he could smell anything.

"Which alley is the rover in, Aja?"

"Back alley, milord."

That bought them a few seconds. He swung around to face the woman who had followed them out of the storeroom. "Trouble's coming, Ferrar. You and Jons are welcome to share the rover."

Ferrar made a dismissive gesture with her hand. "We've been raided before and we'll be raided again. If we turned tail every time a skraelpack showed up, we would have been out of business years ago. Jons!" she hollered, shifting her attention to the center of the courtyard. "Lock us down!"

"This is the Third Guard." Morgan felt compelled to remind her, not doubting Aja's or Avallyn's identification of the marchers.

Ferrar shrugged. "The Third Guard is nothing more than a pack of skraelings from a little bit deeper end of the gene pool."

The sound of moving troops was unmistakable now and growing ever closer. Jons was already moving the Quonset's blast wall into place over the front door. The old *choppes* players slipped through at the last second. The few guests at the inn had heard the call and were up and running. Everyone who used Ferrar's as a safehouse knew the routine, and Morgan noted the goodly amount of firepower being carried out of the rooms.

Jons locked down the blast wall and headed toward the back of the courtyard.

"We'll swing around front and draw them off," Morgan said to Ferrar, signaling for Aja and Avallyn to leave.

He didn't have to tell them twice. They were both out the back door before he cleared the courtyard.

"Damn," he whispered. It was a good thing he had a tracking bracelet on her, or he would lose her for sure.

The sheer idiocy of the thought stopped him cold in his tracks. What in the hell was he thinking? If it weren't for the friggin' tracking bracelet, she wouldn't have been able to hold on to him.

He followed them out the back door, reminding himself that she was his prisoner now. The thought brought him some satisfaction. As for giving her back her lasgun, he wasn't about to have her running around without protection, and he figured the odds of her shooting him had dropped to nil after the kiss they'd shared. She couldn't have been immune to the shock wave of pleasure that had rolled over him, or the odd sense that he'd found something more than what he'd expected. The taste of her was still on his tongue, still beguiling him.

The rover parked in the alley was a Class G, built to house a crew of twelve, with a modified chassis for desert travel. It had two gun ports on each side and a scale-laced overcoat in dun brown. Despite its size—about half of the Quonset—it would be practically invisible in the dunes. Morgan took the amenities in with a glance as he jumped through the open hold door. He punched the "close" panel next to the jamb. The doors slid shut, and he was instantly accosted by the most fetid and horrendous smell known to man: skrael stench.

Standing on the deck, Avallyn looked green. Aja looked abashed.

"York and me had to clean the beasts out," the boy offered by way of explanation for the thoroughly disgusting smell and the mess of goods broken and tossed all over the place. Wires hung out of broken panels. The overhead lighting had been smashed. Burn marks seared part of the bulkhead. "Didn't have much time to tidy up."

Morgan nodded curtly. It was still a job well done, no matter how foul the rover smelled.

"York!" he called. "Take us around front. See if we can give the Third Guard something to think about besides Ferrar's."

With the mercenary at the controls, the rover powered up and rolled smoothly through the alley. Morgan strode across the deck and onto the small bridge.

"Use a half-blast to disperse them, then head east to the Pathian Quarter and see how many we can draw off with us," he ordered.

"Can't go east." York passed his hand over the console and a gridded screen lit up. He planted his finger on a red line. "The local City Guard has put up a blockade with your name on it. They're pretty rankled about the mess ye left in Racht."

Morgan swore; not for the first time since last night, he wondered about their odds of escaping. They'd been running for nigh onto eight hours and had gotten no farther than Pan-shei. The damned Third Guard was still hot on their trail, and now the slags had the damned City Guard to back them up.

"Then go south, toward Magh Dun."

West, into the desert, was out of the question under the circumstances, and traveling deeper into the Old Dominion through the northern provinces was too risky. It was a hell of a long way to the northern border, and even though the City Guard patrols thinned out the farther one got from the Central Quarter, it was too easy for the enemy to call in support troops while they remained in the city.

"Isn't that a bit like jumping out of the frying pan into the fire?" York asked, giving him a sideways glance. The man's beefy face was smudged with dirt and cut in a couple of places. His short-cropped brown hair was dusted with some kind of powder from a busted-open bag that hung off the back of his pilot's seat. The other seat had been ripped from its moorings and jammed under the console. Shards of glass littered the floor, and a rank-smelling, greenish-blue fluid was leaking from a severed hose sticking out of the wall.

It must have been one hell of a fight, Morgan thought.

"Nay," he said. "I think it's time I dealt with the Warmonger, gave him the friggin' dragon, and got him off our backs."

"More 'n likely, he'll just take the damn dragon, skin us alive, and give us to Vishab to boil," York countered grimly.

"Vishab?" Morgan asked.

"Corvus Gei's necromancer," Avallyn said, coming up from behind them and stopping next to him on the bridge.

He turned to face her, intrigued. "Necromancer? As in mage?"

"The witch of Magh Dun will not set you free," she said, discerning his thoughts with damnable ease. "Your man has the way of it. She's ever one to boil and burn, especially Claerwen priestesses. My life would be forfeit in the witch's tower, and the death she would give me would make the endless rot of a sewer snake bite look like a blessing."

The last was added with a chilling solemnity that gave Morgan pause. No fear marred the clear depths of the princess-priestess's eyes, but neither did subterfuge. She was telling him the simple truth.

Mayhap he needed to rethink his plan.

"Skraelings on the starboard," York announced.

Morgan looked through a side window, then moved to the front. More than one skraelpack had joined the group they'd encountered in Racht. The beasts were swarming everywhere. The Third Guard was farther up the alley, readying a cannon.

"Take out the gun," he said. "Let them know we're here."

York lit up another screen with his hand and started setting the coordinates for his shot.

"Morgan!" Aja came running up from the aft deck. "The Second Guard is moving in behind us."

He spun around, his eyebrows furrowed. The Second Guard? Impossible.

"Are you sure?" he asked, and prayed no one else could detect the edge in his voice. It was panic, pure and simple.

"Aye." Aja's eyes reflected the same panic. The Third Guard were truly as Ferrar had said, only a chromosone or two up on the genetic scale from skraelings, a well-organized group of nasty errand boys for the Warmonger. Morgan had been outrunning them since he'd first stepped foot in the Old Dominion. The Second Guard were the Warmonger's elite troops, second only to the First Guard, the Home Guard that never left Corvus Gei's side.

"The Warmonger wouldn't send the Second Guard to pick up a lousy forty-thousand-mark bounty," he said, not sure who he was trying to reassure.

Aja agreed with a vigorous shaking of his head.

"So it's got to be the friggin' dragon," Morgan decided, holding out his hand for the statue, "and pure gold or nay, it's not big enough to warrant the Second Guard's involvement."

"Aye, not nearly big enough," the boy echoed, fumbling to untie the leather bag from his belt. When it fell loose, he tossed it to Morgan.

"I've got their gun in my sights," York said.

"Fire!" Morgan caught the bag and steadied himself against the bulkhead for the rover's recoil as York released their first shot.

There was no recoil.

He looked at Avallyn, impressed. "Nice ship." Shifting his attention to Aja, he slipped the golden statue free of its covering and hefted it in his hand. "What do you think? Is it hollow? And what do you think could be in here that is worth sending the Second Guard after?"

"A clean hit," York announced.

"Give them a half-blast forward. We're going to have to go through them and Ferrar's fence, unless you can get some lift out of this thing." Though he gave the order, Morgan's attention didn't leave Aja.

"Chrystaalt," the boy answered.

Morgan had heard of the strange stuff and its even stranger attributes. 'Twas a salt mined in the Waste, a mineral used by the Psilords of the last dynasty to put genetically superior life-forms into states of suspended animation. Since the Trelawney Rebellion, when the galaxy-wide government had been overthrown, the chrystaal trade had gone underground, becoming strictly black market. Ten grams could make a man's fortune.

He looked at the dragon, a lustrous reddish-gold beast with long fangs and intricately wrought wings sleeping on a bed of writhing gold snakes.

Or worms. The thought came to him as it had so many times since Sonnpur-Dzon. Golden worms. Time worms from the weir.

He lifted his gaze to Avallyn and found her staring at the dragon, transfixed with awe, her eyes alight with desire. Her hand was half lifted toward the thing, though he doubted if she realized it.

Christe, if she would ever look at him in such a way, he would probably go up in flames from the fire it would start.

"It's yours for another kiss," he said softly, giving into insanity and meaning every word. He would give her the dragon, the months of searching to find it, the battle to steal it, and the endless days of drunkenness trying to deal with it, anything to have her mouth beneath his again, sweetly hot and open for his kiss.

Her eyes flashed up to meet his, and a shadow of longing darkened the gray depths.

Satisfaction surged through him. She would be his, the price uncounted. He started toward her, only to be stopped by the slow shake of her head.

"It's not meant to be mine," she said with obvious reluctance, her hand falling back to her side.

"Then whose?" Frustration sharpened his voice.

"The priestesses in Claerwen."

He felt the first stirrings of anger returning. Despite the way she'd kissed him, she would still incarcerate him in a temple of bones. The fact damned him as surely as he'd been damned in the weir.

"They won't get me or the dragon," he said.

"I'll get you both to Claerwen," she corrected him, "have no doubt. But in the end, you are mine. You were sent here to be mine, dread lord."

Of all the things she could have said, that was the last he had expected. He stared at her, dumbfounded, until a niggling suspicion helped him find his tongue.

"To what end?" he demanded, bracing himself for the worst. Slavery, mayhap, or some godforsaken priestess sacrifice.

But her blush and the casting aside of her gaze told him otherwise. He would be hers in the way of a man and a woman.

"Half-blast loaded and locked," York apprised him.

"Fire." His response to the mercenary was automatic. His response to the princess's statement was a confusing mix of anticipation and fear. He hadn't been "sent" to the future. The whole thing had been an accident of battle, one sword against another, and he had lost.

But the chance to have her, to know her, was not one he would put aside lightly.

Priestesses. *Christe.* He must be losing his mind. Mayhap she was working some spell on him. Madron, the witch of Wydehaw, had done a brisk business in love potions.

The half-blast shot out of the forward gun, and Morgan heard York swear.

"They're dispersin', all right," the mercenary said, his voice rising, "with most of them headed this way. Aja! What the hell is going on back there?"

"Second Guard closing in aft!"

"Morgan?" York yelled. "What in the hell are we gonna do here?"

The options had been narrowed down to one, and he swore it wasn't desire making it. He was too old and had been through too much to make his decisions based on a woman's face, even if it was a face that had haunted him for ten long years; or on a woman's kiss, even if her kiss had shaken him to his core.

"Take us west, into the desert," he commanded—*and may God have mercy on our souls.*

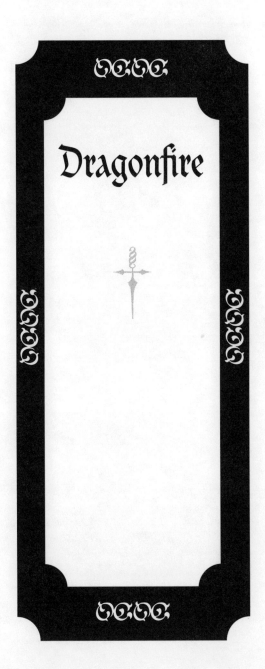

Dragonfire

Chapter 9

Morgan had to concede that Avallyn had been right. The desert had been the right place to come. She'd insisted on a northern route, so he'd given York orders to head south, but either way they'd landed in the middle of nowhere. A full moon shone above them, its light silvering the surrounding dunes and the sheer rock wall at their back. The Medain of Craig Tagen, she called it, part of a stony ridge that stretched for hundreds of miles north to south. Beyond the dunes, the land disappeared into the darkness of an eerily silent night. The rover was parked in the sand at the base of the towering rocks, looking like part of the formation.

Aye, she'd picked a good place. 'Twas a damn good place to die and leave one's bones to bleach. He had his hollow in the rock all picked out for when the time came.

"Friggin' skraelings," he muttered, pushing himself out from under the rover, a welding rod in his hand.

His breath made puffs of vapor in the frigid air. "All right then, York, try her again!"

The fusion block had been mangled during their escape from Pan-shei, giving out about a day from the city and leaving them to limp along on auxiliary power until they'd reached what passed for an oasis in the Deseillign Waste—a half-dozen thrawn shrubs clustered around a narrow crack in a rock wall. Inside the crack was a sinkhole.

Avallyn and Aja were there, hauling water to bring back to the rover, refilling the reserve tanks which the skraelings had fouled during their brief term of ownership.

He should have questioned her by now. Instead, he'd been avoiding her like the plague—at least as much as the tracking bracelet allowed him to avoid her. As for the boy, he owed Aja an apology and probably a debt of gratitude for not letting him drown in wine or self-pity these last weeks— though in truth he preferred either demise to the one he now faced.

Ferrar's small bottle of wine had been broken, the fragile glass of his salvation shattered by a cannon blast they'd taken on the western edge of the market.

He was doomed.

"Fire her up!" he called again to York.

A loud clank coupled with a blast of steam billowing up from be- neath the transport sufficed as the mercenary's reply.

Morgan swore and dragged his hand back through his hair, then glanced over his shoulder at the rock wall.

You were sent here to be mine, dread lord—her words echoed in his mind.

He looked back at the rover. Nothing had been simple since the battle for Balor, when he'd fallen into the weir. He'd not had one simple moment since then, and stealing the dragon from Sonnpur-Dzon had only complicated his life more.

Aye, and what he wouldn't give to have one simple moment of peace.

He started toward the hold door, but was stopped by a stab of pain across his rib cage. Gritting his teeth, he flattened his hand on his chest to ease the ache and continued on into the rover. Ferrar's salves and pills were wearing off. His headache couldn't be too far behind the muscle spasm, and neither could the detox wine fever that had been threatening to engulf him all day.

"Well?" York grumbled.

"The impulse meridians are functional, but without a new fusion block, we can't get more than auxiliary power out of the generator."

"So we're stuck here."

"Aye."

Again he looked to the rock wall, through the starboard window, and this time she was there, a slight figure shrouded against the cold in her tattered black cloak.

You were sent here to be mine, dread lord.

"But at what price?" he murmured, watching her descend the path to the rover.

"What, hey?" York asked.

"Nothing," he replied. "Get ready to lock us down for the night. The temperature is dropping toward zero and it's not going to stop there."

Dinner in the rover's galley was a subdued affair, with everyone, Avallyn included, too exhausted to do much more than eat. The transport's com-cell had been damaged beyond repair, like almost everything else, and there had been no sign of the Night Watchers. If they hadn't been killed—and she didn't think the Third Guard, or even the Second, could kill Dray of Deseillign—they would be searching for her. She had no doubt of that. Her only doubt was whether they would find her. Drunken thief or not, the Prince of Time was blessed with uncanny survival skills and the luck of the stars for making narrow escapes. Elusive didn't begin to describe the path they'd taken since she'd banded him. For all practical purposes, she was on her own in getting him to Claerwen, with or without his consent, and with or without the rover.

Stifling a curse, she took another bite of honeyed seedcake. The fusion block had been half torn from its rigging and crushed on one side. Morgan and Aja had worked on it for hours before even Morgan had given up.

She hazarded a quick glance in his direction. He looked done in and in pain. His face was drawn, his hair raked through. A sheen of sweat dampened his brow. 'Twas more than his fight with the Lyran he was feeling. 'Twas the wine, she knew. The wretched stuff was addictive, and he was without.

She could help him, if she dared. Her fingers went to the pouch on her belt and the crystal vial within.

His hand trembled as he reached for his food, and with a soft sound of disgust he pushed his plate aside and rose to his feet. He stopped next to the wild boy, bending his head down close and saying something that made Aja nod and grip his arm.

The bond there was deep, and knowing of the boy's oath to the priestesses, Avallyn had to wonder at it. She wondered, too, if his sept knew how far he'd strayed in the company he'd been set to keep. After the way he'd drawn on her at Ferrar's, she knew there was more to the boy than she or Dray had thought in Racht. All the wild boys were fast, but she'd never seen one faster than herself, never seen one with *tlas buen,* the ability to "quickety-split." He was fey, for certes, and he'd been making her ears twitch all day.

After giving the boy's hair a quick tousle, Morgan walked away, heading toward the sick bay, and for the first time Avallyn saw pained awkwardness rather than grace in his limping stride. Aja rose as well, but York motioned for him to stay put, and looked at her as if he expected her to do something.

The mercenary was right, of course. She did have to do something. The Prince of Time was hers.

Morgan felt more than heard someone enter the sick bay behind him, the light step telling him it was Aja.

"Well, what do you think?" he asked, staring at the array of drugs he'd laid out on the counter. His hands were splayed on either side of the *materia medica,* both of them trembling with the god-rotting d.t.'s. He'd stopped sweating and started growing hot, a bad sign for certes, the beginning of the wine fever. "Which one is more likely to heal me than kill me?"

He lifted a likely bottle, a drug Ferrar had once given him to counteract an overindulgence in Carillion wine. Would it work for the reverse as well? he wondered.

" 'Tis not more synthetics you need, but an easing of your mind, lord." Avallyn's scent reached him at the same time as her hand touched his arm.

He tensed and made to pull away—he was in no mood and no condition to deal with her—but she held him firm.

"I can help you at least as much as the *chai wallah*," she told him, "and probably a good deal more."

"Do you have wine, then?" he asked, summoning his last ounce of composure and deigning to give her a glance. As always, the sight of her so near startled him with an odd sense of déjà vu, but he didn't turn away.

She shook her head.

Without the daze of the wine in his eyes, he could see she was not so perfectly formed as he'd thought. Senseless sot that he was, though, he found her imperfections even more intriguing.

Freckles—a fair maid's bane—lay like faerie dust across the bridge of her nose, a gift from the desert sun. A scar nicked a bit of hair out of her right eyebrow and lifted it higher than the left one, making her more the mischievous sprite than the golden princess. Another scar marred one of her pointed ears. Her two front teeth were somewhat crooked, one overlapping the other, but that in no way made him want to kiss her less. And thoughts of kissing were bound to be his undoing. He'd offered her the dragon for a kiss and been turned down. Had he no sense left at all?

The biggest difference he noted in her in his new and painfully sober state was her age. Young she was, but not so young as he'd thought, no teenaged priestess.

"How old are you?" he asked. Not the first question he'd planned on asking her, nor the most important one, but the one that came to mind.

"One hundred and twenty-five times has the Earth gone around the Sun since the day of my birth."

He blanched at her answer. He'd long ago learned that in the cosmic scheme of things, human lives were some of the shortest, just as he'd also learned that longer-lived species usually had an arrogance to match, most times for good reason. One hundred and twenty-five years was a very long time for someone who looked no more than simply five-and-twenty, long enough for her to have learned things he probably had yet to imagine. He rubbed at a new pain in his temples. One hundred and twenty-five friggin' years.

"That's more than I would have guessed" was the best reply he could manage.

"My tribe is long-lived, dread lord, on my father's side."

Given the circumstances, he took heart at her continued use of the term "dread lord."

Christe, but his head was splitting.

"And who is your father?" With a death-witch priestess for a mother, he could only wonder at the man who had sired her.

"An Ilmarryn Magia Lord. Tamisk is his name."

Morgan lowered his hand from his eyes and immediately wished he hadn't. The room was starting to soften around the edges, a Carillion illusion. He could almost feel the wine shrinking up into itself and evaporating out of his cells, a circumstance bound to leave a wasteland behind.

"And your father made these?" He lifted his tracking bracelet. Though unfamiliar with the witch Vishab, Morgan had heard of the Ilmarryn, the desert faeries, but only as myth. They were said to live in a Lost Forest on the edge of the Sand Sea, and of course, they only came to Pan-shei to steal naughty children. Given his experience with the Quicken-tree in his past, he'd wondered if there was more truth to the tales than Pan-shei mothers might know, and it seemed he'd been right. If perchance he survived sobriety, it would be good to know whose chains held him.

"Aye. 'Twas Tamisk." She confirmed his suspicion. "He feared I could not otherwise hold you."

"He was right," Morgan said, then wondered if he'd spoken the truth. He could have eluded her, but at what point in their escape would he have left her to the skraelings, or to deal with the Third Guard alone? Even at Ferrar's, where she would have been relatively safe, he wouldn't have been inclined to leave her—especially after they'd kissed.

His gaze slipped to her mouth, and not for the first time he wondered what had made her open herself so completely to him. She'd hardly seen him in his best light, this ancient princess-priestess with the enchanted lineage. Yet when they'd kissed, her hands had settled on his waist, not to push him away, but to hold him. Her body had moved close to his, creating a warmth he had felt seep into his skin.

And her mouth . . . *Sweet Jesu,* her mouth had fit his as if they'd been made for each other.

Looking away, he dragged a hand through his hair. If he did survive his withdrawal from the wine, mayhap he'd have the chance to kiss her again. But not now. Now he needed help. The sick bay was starting to move in unnatural ways.

"Get . . . get Aja for me," he commanded, willing her to obey before he disgraced himself by crumbling to the floor. He'd held on to his mind all day and wasn't yet ready to relinquish control.

"No, milord. I will do." She sounded very sure of herself, showing more confidence than he could offer, what with the room slipping off to one side and doing a slow melt that left him without purchase on the floor.

He lunged to catch himself on the counter before it slid completely away, and found himself caught by her instead.

"Shhh, now, Morgan. Be still." She was warm and amazingly solid, her arms coming around him, holding him. He instinctively followed suit, folding her into his embrace and lowering his head to her shoulder. She smelled so very good, and the mere act of holding her stopped the room from sliding away. He closed his eyes in relief. Enchanted lineage, indeed.

He heard the buckle on his scabbard being released, felt the weight of the sword lifted from his back.

"Let's get you down before you get hurt." Her voice was a sweet breath in his ear. "Careful now." She leaned over and released the bay's examining table from the bulkhead. Another touch on the sensor pad positioned it. He felt the edge come up against the backs of his thighs, but he didn't want to lie down and let go of her. Her tattered cloak was softer than goosedown, the warmth and shape of her body a comfort he wanted to keep close.

"Morgan," she said, nudging him onto the table.

He didn't have the strength to resist, so he gave in—and took her with him, tumbling down onto the bed.

She let out a surprised gasp, filling his arms, and a fleeting smile touched his lips. He wanted her, even in his delirium, and his time was running short. He could feel the fell end drawing near.

"Are you sure you don't have any Carillion wine?" One dram would soothe him, just one dram would see him through, and they could spend the rest of the night making love instead of fighting for what might be left of his life.

Lord, it had been so long since he'd made love with a woman, truly made love. There had been a sweet maid back in Wales when he'd been but a boy. Eiryl had been her name, his first, and his eldest brother's betrothed. She'd searched him out one night in the small room he had claimed over the buttery, looking for love and kindness she rightfully feared she would not find in Damian's bed. Within a fortnight they'd been discovered, and he'd been sent packing off to war, to fight in the Crusades by the Lionheart's side. Many a time since then he'd wondered if Damian's oldest son was his own. Eiryl had never said, and when he'd come back from the Crusades, broken, she'd been content enough in her role as Damian's wife.

Morgan . . . Morgan, wake up. 'Twas a whisper out of the past.

'Twas Eiryl.

Morgan looked to the far side of the sick bay, and there she was, her fair skin paled by moonlight, her long dark hair tangled by the wind and the rain. A storm had been brewing all day.

"Morgan, help me, please. Save me." Eiryl ran to him and threw herself down on his pallet, sobbing. "I canna marry him. I won't. I swear."

"Damian?" he asked, trying to shake the sleep from his head and comprehend the nearly impossible fact that his brother's betrothed was in his room in the middle of the night, and even worse, she was on his pallet—the beautiful Eiryl of Powys, with her flashing dark eyes and sweetly curved figure, was practically lying on top of him. He threw the covers back, intending to leap up, but she grabbed his hand and held him back.

"Aye. Nay. I won't marry him. He's cruel and old, ever so old."

There was no gainsaying the truth of her complaints. Damian was old, nearly thirty, and for certes he had a cruel streak, but no more so than any lord trying to hold the Earl of Chester at bay.

"Eiryl, I—" He didn't know what to say. In truth, he hoped he was still asleep, dreaming. He rubbed a hand over his face and had to admit that he felt awake. Then Eiryl rubbed her hand up his leg, and any doubts he might have had fled on a surging wave of arousal.

"Why couldn't it be you, Morgan?" Eiryl whispered, her hand trailing higher and higher, until she held him within the smooth, warm grip of her palm. "You who are so beautiful, so young and strong and sweet? You are sweet, aren't you, Morgan?"

She answered the question herself, taking him in her mouth and bearing him back down on the pallet where all he could do was groan in pleasure, and, by the second pass of her tongue, pray he didn't pass out before she finished with him.

"No wine, but a potion." Avallyn struggled to a sitting position and pulled a small vial out of a pouch on her belt.

Still feeling the touch of Eiryl's mouth, Morgan forced himself back to the present and squinted up at the liquid stuff. 'Twas green and mossy inside its glass shell, looking more like pond water than a potable potion.

"More binding spells?" he asked, his voice gruff with the fleeting pleasure of memories. Eiryl had been the first to take him in such a manner, and now, thousands of years later, he wondered what it would take for Avallyn Le Severn to be the next. A hopeless hope, he was sure, but once envisioned, the image was hard to dismiss.

"Nay," she answered. "More a loosing spell this is, brewed by Tamisk to contravene the wine."

"Your father is a great mage then?" Aye, to have her mouth on him anywhere would be a blessing, even in his present state, which he feared was taking another turn for the worse. He smelled smoke, and the tremors shaking his body were growing claws, tiny claws of pain snagging on bits of his tissue and bone. 'Twas a distinctly Carillion torture.

"An adept of the Books of Lore," she answered, "including your book, the Red Book of Doom, the *Fata Ranc Le*." Her voice was barely discernible over the growing noise and heat, over the chaos he felt streaming toward him from the far side of the sick bay.

Fata Ranc Le.

Fate. With effort, he concentrated on the desert woman's words. It hadn't been his book, but Ceridwen's. His cousin's red book with gilded marks on its cover. He'd kept it with him one night in Wroneu Wood, and truth be told, 'twas on that night that his life had begun to unravel. He'd held the book and looked through its pages, until he'd reached the end of the writings—but not the end of the book. His hand had rested on the first blank page, and he'd known magic for the first time. Fate, he'd learned that night, was a fiery thing.

His book, Avallyn had said. For certes it had felt like his when he'd held it, but he'd left the book with Lavrans and never seen it again.

You were sent here to be mine, dread lord.

Was that what he'd written in the book that night, during those strange moments when the flames had shot from his fingertips and raced across the page, leaving words in a language he could not read, when his whole hand had felt alive with a power he'd never known before or since?

Too much ale, he'd told himself, a drunken vision, but in his heart he'd known—and Avallyn knew as well, mayhap knew more than he did of all the moments of magic that had touched his life.

You were sent here to be mine, dread lord. He knew she spoke some truth, but to what end? The one threatening to consume him before the rising of another day? Or one that began with her moss green potion?

Of a sudden, a sharp pain dug into him. He gasped, doubling over on his side, then jerking his head back up, the smell of smoke strong in his nose. His heart raced. Battle was upon him. In the distance he saw a ring of fires, and all around him were the sounds of swords clashing and horses snorting, of men crying out and the rush of arrows loosed by long-bows. The sounds of battle from a long-ago age.

'Twas Llywelyn at the Conwy, fighting his uncle, Dafydd, for the Perfeddwlad. Morgan had been with him, sent by Damian less than a sennight after his return from the Holy Land. 'Twas the last time he'd ever tried to go home. He'd sworn himself to Llywelyn and never looked back.

Fires were burning in the camps, sending great clouds of smoke out over the estuary. Morgan leaned low over his garron's neck and urged the horse into the water. Dafydd was on the run.

A pikeman went down on his left, skewered by an enemy arrow. A swordsman came out of the smoke on his right, charging straight at him. Morgan lifted his blade and kicked his horse into a run to meet the charge.

"Llywelyn!" he cried. "Llywelyn!"

"Shh, Morgan." Avallyn slipped off the bed, keeping one hand firmly on his chest, trying to calm him and herself and hold him on the examining table at the same time. Not a moment past, he'd been lucid.

No more. Fever burned through him, and he was trembling again. His eyes stared sightlessly into the shadows darkening the cabinets on the far wall. His breaths were rough and ragged, as if he was expending great effort, making her wonder what vision held him in its grasp.

Shadana. She couldn't lose him now, couldn't lose him to the god-rotting wine after they'd escaped half the Warmonger's army.

"Llywelyn," he moaned, and lashed out as if his sword was in his hand. Falling back on the bed, he moaned again. "Eiryl."

One-handed, Avallyn broke the seal on the vial, then released him to cradle his head in her arm.

"Come now, sweet prince." She tipped the vial and let a portion splash into his mouth.

He choked, then gasped, clutching at her, his fingers digging into her arm.

Sweet Mother! She watched in horror as green smoke roiled up and poured out from behind his clenched teeth. His eyes flew open, one agonized flash of blue before they rolled back up into his head and his body stiffened like a stone.

Be judicious, Tamisk had warned.

Judicious? She'd killed him.

"Morgan," she said, then louder: "Morgan!"

She shook him and he went completely limp in her arms, collapsing back onto the bed. Her breath stopped in her throat. She'd killed him, the Prince of Time. Shock held her frozen in place.

Then she heard it, a soft groan. He rolled over onto his side and released a slow, smoky breath.

"Damn you, Tamisk," she whispered, washed through with relief. The mage could have warned her about the smoke.

She smoothed the hair back off Morgan's brow and ran her fingers down the length of his hair. The time-rider scar was there on his neck, a thin line seared into his skin. His forehead was damp, the fever breaking. His trembling had stopped. The next sound he made was more of a sigh than a groan, and he visibly relaxed deeper into the bed.

'Twas faster than the dreamstone would have worked. She had to concede that much to Tamisk. And there was naught in a dreamstone sleep to deal with the wine.

With the vial open, she touched a drop to her tongue and got another surprise. 'Twas dragon wine, *gwin draig,* with a trace of shampberries and enough haesa to turn the concoction green and mossy.

"Bagworms," she muttered. The mage had cut the dragon wine with Carillion, giving the prince a bit of his own. No wonder it had worked so quickly. He would dream the night away, dragon dreams and dreams of time, and dreams of his past. Could be no worse than what he'd faced without the potion, a raw rehashing of his memories. Memories could trick, but the dragon wine would show him only what truly had been and, if his luck didn't hold, mayhap a glimpse of what was to come.

She couldn't wish him that. With a lifetime's knowledge of the journey she faced, she could not claim any comfort in the knowing. For him, 'twould be worse. Yet for now he slept, and in the sleeping was at her mercy.

And mercy it would be, if she didn't find the other mark she sought. He could return to Pan-shei, none the worse for having been freed of the wine.

With a careful hand, she undid the snaps on his jacket, then the zipseam on the shirt he wore beneath. The wide swath of Ferrar's bandages covered a goodly portion of his chest, but she needed to see only the area above his heart.

His skin was warm beneath her hand as she worked the bandages free at the top and, one by one, pushed them aside. No hesitation slowed her. She would know if he was the prince as foretold—and on the fourth bandage, she did.

The mark was there, the leaf of a rowan tree, and something else besides. The scars she'd thought to find on his face banded his torso in a manner that stilled her hand and made her breathing slow.

Dear sweet gods. She moved more of the bandages aside, until his chest and abdomen were completely revealed. How had he survived such wounds?

"They're bad, ain't they?" the wild boy said behind her, his voice instantly recognizable.

"The worst I've seen," she admitted, and she a veteran of a hundred battles in the north.

"He's a prince, ye know."

She turned to face the boy. "Aye, I know."

He was watching her from across the sick bay, his gaze holding hers with solemn resolution.

She understood his silent message: Morgan was his lord, no matter his sept vows. So the boy might think, but they were in the desert now, and the Priestesses of the Bones did not so easily relinquish their sworn souls. She made a subtle gesture of dismissal used with the acolytes of Claerwen, and the boy responded with a bow and retreat.

Still desert-born then, she thought, despite his years of thievery with the prince. She watched him go before returning her attention to Morgan.

He murmured something in his sleep, a whispering of love and light in an ancient language, and she leaned closer to hear.

"—*sic itur ad astra.*" Such is the way to the stars.

Her brow furrowed. 'Twas a saying chiseled into the stones above Tamisk's tower door, and again in Ilmarrian along the portico of the White Palace and in the great hall of Claerwen. Morgan's speaking it made her wonder if the mage had brewed the prince's dreams to order. She'd had no intention of leaving him, but if Tamisk's hand was in too deep, she dare not. Best she stay close and temper what she could. Dreaming among the stars was no slight thing, and had oft been known to take a man much further than he'd meant to go.

Chapter 10

Corvus stood on the viewing platform of his warship, a rover twelve times the size of any Class G, overlooking the alleys and byways of Pan-shei and the pile of rubble that had once been a Quonset hut. The smell of scorched tea hung in the air.

"Prisoners?" he asked.

"Three, milord," the freshly minted captain of his Home Guard replied, her predecessor having not survived his last summons to the Hall of Tombs. "Including the thief's landswoman."

"Bring them to me."

"Aye, milord." The captain turned on her heel and marched back across the platform, her new epaulets catching the last rays of sunlight, winking and glittering on her shoulders.

"Cachi hwch," Vishab swore, and spat by his side, surlier than usual since the last messenger had come to Magh Dun, though she seemed to have enjoyed the cap-

tain's death as much as any. "Your new piggish sow of a captain will not last a fortnight. Too proud, she is, too proud and pretty. Give the bitch to me for humbling and mayhap she'll yet do you good service."

Corvus slanted the old crone a sideways glance. Vishab usually reserved her name-calling for the priestesses of Claerwen. Ignoring her advice for now, he turned his attention instead to the Lyran in the alley below. She was a powerful beast, pacing along the line of doomed soldiers and skraelings, her flaming orange hair flowing over pale green shoulders. Heads would roll before the sun sank, and she was making her dinner selection. Only one lucky man would be allowed to fight her to his death. The others would not fare so well. Half would go to Vishab, and half he would deal with himself, creating a spectacle of death unlike anything Pan-shei had ever seen.

It was no more than the Third Guard deserved, the whole wretched lot of them, but he couldn't afford to kill the whole wretched lot. By all accounts, there had been only two men with the thief, and no more than a half score of Night Watchers with Avallyn Le Severn. Yet all had escaped two days earlier.

But not for long.

The Second Guard was on their trail, heading west into the desert. If nothing else, they'd been smart enough to get out of Pan-shei before he arrived. The Third Guard had no such strategist in their ranks. They had stayed and leveled the Quonset hut, and for that misjudgment, they would pay in lives.

Van the Wretched would demand some payment for the skraelings Corvus was going to destroy, but their failure had been no less than his own soldiers', and the lives of skraelings came even cheaper than guardsmen. Maybe next time, Van would send only the best of his line.

"Milord Most High, Warlord of the Waste, and Exalted Ruler of Magh Dun," a muffled voice came from the vicinity of his feet.

Corvus cast his gaze downward at the prostrate messenger who had been waiting on the deck, his face pressed into the riveted planks of twenty-aught steel.

"Aye?"

The battle lackey rose to a kneeling position. "The most honorable captain of your Second Guard sends his greetings and would have you know that he has tracked the thieves to Craig Tagen and is even now scouring the ridgeline for their rover."

Corvus's mood, never overly bright, took a dark turn. Craig Tagen was over two hundred miles long and twenty-five miles deep, big enough to conceal a whole battalion of rovers.

"For your sake, I pray you have better news than that to relay," he drawled, arching a brow. The lists for the evening entertainments were already full to bursting. One more death would only drag the night out too long.

"Their rover is damaged, milord, and sure to have run its last."

"The skraelpack lieutenant who lost the transport told me as much on his dying breath," Corvus said dryly, giving the commissionaire fair warning and one last chance.

The messenger continued on, undaunted, his next words proving him ripe for promotion. "My captain has sent troops to the two caravanserais nearest to where the trail was lost, Rabin-19 and Cere. The slackers have no other choice for repairs or supplies, and we are assured that they will need one or the other if they are to cross the Waste. The captain vows to have them before nightfall tomorrow, milord."

"As well he may, or face my wrath," Corvus promised with a dismissive flick of his blackened hand.

The messenger paled at the gesture and backed away, his gaze never leaving the black and wispy thing that had bade him go.

"Tell your captain I will have the two I seek, or I will have his head. Nothing less," Corvus added more loudly, watching the commissionaire slink out of sight into the gloom and shadows of the upper deck.

"Heads." Vishab spat again, her voice rusty and cracked from too many hours spent over her cauldrons, inhaling smoke and vile emanations. "It's hearts I'll take this night and drain them into my pots, and in that boiling blood I'll find what ye seek—but for this, Corvus, I'll have a boon."

Corvus turned fully to meet her gaze, and was surprised to find it boring into him with untoward intensity—a feeble witch trick unlikely to wield influence in his quarter. Something had set her off kilter for her to even try it.

" 'Tis no more than you can spare, lord. No more, and for certes no less than you dare give," she went on, holding him with her yellowed eye.

"A threat, Vishab?" He would not have the old woman forget who held the reins of power.

"No threat, lord, a request only, from one whose heart's desire is the same as your own, to destroy the priestesses of Claerwen and all their line."

"My desires are not quite so simple, woman. I would have some salvation with my vengeance."

"And so you shall, so you shall." She nodded her bony gray head in obeisance. "Together we have killed many a priestess, lord, and with the vision I will seek this eventide to find the Lady Avallyn, we will kill again, mayhap for the last time. This is all I meant, nothing more."

Avallyn, was it? Whatever the stakes, Corvus didn't like the sound of his nemesis's name on Vishab's withered lips, but this was not the time to press her. The captain of his Home Guard had returned on deck with the prisoners.

One was a giant of a man, bald and muscular and bound in chains. Blood ran from the wounds he'd taken in the battle for the Quonset. Even when the place had been leveled around him, he'd kept up the fight. A woman stood by his side, the *chai wallah,* small with graying blond hair, her gaze fearlessly meeting Corvus's despite the lasgun wound on her arm.

There was something familiar about her, something he could not place. Not her face, he decided, but perhaps her expression. It wasn't often that someone met his gaze. Certain zealots managed it, secure in their salvation from whatever hells awaited nonbelievers. Yet the woman didn't have the look of a religious zealot. No manic fire lit her gaze, only a steady, glowing ember.

Which he would soon extinguish.

Her fearlessness would pass quickly enough, he thought, casting a glance at the third prisoner, a Pan-shei rumrunner from the looks of him. Narrow-faced and pockmarked, his surfeit of fear more than made up for the woman's lack.

"Have they been questioned?" he asked of no one in particular.

"Thoroughly," came the captain's reply.

"And?"

"They have told us nothing."

"Not true! Not true!" the rumrunner cried, lunging forward to the end of his chains. "I have told all, lord, all! And if you desire, I will tell you more! Anything!"

"He knows nothing, milord," the captain said over the man's protestations.

"Then he's mine." Vishab reached out and marked the man down the side of his face with a clawlike fingernail.

Within seconds, the scratch began to bubble and froth, with the rumrunner's blood turning blue. The man fell to his knees, his eyes growing wild, his limbs twitching, until he collapsed in a heap.

"Take him below," Vishab ordered.

One of the guards strode forward and hauled him away, and Vishab turned her gaze on the woman.

"You," she said, her voice a wicked rasp. "You've run your last, and well you know it."

The crone sidled closer and sifted her fingers through the woman's fair hair, then grabbed a fistful and pulled it up, revealing a pale streak of hair and a matching scar running the length of her neck—the mark of a time-rider. Corvus stared at the scar, thoroughly intrigued.

The *wallah* didn't flinch, but the giant lunged forward and would have crushed the witch with his bare hands, if not for the electric shock a guard sent through his chains.

The man roared, and at that Corvus noted the first sign of distress in the woman's eyes. The giant was her companion, he realized, her consort. He would have to thank the witch for the revelations about his prisoners. Certainly his new captain had not ferreted the information out. Maybe Vishab had been right in that quarter as well.

As the witch left to go below, his gaze went over the woman again, and an unsettling thought came to him. He'd gotten a description of his thief months ago, and the man had a white stripe in his black hair. An insignificant fact by itself, given the sycophantic fashions of the Old Dominion, but of disturbing import if he should prove to be a time-rider as well.

"Are the crowds assembled?" he asked, ready to be done with the night's work and on his way to Craig Tagen.

"Aye, milord, from every quarter of Pan-shei," the captain replied.

"And the sacrifices chosen to join the doomed Guard?"

"Aye, milord, from every quarter of Pan-shei."

The next time he or his Guard came to this rathole on the edge of the Old Dominion, no one would bar his door, and no one would offer safe harbor to his enemies. He had left Pan-shei alone all these years, seeing little profit in the ragged market, but now they would pay tribute directly to him. They would know who their true master was—as would the woman facing him. Ferrar was her name, and if he had known there were time-riding souls of such courage in Pan-shei, he would not have dismissed the place so lightly.

With a sweep of his left hand, he lofted a wisp of smoke into the air, a wisp of his own corporeal being; with another gesture he set it to twisting, a black and noxious funnel that sucked the very light from the sky.

It would cost him, this deadly deed he contrived out of his own destruction, and for every soul he took another piece of his own would be lost. But the price—a spark of fierce, raw power flashed up his arm and through his body, riveting him to a razor's edge between ungodly pleasure and torturous pain. Ah, the price had its own sweet rewards.

From deep within the warship, Vishab heard the terror begin. Corvus unleashed was a sight not soon forgotten. In truth, none of the populace of Pan-shei would ever be the same again after witnessing the Warmonger's dark power. 'Twas enough to lift the hairs on her neck, but no more than that. She had been to the depths of nightless chaos, been to the depths of sunless, unformed worlds, cast there by White Ladies who had found her own colors too impure, and she had survived.

The priestesses would not.

The fools had taken their most precious jewel and set it adrift on the sands with no more protection than a peach blossom on the open sea. Vishab would pluck the hapless gem from the dunes, grind it into dust, and let it be blown to the four corners of the earth.

She could think of no sweeter revenge.

Chapter 11

Avallyn woke with a start. She'd fallen asleep in a chair, but was now in the sick bay bed. Besides herself, the bed was empty—or rather, almost empty. Morgan's tracking bracelet lay on the rumpled blankets next to her, its lights turned off.

Her heart plummeted.

He's gone. She slipped off the bed, ready to race through the door, but was stopped by the sight of the wild boy leaning negligently against the hatchway.

"Morgan?" she asked, knowing all too well that she'd lost. She only prayed that reason would work where physical restraint had not.

"He's taking a bit of a stroll," the boy said, his mischievous grin telling her his earlier deference had not gone beyond the hold she'd had over his lord, and that he was the one who had broken that hold.

For no good reason she could think of, she relaxed. Morgan had won, but he hadn't abandoned her, and what was written was written. On the other hand, for all intents and purposes she'd been kidnapped and her rover pirated by a band of tech-trash thieves from Pan-shei.

"Can I see him?"

Aja's grin widened. "Aye, he's waiting for you up by the spring," the boy said, and pushed away from the doorway, sweeping his arm out in a gracious bow.

Morgan shrugged into a clean shirt he'd found in the rover and towel-dried his hair one more time. The sinkhole was spring-fed with cool water rising from an aquifer deep below the desert floor. He'd submerged him-self in it naked, letting the coldness seep through him and clear his brain.

'Twas well past time for clear thinking.

Floating down through the sinkhole, he'd looked up and seen beams of sunlight shimmering through great cracks in the ridgeline above, trails of golden light that reminded him of his dreams. He'd gone through the wormhole again in the night, but in a way far more real than any Carillion memory run. He'd felt the glaciation of his body, the bitter, numbing cold. He'd seen the clouds of wind-borne frost and the jacinth bolts of lightning—and the golden worms swirling like liquid light be-low him, waiting for him.

The dream had been simply linear, one moment turning into the next with no intrusions from other times or other places, and the whole of it had unfolded with a clarity he could not fault. Thus it had been, down to the last crystal of ice formed in his veins. Avallyn's potion had done him no favor in that, but neither had it done him any harm. He felt more whole than he had since the battle for Balor. Her father was a great mage indeed, and she was— He looked up as her shadow fell across the sunlight's path. She was the death of him.

Aye, he'd seen that too.

"Malashm," she said in the Quicken-tree tongue, and he knew all his dreams to be true.

"Malashm." Without taking his eyes off her, he finished buttoning his shirt.

"Did you sleep well?"

He laughed and sat down on a rocky ledge to pull on his boots. "There was no sleep in what I did in the night."

"Dreams then?"

"A thousand of them." He looked up from his boots. She appeared rested, her hair rather wildly sticking out where it had been pressed into the bed. She also appeared distinctly ill at ease—as well she should. "We are to be lovers."

"My mother says not."

"Then your mother is wrong." He reached for his lasgun holster and buckled it around his waist, then stood and wrapped the lower strap around his thigh.

"She won't be glad to hear it."

"For what your mother asks of me, your virginity is a small price to pay." He tightened the strap and straightened to his full height. "Or would you have it otherwise?"

"No." She shook her head, which gave him no satisfaction. Whether he made love with her or not, there was no winning in the dreams he'd had, only a steady decline into desperate danger.

"Would you have someone else?" he asked, picking his munitions belt up off the ledge. He shrugged into it and settled his carbine and scabbard down the middle of his back. "There are other time-riders in the Old Dominion. Ferrar is one, and so is Jons. Or have you already been through the wormhole?"

"No, not yet." She shook her head again.

He walked down the path toward her, his expression as grim as his thoughts. To her credit she held her ground and even tilted her head to give him a better look when he lifted a swath of her hair. There was no scar on her neck, only a silken expanse of skin, creamily smooth, and he had to resist the urge to run his hand over it. At such close quarters, her scent filled his nostrils, the green grass smell of her, the freshness so at odds with the desert.

She was meant to be his—unless he walked away. Thanks to Aja, he had the choice.

Or did he?

He pulled his hand back without touching her.

"How did you get the bracelet off?" she asked.

"The boy. He's more than he seems."

"Much more," she conceded, "if he can undo Tamisk's magic."

"And what magic is it that would send us both to our deaths?" He couldn't keep the bitterness out of his voice. "Your own mother would send you into that hell? Into the dark night I saw? And for what? To save one corrupt and pathetic world when there are so many others?"

"It is our world," she said, a weak defense, to his way of thinking.

"And there are thousands upon millions more."

"None like this."

"Aye, mayhap none with such decay at its core." He turned away in disgust.

"If you are afraid—"

"And you are not?" he cut her off, spinning around. "Christ save you, Avallyn, going through the wormhole alone is nigh unto death. As for this black chaos locked in the earth, I say leave it there. Live your life here, where you were born, and leave the past to its own making."

"There are other lives at stake."

"More important than yours?" His voice rose on a harsh note, his anger barely controlled.

At that she looked away, and he felt needlessly cruel. If her own mother and father gave her such little worth, what was she to think?

But he had underestimated her.

When she raised her head, it wasn't self-pity filling her eyes, but anger of her own.

"Aye, there are lives at stake more important than mine, and I do not count myself lightly. But with you at my side, I had not planned on dying. You were to be my protector, a barbarian from out of the past sent to save the future, a great warrior sent to save me."

Her protector? No wonder she'd kissed him as if her life depended on it. Her life did. He held his own in a fight, but "great warrior"? Even at his best, the designation didn't hold true. Dain Lavrans had been a great warrior, capable of killing with more grace than most people prayed. Morgan would give himself no higher marks than efficiency and enough success to have kept his head attached to his shoulders.

"You've been deceived." The words tasted like dust in his mouth, but he would say them, and he would have her kisses given for another reason.

"You got us here," she reminded him, her gaze meeting his square on.

"The only fight I've had all week has been with the Lyran, and *you* were the one who saved *me*." Dustier and dustier, he thought, hating the truth for what it was, and hating even more so what he'd seen in his dreams.

"I only know that you are the Prince of Time, and that we face nothing that has not been faced before. Mychael ab Arawn fought the everlasting night of Dharkkum, and he prevailed. Llynya of the Yr Is-ddwfn did the same."

The names gave Morgan a heart-jolting pause.

"I knew them both," he said, and wondered what had become of the world after he'd fallen into the weir, that Mychael and Llynya would have been pitted against such evil.

"Come with me and you will know them again," she said as if in answer to his thoughts, implying a promise he would be hard-pressed to refuse. "It is your path we will follow into the past. It is your time where the darkness lies sealed behind the nascent crystal. If we can put ourselves in Kryscaven Crater before the seal is tempered by time, we can save the five that were lost, and the world will not be what it has become, a wasteland of war, but will be what it was, a planet of blue seas and green forests where life prevails and the miracle of each day is blessed by nature."

Her impassioned plea did not fall on deaf ears. She was offering him his heart's desire—to go back to his own time.

But the price.

Sweet Jesu. 'Twas more than he could ever have imagined.

Dharkkum, she'd called the darkness, but no single word could sum up the horror he'd seen. Dharkkum was a devourer. It was pestilence and plague and thinning screams of ungodly terror. It was chaos in its most virulent form, distending atoms on a quantum level. If it was sealed in the earth by some miracle of crystal, then that was where it belonged.

He had a life in the here and now. Imperfect? Aye, but not unbearable. He remembered that now, remembered what the wine had made him forget: that life in any form was sweet, a blessing not to be squandered.

Avallyn had saved him from the wine with her potion, but he could not save her from Dharkkum, except by keeping her in the present. Gods, but he should have thought twice before he'd set Aja to breaking the tracking bracelet code.

"Worlds die," he told her. "Stars go supernova every day. Change is the only constant in the universe."

"I have a duty," she insisted, much to his amazement. "I was born to make a difference."

A hundred and twenty-five years old and she was still clinging to youthful ideals? Perhaps he was older than she after all.

"Aye, well, my sense of duty is threadbare and unlikely to carry the day," he said, finishing the conversation. He strode by her, heading for the sick bay and the tracking bracelet he'd left on the bed, praying it was still there. He'd lock her to him, if need be, to keep her from the death he'd seen. She'd be safe by his side, aright, because he sure as hell wasn't going down any wormhole.

Aye, and wasn't that a shocker.

There it was, his heart's desire, laid out before him like a banquet for a beggar—and he dare not partake of the feast.

Dharkkum.

Even the name sent a chill through him. Yet she'd stood there in front of him and talked about duty, her duty to face the black horror and save the five that were lost.

What five? he wondered. Five Quicken-tree? Or mayhap Dain and Ceridwen were part of the company.

God, he hoped not. For certes they'd both been into magic up to their necks, and he soon would be as well if they were trapped in some magical crystal crater. Ten thousand years, and his debts on that front had not yet been paid. Avallyn had already told him that Mychael and Llynya had prevailed in their battle with the darkness. Given a little thought, he could see the two of them together, the too-serious boy and the elfin sprite. No doubt they had saved each other more than once from disaster.

He strode through the open hold door and turned right for the sick bay. She'd called him a barbarian and mayhap she was more than half right, but if so, it was what he'd become in the future, not what he'd brought with him from out of the past. Her world was barbaric, made so by men like the Warmonger and the crude and vile beastmen called skraelings. What there was of art had been stolen from someplace else or created in some other century. There were no gatherings of people for a common good, no harvests, no Christ's mass, no religion untainted by greed. 'Twas utter barbarism, to Morgan's way of thinking, that people would choose to be so alone.

He swung through the sick-bay hatch and was relieved to see the tracking bracelet right where he'd left it, but his relief didn't last any longer than it took for him to cross the room and pick the thing up.

Damn. He looked down at the band of *thullein,* caught in a quandary.

If he was going to leave her, now was the time. Rabin-19 was not so far away. He and York and Aja could take the rover's tender and make the caravanserai in two hours. From there he could negotiate the final price for the Sonnpur-Dzon dragon. The Warmonger's spies were everywhere and easy to find. Any fly-blown bar in the Waste housed half a dozen.

But he couldn't leave her alone in the desert, and he couldn't leave her in Rabin-19, because every fly-blown bar in the Waste housed half a dozen of the Warmonger's spies.

Nor could he take her to Claerwen, for fear her mother would drop her down a weirgate with or without her barbarian warrior from the past. He didn't consider her father, wherever he was, any more reliable.

Fine, he thought, slightly disgusted with himself. Now was the time to leave her, and he couldn't leave her. She'd saved his life with the Lyran, and he owed her his protection.

No more than this tied him to her, he assured himself, no more than fair play. It had nothing to do with her kiss or his dreams or the book called *Fata Ranc Le.*

"Well?" she asked from behind him, breaking into his reverie.

Well, hell, he wanted to answer.

Instead he said, "Do you know Rabin-19?"

"Aye. Claerwen considers all of Craig Tagen within its jurisdiction. We patrol there."

He took one last look at the tracking bracelet, then shoved it into the leather packet with the gold dragon before turning to face her.

"York thinks we can get spare parts for the fusion block from one of the mechanic shops on the south side." The whole south side of Rabin-19 was a salvage yard full of junked rovers and ditched chassis, broken tenders and crashed air cargoes. Any piece of junk found out on the dunes was dragged into Rabin-19 or Cere.

"You won't find a Class G," she told him. "The Night Watchers never abandon their rovers."

"It doesn't have to be a perfect match for York and Aja to get it to work," he said, dragging his hand through his hair and not quite meeting her gaze.

He was taking her with him, and leaving York and Aja to prepare the rover for the new fusion block. It only made good sense, he told himself. She knew the caravanserai, and he always did the reconnaissance.

So if it made so damn much good sense, and he was the one making the decision, why did he feel like the whole damn situation was out of his control? He didn't want her out of his sight, and it wasn't because he didn't trust her. Hell, she was savvy enough not to leave the rover, and she'd more than proved she could take care of herself. They weren't bound by the tracking bracelets any longer, so why did he feel compelled to keep her by his side? And was this the sort of reasoning that would eventually find him sliding down some cosmic worm gullet?

"It won't be like it was the last time," she said, and he knew exactly what she was talking about.

Christ save him, if she was going to read his mind.

"I'll be with you," she went on, taking a step closer, her voice softly earnest. "And you'll be prepared."

Prepared? 'Twas impossible to be prepared for what he'd seen and felt and heard in the weir.

"The priestesses will give us chrystaalt to ease our way, and the Sha-shakrieg will bind us *en chrysalli.* You'll not be alone this time."

Frankly, he didn't think having someone to share the terror would be much help, but he didn't tell her that.

"You've got an hour," he said. "Then we leave for Rabin-19."

He left the sick bay without waiting for an answer. He knew she'd come with him. She'd been waiting her whole life to follow him into the blackest bowels of hell. She wasn't likely to balk at a cakewalk into Rabin-19.

Chapter 12

Approached from the southwest, Rabin-19 looked like a war zone. Rusted heaps of metal jutted out of the landscape, some soaring hundreds of feet into the air, others bunched and piled like tide wrack in long, twisting lines. Beyond the salvage yards, the mud brown buildings of the caravanserai shimmered in the heat, seeming to float above the desert floor. Walls had been built on the north and west sides of the town, sunbaked ramparts snaking a path through the dunes, meant to hold the wind-driven sands at bay—and failing. Hillocks of sand building up on the windward side of the wall sporadically crested and poured over into the streets, giving the outpost an air of quiet desperation as it was slowly swallowed by the dunes. The people in Rabin-19 had the same desperate look about them, furtive and edgy, as if they didn't expect to survive the day.

Morgan understood the feeling. There were an uncommon number of Rift dogs roaming in the surrounding hills, striped wolflike animals capable of taking a man down and stripping his bones clean. He and Avallyn had seen half a dozen packs of thirty or more animals within two miles of the city's walls, all of them seemingly heading toward Rabin-19.

The outpost itself was stark, emptied of litter by the ceaseless wind and overlaid with a thick layer of dust blown in from the wasted plains to the south. No trash piled up in its alleys, no clothes were left out to desiccate in the fiery sunlight. No one lingered in doorways or courtyards. Everyone was inside somewhere, emerging into the day only to submerge into another covered market, another tavern, or their transport. The exception was the wild boys. They ruled the desert streets with cocky confidence, their sandskiffs battened down and anchored to great iron rings bolted into the breached walls, their masutes—the shaggy-headed quadruped mounts of the Deseillign Waste—harnessed to the same rings.

Seeing gangs of the boys gathered by their tents on the western outskirts, Morgan had steered the rover's tender on a more southerly approach. The fewer people he and Avallyn encountered, the better. He wanted to finish his business and be gone. They'd barely passed the outlying boundaries of the town before he'd begun regretting his decision to bring her with him. Virgin princess or nay, she was a desert mother, and she'd told him Rabin-19 was under Claerwen's jurisdiction. The place could be crawling with the priestesses' spies, and unlike the Warmonger's, Morgan didn't have a clue as to who they were or where they might be found—though he suspected they were hidden among Claerwen's allies, the wild boys.

He and Aja had been to the caravanserai a few times in years past, when they'd still been scavenging most of their hardware. Besides transport junk, the salvage yards in Rabin-19 stockpiled used and discontinued sensitized equipment, the small stuff that made Morgan's jobs go so much more smoothly. He and Aja had tipped a cup or two with the wild boys in Rabin and never noticed anything amiss, but now Morgan wondered if they'd been watched and reports had been filed—and he wondered which desert sept had found him so many years ago and set him on the road to Pan-shei.

"There," Avallyn said, pointing an authoritative finger toward a low-slung building with a large open bay. "Stoell's is the place to find a fusion block."

Morgan nodded in agreement and stopped the tender in the small slice of shade afforded by the salvage shop. A few cannibalized scant-ton chassis were piled together in a heap just outside the bay, with most of the good parts missing, from what he could see. Before opening the hatch, he took a quick look at his companion. She was angry—nothing new there—her eyes flashing silver in the bright light, her mouth tight. A tiny muscle was working in her jaw, and she was avoiding him with studious disregard. No mean feat when they were jammed together almost shoulder to shoulder in the tender's cockpit. Other than her mood, she looked fine. In truth, she looked better than fine, even dressed in Aja's old clothes—rust-colored pants, faded yellow shirt, an even more faded green quilted jerkin, and a turban they'd fashioned from part of an old white cloak. Without her Night Watcher garb she looked far more nomad than priestess, more wild boy than princess. All she needed was a quirt to look the perfect masute mahout.

"Where's your tech-jaw?" he asked. Angry or not, he wanted to kiss her, but it was pretty damned unlikely that he was going to get the chance.

She slanted him a long look, then pulled one of York's tech-jaws out of her pocket and stuck it in her mouth. Still holding his gaze, she bit down hard, real hard, and he winced at the skittering of static through his ear.

Aye, pretty damned unlikely, he thought, and wasn't he the perfect fool for still wanting her after what he'd seen in his dreams. But his dreams had not all been of horrors. They'd been lovers in the night. The taste and feel of her was still imprinted on his brain, a vision made real by her potion, and a part of him ached for her.

"If you would put your tracking bracelet back on, we wouldn't have to worry about getting out of shouting distance," she said loud enough to make him wince again, making sure he heard her inside and out.

He heard her, all right, every peevish word. She'd been peevish since he'd walked out on her in the sick bay, and she hadn't wasted any time in letting him know. He'd gotten no farther than the hatch when she'd tried her royal tone of voice on him with her imperious command: *"Hold."*

He'd done no such thing and had been suffering her mood ever since—which was probably for the best. If she'd been at all amenable, he'd be making love to her right now in some hidden cove of Craig Tagen, and dragons and Dharkkum could go to hell. Which, of course, was exactly where making love with her was going to get him. All in all, 'twas best she was angry.

"Do you remember the protocol?"

Her eyebrows rose at that, the nicked one going a wee bit higher. "Protocol? Do you mean the part where you give the orders and I obey?"

"Aye." His gaze was unflinching. "That's exactly what I mean." His reconnaissance protocols were tried and true, proven to glean the greatest amount of information with the least amount of effort and personal danger.

"And the part where I keep my mouth shut and you do all the talking?"

"Aye," he said, still unflinching.

"You'll be lucky to walk out of Stoell's with your shirt, let alone a fusion block," she informed him with the slightest of sneers, turning away to look out the tender's windshield.

"I've traded here before," he assured her, starting to feel a bit peevish himself. Her lack of faith in him was annoying, considering that he was supposed to be her great warrior barbarian, sent to fight off her enemies and unimaginable evils.

She shrugged, an elegant lift of one shoulder that told him he was a fool, a doomed, soon-to-be-fleeced fool whom she couldn't be bothered to save.

It made his teeth hurt, that little shrug, to have himself so neatly summed up and dismissed. 'Twas no more than he deserved, he was sure, for he'd pretty neatly summed up her whole life as a lost cause and thrown it back in her face.

Still, her shrug hurt. He wanted her, and he couldn't have her, and it was going to drive him crazy until he could figure out a way to get rid of her—and probably even longer than that.

"Let's get this over with." He coded in a lock sequence on the console and flipped open the tender's hatch. He'd taken another part of the white cloak for his own turban, and when the wind and sand caught at him, he fastened a swath of the worn cloth over the lower half of his face, leaving no more than a slit for his eyes.

The tender was a small subclass hovercraft that had seen too many desert days attached upside down on the rover's underbelly to be anything but a sandblasted rattletrap. It looked little better than the scant-ton chassis piled up in front of Stoell's, which Morgan thought gave them an added measure of security. No one was likely to try to steal something that looked like it was on the verge of collapse, and in the case of the tender, appearances weren't deceiving. Besides a fusion block for the rover, they were going to need a pair of short-shanked meridians to replace the ones on the hovercraft, if they wanted to get back to the rover sometime before next week. They were lucky to have made it to Rabin-19. He figured the lot would set him back about three hundred and fifty Old Dominion marks.

Seven hundred marks later, he and Avallyn stalked out of Stoell's, neither of them speaking. Morgan because he couldn't—he was gritting his teeth too hard—and Avallyn because she didn't dare. Or so he thought.

"Your first mistake was talking to Stoell."

Knowing she was right, Morgan didn't bother to reply. He just kept walking, wanting to get to the tavern a block up before the sun fried his brain.

"Dray and I always deal with the mechanics in the yard."

Again he had to admit—silently—that she was right. He and Aja had always dealt with the mechanics in the yard too. But Stoell had waylaid them the minute they'd walked into the bay, and for the life of him Morgan hadn't been able to shake the old codger or get anywhere near one of the mechanics. They had all been in the back of the bay, huddling around a pile of Class S junk.

"And you hardly made eye contact with the crikey bastard," Avallyn went on, oblivious to his silence, "let alone give him that damned intimidating look which you are so damned fond of giving me."

Morgan stopped at the tender and locked the fusion block and the short-shank meridians inside. Seven hundred marks. He'd been taken and he knew it, and so did Avallyn. However much it was bothering her, though, it wasn't what was bothering him. He turned the latch on the tender's cargo hold and took off at a fast walk.

"He wouldn't have dared to overcharge *me*," she said, lengthening her strides to keep up.

Once again, Morgan was absolutely sure she was right. The old man wouldn't have dared to overcharge a White Lady of Death. He'd seen the little bag of bones hanging from Stoell's belt, the nervous dampness on the old man's upper lip, the way his glance kept darting to the windows and any door that led to the outside. When the parts had been found and Stoell had named his outrageous price, Morgan had been glad to pay just to get out of the place.

He needed to get to a tavern and a comstation. The mechanics hadn't been merely huddling, they'd been watching the morning news broadcast on the Class S's comstation, and as Stoell had been going on about the price of parts, Morgan's attention had wandered to the back of the bay. He'd seen a woman's face—Ferrar's face—flash onto the comstation screen, just before a horrifying darkness had swirled down out of the sky and the screen had gone black. His heart hadn't stopped pounding since.

Something terrible had happened in Pan-shei, something that was straight out of his dreams.

He'd paid the old man, grabbed the parts, and gotten the hell out of there.

"Stay close to me," he said to Avallyn when they were within a few yards of the tavern door.

"How close?" she asked warily.

The question stopped him in his tracks. *How close?*

With one move, he took her by the arm and pulled her off the street, into the band of shadows darkening the alley.

"Close enough for me to touch," he ground out between his teeth, grasping her other arm as well and almost shaking her. "When I reach out my hand, *I want you there.*"

Her eyes widened, perhaps in fear, perhaps in surprise. He couldn't tell. For certes he was awash in fear, and he couldn't keep the intensity of it out of his voice. It was running like ice water through his veins, chilling him to the core despite the searing heat of the sun. He felt cold everywhere except where he was touching her.

"Close enough for me to hear you breathe." His voice softened to a menacing whisper even as he pulled her nearer. "Close enough for me to feel your pulse."

And even that wouldn't be close enough if the darkness came for them. They would be torn apart by the black storm—unless her father had a binding spell more powerful than the tracking bracelets. Aja had unlocked the one on Morgan's wrist with a strange ease, surprising even himself.

"Close enough . . ." he started again, but staring down at her upturned face and suddenly solemn eyes, words failed him. What could he tell her? And what did he dare not? That Dharkkum was here and no longer part of the past? That whatever battle they had been meant to face in a bygone age was upon them now?

A fleeting shift of shadows at the mouth of the alley caught his eye. He jerked his head up, stiffening in alarm and reaching over his shoulder for his sword.

Avallyn turned quickly as well, but there was nothing, only dust motes filtering down through the band of sunshine cutting through the shade. Morgan lowered his hand even as he wondered what he'd been about, going for his sword instead of his far deadlier lasgun. *Christe,* he could wipe out half a dozen soldiers with one well-aimed blast off his lasgun. He couldn't begin to touch those kinds of odds with a sword, not even with Scyld. Still, he'd seen the shadows move and instinctively gone for the sword.

"Come on, then," he said, pulling Avallyn toward the door. "Let's get inside." And God save him if he was going to be suffering from any more atavistic tendencies. The future was a place of carbines and lasguns, not swords.

"Oy, Lannikan, and there they be," a chirpy voice said from behind them. "I told ye we'd find 'em."

Morgan spun around, pulling Avallyn close and drawing his lasgun before the boy half finished saying "Lannikan." There were eight of them, all wild boys dressed in sun-faded tatters with looping turbans draped over their heads and around their faces. Most of them were armed with lasguns. All of them had quirts and quarrel slings, a digitized shortbow used to shoot razor-ridged arrows. Unlike a lasgun, quarrel slings couldn't be detected with a power scan. The wild boys used them for ambushes out in the dunes, ambushes that weren't always directed against the Warmonger's soldiers. Legitimate trade caravans were known to attract their attention now and again. Priestess allies or not, they were still wild boys.

The tallest stepped forward, a shock of dirty blond hair falling across his forehead, his eyes a piercing blue above a pug nose that looked as if it had been broken more than once. All the boys were burnt brown by the sun, their skin dusty and parched-looking.

"Commander." He addressed Avallyn with a formal bow. "I'm Lannikan of Sept Rhymer, and aye, ye'd be safer inside."

Morgan felt Avallyn relax beside him, but he didn't lower his guard or his lasgun. *Commander?* She was quick for a princess and damn good with a weapon, but a commander? 'Twas a rank reserved for only the most seasoned warriors, the true leaders of the Waste.

As interesting as this new information about Avallyn was, Morgan was more concerned about the boy facing them. Lannikan looked no different from the hundreds of other ragged wild boys he'd seen in Rabin-19 or Pan-shei, but this wild boy had been looking for them. Not a good sign in Morgan's book. Only the Night Watchers could have set the boys on their trail, and only somebody who knew her would have recognized Avallyn so easily.

"Sept Rhymer was valiant in their defense of Holy Well," she said to the boy, confirming Morgan's suspicion. " 'Tis good to see you again, Lannikan."

"Prince." The boy made a short bow to Morgan before meeting his gaze. "We've been charged with your safety."

"By whom?" Morgan asked, further unnerved by the boy calling him prince. He knew Lannikan meant the Prince of Time, what Avallyn had called him that morn, not his true title as a prince of Wales.

A noise behind him and a brief shift of Lannikan's gaze warned him there were more wild boys coming down the alley, and he felt his first bit of relief. It had been boys in the shadows that had caught his eye a minute earlier, not just black, moving shadows.

"Dray of Deseillign," Lannikan said in answer to his question. "We can talk more inside."

Morgan swore to himself and glanced over his shoulder, quickly noting the newcomers. There were four, and despite his misgivings, he nodded in agreement with Lannikan's suggestion. The wild boys posed no immediate threat, and the odds were against him twelve to two—or more likely, thirteen to one, with Avallyn bound to side with Lannikan. Even more important, he still needed a comstation. He needed to know what had happened in Pan-shei, and if it truly had been Ferrar he'd seen.

A narrow door opened onto the alley near where the Rhymer boys stood, and another boy stuck his head out. "Nain't here, Lannikan, but the pubby's gone and made a loovely chip-butty and shamp mash."

"We've found them, Sakip. Go on now." Lannikan jerked his head toward the door and the other boys started piling in.

Sakip turned to stare at Morgan and Avallyn and let out a low whistle, and for the first time Morgan realized that not all the wild boys were boys. Little could be seen of Sakip's figure beneath her layers of rags, but her face was decidedly feminine, framed by a curve of sable hair that had escaped her turban.

"Commander?" Lannikan said, looking back at Avallyn and gesturing toward the door.

Keeping a firm grip on Avallyn's arm, Morgan led the way through the opening. The tavern was dimly lit, and the faintest breeze of cool air wafted out of its floor vents. He chose an isolated table with a comstation built into the wall next to it, and punched in a number sequence to give him a repeat of the broadcast out of the Old Dominion.

The announcer started with the weather forecast.

"How did you find us?" he asked Lannikan when the boy—who truly was not a boy, but a young man of no less than twenty, by Morgan's reckoning—sat down across from him at the table.

"We were alerted by the Night Watchers to look for you." Lannikan glanced over his shoulder and made a hand signal. Four other boys responded, taking up positions at the doors and windows.

Morgan was uncomfortably reminded of Stoell's nervous glancing about. He took a quick look himself around the tavern. Pieces of masute tack hung from a line of hooks on one wall, and beneath each narrow saddle lay a pack of gear. A few patrons were scattered here and there, enough to start a ruckus if he decided it was time for him and Avallyn to make a run for their rover. With or without the new short-shank meridians, the tender couldn't outrun a sandskiff, but he might be able to outmaneuver one or two.

"Dray is farther north in Cere," Lannikan went on. "He thought it more likely that you'd taken a northern route and would show up there. We knew the rover had been damaged and that you'd need parts. He sent three Night Watchers to Rabin-19 just in case. They arrived at dawn. One is wounded. We have her in our tents. The other two are searching the streets even as we were, until Samm here picked up the lady's scent and spotted you coming out of Stoell's."

A grinning boy popped up by Lannikan's side, the same one who had announced their presence in the alley. "She smells like grass, she does, new blade grass."

'Twas true, but Morgan was amazed the boy had discerned the subtle scent from a distance, and he was damned grateful it had been the wild boys and not the Night Watchers who had found them.

"Who was wounded?" Avallyn asked, leaning forward, concern knitting her brow. She'd sat down next to him—close enough to touch—and Morgan felt a mild, probably misplaced, encouragement.

"Mepps," Lannikan answered. "They ran into a skraelpack working off the Second Guard last night. We're preparing a sandskiff to take her to Claerwen." At another hand signal from him, the boys began clearing out the other patrons, even the bartender, and taking over the tavern.

Now what? Morgan wondered.

"And us?" Avallyn asked.

"I don't know." Lannikan kept his voice low, his gaze constantly alert and moving. "Plans have changed. Sakip is contacting Dray now, but there isn't much time, and it might not be safe to wait for him here."

"Where was the skraelpack?" Morgan asked, not liking that the girl was disclosing their location to the Night Watcher captain. After what he'd seen in Stoell's, he'd already rethought his original idea of negotiating with the Warmonger's spies for the sale of the dragon. His new plan was to attain as much information at Rabin-19 as he could and to get the hell out before anybody else caught up with them.

"Forty miles north," Lannikan answered. "The whole Second Guard is swarming into Craig Tagen along the main routes, and they're sending out skraelings to herd in the Rift dogs, preparing for a bloodbath. It don't look good. You must have come in from a lot farther south to have missed them."

They had purposely avoided the main routes for just that reason, but Morgan was surprised to learn that the whole Second Guard was after them.

"We saw the dogs, a half-dozen packs," Avallyn said.

"What do they want?" Morgan asked the boy. If it truly was the dragon, he was ready to just give it to them, leave it on a rock somewhere and let them have it.

"Dray says there is only one thing that would bring the Second Guard out in such force. He fears the Lady Avallyn was recognized in Racht, and without the protection of Claerwen about her, she's as near to capture as she's ever been. As for the rest of it . . . what happened last night in Pan-shei . . ." The boy's voice trailed off. He shook his head and lowered his gaze.

"What?" Avallyn asked. "What happ—"

Morgan silenced her by putting his hand on her arm. His attention was focused on the comstation and the sudden warning bulletin flashing at the bottom of the screen. The dateline showed that the report had first come in the previous night, about the time they'd reached Craig Tagen. All the wild boys had grown silent, except for Lannikan.

"We been watchin' this thing go around the comstations all morning, and like I said, it don't look good."

The Warmonger's warship took up most of the screen, with the background filled in by line upon line of skraelings and soldiers wearing the Third Guard's insignia. The audio was being broadcast in fifteen languages, one of which was supposed to be dominant, with the others relegated to a droning hum. Three languages were coming over the tavern's comstation, fading in and out, jumbling the news. One of the boys leaned across the table and thumped the screen, and for a few seconds they heard the rising panic of the news reporter's voice: "—*arrived not an hour past. The City Guard has fled to the eastern provinces, and no Overlord has been seen since midday, when Ference Lieq announced the closure of all Old Dominion banks, an unprecedented move which resulted in widespread rioting throughout the quarters. The remaining force has taken over Pan-shei, blocking all roads out of the market. An earlier explosion on the East-West Ninety shut down . . .*" The reporter's voice faded out, but was not missed. The pictures flickering across the screen spoke for themselves: a pile of crashed scant-ton chassis lying off the Ninety; the Lyran stalking through the ranks of soldiers and then devouring her meal in front of the demolished Quonset; long shots of the steely black warship with its battlements and gunports, spiked rams and strafing lasers; and Corvus Gei standing on the ship's viewing platform, flanked by his captain and two guardsmen holding the chains of two prisoners: Ferrar and Jons.

A sick dread washed through Morgan. He had not been mistaken in Stoell's.

"*Mother,*" Avallyn whispered beside him, her gaze riveted to the screen.

The camera slid away to follow the entrance of another batch of prisoners, denizens of Pan-shei, recognizable by their dress. Morgan instantly thought of Klary, but as the prisoners filed by, he could see that no children had been rounded up. Still, it was impossible to feel any relief with Ferrar and Jons in chains and the Quonset demolished.

The camera panned back to the Warmonger.

"This is it," Lannikan whispered. "This is what we'll be fighting, just like when we faced the fiend at the Holy Well in Claerwen."

"No," Avallyn breathed out. "Corvus has *never* debased himself except in the Northern Waste. The price he pays is too high. I saw what it cost him to destroy the well at Claerwen."

"As did I, lady," the boy said solemnly.

The camera pulled in tight on Ferrar's face, and Morgan saw the fear in her eyes. The sick dread in his gut churned and tightened. Whatever debasement the Warmonger had planned, Ferrar didn't expect to survive it.

That's when he saw what he hadn't seen in Stoell's: the Warmonger's blackened hand and the wisp of smoke rising from his fingertips.

"Sweet Jesu," he whispered. He'd heard of the left hand of the Warmonger, but the tales had not prepared him for the abomination he saw on the comstation screen.

"Aye," Lannikan agreed. "If Sweet Jesu be your god, now is the time to pray."

"No," Avallyn said again, her face ashen. "He cannot."

But he did. The wisp of smoke spiraled up into the sky, quickly growing huge. Screams arose from the crowds of prisoners corraled below the warship. The camera filming the scene jerked upward to capture the swart, swirling cloud. For the briefest moment, Morgan saw flesh-colored ribbons winding up into the cloud, the bodies of the doomed getting thinner and thinner, then all went black. Long seconds passed, but nothing came back on the screen.

"Crikey," Samm choked out.

Morgan turned to Lannikan and grabbed the boy's arm. "The two prisoners on deck with Corvus. Do you know what happened to them?"

"Nay," the boy replied, remaining calm despite the tension Morgan felt tightening his muscles. "We ain't been to Pan-shei for months, and now most of it's gone."

Morgan released the boy and slumped back in his chair, his thoughts whirling. He needed to think, and all he could see was Ferrar's fear-filled eyes and the ghastly flesh-colored ribbons. He'd offered her a chance, a chance she hadn't taken. *Sweet Mary.* Ferrar and Jons had been riding time since the twenty-second century. Of all the people he'd met in the future, she understood more than any what he'd gone through, and her advice had always been the same: Take care with your life, take care not to overestimate your power.

It was easy to fall into a false sense of immortality after having survived the weir and traveled ten thousand years—and indeed, a certain power was conferred by the journey. He'd been skirting the edge of danger for ten years, falling off more than once, and yet always coming out in one piece.

Had Ferrar miscalculated this time?

"If they was friends of yours, I'm sorry," Lannikan said, "but there ain't any goin' back—not for any of us."

"Aye," Morgan agreed softly. If Ferrar and Jons were gone, there was naught he could do to bring them back, and if they'd survived, he had a feeling he'd know soon enough. The Warmonger hadn't put them with the other prisoners, and 'twas unlikely he'd destroyed the deck of his own warship. So there was reason to hope, and reason to dread. If he'd kept Ferrar and Jons alive, it could only be because of their connection to him, and through him, their connection to Avallyn.

He slanted his gaze in the princess's direction and found her watching him, her eyes dark with distress. Lannikan was right. She was the true prize in all this, not him and his golden dragon.

"I'm sorry, Morgan," she said quietly, shakily, and he realized that the mere sound of her voice was a balm.

Her turban had slipped back off her head, revealing the faerie curve of her ears, and he wondered if it was possible to truly fall in love in a night and a day.

He wanted to kiss her and had to restrain himself from reaching for her—because he knew she would kiss him back. She would melt into him, sweetening his mouth with her own, and then he would be lost, truly lost.

Chapter 13

A door was flung open on the far side of the tavern, and Morgan turned at the sound, his hand going to his lasgun. Sakip raced into the room, breathless, her face flushed beneath a coating of dust. He relaxed his grip on the trigger.

"Dray says . . . says . . . *ride,* and he be right." The girl gulped in a breath.

"I seen 'em myself . . . on me trackin' screen, not a hundred miles distant."

"Who?" Lannikan came out of his chair. No one was left in the tavern except the band of boys, and they all rose to their feet, alert and waiting.

"Sec . . . Second guard. Coomin' out o' the north, 'tween us and the Night Watchers, with the Home Guard not far behind. Dray says we cain't be headin' for Claerwen with Corvus on his way. The temple is the first place the Warmonger is like to strike."

"Sept Rhymer then?" the wild boy asked, gesturing to the others to move out.

"Nay, Lanni," the girl said. "Not to no sept we ever seen before."

Lannikan held up his hand to stop the boys and threw her a questioning glance. The girl nodded, her eyes taking on a luminous sheen.

"For certes?" An edge of excitement ran through the boy's voice, and Morgan realized that some silent understanding had taken place.

Sakip nodded again, and another swath of dark hair fell loose from her turban. She gestured toward Avallyn. "He says she'll lead the way."

Lannikan turned to Avallyn with an assessing gaze. "Aye," he murmured, "and who better than a White Lady to take us to the edge of the Sand Sea."

Morgan didn't like Lannikan's assumption any more than he liked the news about the Second Guard. They didn't need any more of the Warmonger's beasts breathing down their necks, and he sure as hell wasn't taking up with a bunch of wild boys on the run. Especially if they were running to the Sand Sea, a desolate expanse of sand and salt flats that made the Deseillign Waste look like an oasis.

"This party is over, *cariad*," he whispered to Avallyn. He slipped his hand back into the lasgun's grip and started to rise. He knew they wouldn't shoot her, and he was pretty sure they wouldn't shoot him. It was just a matter of easing out the door without having to shoot any of them.

Eleven wild boys turned on him at once, lasguns and quarrel slings drawn. Mayhap he'd been wrong about their willingness to shoot. Lannikan didn't move, only continued to stare at Avallyn.

"Commander?" He lowered his head in a brief bow. "Time is short. What would you have us do?"

The concession was direct and clarifying. 'Twas only him they were likely to take out. As for Avallyn, hell, the boy was waiting for her to take command. And of course she did so with regal grace, rising and moving away from him.

"Dray would not send us west without good reason," she said, her voice strong despite the paleness of her face. "But for wild boys, the honor of traveling to the edge of the Sand Sea has a—a price."

Her voice caught on the last words, losing its sureness, and Morgan saw her hand tremble. She balled it into a fist and continued on.

"Are you willing to pay?" she asked, lifting her chin.

He, too, was feeling the horror of what they'd seen, and like her was doing his best to block it out. Escape first, collapse later had always been his motto.

Lannikan glanced back at Sakip, and the girl nodded without hesitation.

"Aye, Sakip and me will pay," the boy said, returning his attention to Avallyn. "We'd pay thrice over to end our days in the Lost Forest."

"And to the end of your days it will be, until your last breath is taken by the Ilmarryn and released on the desert wind," Avallyn assured him gravely, and Morgan thought, *God's blood, what were they getting into now?*

A moment's silence descended on the boys as the import of her words sank in.

"Will we get to see the caves of Rastaban?" Samm asked, curiosity getting the better of apprehension.

"Aye, 'tis there."

"And the White Bitch's icy tomb?" another boy asked.

" 'Tis frozen still in the Dangoes," Avallyn confirmed.

"What o' Dragonmere?" another asked.

"Aye," she said. "All you have heard about is true and can be seen where the Waste meets the sand, but to set eyes on the White Palace is to never return."

Friggin' hell, Morgan thought. She'd told him at Ferrar's that she was a princess of the White Palace as well as a priestess of the Bones. If he hadn't been so wine-drunk, he might have had the forethought to find out exactly what in the hell that meant. Apparently the White Palace was a place of wonders and home of the Ilmarryn, and no doubt of her magi father as well, but not of the weirgate. The weir was in Claerwen, guarded by the White Ladies of Death, which made the White Palace the less dangerous of the two. Having Tamisk near might not be such a bad idea either, after what they'd seen on the comstation.

Be safe, Ferrar, he prayed. If she was truly gone, if she and Jons had been taken in such a strange and violent manner, he'd be years recovering from that anguish. Far better to die well loved in one's own bed. 'Twas what he hoped for himself when the time came, however unlikely the possibility might be. An ill end had come to him with the Boar of Balor's blade, and Morgan had no doubt that another equally ill and far more final end awaited him someplace else.

"To each his own," Lannikan announced, gazing about the room.

"Tell the others I'll think none the less of any of ye for not going. 'Tis a far pass with no return, but go or stay, I'd have ye all with me until we cross Botting Chasm west of here." He looked to Avallyn and asked, "Where is your rover, Commander?"

"In the lee of the Medain." She didn't hesitate to reveal their transport's location, didn't cast Morgan a glance, and he swore under his breath. She had a damned unnerving way of undermining his plans. He was used to being in charge, no questions asked and none answered.

"I know the place," the boy said. "The sandskiffs won't be at their best among the rocks."

"Head them southwest out of Rabin-19 to meet us at the edge of the Waste. We'll come through Craig Tagen on the twelve second line." Despite the strain evident in her stance, she was holding to the unspoken rule—escape first, fall to pieces later.

"And the tender?"

"Is carrying a fusion block for the rover. Send a mechanic with it. We'll take masutes."

A flick of the boy's hand had the mechanic on his way and the rest of the band once again on the move, gathering up tack and gear. He made an inquiring gesture toward Morgan.

Avallyn shook her head. "Saddle our mounts and wait outside."

Morgan thanked the gods for small favors.

"Masutes?" he asked when she didn't say anything after the last boy had cleared out. Her back was toward him, her head bowed. Time was short, but he was hesitant to rush her. He'd learned more than he'd bargained for in Rabin-19: Pan-shei was destroyed; Ferrar was gone; his damn dragon wasn't going anywhere; and every time he thought he had the upper hand with the priestess-princess, he was guaranteed to be wrong.

Rallying, she swiped a hand across her face and straightened her shoulders before turning to face him.

"Night Watchers never abandon equipment we might be able to salvage, milord," she told him, "a law that has saved us on more than one occasion, and the tender will fare better with a mechanic on board. The sandskiffs are going the wrong way, if you want to return quickly to your crew. That leaves us with masutes."

"*My* crew?" he asked, walking slowly forward, closing the distance between them, not liking her being so far away. He shouldn't mind. He knew it. 'Twas no more than fifteen feet separating them, but it felt like more, and in an odd way he didn't care to overanalyze, he felt better when he was closer to her. She was safer when he was closer.

Her gaze slid away from his when he stopped in front of her. "Aye."

"But *your* rover now."

She nodded.

Fine, he thought. He'd ridden a masute or two. Bigger than garrons, they were the size and shape of draft horses, shaggy as highland cattle, and amenable beasts, surprisingly swift and surefooted. Like Avallyn, he considered them superior transport for traveling in Craig Tagen, and he was sure he could outride any Sept Rhymer boy in Rabin-19.

What he couldn't do was not touch her, not when her face was damp with hastily wiped tears. He was no young boy. He could offer solace without losing his head.

"Geneth?" he murmured, smoothing his fingers over her cheek and marveling at her softness. She was delicate and strong and so very female.

"What you saw," she said, still not looking up at him, "what we saw, the black strength of the Warmonger, it's—it's as naught to what we will face in Kryscaven."

"Aye." He knew as much. The swirling cloud over Pan-shei had been a child of Dharkkum, the merest wisp of offspring. No man, no matter his dark might, could summon or control what Morgan had seen in his dreams. Any man would be signing his death warrant to try. So would any woman.

A broken sigh escaped her, a pause before weary confession. "There's more, Morgan. Far worse."

Of course there was.

"The destruction of Pan-shei was foreseen in the Red Book," she said, "and Dray . . . Dray would not send wild boys to the White Palace for anything less than the beginning of the end. I fear our time has run out."

Her verdict passed, she started to pull away, but he stopped her. His other hand rose to cradle her face, and he wondered if ten thousand and thirty-odd years had left him still too young to deal with some women. Certainly he'd shown no sense or wisdom in dealing with Avallyn up to this point.

After a moment's pause, she lifted her gaze to meet his, her eyes a dark gray in the tavern's dim light, and Morgan's heart filled with a heaviness that spilled over and pooled in his groin. 'Twas a slow, flowing surge of desire he could no more control than the rising of the sun. It was nothing so simple or pure as lust, but a wanting he felt to the depths of his bones.

"All may be lost," she said, looking at him with such a mixture of fear and longing that he was compelled to acts of sacrifice.

Damning himself on every breath, he ran his hands up into the silky twists and braids of her hair and lowered his mouth to hers. He was her savior, the poor chit, when likely the greatest act of heroism he could manage was the kiss.

Her mouth was open and waiting for his, granting him an access that only hastened his doom. She softened in his arms, moving closer, her response everything he had hoped and feared.

The taste of her flowed into him, a warm earthiness laced with an intoxicating flavor too elusive to name. 'Twas green like her scent, but more reminiscent of flowers dampened by morning dew. He wanted to lick it off her and drown himself in it. Her hands tunneled through his hair, holding him closer, and he was bound by the succor of her touch. Aye, 'twas heaven he held in his arms.

He could have her. He could have all of her, every gently rounded curve, every quickening response. He felt the truth of it with every trespass she allowed, the slide of his hand over her buttocks, the press of his hips against hers. He sucked on her tongue, a sweet lewdness he couldn't resist, and her groan nearly undid him on the spot.

Kyrie eleison . . . Lord have mercy. Even as he sank deeper into the haze of desire she wove, his mind started cataloguing practicalities: locking the door, clearing a table, getting rid of their clothes. It was all possible, well within his capabilities, but not within any bound of reason he could claim.

The slamming open of the tavern door proved the point. Morgan broke off the kiss, whirling toward the sound, his lasgun drawn and cocked.

"Commander, we ride." 'Twas Lannikan, giving them a curious look, as well he might, considering how they were wrapped around each other.

Avallyn nodded curtly in acknowledgment, and the boy slipped back into the alley, leaving the door open.

Morgan looked down at her, his heart pounding, his body aching. She was more than doom and desire. He had felt salvation in her kiss, a trace of it winding through his senses and beckoning him to come forward, to lay his life at her feet and claim her for his own. All he had to do was sacrifice himself, and she would make him whole. The irony of what she represented was not lost on him. In truth, it was probably the only thing that saved him.

He forced himself to step back and break contact with her. He couldn't think clearly when they were touching.

"Aye," he said roughly. "You may be right, princess. All may truly well be lost."

God knew he was.

Avallyn watched him turn and leave, and took a great breath to pull herself together. *Shadana.* Her mother's warnings were as naught compared to Morgan's kisses.

She raised her fingers to her lips and felt the warmth he'd left on her skin. The taste of him was everywhere inside her mouth, strangely wonderful, both soothing and exciting. 'Twas time to deep-scent the prince and find out all that she could about the man fate had delivered into her arms. After what they'd seen in Pan-shei, she dare not leave anything to chance. If there were other weaknesses in him beside the wine, she would know of them before Tamisk. Her father would not treat lightly any additional failings, and she would not have Morgan subjected to too much of Tamisk's meddling and transforming magic. Nor would she have him given to an Ilmarryn maid to be bent to her father's will. 'Twas bad enough that her mother's will must govern her dealings with him, for if left to her own devices, Avallyn knew she would be tempted to sample much more than just the thief's kiss.

Leagues south of the White Palace, beside a dune cove washed inland by the Sand Sea, Tamisk pulled his masute to a halt. Red dust filtered down through the fading sunlight, muting the landscape and giving an ochre hue to the stone ruin jutting up out of the Waste. He'd left the palace in a rover at dawn, shortly after the accounts from Pan-shei had been confirmed. Only three items of business had detained him from heading south immediately: having Avallyn's course changed from Claerwen; sending a call to arms to every sept in the Deseillign Waste; and convincing Au Cade, the reigning Queen of Deseillign, to at last relinquish her hold on the Orange Book of Stone, the *Gratte Bron Le,* and give it to him.

The time had come, and he must make haste.

Swinging down off his mount, he removed the book from his saddlebag and whispered a command for the animal to stay. He'd picked up the masute in Sept Siell and continued on alone to the ruin hidden amongst the dunes and a trailing outcrop of granite. 'Twas a closed place, Nemeton's Hart Tower, kept veiled by mirage and unknown to all except Tamisk, the lord of Sept Siell, and the one who had helped him dig the tower out of the sand, Rhayne. Her presence was greatly required again if he was going to succeed in his task. She had one of the three missing Books of Lore. He needed them all.

He entered a darkened doorway banked into a dune and climbed the spiraling stairs two at a time, taking in one crumbling black step and one crumbling white step with each stride. Shafts of reddish light moted with windblown sand slanted down through the arrow loops ringing the tower, heating the stone in small patches on the opposite wall. Tamisk felt the warmth on his skin as he passed through each luminous band, and he felt the coldness that emanated from the stone left in the dark. Light and darkness, heat and cold. They rippled over him in contrasting waves, a pattern of what had come to pass too soon.

Upon reaching the landing, he strode over tumbled rocks and drifts of sand to the remains of the Druid Door. On the centermost plank, a gargoyle of hideous countenance glared at him, its rock crystal eyes undimmed by the eons since their making. Iron fangs rusted to bloody red clutched a bronze knocker hanging from the gargoyle's mouth. Tamisk used the piece lightly, pushing the door a bare quarter inch to realign it with its frame. Decrepit though the door was, its locks still held. He worked them with a skilled hand, and only after gaining entrance into the main solar did he allow himself to feel the dull pain that had threatened to engulf him all morn. He squeezed his eyes shut and slumped back against the door. Pan-shei had been destroyed. The fool, Corvus Gei, had unleashed his murky cloud over the slum, and every hovel and denizen within a mile radius had been sucked into the naked singularity of Dharkkum's black hole. For miles beyond ground zero, the city of rags had become uninhabitable. Even the Old Dominion had felt the Warmonger's wrath, with black wisps of the fell mist blown eastward by the wind, consuming the first thing or person to cross their paths.

And it was all happening too soon.

He swore beneath his breath, an ancient, powerless curse, and opened his eyes, looking to the center of the room where a desiccated oak tree pushed up through the floor and out through the ceiling into the eyrie above. 'Twas Llynya's oak, preserved in its sandy tomb for thousands of years, petrified into stone.

Across the room, on the lintel above a deep-set door, were the words written to guide him. *Amor . . . lux . . . veritas—sic itur ad astra.* Love . . . light . . . truth—such is the way to the stars. Nemeton's words marked the path into the heart of the bargain he had made ten thousand years ago to seal their fate this day.

Blood to save the world, Tamisk thought, placing his hand over the small vials secreted in a pocket on his chest. 'Twas always blood, the elixir of salvation.

The *Beirdd Braint* of the Quicken-tree had seen his own bloody death at the hands of a Dark Age brute named Gwrnach the Destroyer. Arch Druid, Magia Lord, and adept of the Books of Lore, Nemeton had not tried to avoid his fate, but had left the sanctuary of the White Palace and gone back in time to ancient Carn Merioneth, setting the wheel turning toward the day that had come too quickly upon Tamisk—this day.

He crossed the floor to the deep-set door, pushed it open, and was engulfed in a sea of green. Shimmering leaves of a hundred verdurous hues canopied the stairwell leading upward into the eyrie, growing from branches Tamisk had brought to life with his nurturing magic. He blew his breath into the air as he climbed, swirls of blue and green exhalations, and the leaves fluttered in response to their maker, reaching for him. Crumbling stones and chunks of mortar littered the steps, but did not hinder his ascent.

Veritas—truth—he knew. Tamisk lived his days distilling and applying truth. But of light, he knew only what was written in the Books; and of love, he would be the first to admit that he knew nothing.

Nemeton had dared much and lost much in his travels through time in search of the Books and a way to rid Earth of Dharkkum. No one had dared to dabble in the Books' pages with such bold confidence before or since, except for their maker, she-whose-name-could-not-be-spoken, once called Ysaia and now called Rhayne, White Bitch of the Dangoes. The greatest of all the Prydion Magi, she had conjured the dragons in her cauldron and forged the Magia Blade, some said with Nemeton as an acolyte by her side. Nemeton himself had never confirmed as much, not to Tamisk anyway, and they had spent nigh onto a year together in the White Palace. Nor was it Rhayne's way to speak overmuch of things in the deep past. Sometimes Tamisk wondered if, in her many incarnations, she'd simply forgotten parts of her past.

All of Nature had been grist for Nemeton's mill, a place where physics and magic were differentiated only by the skills of the practitioner, a place where a sorcerer became the bridge between the metaphor and reality. He'd taught inquiry in all its permutations of religion, science, and philosophy, and he had taught Tamisk to look for truth only where seemingly disparate beliefs crossed. Light lay at the intersections of harmonic accord, he'd said, like the jewels in Buddha's net. The rest was man's dross.

So Nemeton had died by a brutish hand in an unsung age, the man who had bargained with blood to give the world the Hart's eyrie, the world's hope of salvation when its end came nigh—but just a man, no god as others might have claimed.

And now the end had suddenly come nigh. Corvus had proven more powerful than Tamisk had calculated, a fact which must have surprised the Warmonger at least as much as it had surprised the Ilmarryn mage. Tamisk was not one to underestimate his enemies. Yet Corvus Gei had taken the scrap of mystery that was his left arm and created chaos on an unprecedented scale. Something had goaded the Warmonger beyond his usually keen sense of self-preservation, and Tamisk knew it could only have been one of two women: Vishab or Avallyn.

No one else held any sway over the man, though not much of Corvus the man could be left after his Pan-shei fiasco. 'Twas what had always held him in check, the dear price he paid for giving in to his anger. Strange beast that he was, he'd brought the pestilence upon himself by carrying a vile rot with him through the weir—and now he'd let it destroy him.

Vishab could have pushed him to such, if she'd found something in the *Chandra Yeull Le,* the Yellow Book of Chandra, to make Corvus's destruction a means to her own ends. The exiled priestess had intercepted Corvus ten years ago on his return from the past, finding him before the White Ladies and saving him from certain death. Corvus had brought the book with him, and given it as a boon to her. Tamisk had let her keep it all these years. Indestructible as it was, she could do naught to harm it, and letting her keep the book had kept her from other mischief. But 'twas time for Tamisk to bring the Yellow Book home. It had always been within his reach, and never more so than now, when light and darkness were flickering side by side and rousing the dragons to wrath.

At the top of the steps, Tamisk paused, his gaze taking in the forest he had conjured in the tower, greenery to cover the walls, a glade for his scrying pool, the myriad paths. In the center of it all was the wondrously crude yet infinitely refined contraption encased within the oak's boughs, Nemeton's armillary sphere. Each chunk of rock crystal on the pedestal shone with an inner fire, starfire from the first Star, dreamstone chiseled from Deseillign's fallen vault of heaven. The front of each hand-fashioned piece of copper was aged with rich verdigris and washed in thick layers of color—turquoise, brown, and blue shadowed with gray turning to black. The backs of the pieces were acid-etched with patterns of conductivity. Like the books, the sphere was impervious to man's meddling. For thousands upon thousands of years it had held its place in the Hart Tower, waiting to complete the task Nemeton had set for it—and for Tamisk—in another long-ago time:

A star fell to Earth in Deep Time and birthed an Age of Wonders. Then the darkness came, following the star, and the whole planet went to hell. So had begun Nemeton's first lecture.

Tamisk stepped forward, lifting branches out of the way with his upraised arm. There had been rain earlier, Ilmarryn rain conjured by clouds he had set adrift years earlier like mist among the oak's branches. Fine rivulets of water sloughed off the leaves onto his arm, dampening the fine lawn of his shirt.

Four of the ancient Ages passed before the true nature of the darkness was understood. Called Dharkkum *by the descendants of the Starlight-born and fought with all manner of courage and talismans by Stept Agah and men and women whose names are forever written on the stone doors of the Court of the Ilmarryn, 'twas discovered to be an anomaly, a cosmic mischance, a naked singularity bound by no event horizon and no law of Nature beyond its own smoky form and its unpredictable and terrifying power. The whole of Earth's history is no more than a passing nanosecond to the eternal cusp of destruction birthed in a black hole in the NGC 2300 cluster of galaxies and sent careening across the universe. It's Earth's bad luck to be riding that cusp with no hand of God to push it out of harm's way.*

No hand of God, but the hand of Nemeton, and through him,

Tamisk. That billions of creatures would die if he failed did not mean that they lacked God's grace, only that like all other matter, the creatures of Earth were subject to change. 'Twas true the coming change was profoundly cataclysmic. There would be no Earth left, and no creatures left to worry about the lack, but still 'twas merely change, the lifeblood of the universe.

Tamisk knew the broad view as well as any mathematician, astronomer, or physicist, but he also knew Earth to be a wondrous cradle of intelligent life, a rare, nurturing pool of sentience in the cold vastness of space. The creative potential of this one star-wrought planet was equal to the chaos of Dharkkum. 'Twas what had held it together in the past, and Tamisk would save it if he could. All he needed was for the rest of Nemeton's machinations to fall into place.

Thus I traveled to the home of darkness itself and was washed upon a strange and hostile shore. The galactic beings there knew of Dharkkum and the Star that had come before. The Star they wanted returned, but it had embedded itself too deeply into the earth to be retrieved without tearing the planet apart. The darkness they were content to let lie. For a price, I convinced them otherwise.

Seven small measures of blood had been the price. Blood from the place that had birthed the Starlight-born from the very star the galactic beings had lost. Life had not been their purpose when they'd made the star, but they were fascinated by Nemeton and the world he described. So they'd bargained, and in the end, they'd devised the sphere.

Tamisk's brow furrowed, and he crossed the final steps to the telluric pedestal that held Nemeton's prize, an odd, zodiacal assortment of dangling rods and orbs that formed the outer shell of the armillary sphere. The Arch Druid had built it in an ancient age, and it had the look of its time, an intriguing guise for such a timeless thing, for at its core was science beyond any the earth had achieved—a break in the time-space continuum, paid for with the promise of Avallyn's blood, an elixir distilled through countless generations to a richly complex brew not so very different from Tamisk's own, yet different enough that only the young priestess's would do. Nemeton had calculated the genealogy of the galactic beings' price, and he'd known it would take millennia to achieve, a span of time that barely registered on the beings' collective conscience. To them, ten thousand years was as naught. To Earth, now without her forests and oceans, it had almost been a death sentence.

But the time was nigh.

Of Avallyn, Tamisk had no doubts, just as he had no doubts that it was she and not Vishab who had pushed Corvus beyond the edge of reason. Sent into the Old Dominion, unprotected by the great walls of Claerwen or a thousand ranks of her soldiers, she had been his for the taking—and Corvus had somehow found out.

Palinor had never understood the depths of a man's lust or love, or how the two entwined, how one woman could become a need as great as breath. The Claerwen priestess was beyond such lowly sufferings, as Tamisk had discovered for himself, but then, so was he. Yet they'd mixed their DNA in an act of physical union as Nemeton had prescribed, and Avallyn Le Severn, Priestess of the Bones and Princess of the White Palace, had been born to grace the last days of Earth and make the sacrifices of salvation.

Setting the Orange Book aside, Tamisk chose one of the rods from the constellation Draco, the dragon's eye, pulling it out of the pedestal and removing the copper orb on the end. With a softly blown breath and the spoken words *"Llagor, Rastaban,"* he sent the orb floating off among the boughs on a lazy, spinning path, trailing a silver cloud, the first of eight he would set in the air. 'Twas a minor skill as magic went, but an important one in this instance. The spinning orbs were the initial key to unlocking the pedestal. When all were set afloat, the pedestal would open and he could make his offering of blood and put the Orange Book in its place—unless he was accidentally incinerated by a stray tendril of the sphere's force field.

With the first orb removed, Tamisk felt the power of the sphere shift and come to life. The low hum of its energy reached out beyond the pedestal and set the hairs on his nape on end. He knew that by the fourth orb, the hum would be vibrating in his veins. By the eighth, he'd feel it like an endless wave rippling through his brain.

Nemeton had been near like a god, and he had brought much to pass as he had written. Three of the seven Books of Lore were already safely shelved in their crystalline slots inside the pedestal, according to the Bard's plan and awaiting the moment of final triumph—or final defeat: the Violet Book of Stars, *Sjarn Va Le,* wrenched at great cost from a troll's hand on Inishwrath in the Fifth Age and known to some as Shay's Bane; the Blue Book of the Magi, *Prydion Cal Le,* kept in Merioneth after being found by Madron, daughter of Nemeton, also during the Fifth

Age; and the Red Book of Doom, *Fata Ranc Le,* sent spinning through the time weir, gathering its fates, until it had come to Avallyn. The last story to be written upon its pages was of the priestess-princess and her Prince of Time—and there was Tamisk's sticking point: Morgan ab Kynan.

Despite Palinor's demands, he had a need to see this thief for himself before the White Ladies of Death fed him to the time worms.

Of the three missing books, the Yellow Book, *Chandra Yeull Le,* was nearly in hand, left unguarded at Magh Dun. The Green Book of Trees, *Treo Veill Le,* would come in time, delivered as a gift from Rhayne. Tamisk awaited its arrival on faith, but also with impatience. She must know what had happened in Pan-shei. She must have felt the dark wave of terror reverberating through the firmanent even as he had, a tremor of anguish that had opened the dark abyss of eternity for a seemingly endless moment—yet the day was already passing into a gloaming dusk and she still had not come.

The Indigo Book of Elfin Lore, *Elhion Bhaas Le,* was another matter. It had been locked inside Kryscaven Crater with the Prydion Mage, Ailfinn Mapp, during the last plague of Dharkkum. 'Twas Avallyn's task to free it and the Lost Five. 'Twas she who would place the Indigo Book between the Violet and the Blue and seal the spectrum of color into the pure white light of the first fallen Star. Whence went the light of the Star, Nemeton's galactic beings had revealed, so would go the naked singularity.

For all its rough appearance, the celestial sphere was an exquisitely balanced electromagnetic radiation chamber with high internal reflection, tuned to the distant cluster of galaxies designated as NGC 2300, with every single atom in harmonic accord for its task of sending Dharkkum back to said cluster and letting the far-flung galaxies deal with their own black-hole spawn.

It *should* work, Tamisk thought. Though with so much at stake, 'twas hard not to harbor some doubts—especially about the thief time had sent to stand by Avallyn's side. Morgan ab Kynan was a man, no more, and mayhap far less. Even the least learned Ilmarryn knew more about the workings of Earth than he; even the least skilled sprite had more practical magic to wield.

"*Llagor, Etamin.*" He released another orb and sent it sailing through the sea of leaves.

Aye, Tamisk would see this man, this thief, and perhaps rearrange some of his atoms to more finely harmonize him with Tamisk's accord.

The thought brought a faint smile to the mage's mouth and eased a measure of the dull pain in his head. Prince of Time or nay, the man would not win the Princess of the White Palace without first running the gauntlet of her father.

Chapter 14

The camp in the lee of the Medain was full to overflow-
ing with wild boys and masutes, the four-legged animals
crowding around the rover to warm themselves with the
last of the day's heat coming off the metal bulkhead. Soft
circles of lantern light and the flickering flames of camp-
fires dotted the nooks and crannies of the surrounding
rocks, illuminating the tents and lean-tos of the Sept
Rhymer band. More than fifty wild boys had joined
them, including a fair share of girls who looked little different—except up close. Up close the differences were
undeniable—softer voices, gentler facial curves, smaller
hands—and Morgan wondered if it was the wild girls
that had given the Sept soldier bands their reputation for
being made up of youths. A good portion of the men
were young, but men nonetheless, like Lannikan. Many
of the soldiers were paired up. Lannikan and Sakip had
a tent separate from the others, and Morgan had noted
the care the wild boy took with the dark-haired girl, and

how often Sakip splayed her hand low over her stomach. No doubt she was with child, which explained their eagerness to go to a protected place from which they could never return. Their only other option was to settle in Sept Rhymer, but none of the open-desert Septs would be safe from the horror in Pan-shei, and they knew it.

The wild boys had put up a pavilion tent for Avallyn, much to Morgan's aggravation. She'd slept with him the night before, and if he hadn't taken off the damned tracking bracelet, she'd be sleeping close to him tonight—a heaven-and-hell situation he was more than willing to endure to have her with him through the dark hours.

He could put the damn thing back on. It only needed contact to reactivate. But he hesitated. Not because he thought the leash would hinder him, but because she would know exactly what he was about, and he wasn't ready for such a blunt confession of need.

So he stood next to the rover, wrench in hand, staring up at where her tent was pitched in a sand-filled curve of the rockface, halfway up the rise to the grotto. The tent was protected by the two Sha-shakrieg Night Watchers they'd brought with them out of Rabin-19, and on three sides by the curve of stone. Nevertheless it wasn't as safe as the rover, and—putting his own feelings aside—he felt obligated to go up there and point out that fact. She should be inside the rover, *her* rover, she and her damned desert wraiths. She had no business sleeping inside a couple of flaps of tanned masute hide when half a galaxy's worth of beastmen were on her trail.

Aye, he thought, the whole tent idea was as flimsy as the thing itself.

"Crikey," Aja swore, sliding out from under the rover just as one of the masutes ambled past and nearly knocked him over. They were working on the fusion box with the wild boy mechanic, with York at the controls inside.

Aja was in a fine glower, and had been ever since Morgan had returned with the pack of desert nomads. Not even the promise of seeing the legendary Lost Forest of the Waste had softened Aja's view of his and Morgan's new situation or their destination. "Aye, now," the boy had said with uncharacteristic churlishness, "mayhap there's adventure on a grand scale for us, milord. And mayhap there'll be naught but more friggin' trouble."

Morgan hadn't dared to tell him just how grand an adventure the

White Lady truly had planned. Something was eating at the boy, something more than recalcitrant masutes and wild boys to have put him to such an edge.

"Are they blind or what?" the boy groused, sidestepping a pile of dung on his way to the toolbox.

"No," Morgan answered. "Just single-minded. They know it's going to get damn cold, real quick, and they all want a spot next to the rover."

"Bloody-minded, if ye ask me."

"Aye," Morgan murmured, thinking that it really was going to get damn cold, real quick. Avallyn would be warmer in the rover, not just safer.

"Ye oughta just go up there and see her, Morgan, before ye burst a friggin' eyeball or something worse."

"What?" He turned and found the boy looking at him with a grimly purposeful expression. Aja had obviously worked himself up to having his say, and Morgan thought 'twas about time. If anyone was in danger of bursting anything, 'twas the boy.

"I've never seen ye so cross-eyed over a woman, milord," Aja started mildly enough, though his teeth were gritted, "and for all that she's a pretty piece and a princess to boot, she's trouble. Look at us." He gestured at the camp. "Less than three days we been with her, and we're knee-deep in wild boys and masute shit and headed off to a place that any sane folk will tell you probably don't exist. So I say, go." His voice dropped to a disgusted pitch. "Go up to see her if ye must. Have her if ye can, by God, and then, by the Bones, let's be gone from this place."

So 'twas Avallyn that stuck in Aja's craw. He'd guessed as much. The boy, by nature, was not given to outbursts, and if it had been anything or anyone except Avallyn he'd latched onto, Morgan would be inclined to agree that they'd come a ridiculously long way under the worst of circumstances and could best serve themselves by cutting their losses and running hard in the opposite direction.

But it *was* Avallyn, and she was the crux of it all.

" 'Tis not so simple" was all he could say.

"What isn't simple?" the boy demanded, clearly unmollified. "The seeing her, or the having her in your bed?"

"Nay." Morgan shook his head. "She'll have me, aright. It's the leaving of her I can't see my way clear to do."

A moment of stunned silence met his announcement, then the boy swore. "Sweet gods. Don't go telling me you've gone and fallen in love with a woman who trapped you with a friggin' bounty bracelet?"

'Twas a question without an answer. So Morgan gave what answer he could, knowing the boy should know where they stood. If the situation started to change fast, he didn't want Aja making his lightning-quick decisions without all the facts.

"She wants me to go through the time weir with her, Aja, to go back from where I came, to Wales. 'Tis her destiny, and also, she says, mine."

The boy's face paled, the vinegar going out of him of a sudden, making him seem years younger.

"You wouldn't do such a thing . . . would you?" That 'twas a question at all in the boy's mind spoke of his fears.

"Not by choice." Morgan's gaze strayed again to the tent on the hill.

"Then we leave tonight," Aja said crisply, rallying back to his plan. "Let her find another time-rider for her destiny. We can leave the rover here. Take a couple of the masutes and ride south, out of the line of battle. We can slip back around into the Old Dominion and pick up our stuff in Pan-shei, then—" The boy broke off with a virulent curse.

Morgan understood. With more grim news piling on the last at every turn, 'twas hard to remember just how much the world had changed in a day, that Pan-shei was gone.

Aja brought a hand up to cover his face and swore again. "Gods, Morgan. What about Klary . . . and the others?"

Morgan shook his head. The question had plagued him as well. He didn't know what had happened to the other friends they had in Pan-shei, and he for certes didn't want to think about Klary and her brood.

"She scored on me before the Warmonger arrived in Pan-shei," he told the boy. "She wouldn't have stayed in the Northern Quarter, but gone home with her money and her booty. Chances are she was well out of it." 'Twas a balm spoken for Aja's sake, though the odds on it being true were no worse than even.

"We should leave," the boy said, lowering his hand and lifting troubled green eyes to meet Morgan's. "No good can come of this. We've always worked alone and done right well by ourselves. As for this other . . ." His voice trailed off.

"As for this other." Morgan grasped the boy's shoulder with one hand. "Fate may not be a matter of choice, but the time weir is in Claerwen, the northern temple of the Priestesses of the Bones, and we are off to the west to the White Palace." A faint smile curved his lips. "Home to fierce and wondrous dragons, if the rumors flying around camp are to be believed, and also to this Lost Forest. I've heard ye speak of the place, in your cups and out of 'em. About how there are trees growing out there in the sand that haven't been seen on Earth for thousands of years. Greenwood trees, you called them. Like what we've seen through the wine."

"I'd not lose you just to see a bunch of friggin' trees, Morgan." The words were heartfelt, gruffly spoken.

"Milord!" They were hailed by one of the older wild boys making his way through the masute herd.

Morgan tightened his grip on Aja's shoulder. "I'll not leave ye, unless the choice is taken from me." He spoke as honestly as he could. "And if it is, you'll know before I go." 'Twas more than Morgan had been willing to admit to himself, that there was even the remotest possibility of his returning to the weir. *Christe,* it made his blood run cold even to think of it.

"Milord." The wild boy halted in front of them. "Commander Avallyn requests your presence in her tent."

Aja's expression became grim again, but for all the risks involved, Morgan could only be heartened at the invitation. Picking up his munitions belt, he nodded his assent to the messenger, then slipped his carbine and Scyld over his shoulder.

Aja watched until Morgan disappeared inside the sand-colored tent, all the while forcing himself not to follow. He and Morgan had saved each other's lives more often than he could count. 'Twas part and parcel of their work, and a measure of their skills that they'd gone unscathed as long as they had, but he could not protect Morgan from a woman. Especially not Avallyn Le Severn, for he'd known she was a threat beyond reckoning even before Morgan had revealed her views on destiny.

While the two of them had been in Rabin-19, Aja had cast his mother's bones in the sands of the Medain beneath the noonday sun. He'd seen his lord's path crossed with wicked terrible danger, a danger that could only have been brought down on his head by the princess. A Princess of the White Palace was not to be fooled with, nor was a Priestess of the Bones, and Avallyn Le Severn was both. For certes they'd been running for their lives since she'd captured Morgan in Racht Square.

She was a priestess, aye, and Aja had been sworn through his sept to the priestesses of Claerwen, but the vow would be broken if the cost was Morgan's life. For even more than Claerwen, he'd sworn himself to the lost prince of the Cymry.

Mayhap 'twas the journey through the time weir he'd seen in the bones. Aja knew what destruction the time weir had wrought on his lord. A second journey might well kill him.

Or mayhap 'twas not the time weir at all, but something else that threatened. Aja looked up to the surrounding ridge of rock, his gaze scanning the cliffs, his senses twitching. The time weir was hundreds of miles to the north, and the danger he'd seen in the bones had felt much closer, more imminent, and far more personal than a cosmic force.

Aye, 'twas this intimate quality of the casting that had set him on edge. The coming danger Morgan faced was for him alone, and Aja feared there was naught he could do to stop it.

The scent of lavender and oranges surrounded Morgan as he entered the tent, the heady fragrance steaming up from a pot set over a brazier of hot coals. Soft light fell from lanterns hung from the tent poles, and the perfumed air and quiet ambience eased a measure of his tension. The only thing missing was Avallyn.

"My Lord." The Night Watcher who had led him in gestured to another opening farther back in the tent.

The same scent and soft light emanated from the far room, and Morgan approached it with growing anticipation. She would be waiting for him inside.

And indeed she was.

He stiffened on the threshold, his anticipation turning to wariness. Avallyn sat on a thick-piled rug next to another brazier brewing the same heady mixture of lavender and oranges, but she was not the desert-bedraggled princess he'd last seen. Priestess garb robed her from head to foot in swaths of calcimine white, the color of Claerwen, the color of sun-bleached bones. A medallion hung from a silken cord around her neck, a silver disk incised with a square rimmed in gold and inset with a triangle of carnelian—a symbol of the alchemist's quest, a design he'd seen long ago on the walls of Dain Lavrans's Hart Tower.

"Come in," she said, her voice a study in solemn authority. "Be seated." She lifted her hand to indicate a place for him across from her on the rug. Flamelike shadows shifted in a sinuous dance across her face, playing with the light from the brazier's fire and casting her in mystery. 'Twas witch's glamour and well within the White Ladies' arts, and for certes he found it disconcerting for her to be using such on him.

"Milady," he said, not without a trace of irony in his voice. That she was playing the priestess again could bode no good.

Her nicked eyebrow lifted slightly at his formality, and he allowed himself an inward smile. They had kissed, and what he'd learned of her in those moments could not be cast aside like Aja's worn tunic. She was Avallyn, and she was his for the taking if he was willing to pay the price.

For the first time he found the thought steadying, one sure thing in a quickly changing world. Thus reassured, he again started forward.

Avallyn watched him finish crossing the inner sanctum she'd created inside the pavilion, his strides long and imbued with the easy grace he'd used so effectively to get them out of Racht. Barely a trace of his limp remained since he'd taken her father's potion. 'Twas a temporary surcease, she was sure, but she was glad even for a brief easing of his affliction, and she hoped he would not hold against her what was to come. Being deep-scented was not unpleasant, provided the subject did not find the mere act of being searched in such a manner offensive—and Morgan was unlikely not to notice. For that reason, she'd decided to tell him beforehand.

"My mother is a formidable woman," she began, ladling a cup of lavender-orange tea out of the pot on the brazier.

When he'd seated himself on the rug in front of her, cross-legged, his elbows resting on his knees, his sword and carbine angled across his back, she handed him the cup and dared for a moment to meet his eyes. To her surprise, he was watching her with an intensity not too far removed from the level she was about to turn on him, his darkly indigo gaze seeming to look beyond the facade of calm she'd so carefully built in preparation for what she must do.

She glanced away, busying herself with ladling another cup of tea.

"But within the bounds of her priestess vows, my mother would not cause you harm," she continued, then paused for a telling second. "The same cannot be said for my father. Tamisk is not bound by any creed other than knowledge, and he employs a vast array of methods for gaining his precious truths, some of them decidedly unpleasant."

"Has he used those methods on you?" 'Twas not a casual question, but one spoken with a subtle edge of threat.

He was her protector, she thought, carefully sipping her tea from a clay cup. Whether he claimed it or not.

She hazarded his gaze again.

"No," she said, and saw him visibly relax at her answer. "Nor would he, so long as my mother draws breath. It is for you that I fear."

His only reaction to her warning was to take a sip of tea, which made her wonder if he understood the potential difficulties awaiting him in the White Palace.

"My father is an Ilmarryn mage, a Magia Lord adept of the Books of Lore," she said succinctly. "Even the Queen of Deseillign bends her knee to him on occasion, and though by rights of the *Fata Ranc Le* you fall under the patronage of the Claerwen priestesses, Tamisk also has a stake in your fate. I fear with this change in our course, he will bring undue pressures to bear on the situation."

Pausing in the act of taking his second drink, he lifted his head. "Undue pressures?"

"Magic." 'Twas an inadequate word to describe the complex dimensions of Tamisk's skills, but Avallyn knew none better. Magic, by its very nature, defied definition or explanation—except in the hands of her father, who knew quite well what he was about.

Magic, Morgan repeated in his mind, feeling his heart sink to the vicinity of his stomach. Having been subjected to unpleasant inquiries by life-forms with no stake in his future, he hadn't been overly concerned about her father's interrogation—not when the man needed him, and not when he'd already decided that they needed Tamisk to hold off the Warmonger.

But magic. He remembered all his brushes with the stuff, what little good and what great harm it had brought him.

"Magic," he said flatly. "Against me."

"Aye, milord."

'Twas only fitting, he thought with disgust, that at this great juncture in his life he should find himself in danger not only from the Warmonger and universe-devouring black plagues, but from friggin' magic as well.

"No sleight of hand, smoke, or mirrors?" he asked, keeping any trace of hope out of his voice. He'd not have her know that magic unnerved him. When he'd found none in the future, he'd been disappointed—he had desperately hoped to find an explanation for what had happened to him—but he'd also been relieved.

"Nay," she answered. "Tamisk is no Pan-shei juggler or Pathian illusionist. When he makes something disappear, it is truly gone, its atoms dispersed into the cosmic fold."

"And you fear he might disperse me?"

"He would not dare," she said quickly. "But that could well be the only constraint he puts upon your meeting."

Well, hell, Morgan thought, his mood sinking even lower.

"I can help you, though, milord."

Of course she could. For a price, he was sure. Probably his soul or some other equally pertinent part of his existence. It seemed the only tender that held her interest.

"How?" he asked, setting his cup aside.

"By discerning your weaknesses for myself beforehand, mayhap I can ameliorate any problems that may arise."

He wasn't fooled by her wording. There was a cost to him somewhere in her amelioration, and he wondered if there would ever be a time when things between them were simple.

"What kind of weaknesses?" The list was nearly endless as far as he could tell, and she may well have been getting in over her head trying to sort them out.

"I could not say, milord, not without looking first."

Quite diplomatic, he thought, for someone who had seen him in the midst of a Carillion wine fever.

"And your method of discernment?"

"Scenting, milord. Deep-scenting."

"Deep-scenting?" He'd never heard of it.

"A highly refined use of the olfactory sense," she explained.

"You can smell my weaknesses?" he asked skeptically.

"What I can actually smell is your past. It's locked into your cells in a complex pattern of minute chemical deviations, and these historical deviations ofttimes reveal a person's predilections and weaknesses."

And if that wasn't enough to put him off the idea, Morgan didn't know what was. Having his weaknesses exposed through his chemical deviations on a cellular level would hardly put him in a bearable light. In truth, the mere thought of it made him want to hightail it back to the rover and lock the hatch door behind him. *Sweet Jesu,* and she thought her father was a magician.

But he didn't jump up.

And he didn't run.

In truth, he made no movement other than to breathe and consider his options—and it didn't take him long to wonder if she hadn't already done some of her deep-scenting on him. They'd surely been close enough, and more than once.

"All you have to do is smell me to find out my predilections?" He hated repeating the word "weaknesses" out loud in connection with himself.

"Deep-scenting is a way of using the olfactory system with specific guided intent," she said. "It can quickly, almost instantaneously, go beyond what would normally be considered a person's smell into subtler dimensions."

"And then the person you're deep-scenting is pretty much an open book for you to read?"

He watched her hesitate before the truth won out.

"Aye," she admitted, then clarified her answer. "Providing there are no complications."

"Such as?"

"No one can read the past through a muddle of cells soaked in Carillion wine," she said bluntly.

His mood lightened somewhat at that. "Then you've only had today."

"And there's been no time," she said, answering his unasked question.

"When we kissed?"

A blush bloomed on her cheeks, staining them the palest pink, but she didn't look away.

"I . . . I was too distracted, milord."

Satisfaction filled him at her answer, satisfaction and a longing made even sweeter by her confession.

"And now?" He leaned close and cupped her chin in his hand.

Her blush deepened, and her golden brown lashes swept down to fan across her cheeks, enchanting him. He wanted to kiss her ears, run his fingers through her hair, and lose himself in the lovely scent that was hers alone.

"If I kiss you, it will be as before," she said softly, "and we'll be no safer for my having failed to search your mind."

Gods. Even the cost of a kiss had grown steep, if she felt her safety was the price. On the other hand, he felt exactly the same way, that her kisses would probably be the death of him.

Releasing her, he leaned back and consigned himself to the inevitable.

"So you must look," he said, "and I must endure, and we both must live with what you find."

"Aye." Dove gray eyes peered up at him from beneath her lashes, their expression unreadable.

He offered his own warning. "I fear it will not be a pretty sight, what you see in my mind. And I doubt if it will do anything to make you feel safe. Quite the contrary."

And this was where he lost her, he thought. He knew his past better than most men, having relived it countless times through the wine, and there was little enough there to give a person heart—unless, like him, she went beyond the brief past of his future into the deep past of another age. He'd been a good man then, even a hero to some. But God knew he'd had weaknesses then too, and for certes there had been nothing in his old life to indicate he was capable of saving the world from a terror like Dharkkum. At his lowest point, in the deserts of Palestine, he hadn't even been able to save himself. That job had been left to Dain Lavrans.

He nearly smiled. The fears of his past paled considerably compared to the trials he'd faced in the future, but he had no doubt that Dain could have met the challenges of the weir and the Waste with the same cool competence that he'd used to establish himself as a mage of renown in ancient Wales. The man had been reforged in the heat of the desert, and naught had ever touched him afterward, until Ceridwen.

"Tell me about your sword," Avallyn said, the sound of her voice bringing him back to the present, her words making him wonder if she could read his thoughts. The sword had been Dain's.

"'Tis called Scyld, after the first king of the Danes," he said, unsheathing the sword and lifting it over his shoulder, laying it across his lap, "and is mine only by an accident of fate."

She reached out and ran her hand down the sword's hilt. "Fate makes few mistakes and tolerates even fewer accidents. If this weapon came through the weir with you, more likely than not 'twas meant to be yours." Her hand slid over the curved cross-guard to the blade, and she looked up, her brows knitted together. "Who wielded this blade before you?"

"Dain Lavrans, a friend and soldier, and last I knew, a sorcerer as well."

She nodded. "Aye, it has the feel of enchantment, faint but there. And these? What do they say?" she asked, running her fingers over the runes on the blade.

"They're Norse, an invocation to a long-dead god."

"All gods have ever been the eternal One. What was this god's name?"

"Odin, a god of war."

"And also of magic and wisdom. Aye," she said at his questioning glance. "I have heard of Odin the one-eyed god. His Valkyries brought heroes slain in battle to Valhalla, where they awaited the coming of Ragnarok, the cataclysmic end of the world and the doom of the gods."

"We seem to have apocalypse as a recurring theme," he said, smiling wryly.

"Aye." Her gaze returned to the sword. "Ragnarok and Dharkkum seem much alike." She leaned closer to inspect the rune staves, her braids and twists sliding over her shoulders. "Odin was ever one to carve magic runes on his weapons in hopes of fending off the fateful moment of his death. Mayhap a bit of his magic has rubbed off on this god-blessed blade."

"Mayhap," Morgan agreed, his voice roughened by a surge of desire—inevitable when she was practically in his lap. Whatever the dangers, he had to kiss her, his need far outweighing self-preservation.

With his sword between them, he lifted her chin and lowered his mouth, and with only the slightest hesitation, she allowed herself to be captured.

Sweet Jesu, no lips had ever been so soft, no mouth so made to match his, no flick of tongue so erotic as she pressed herself closer and kissed him back. Her hand came to rest on his chest, and he wished his skin was bare to feel her touch.

"Morgan," she breathed, her lips sliding away from his to press a silken trail of kisses across his cheek, caressing him with a tenderness he was sure was undeserved—as she would undoubtedly find out when she deep-scented him.

And she would, he knew. Distraction or nay, the fey woman had been single-minded in her purpose from the moment they'd met.

Better to enjoy her kisses now, he thought, when they were still so easily to be had. In Rabin-19, he had pulled away, but no more. 'Twas time to stop and indulge himself, while the scents of lavender and oranges filled the air and her lithe body was his to be had on the soft rugs in her private bower.

He angled his head to kiss her throat, but his lips no sooner touched her skin than he sensed the first soft tread of her deep-scent invasion.

He stilled, one hand on her waist, the other tunneled into her hair, and he waited, knowing there was nothing he could do to stop her, fearing there was no place left for him to hide.

'Twas a strange sensation, wondrously strange, having her search him from the inside out. He felt her presence move through him, lingering here and there, especially near his heart, where Llynya's rowan leaf graced his skin. For long, silent minutes, she wandered at will before focusing on his mind, and with each minute that she looked, his unease increased, the novelty quickly wearing off and leaving him uncomfortably aware of what she was finding—a truth about himself that perhaps he didn't even know.

"Avallyn." Her name was a whisper on his lips, half contrived as a plea. She was getting close to something, and though he hated to think there was danger for her inside himself, he felt she was heading somewhere she should not go.

He knew instantly when she took the one fateful step too far. A gasp was torn from her throat. She clutched at him even as his hands tightened on her. Then she fainted into a heap in his arms.

"Avallyn!"

Avallyn heard the cry of her name echo across the timeless abyss, but she could not answer. She was falling, falling into the fathomless canyon that snaked across the inner landscape of Morgan's mind.

She'd deep-scented a time-rider once before and had known what to expect: the faint scent of knowledge twined into a wavelike ribbon; the growing storm of wind; then the fall into the canyon, the weightless traverse of space and years. Such was the trail into the prince's deep past.

There had been love in his other life, an abundance of it, and a surpassing amount of innocence for a thief, and all the passages of a life well lived.

But there was something else as well, an elusive thread running through the ribbon that was pulling her deeper than she'd meant to go. Deeper than she'd thought 'twas possible to go, past his cell walls into their nuclei and into the threadlike bodies of his chromosomes.

'Twas there she found the unexpected, a gene sequence that marked him as the warrior they had long awaited, more surely than any time-rider blaze or rowan leaf. Morgan ab Kynan had been bred to the sword, to one special sword, the Magia Blade. With it in his hand, he would fight to the death and beyond—like his ancient forefather, Stept Agah.

She saw the place of Stept Agah's birth in a deep cavern, and she saw his long-ago battle with Dharkkum, how the Magia Blade had molded itself to his hand and fought on even after he'd died—and she feared the same fate for Morgan, that he would die and still fight.

"Avallyn. Avallyn."

She roused to the sound of her name, coming back from the abyss to find herself cradled in Morgan's arms. Looking up at him, she was washed through with fear. Stept Agah had defeated the darkness in his own time, and a son of his had been sent to save the world in her time, but the price was too high.

Dread lord, indeed, and dread warrior with a star-crossed blade.

"Morgan, you are—" She started to tell him what she'd seen, but was interrupted by a commotion in the outer tent.

They both turned toward the noise, rising to their feet in one graceful movement, the sheer fluidity of the action making her wonder if they were still somehow connected on a cellular level. The look he gave her showed the same intrigued awareness.

"Commander." One of her Night Watcher guards rushed through the tent flap, his black-and-gray robes whipped up by a gust of wind following in his wake. The flames in the brazier danced and flickered, casting wild shadows on the tent walls.

"Petr. Who is here?" She no sooner addressed him than the telling scent reached her nose.

"Sha-shakrieg, a corps of Night Watchers from Tamisk."

Aye, she thought, detecting the fine, bitter smell of the spider people. A corps' worth at least, if not more.

But this other, what she'd learned of Morgan, it set her reeling. The blood of Stept Agah ran in his veins—for the good of the world and his own doom.

Shadana. Palinor must have known.

"He commands your presence, and that of the time-rider. The corps is to be your escort."

Other shadows from the outer chamber danced on the walls, too many for her to count. She was being invaded by her father's troops just when she needed time to think. If Palinor had known about Morgan and deliberately kept the information from her, there must have been a reason.

The first one that came to Avallyn's mind hardly bore contemplation, yet it had a disturbing ring of truth about it. He would not save the world as Stept Agah had. The whole world, including the two of them, would be destroyed no matter what they did.

So why suffer the agonies of the weir? And why would Palinor sacrifice her only daughter when fate had already doomed them out of hand?

The answer to that was a bit more complex, but easy enough for Avallyn to surmise. Perhaps the world would survive through their efforts, but only with sacrifice. She and Morgan would perish, with him fighting like his forefather before him, wielding his blade even beyond death to secure the destruction of Dharkkum.

'Twas a grim conclusion, but not too difficult to fathom. Palinor had ever been a priestess before she was a mother, and Tamisk had been even less of a father. Easy enough to understand how their duty had overcome any maternal or paternal instincts. Avallyn had been born of their union, but not of their love—and in all her years love had not grown between them nor for her.

Her mouth tightened. Mayhap Morgan had known the right of it, after all. Mayhap she did count her life too lightly, a trait well learned at her mother's knee. 'Twas an old and worthless hurt, and one she'd long outgrown.

Or so she'd thought.

What else was her mother keeping from her? she wondered.

"Commander." Petr interrupted her thoughts. "We must leave now."

Aye, 'twas true. Time was running out.

Within the voluminous drape of her robes, she made a sign of protection.

.   .   .

"Dragonsss," Corvus hissed, drawing out the word on a sibilant exhalation even as he drew himself in as best he could.

A wisp of his left leg escaped him, and he swore viciously. How could he survive if parts of him were ever drifting away?

It was a question with an obvious answer: He wasn't going to survive.

"Vissshhhab." He snarled the witch's name, staring at her across the dark expanse of her workroom in his warship's hold, willing her to look at him, to look at what little was left of him.

The crone lifted her gaze from her cauldron of boiling blood, the light from the fire reflecting red in her eyes, the nimbus of her hair looking like the fires of hell.

"Lord?" she inquired, almost sweetly, if he was any judge. No doubt she was reveling in a misconception of her own power now that he was so disturbingly discarnate. Parts of him were still corporeal, though, mostly on his right side. He still had an arm, a hip and thigh, nearly half his face, and a bit more.

The ancient bitch would go too far someday, and then he'd have her, by God, and take her with him to their doom. Only the thought of spending eternity attached to the ragged woman stopped him from shredding her into the cosmos—that and the hope that she could contrive some foul conjuration to hold him together.

"Dragonssss," he hissed again, reminding her of what he needed, staring harder with his one good eye to get his point across. Of course, he wasn't even sure if dragons could save him now. He'd been willing to sacrifice an arm, if being free of the black smoke would keep him from destruction. But more than his arm had been consumed by his deeds in Pan-shei, so very much more than his arm.

"Aye, the beasts are cauldron-born, milord. The book is very clear about it, and I'm stirring, I am." She cackled, a harsh, maleficent sound, and his patchy skin crawled. "Oh, aye. I'm a-stirring."

"Crysssstal." She'd promised him crystal to seal in the darkness and the smoke, enough to see him through until they reached Claerwen, the only place on Earth where he knew a time weir existed. It was filled with sand, as was everything on the goddamn planet except the Old Dominion and the Middle Kingdom, but it still was a time weir, still a place where the time worms came.

And he needed worms, golden worms—and dragons, and crystal, and whatever else it would take to keep him from his self-inflicted doom.

Chained in a corner of the workroom were the two prisoners he'd taken in Pan-shei, the woman time-rider and her giant. Grim-faced, they were, but not beaten, not yet. Corvus was saving them, his instincts telling him they had value beyond fodder for his dark, smoky power. Perhaps he could bargain their souls for Avallyn's.

"*Avallynnnn,*" he moaned at the reminder of his demon-witch. As much as he needed worms, dragons, and crystal, he wanted her, now more than ever. It was a fiery desire incinerating the last shreds of his reason. Nothing could be sweeter than to take her with him into a hellish eternity.

Ah, yes, that place by his side was reserved only for Avallyn Le Severn, the damned bitch he loathed . . . and loved. A pain stabbed through him where his heart had once been, a vicious, tearing pain that would have put him on his knees, if he had any. As it was, he writhed with the pain, a shadowy twisting, and his loathing doubled over and increased. Such were the rewards of love.

He cut his gaze to the rigid form of his First Guard captain.

"*Find herrr,*" he commanded.

"W-we will, m-master," the captain stammered. "W-we have over a h-hundred search v-vessels combing the W-waste, and five hundred ss-sseeker d-droids."

It would be enough. It had to be enough.

Avallyn had brought him to this horrifyingly nebulous existence, and it was only just that she share his fate. To that end he would search her out wherever she'd gone to ground, search her out and devour her.

Chapter 15

Morgan felt the Night Watchers' rover slow, but he saw nothing in the vast expanse of the Waste to tell him why. They'd traveled most of the night, with dawn just beginning to break behind them to the east.

Twelve rovers had been sent to the Medain—two to pick up Avallyn and him and bring them here to the middle of nowhere, the other ten to reinforce the troop of wild boys from Sept Rhymer. All the desert Septs had been summoned for battle. The Second Guard was to be fully engaged on Craig Tagen. The First Guard was to be harassed and kept north of Rabin-19, but not engaged, not after what had happened in Pan-shei.

The dragons were rousing, Morgan had heard one of the Sha-shakrieg captains tell Avallyn. Dragons. It scarce made sense, but Avallyn had assured him that they were real, the dragons of Merioneth, fighting dragons meant to fight with him and her.

He knew Merioneth, and he remembered a cavern

by the Irish Sea known as the Dragon's Mouth, but he'd never dreamed the name referred to actual dragons. Even when he'd been in the deeper caverns, there had been only *pryf,* strange enough for any man of twelfth-century Wales to comprehend, less strange to a man who'd fought with skraelings and Lyrans and other manifestations of galaxy offal.

A man revered as Saint George had killed a dragon once, in a long-ago and faraway land. Morgan had seen a drawing of their battle in Dolwyddelan Castle. Saint George had been mounted on a horse, and the dragon had been writhing about the destrier's feet, a serpentine beast looking to be twelve feet in length and weighing nearly a quarter of a ton. In the future, he'd seen all manner of dragonish beasts: crocodiles; Komodo dragons, lizards as big as Saint George's nemesis; the giant tuataras and snakes from the Friina Group—none of which he would particularly care to have by his side in a battle, and for certes none of which he wanted to fall through ten thousand years with in the weir.

The rover came to a complete stop, and still there was nothing to see but the rolling crests of dunes.

Nothing to see, but Morgan felt something, an odd familiarity. His brow furrowed.

"What, milord?" Aja asked, standing next to him on the forward deck. York had chosen to stay and fight on Craig Tagen, but nothing could have kept Aja from Morgan's side. For himself, Morgan was glad to have the boy with him. If there was to be a parting, he'd as soon it was later.

"I've been here more than once in my dreams, but it did not look like this," he said, glancing over his shoulder at the boy. "Have you ever followed me to such a place through the wine?"

Aja looked out the starboard window and shrugged. "We came out of the desert, milord, and from any direction 'tis all very similar, but I like not the feel of this particular pile of sand."

" 'Tis true there is more here than meets the eye," Avallyn said, coming up behind them.

"Is the White Palace buried beneath the dunes?" Morgan asked.

"Not yet, thanks to the sweepers. It lies farther to the west, on the edge of the Sand Sea. Captain." She turned to the nearest Night Watcher. "Tamisk undoubtably knows we're here. What's the delay?"

"No delay, Commander." The Sha-shakrieg lifted a large, callused hand and pointed to the nearest dune.

Before Morgan's eyes, the sand began to flow like water, illusory sheets of it sloughing off to reveal a jutting protrusion of stone—but no mere protrusion. The stone had shape and, Morgan realized, purpose. 'Twas a tower, one he feared he recognized.

"How?" he whispered, taking a step toward the window, his hand rising to touch the glass.

Second by second, the ancient tower was stripped of its protection until it stood like a beacon in the Waste, a beacon of the past. The rest of Wydehaw Castle was little more than rubble, but the Hart Tower stood tall, Dain's tower of magic and alchemy. Any doubts Morgan had harbored about the priestess-princess and her Book of Doom evaporated in the face of reality. Even without the weir, she'd brought him to a place in his past he'd never thought to see again, a place he'd thought long destroyed. That it still existed, even in a ruined state, attested to the power of the Hart. Naught but the abiding grace of magic could have saved it from the destruction of the wars that had ravaged Earth and made the Deseillign Waste.

"You know this place, then?" Avallyn asked.

He slowly nodded. "Aye, 'twas a castle in Wales, where Ceridwen was healed by Dain Lavrans before they opened the time weir beneath Merioneth, and where my sword was kept in the years between our Holy Crusade and the Battle of Balor. Why have we come here?" he asked, wondering if he would have been better served to stay and fight on Craig Tagen with York. Not that he'd been given a choice. That he was caught in the inexorable pull of destiny was a truth he could no longer deny.

"Tamisk." Avallyn's answer to his question was succinct and exactly what he'd expected.

"The Magia Lord awaits," the Night Watcher captain said, gesturing for them to descend the rover's ramp.

Aja started forward with them, but the Sha-shakrieg man stopped him with an outstretched arm covered with whorls of fighting threads.

"Only two have been granted leave to enter the tower."

"Then let his admittance be on my head," Avallyn said.

"So be it." The captain stepped back and allowed them all to pass.

The desert dawn was a frigid thing. Though warmly dressed, Morgan was grateful when they had covered the stretch of open dune between the rover and the tower. At an arched doorway banked into the sand, he stopped and turned, surprised to hear the rover engines winding up.

"Are they leaving us?" he asked.

"Aye," Avallyn said. "Rovers are not usually allowed this close to the tower. They're too easy to track. They'll wait for us beyond the ridge we came over two miles back."

"I don't like it," Aja said.

Neither did Morgan, but he continued on.

He had climbed the parti-colored stairs a few times in his other life, but never with more misgivings. Aja's fretful grumbling at his side did nothing to alleviate his dread of what they might find awaiting them within the tower walls.

"By the Bones, Morgan, I swear no good can come of your being here. I'll watch your back, milord, but you must stay sharp!"

" 'Twas the home of my friend for many years, a man who saved my life." He mounted the first black stair and felt a tremor of reminiscence. A white stair followed, then another black, the whole curve winding upward into darkness. Barely a trace of the dawn's light penetrated the narrow arrow loops.

"As no doubt I will have to do before we are free of this block of stone," the boy mumbled, his lasgun drawn and cocked with its trigger unlocked.

Christe. The boy was serious to the point of trouble.

"Lock down, Aja," he ordered. "If there's one thing I'm sure of, it's that we don't want to shoot anyone who might be in this tower."

He was rewarded with a narrowed gaze and a scowl, but the boy locked the trigger on his lasgun.

For a moment, Morgan breathed easier, then Avallyn reached the Druid Door. The sight of the crystal-eyed gargoyle and its blood-rust fangs was enough to chill him to the bone.

The princess pushed through the door without hesitation, which was more than Morgan could manage. It took a steadying breath for him to walk past the leering beast. Aja gave the gargoyle as wide a berth as possible, scooting by close to the opposite doorjamb.

" 'Tis called Llynya's Oak," Avallyn said, indicating a gnarled, desiccated trunk pushing up through the floor of what had once been Dain's main solar. None of the furnishings remained, but even with the room dominated by the dead tree, it was painfully familiar.

As for the tree itself, it seemed perfectly in keeping that the elfin sprite would have planted such an unruly acorn and conquered the tower with her deed.

Morgan forced himself to walk deeper into the room. The windows were the same, with stone embrasures set into the walls and the eastern window catching more of the rising sun with each passing minute. The floor had been rebuilt to accommodate the great tree. He couldn't imagine what had kept the Hart standing for all these thousands of years, until he was close enough to see that the trunk had been turned to stone, petrified in a palette of oranges and browns and becoming a support for the very building it had undermined.

He put his hand on the trunk and turned to look around the room. The walls in the chamber below were incised with all manner of alchemical formulae, many of which Dain had never deciphered. The current occupant had undoubtedly surpassed all the previous ones and achieved the alchemist's quest—the art of transformation through the mastery of time.

With that realization came a disconcerting thought. Tamisk could have time worms lurking beneath the tower, their serpentine forms winding through the roots of the ancient tree.

Morgan sniffed the air and smelled naught, and he heard naught. For certes the beasts seemed to recognize him as one of their own. If the tower had become a time weir, they wouldn't have missed the opportunity to torture him with their keening cry.

"What do you call this place?" he asked Avallyn.

" 'Tis the Hart Tower, Tamisk's desert abode."

So the name had not changed, Morgan thought, only the sorcerer who ruled it.

"You've been here before?" he asked.

"Many times. If we are successful in the past, our journey will end here, in the Hart of Wydehaw Castle while it was still new and whole."

"So the tower does have power, as Dain thought?"

"Enough power to save the world from Dharkkum," she told him grimly, "if we can but deliver the energy source."

"Which is locked in Kryscaven Crater." He'd seen the place in his night of dreams, a cavern sealed by an amethystine wall, the deep purple crystal stretching in a jagged, sharp-edged expanse across the stone face of an underground mountain—the home of darkness.

"Aye," she said, her expression growing even more troubled. "Dread lord . . . whatever happens here, remember that even without magic, you hold an edge over Tamisk. You are the Prince of Time. You have strengths he does not."

"And you saw these strengths in my cells?" he asked, wondering at her renewed formality. She hadn't spoken of what she'd discovered with her deep-scenting, but she'd been keeping her distance from him ever since their time in the tent. 'Twas what he'd expected—that she would see him for what he was and lose heart—but it still pained him. For a brief time, she could have been his, and he'd spent most of that time trying to get rid of her.

"Aye, that and more." She turned away, and he reached for her, taking hold of her arm.

"Was it so very terrible, then? What you saw of me?" He'd long thought that he harbored no illusions about himself, but she had seen something beyond his worst imaginings if it made the very sight of him unbearable.

"Terrible and terrifying," she admitted, avoiding his gaze. "I fear it means our doom."

"My strengths will be the death of us?" Now he was truly confused.

The scrape of wood on stone brought his head around before she could answer. A door with words carved on its lintel was opening in the far wall, seemingly of its own accord. The trick had been one of Dain's favorites, but Morgan didn't think what he was seeing had anything to do with trickery. A mage capable of dispersing items and animals into the cosmos could probably just as easily manipulate the atoms in a door.

Aye, 'twas time to meet Avallyn's father and hope the man had more need of him than not.

Without releasing her, he started forward, only to be brought up short by a scent he had not known since he'd been lost to the past. 'Twas the smell of a forest, a rich, lush forest, and it was coming from Dain's eyrie.

He closed his eyes and let the green redolence wash over him, filling his senses.

Avallyn. Her name soughed through his mind. 'Twas her scent, only intensified, and it took him home more surely than any cup of Carillion wine. He'd lived in the wild forests of Wales, and was ever used to waking up to the smell of pine and dew-wet grass. 'Twas what he'd longed for so many nights in the future.

"I bid you welcome, Morgan ab Kynan." The voice came from above, rippling through the open doorway like the gentle waters of a stream. 'Twas soothing and harmonious, and utterly enchanting.

Reason enough to beware, he told himself, opening his eyes. Sliding his hand down Avallyn's arm, he entwined his fingers with hers and walked toward the door.

"Aye, come then," the voice beckoned, "and see your destiny."

The man remained hidden from view, but as they neared the doorway, the source of the scent became abundantly clear. Leaves, thousands of them, every one a sylvan shade of green, hung from richly brown branches and filled the stairwell leading up from the door. As they mounted the steps, the leaves reached out to caress them, quick light touches like butterflies landing and taking off again.

"Aja?" Morgan said.

"Here, milord. Not a half-step behind." And sounding far more intrigued than cautious.

Morgan didn't blame the boy. For someone who had never seen a forest, this one tree must seem like a whole woodland. Tamisk truly was a mage to have made a stone tree blossom with such greenery.

At the top of the stairs, Morgan realized Tamisk had conjured much more than a tree. The interior of the Hart's eyrie was lush to the point of unbelievability. No forest of home had ever been so chockful of vines and plants. Layer upon layer of vegetation covered the walls and spilled toward the oak, giving the illusion of an endless wood.

He closed his eyes again, breathing deeply, and a pang of longing went through him, so sharp, his heart ached. 'Twas much of what he'd lost, now found again, the ancient forest where he'd lived, traveling from one end of Wales to the other, the mission changing with each traverse but the landscape always welcoming, be they camped in a snowbound valley in the north or winding along an overgrown track in Wroneu Wood. The scent of leaves, and sap, and loam had permeated his days, along with the sharper smell of new cut wood for their fires and the sounds of wild rivers cascading through mountain gorges. 'Twas all here in this lost place.

The eyrie was full of branches and leaves, yet there was a trail of sorts leading around the trunk. Morgan followed it, and in a surprisingly brief passage of time—hardly a minute, and certainly not two—realized he was lost, if such was possible in a tower that measured no more than thirty feet across.

"Aja." He turned to question his captain, but Aja was gone, disappeared.

He swore and turned in the other direction.

"Have no fear for the boy, dread lord," Avallyn said. " 'Tis you Tamisk wants, not him."

"Where is he?" Morgan demanded, cursing himself for not taking more care. They were in a sorcerer's tower. He'd known the truth even thousands of years ago.

"I'm sure Tamisk has him tucked up in a branch somewhere, safe enough for now, wandering through the forest of his dreams." She looked up and, after a moment of searching, pointed to a branch high, high above them. "See. There he is, safe and sound, and sleeping."

And so he was. Morgan saw the bright shock of red hair nested on a pillow of leaves, the relaxed curve of the boy's spine as he slumbered on a branch, entranced, and something inside him turned cold. Aja was not so easily overcome; nor could he have been moved so quickly by any mortal means. Magic was thick in the tower, potent and adverse, a far cry from the alchemist's conjuring in Dain's time.

"Tamisk," he called out, keeping a tight rein on his anger. "Release the boy. He has nothing to do with this."

As if proving his thoughts on magic, a small copper orb came out of nowhere and floated over his left shoulder. Ten thousand years ago, he would have quickly made a warding sign. In the future, his lasgun usually took the place of superstition—but not in this instance. Blasting the mage's conjuration to smithereens was unlikely to get them the help they needed against the Warmonger.

"Even on first glance, I would have been disinclined to agree," the most mellifluous voice informed him, sounding closer with every spoken word. "After a second, deeper look, I can assure you that the boy is quite involved. And so you both arrive here cloaked in mysteries where I would have preferred to find none."

A man appeared on the shadow-darkened trail, his form barely distinguishable from the leaves and branches overhanging the path. Long brown hair fell to his shoulders and beyond, with an intricate braid twisted into the gray stripe that marked him as a time-rider. His clothes were in shades of green and brown. A thin silver coronet graced his brow. The bracelets coiled around his wrists were also silver, a matched set of snakes. Or worms, Morgan thought.

"Why did you have us brought here?" he demanded.

"To give you gifts," Tamisk replied, continuing forward.

Before Morgan could retort, his gaze was drawn to the elaborate blue tattoos swirling in runes and curves over the right side of the mage's face, and to the ears as gracefully shaped and pointed as Avallyn's. The mage's features bore a marked similarity to the priestess-princess's, though they were not so feminine, and like her, he was slender, but not slight.

Nay, there was substance to the Ilmarryn, especially to his presence.

"Lady Avallyn," Tamisk said. "Priestess of Claerwen."

"Magia Lord." She bowed her head and touched her fingers to the middle of her chest, speaking the title with due reverence.

For himself, Morgan decided to forgo any gesture of respect.

"Prince." Tamisk addressed him with a brief lowering of his gaze. His eyes reminded Morgan of Aja's, except Tamisk's were much greener, preternaturally green, almost glowing.

And his bracelets were moving.

God's blood. Morgan went perfectly still. The movement was subtle, but definite, a fluid rippling that quickly subsided, so that the bracelets looked to be solid silver.

"Come. I have gifts." Tamisk walked by them, and Avallyn turned to follow.

Leery of leaving Aja, but damned if he'd leave Avallyn, Morgan hesitated. "The only gift I want is my captain back."

"In time," the mage said, continuing on without so much as a backward glance. "After you receive what else I have to give."

As promises went, the mage's words sounded more like a threat. Morgan looked up into the tree where Aja slept, and though he perceived no immediate danger, he wanted the boy back, and sooner rather than later. Before Tamisk and Avallyn could disappear in the thicket of branches, Morgan took off after them, reminding himself that he and the mage were supposedly on the same side.

Tamisk kept to the trail, though how so much trail could be enclosed inside one room of the Hart was beyond Morgan's reckoning. 'Twas more enchantment, of course, as was all the lush flora. Now and again he could see the stone wall behind the greenery, but for the most part, Tamisk's conjuration was complete, especially when the audience was willing.

"You have the Sonnpur-Dzon dragon?" the mage asked as they walked, though 'twas more a statement than a question.

"Aye," Morgan answered.

"The High Priestess of Claerwen would be grateful for its return," the mage suggested, though, in truth, it sounded like a command.

They came to a small glade beneath an opening in the oak's branches, where the floor beneath his feet was loam and grass. Another copper orb drifted by, brushing through leaves and winding its way around the eyrie. A stone pedestal stood in the middle of the glade, surrounded by saxifrage and supporting a broad, maple-rimmed bowl of purest silver, a mazer full of water.

"Come and look in the scrying pool," the mage directed, stopping next to the pedestal and running his fingers across the top of the water. Ripples blossomed from the middle of the bowl to its edge and rolled up the sides in waves of mist.

'Twas enough to keep Morgan in his place.

"Come," the mage cajoled. "The first gift is one much to your liking, prince. 'Tis the past. I give it to you free of the complications of Carillion wine."

Crikey bastard, Morgan thought, not forgetting it had been Tamisk's potion that had saved him from the wine fever.

"You can keep the friggin' past and your—" He came to a startled halt.

Tamisk's snake bracelets were on the move again, gliding like quicksilver around his wrists and sliding off into the water. The serpents swam to the rim and began circling 'round and 'round, growing longer and thinner with each lap, until each could take the other's tail in its mouth.

Cold sweat broke out on Morgan's brow, and he glanced up at Tamisk. *Christe.* The mage had time worms at his command, but smaller worms and silver, not golden like the worms in the weir. He looked back at the pool, captivated in spite of himself. Faster and faster the serpents swam, until they were naught but an undulating ribbon beneath the small waves set in motion by their efforts, a silver ribbon streaking around a silver bowl.

Avallyn had called her father a Magia Lord, and indeed he was a lord of magic. No scientist or mechanic, however skilled, could conjure marvels with such ease. Nay, a higher power was needed than science, and Tamisk knew the way of it well.

Well enough, Morgan wondered, for the worms to suck him into the vortex?

"No," Tamisk said. "The pool is only for viewing, not for traveling."

"You can read my mind?" Morgan jerked his head up, grateful for the spark of anger he felt, for it helped assuage his growing fear.

"Not exactly." A fleeting smile curved Tamisk's lips. "And what need, really, when the expression on your face tells me so much?"

Perfect, he thought with disgust.

A flash of yellow light streaked out of the pool, drawing his attention back to the bowl. He fixed his gaze on the water, and as he watched, a nightmare vision floated up from the shallow depths.

Chapter 16

The nightmare was Caradoc, lying on a beach with a dreamstone-encrusted sword thrust through his chest, his blood pooling in the sand. Caradoc the betrayer. Caradoc, his murderer.

Morgan stiffened.

"Ah, so you recognize the man," Tamisk murmured, sounding pleased.

Morgan did naught but stare into the water, a thousand emotions flooding through him, dragging a thousand memories in their wake.

In all his drunken journeys he'd never seen the Boar of Balor, the man who had nearly cut him in two with his blade. The power of that last stroke had pushed him into the time weir. He'd relived the fall more than once while under the influence of Carillion wine, but mostly he'd seen Dain and Llynya and the agony on their faces as they'd watched him slip from their world into the next.

He'd never seen Caradoc—until now.

The Boar is dead.

In truth, he'd been dead for thousands of years. Morgan had thought about that more than once. But this was fresh death, the blood still pumping out of him.

And whose hand had wielded the blade?

He saw someone reach down and take a gold ring from Caradoc's finger. The band was incised with a circle, the four lines of a square, and inset with a reddish triangle, the same symbol as on Avallyn's amulet.

Deeper and deeper, he thought, feeling a creeping edge of panic seep into his veins.

"Has any part of my life been untouched by magic?" he asked.

"Mayhap." The mage seemed unconcerned, though the question burned a hole in Morgan's mind.

"What of free will?" he demanded, looking up. "Have I had none?"

"You're a thief, aren't you?" Tamisk replied with undisguised distaste. "The Red Book said nothing of that."

"He has the blood of the Starlight-born from Stept Agah's line," Avallyn interjected. "Did the Red Book say anything of that?"

The mage stared hard at Morgan, his interest obviously piqued.

"Stept Agah? Did you deep-scent him, then?" Tamisk asked his daughter.

"Aye," Avallyn said.

"After the wine was out of his system, I hope."

"Twenty-four hours after I gave him your potion."

"Good," the mage said succinctly, and in the next moment, Morgan felt Tamisk's invasion of his mind. 'Twas no light step like Avallyn's but a bounding leap that set him staggering. Avallyn grabbed him as he was nearly knocked off his feet. It was all over in a second.

"So he does," Tamisk said, not looking at all as though he were going to faint from the effort.

Left feeling slightly nauseous and thoroughly trammeled, Morgan found his balance and enough wherewithal to glare. "Bastard," he ground out. "I can trace my family's lineage back two hundred years to Gruffudd ap Cynan without once coming across anyone named Stept Agah."

Tamisk appeared nonplussed. "To get to Stept Agah, you would have to go back to the end of the Dark Age of the Starlight-born, an un-likely journey even for you, time-rider."

"So you didn't know?" Avallyn asked her father.

"No." The mage considered Morgan. "Perhaps 'tis of no import. Blood alone does not make the man, as any king with sons can tell you."

"And perhaps it is the difference between life and death for all of us," Avallyn said.

"Stept Agah had many children, with the last child born from Ar-ianrod's line after his death." A frown marred the mage's smooth brow. "We know that line was carried only by the females until Mychael ab Arawn was born, and the other branches spawned as many cowards as heroes."

Morgan had his sword drawn and laid against the mage's neck be-fore he finished his sentence.

"Give me back my captain," he demanded through gritted teeth.

"You're fast," the mage said thoughtfully. "Very fast. Journeying through the time weir has given you speed."

"His sword, Scyld, is marked with runes," Avallyn said, neither of them seeming the least concerned that the blade in question was pressed against Tamisk's fair skin.

"So I see," the mage said.

'Twas a slender, elegant neck, and easy enough for Morgan to sever if he so wished—but he didn't wish, and the mage knew it. Nay, he wasn't going to cut Avallyn's father's throat. Not yet.

With a muttered curse at his own rashness, he lowered the sword.

"At last, a sign of wisdom," Tamisk said drolly. "Mayhap all is not yet lost. Come, prince, look into the pool, into the past. I swear no harm will come to your captain, and perhaps you will learn something to in-crease your own odds of survival."

The mage was speaking the truth, and Morgan knew it. He had to look, had to know, and anger was a luxury he could no longer afford.

Neither was fear.

But when he looked, he discovered he had some fears not so easily put aside. Mychael ab Arawn, Ceridwen's twin brother, had taken the ring from Caradoc's hand. The boy looked older than Morgan remem-bered him, and fiercer, far fiercer, with a wildness in his eyes Morgan had never before seen in a man. His face was grimly stark, his hair a wind-whipped mane cut through with the copper blaze of a time-rider. Flying in behind him, looming up out of the darkness of sea and cave, were dragons—beasts of enormous size and magnificent fury, their visages carved in clean, reptilian lines, their screams echoing out of the past. Scales with the shimmer of abalone covered them from their long, bewhiskered snouts to their serpentine tails, one in crimson limned in shades of blood and flame, the other in pale green underscored with watery blue.

"Ddrei Goch," Avallyn whispered by his side. "Ddrei Glas."

"The dragons of Merioneth," Morgan said, fascinated despite the purely primal fear that told him any flying serpent-lizard that big was a monster, far more so than *pryf*.

The dragons had teeth, incredible teeth. Fangs the size of ship's masts bracketed their jaws. Flames roiled out of their gaping mouths, and smoke trailed from their nostrils.

"They live in the White Palace?" he asked, the truth of what he'd been told almost impossible to believe when faced with the beasts themselves.

"In Dragonmere," Avallyn answered, "the last remnant of Mor Sarff, the Serpent Sea that lies beneath the carn. There are always only two, genetic replicas of the first dragons conjured in Ysaia's cauldron."

" 'Tis a name she chooses to forget, priestess," Tamisk interjected in a pained voice. "A name the wise refuse to speak. 'Tis better to call her Rhayne, as she has chosen for the incarnations of this Age."

"Nothing is forgotten in Claerwen," Avallyn said. "And so Rhayne knows."

"Rhayne?" Morgan asked, a faint memory tugging at his mind. In the pool, the dragons beat their wings against the dark sky, and he swore he felt a gust of wind blow across his face. He nearly retreated. These were the beasts he was supposed to fight with against Dharkkum? Gods, he'd never heard of anything more insane. Yet there was Mychael ab Arawn, the look on his face telling Morgan he knew exactly what was coming down out of the sky behind him.

"The White Bitch of the Dangoes," Avallyn explained.

"And your threat to the Lyran," he said, remembering how she'd invoked the name Rhayne and the Lyran had backed off.

"Aye. The Lyrans remembered her wrath when they would have destroyed the last of a rival species, and they know where their bones lie in the walls of Claerwen. The White Bitch still strikes fear in their hearts."

Morgan barely heard her explanation. The dragons were descending on Mychael, dwarfing him with their size. No Saint George's beast of a quarter ton, they were sea dragons with dorsal fins rising ten feet off the crowns of their heads and cascading down their backs. Their wings were like thunderclouds, with a single claw at the apex of each scapular arch. The long fangs gracing each side of their upper jaws were curved scythes of pure ivory running green with seawater.

"Mychael," he whispered, a warning that was ten thousand years too late. Smoke bellowed out of the beasts' razor-toothed maws with every breath, smoke shot through with flashes of flame. Mychael had to feel the heat—yet the boy's attention was firmly fixed somewhere beyond Morgan's sight.

The dragons screeched in fury, flying in closer, their wingtips grazing Mychael, but to no effect. Mychael stood like a tower of rock on the beach, resolute, as if receiving only his due—until the dragons roared, a rumbling, all-consuming sound rising from the depths of their wyrmish souls. Mychael responded, opening his mouth and answering the call, lifting his sword into the light of the cliffs guarding the gates of time. Aye, he lifted his sword and roared, a sound no less gut-wrenched than the dragons', a call to blood, a primal scream of fury that belonged in no man's mouth. And within that fearsome, chilling roar, Morgan felt his own blood catch fire and race through his veins, urging him on to the fight. A fight to the death.

His breath came hard. His hand tightened on his sword, and he felt Scyld grow warm and come alive with power—and he feared he would go, that nothing could keep him from the battle awaiting him in the past. No fear of time worms or the weir; even the Warmonger was as nothing compared to the insistent, blood-churning lure of the dragons' cries. They were his, and he was theirs, their destinies entwined beyond fate.

Closer and closer the dragons flew, louder and louder they roared, until Morgan could feel nothing beyond the beat of their wings and the scorching heat arising with each ear-shattering screech. Sweat poured down his body, steam rose from his clothes, and still he couldn't tear his gaze away from the pool. Within its watery depths Mychael was being consumed, his clothes giving way to tatters in the growing maelstrom, the blaze in his hair seeming to come alive. Smoke and flames swirled around him, fed by the bellows of the dragons' breath and turning the sand at his feet into glass.

The blaze of flames streaked up Mychael's body. Morgan watched,

horrified, as the fire pouring out of the beasts and the fire engulfing Mychael became one, a single inferno into which the man vanished—only to
be reborn in the red dragon.

The giant animal tossed and twisted in the flames, its wings flapping, its cry strangled in its throat, until Mychael's voice became its own,
the scream of Mychael's fury breaking free from the mighty jaws to ring
out against the cliffs and shore. The maelstrom of fire ran back into the
roiling waves of Mor Sarff, and a wash of gray flooded into the beast's
golden eyes, the beginning of a thousand shifts of shape confirming the
frightful transition taking place by the dark sea.

The man was gone, and so was the dragon, and in their place was
a creature far different than either. It looked like a dragon, but the heart
beating inside its scaly breast was that of a man, Mychael ab Arawn's.
Morgan felt its rhythm match his own beating heart's.

"Fight with me." Mychael's voice, edged with a dragonish rasp,
spoke out from the pool. *"Fight with me so that we may live!"*

'Twas a call to arms, a call for the death of Dharkkum, for the
great devourer to be devoured by Ddrei Goch and Ddrei Glas. Mychael's
sword had fallen to the shore, and another hand came into view to lift it
up. Morgan knew who grasped the blade before the pool showed him
Llynya's face. She'd been wounded. Blood ran from a bandage on her
arm and from a fresh cut marking her from elbow to wrist. Sweat dampened her brow. Her hair was a tangled riot of braids and twists stuck
through with green leaves. Behind her was chaos, the coming of
Dharkkum, a blanket of whirling threads warped in darkness.

The undulating vortex flattened and flowed through the cavern of
the Serpent Sea, and everything it touched was consumed, stretched to an
excrutiating thinness before being dissolved into Dharkkum's black core.

'Twas Pan-shei again, but worse, far worse. No malfunctioning
camera or comstation blacked out the harrowing truth of Dharkkum's
destructive powers. Terror made the elfin maid's face stark, but she did
not cower in the face of such dreadful death. She lifted Mychael's blade
with a cry of *Khardeen!* and urged the dragons on to their duty.

Ddrei Glas, the smaller green dragon, dropped out of the air,
swooping in behind the sprite. With a leap, Llynya was upon the
dragon's back, the sword still held high to lead the beasts into the fray.

As if sensing the coming of its foes, the blanketing vortex rippled
backward along its length, wiping out half a score of Light-elves on the
beach. Farther down around the headland, a strange sight met Morgan's

eyes—skraelings, dozens of them, fighting their way down to the sea and dying in the swart grip of Dharkkum.

Sweet Jesu! Skraelings in his own time.

'Twas a revelation he had little time to dwell upon, for the battle was engaged. Threads spiraled out of the darkness to ensnare warriors and snatch away their lives. The dragons retaliated with fire, flames unlike any Morgan had ever seen—ephemeral washes of color that stained the ether of the beasts' scorching breath, all of it coalescing into a white-hot core of painfully bright, darkness-eating light.

With each advance the dragons made, the light grew brighter and hotter, until Morgan felt the heat of it licking at the air around him, more intense than what he'd felt before. Dharkkum flowed forward to meet the beasts, skimming along the face of the damson cliffs, stealing light from the crystalline wall and picking off soldiers, and growing larger with each death.

Then, in a sudden about-face, Dharkkum retreated, imploding upon itself and drawing back into the deeper reaches of Mor Sarff. Like an arrow, it shot back into the labyrinth of fjords and tunnels fronting the blackened sea. Enraged, the dragons followed, and in the lost land of the deepest caverns, the true storm broke.

Morgan witnessed the ferocity, the tearing asunder of both the light and the darkness as time sped by in the pool, days falling away in the space of minutes. Clouds of smoke covered the sea and scoured the cliffs; the dragons' fiery breath flashed like lightning through the banks of endless night. In his mind, Morgan knew the dragons had won in the end, for he was alive and standing on Earth, though 'twas a wasted shell of the green paradise it had been—but in his heart, he feared for Mychael and Llynya. Each glimpse he caught of the sprite showed her weakening, her clothing scorched, her face haggard with exhaustion, the sword she wielded growing too heavy for her to bear. He feared she would soon die.

For Mychael, his fears were of a different nature. Not that he would die, but that he would forever be trapped in his dragon form, a beast and no longer a man.

At the dawn of the fifth day, the tide of battle shifted in the dragons' favor, with Dharkkum retreating ever faster and ever deeper into the earth. As the dragons raced in pursuit, a voice could be heard rising out of the depths.

"Heln heln criy-darr . . . ba!"

A woman's voice, growing stronger.

"Ailfinn Mapp," Avallyn whispered.

"Aye," Tamisk confirmed. "Chanting the Doom of Dharkkum."

Morgan watched the dragons chase the darkness through tunnels carved from the mother stone of the planet, until a great, broken wall rose up out of an even greater cavern. 'Twas the underground mountain of Kryscaven Crater, with its broken western face made of rock crystal, deep purple rock crystal shattered into thousands of jagged-edged boulders.

Five people stood on the crater's silvery floor beyond the broken wall, a rainbow-hued fire blazing at their feet. 'Twas their protection, Morgan knew, because Dharkkum swirled all around them, the black threads twisting and turning, the vortex shuddering as it was pulled into the crater, and yet the five were untouched by the darkness.

"*Luenn luenn criy-darr . . . ba!*" The woman's voice rose, and an edge of darkness fell in upon itself and disappeared into the crater. It would soon escape, Morgan was sure, unless the old woman could rebuild the crystal wall.

Ddrei Goch roared out of the tunnel first after Dharkkum and leveled a mighty blast at the shreds of smoke snaking through the shattered crystals on the passage floor. The smoke vanished, consumed by the fire, and the purple stone turned to molten glass in the heat. Ailfinn changed her chant into a soft murmuring, and the fiery purple rivers began running together into pools. The words were unintelligible at a distance, but the effect was immediate, with the pools washing together into a tide-racked lake a hundred yards across. As her chant grew in strength, the tide rose, flowing up onto the wall and cooling into hard rock.

The dragons breathed again, a fierce expulsion of flame, and more of the crystal boulders melted. Once again Ailfinn drew the molten tide up onto the wall with her chant.

'Twas a mighty task she had taken upon herself. With each word, she dragged Dharkkum in deeper and built the wall higher, until it became obvious to Morgan that she was walling herself and the four inside.

The woman knew. She had to know what she was doing, and what kind of death Dharkkum would deal them. Yet as he watched, the wall grew higher and higher. 'Twas a nightmare fate far exceeding the vision of Caradoc in the pool. How long, he wondered, would the rainbow fire last? And how was such a sacrifice made when hope must die with the last embers of the flames?

The five were doomed.

His gaze slid over them, their scorched clothes, their faces hardened by determination, yet weary with despair: the old woman with her cloud of long white hair and rune-marked cloak, a book held open in her hands; a Night Watcher—to his surprise—a Sha-shakrieg recognizable by the whorls of fighting threads on his arms and his desert countenance; a Quicken-tree man he faintly remembered, Wei was his name; and another of the Quicken-tree he remembered all too well—Rhuddlan, King of the Light-elves. 'Twas the last of the five, though, that caused his breath to catch and his heart to seize up with fear. 'Twas Owain, his own man, a Welshman with no business dying in the midst of magic and horror.

Owain had been his captain in the past, his responsibility, and Morgan had led him into a world of enchantment when he'd committed his small force to the taking of Balor. The man had been like a father to him, and he'd died a death of terrors—stark, raving terrors by the wild look in Owain's eyes and the tears streaking down his cheeks. The sheer dread and fear on the man's face stripped Morgan's emotions to the bone. There was no defense for leading his men into a situation so far outside their comprehension. Owain would have bravely died by the sword in any battle with the Norman English, the warrior's death he'd expected, but Morgan's choices had reduced him to less than a warrior, to less than what Owain would ever have considered a man.

He'd deserved so much better for his loyalty. He'd deserved better for following his prince.

A numbing wave of guilt forced Morgan to look away.

"You can save him and all the Lost Five by going back," Tamisk murmured, and Morgan suddenly understood why the mage had brought him to the tower.

"It's the old woman, the priestess, you want, isn't it?"

"And her book, the *Elhion Bhaas Le,*" Tamisk admitted. "It is of the most importance."

"And the others?" Morgan demanded. "Why did she take so many with her?"

"So many?" Tamisk repeated blandly. "There were only four. Ailfinn's ordeal in the oubliette at Rastaban had left her weak. She needed the strength of their life force to sustain her, mayhap for eternity. Believe me, if there had been a hundred at hand, she would have taken them all."

Tamping down his anger with himself, Morgan replied, "I was

won to the cause with Mychael's first dragon cry." But 'twas true that seeing Owain took away even the possibility of doubt, or of hesitation when the time came. He had no choice but to go back through the weir and breach the prison Ailfinn Mapp had made for herself and her companions—and for Dharkkum.

If he could.

"Won, aye. But ready?" Tamisk asked, and in the pool the dragons roared.

Shaken, Morgan looked back at the water. Flames shot out of the beasts more immense and fierce than before, with more hot white core than haloing rainbow colors. He stepped back, feeling the shocking heat of the blast like a violent desert wind. The dragons' next blast licked up the sides of the bowl and broke free of the vision, dancing upon the water in a scorching conflagration. He retreated again, wary of the mage's power, but there was no escape. Tendrils of the dragons' white-hot fire leaped out of the mazer and snaked around his arms, cutting him like razor-sharp blades. Morgan gasped with the pain.

"Stop it, Tamisk!" he heard Avallyn cry out. "He is no Dragonlord."

"No, he is not," the mage agreed coldly. "He is only a man with the fate of the world in his hands. If there be any chance for him to live, let him be tempered by dragonfire, and let us see who forged his runechased blade . . . *Scyld*."

The mage no sooner invoked the sword's name than the flames snaked down Morgan's arms and leapt onto the sword's grip, turning it into a searing brand in his hand. Blood followed the fire snake's path, running from his wounds. The wide ivory rings fitted around the sword's tang cracked and crumbled to the grass, smoking. The metal on the grip turned soft, then liquid, melting away between Morgan's fingers in agonizing streams of molten gold and silver, burning him to the bone. Yet his fingers remained whole.

Pain dragged him to his knees, and he doubled over, a silent scream lodged in his throat. *Gods save him!* How could his flesh not be charred to ashes? What magic could create such vile torment?

He tried to let go of the sword, but 'twas melded to his palm. When the last of the precious metals poured out onto the blade, there was naught left of the grip but a burning rod of sky blue crystal with a violet core.

Gasping for breath, in agony, Morgan stared at the sword as if seeing it for the first time. Gold had run into every rune, making them glitter and shine. The silver had hardened in beads along the length of the blade's channels, giving the sword an odd aspect. The cutting edges were stained a smoky dark purple.

"Edge of Sorrow," he heard Tamisk say. "The gridelin poison conjured in the Waste from the sap of the bia tree."

"Release him, Tamisk," Avallyn cried. "He is Claerwen's, and as a Priestess of the Bones, I demand it!"

"In time" was the mage's reply.

In time, Morgan would die of the pain. In time, he was certain his hand would char and he would suffocate from the searing heat.

"A Magia Blade," Tamisk murmured. "Do you not see it, priestess?"

"I see you hurting him for no reason."

"No reason?" the mage exclaimed. "How else is a Magia Blade to be revealed except by the hand that wields it?"

"It will do us no good, if he's dead or—" She stopped, not finishing her thought.

"Or broken?" Tamisk finished for her. "Is that your fear? That I'll break him with one test of valor? And what good would he do you then, Lady Avallyn, when you stand before Kryscaven Crater and contemplate the unleashing of Dharkkum? Will he stand then? Or flee?"

Flee, Morgan silently screamed, if he had any sense, but sense was quickly being burned out of him. He would flee now, if he could, but pain held him in its fiery grip, and he could not move.

"No?" Tamisk asked him, one eyebrow lifted, his eyes wickedly bright and green. Green. The color of Old Earth. "Are you so sure?"

The bastard *could* read his mind.

"Well, let us see," the mage said, turning to Avallyn. "If you would not have him tempered, Priestess, then take the dragonfire upon yourself." Tamisk made a small gesture, and a ball of fire burst into flames at her feet.

"No!" Morgan roared, leaping up and swinging his blade in a killing blow against the mage and his magic.

The blow never landed, but was stopped in midair by a lift of Tamisk's hand and a spoken word. Morgan's arm trembled with the force of power pushing the blade back from the mage's body. Sweat ran down his face, stinging his eyes. The fire at Avallyn's feet vanished, and the fire in the crystal grip was gone suddenly as well, and the burning pain. Scyld was yet a sword again, albeit one far different than before.

Morgan knew dreamstone, and dreamstone was Scyld's core. The light pulsed from its violet heart and streamed through his fingers.

"Your instincts are good, prince," Tamisk said, releasing him with another gesture and word.

Scyld fell to his side, its point embedding in the dirt, his arm too tired to hold it. With his other hand, he wiped the sweat from his face. His gaze was riveted to the mage, while in his mind, he debated whether or not to kill the bastard.

He could.

With Scyld, he could. He knew it, and his eyes bored into Tamisk, willing him to read his mind yet one more time and see what truth he may.

"Perhaps," the mage conceded, "but you have far more deadly enemies than me, Morgan ab Kynan, and we are all best served if you deal with them. Don't you agree?"

Ignoring Tamisk, Morgan turned to Avallyn. "Are you hurt?" His voice was hoarse, barely intelligible.

"I am unharmed, dread lord," she said softly, looking stricken. Her face was pale, her eyes wide. "I fear I have not served you well to bring you here."

"No." He shook his head. "I am served in this."

He hated what they faced and loathed the mage for giving him such excruciating pain, remnants of which were flashing beneath his skin and shooting up his arm—but he was served.

Dragons.

"I want to see them," he said to Tamisk, and the mage nodded.

"They await you in the past."

"And Mychael ab Arawn?"

Tamisk shrugged, a slight, graceful lift of one shoulder. "He survived the battle, but the cost was high in terms of the years of his life. For certes Llynya of the Light-elves will still be living when you return to Wales. Their fight with Dharkkum in the Fifth Age did not take so much from her. Of course, she was Yr Is-ddfwn, from Rhayne's own line of the Starlight-born, the purest line of descent for the fair folk. Mychael's blood was much mixed with that of men, with his strongest line coming down through the priestesses."

Morgan wiped his face again and returned his gaze to the pool. Instantly, he felt the lure of the beasts. His blood sang when they roared, and the fiery remnants of pain became easier to bear, for 'twas dragonfire.

Tamisk's gift.

"The weir will be destabilized if you are successful. There is little chance that you will be able to return—but mayhap once more through the weir is all you'll wish."

Morgan slanted the mage a considering glance, meeting his too-green eyes.

Tamisk smiled faintly. "Neither Palinor nor the High Priestess of Claerwen will thank me for awakening the dragonfire in you, but the Priestesses of the Bones have forever known more of death than of men."

Morgan looked to Avallyn and saw her stricken expression turn to one of wary concern—as well it should. The barriers had been destroyed. The decision had been made, whether 'twas by Tamisk's magic or a true writ of fate. He would have her.

"She is a willing sacrifice," Tamisk said, "but I trust that you will put her life before yours."

"Aye," Morgan answered, not taking his eyes off her.

"And that you will protect her to your dying breath, and if the sword so allows, even beyond your death."

"Aye." There was no hesitation. She was safer with him than any-where in the galaxy or beyond. And for what she must do and where she must go, to the past to battle Dharkkum, he was the one, the only one, who had a chance of bringing her back alive.

"And that her quest will be yours, the banner for you to take up whether she lives or dies."

"Aye." But she would live. She had to live. They were bound by fate, and blood, and fire, dragonfire, and she was his. Avallyn Le Severn, Princess of the White Palace and Priestess of the Bones, was his in this world and the last.

Chapter 17

Avallyn sensed the change in him, and it was not one she welcomed. She now had what she had professed to want, the Prince of Time committed to Claerwen's goals. He would journey through the weir and return to his own time. He knew now what danger they would face, and he was willing to face it. But the cost to her was greater than she had foreseen.

The balance of power had shifted.

She was no longer in charge.

"What dragon's fire have you given him, Tamisk?" she asked. "He is not a Dragonlord. Nor is he meant to be."

"Not even I can confer dragonfire where it is not already present," Tamisk said. "You see the Magia Blade in his hand. Dragonlord or nay, the sword is his, and we should thank the gods it is so."

"So Stept Agah's line ran true?"

"True enough, it seems, for our purposes. All may not be lost."

His words sent a chill down her back, reminding her of her suspicions when she'd deep-scented Morgan.

"You thought it was?" she asked. The outcome aside, the journey itself was too fraught with danger for it to be embarked upon as a fool's mission.

"I have wondered," the mage admitted, "and I have doubted, and of late my biggest doubt was that you could even lay your hands upon such an . . . unexpected prince, let alone bring him to me. In truth, I did all that I could to have another sent in your place, an Ilmarryn maid whose magic is less naive and whose loyalty to the White Palace supersedes that to Claerwen. Your mother was adamant in your favor, though, and so we are here. But come. Time is short."

With a gesture for them to follow, he turned and walked out of the glade. Avallyn hazarded a glance at Morgan and was again unnerved. The differences in him were subtle, but telling. The white blaze in his raven black hair shone brighter. His eyes were an even deeper shade of blue, like the night-dark sea of Dragonmere by torchlight. The energy of his life force nearly arced off him. For ten years he had lived in her world, a stranger surviving by his wits and thievery. Now he was going back to his. Tamisk had shown him his purpose in the pool, and in purpose was power. More than the dragonfire that had tempered his hand and revealed his sword, 'twas purpose she saw lighting the depths of his eyes—and she instinctively felt that she was part of that purpose, a great part. Verily, her sense of alarm grew with every heated look he sent her way.

Reason enough to be unnerved, and to be wary. His kisses were wondrous, but Palinor had forbidden any congress between them, a fact he had already dismissed as meaningless. Yet mayhap her mother had been right. Mayhap to mate with him was not in her best interest, despite the wonder of his kisses. 'Twas no loss of virginity she feared, but further loss of power. In his current state, Morgan would consume her.

Sweet Mother, what woman wouldn't be leery? The High Priestesses of Claerwen were always virgin, and Avallyn knew a part of Palinor resented the sacrifice she'd been chosen to make—to breed a daughter to save the world, and with an Ilmarryn Magia Lord, her last choice, if there had been any choices to be made; and to always be relegated to the second tier of priestesses, to know she could never rise any higher, despite her talents, her intelligence, and her yearning to rule.

Palinor had not been given a choice, but Avallyn could make one.

Palinor had forbidden her to have any sort of physical intimacy with the Prince of Time, and she expected to be obeyed. Avallyn, though, had already taken it upon herself to kiss him. She could as easily take it upon herself to choose power over a man's love—if 'twas love she saw burning in his gaze. Her inexperience gave her no way of gauging the difference between love and lust. Perhaps the dragonfire had ignited some beastly desire in his heart that was far outside the bounds of a love-filled joining.

The thought heightened her alarm and sent her hurrying after Tamisk. Best then to choose power, she assured herself, and save herself from ravishment.

Morgan smiled to himself, sheathing Scyld. Avallyn was thinking too hard. He could see it on her face. What was to happen between them was inevitable and not to be feared. What was to happen to them in the past, though, was a different matter. If he was truly to be her protector, the greatest protection he could offer would be to leave her behind when he went through the weir. He would have Llynya to help him, and possibly Mychael, and Owain and the mage, if he and Ailfinn Mapp had survived their years in Kryscaven Crater. If not, he would have the old woman's book.

Aye, it all came back to the books. The mage's, which Tamisk wanted, and Ceridwen's, the Red Book which had brought him to such a pass.

Tamisk had said time was short. Morgan felt it as well, but there were things he had to learn before they left the mage's tower, especially if he was going back alone.

He brushed aside an overhanging branch and saw another copper orb skimming through the leaves. Two more followed, drifting down from higher up, one spinning in from the outer expanse of the tree, all of them seeming to trail after Tamisk.

Or not seeming, for when Morgan caught up to the mage, the orbs were lined up behind him, hovering in midair in front of an ancient spherical contraption Morgan remembered from Dain's time in the tower. In the twelfth century, no one save Dain had dared the Hart's eyrie for fear of the mechanical mystery lodged within its curved walls. Facing it now, Morgan realized the wariness had been well deserved. A strange hum of energy emanated from the sphere, making the hair on the back of his neck rise. The dreamstone encrusting its surface glowed with an odd light.

"Do not be alarmed," Tamisk said, reaching for another of the orbs hanging off the pedestal.

Morgan didn't think Tamisk could do too much more to alarm him after what had happened at the scrying pool.

He was wrong.

"Llagor, Rakis," the mage murmured, releasing the orb into the air.

The energy hum instantly rocketed upward to a far more disturbing degree. Morgan felt it pulsing through his veins.

"Once Ailfinn's book is retrieved," Tamisk said, raising his voice to be heard above the hum, "Avallyn must bring it back to the Hart and place it in the chamber that lies within the sphere's pedestal."

"Why Avallyn?" he asked.

"Because her blood is the price of Earth's salvation."

There was no equivocation, only a blunt statement of an unacceptable truth. His thought to leave her behind was no good.

"How much blood?" Morgan asked, holding himself in check, his sword hand tightening into a fist at his side.

"A small measure to open the chamber each time we set a book into the pedestal," Tamisk said without bothering to glance in his direction. The mage's attention was fully on the orbs. He sent another spinning into the air, then another, and another, until there were eight in all, each with a name. The energy leapt to new heights with each release.

Morgan was rooted to the spot where he stood, his whole body— right down to the cells in his brain—in thrall to the rhythmic pulses coming from the sphere.

Tamisk did look at Avallyn as he pulled three small vials out of his pocket. The potions inside were deep red, her blood. Of them all, she seemed least affected by the sphere's force field. For himself Morgan wasn't sure how much more he could take.

One by one, the five newly released orbs finished their paths and lined up with the others, until all eight had formed a ring, a spinning wheel on the surface of the pedestal. As the ring spun, a portal opened and revealed a bracket and a hand's-width tunnel bored out of the crystal on the sphere. Tamisk set the vials into the bracket as if placing them in a vault and looked to Avallyn again.

"Priestess?" He extended his hand to her. "Will you open the chamber yourself and save the vials for my use?"

Her expression grimly resigned, Avallyn stepped forward.

Morgan caught her with his hand on her arm. "You don't have to do this."

"But I do," she said simply—and he knew it to be true.

Whatever love they found was secondary to their purpose, and perhaps of all the truths he'd been forced to face, Morgan resented that most of all. Dharkkum and the wormhole terrified him, but those were his battles. This thing with Avallyn's blood was outside of him, and he didn't want any part of her outside of him—especially if it could bring her harm.

Steeling himself for what might happen, he watched her approach the armillary sphere and put her hand and arm through the spinning wheel and into the crystal tunnel. All of her muscles tensed, and a sharp gasp was wrung from her.

Morgan stepped forward, but was stopped by Tamisk taking hold of him.

"It's a small amount they take," the mage said, not looking away from Avallyn. "And the prize is well worth the price. Look."

Morgan did, and watched in wonder as a window opened in the pedestal, a window of light; behind the window, a chamber was spinning. Round and round it went until Avallyn removed her arm, and it coasted to a stop.

He looked at her, and with a nod she reassured him of her well-being. Then he looked at the chamber and what it held.

Books. One he recognized, the *Fata Ranc Le,* the Red Book of Doom. The other two were equally as grand, their worn covers marked in gold, their bindings reinforced with silver plackets.

Over the course of the next hour, Tamisk unraveled the mystery of Nemeton's celestial sphere, revealing to Morgan the tower's secrets. Indeed, their salvation did lie with the books. There were seven. Three were already locked in place, and one was to be taken by Tamisk from the Warmonger's stronghold—Morgan was profoundly grateful the task to enter Magh Dun had not fallen to him. One was to be given by the dragon conjurer, Rhayne; and the last was to be recovered from the grip of Dharkkum and set into the telluric pedestal.

That task complete, hell would be conquered. The earth would be saved.

So simple.

So fraught with potential disaster and the specter of failure.

With due ceremony, Tamisk put the *Gratte Bron Le* into place, the Orange Book of Stone from the Queen of Deseillign. It was the fourth book, Morgan noted, and there were still three vials of Avallyn's blood left in the sphere, one for each of the remaining books. If he could get the friggin' *Elhion Bhaas Le,* he didn't need her to open the chamber. He could put the Indigo Book in place himself.

There was relief with the realization, nearly enough to overcome the sense of loss.

When Tamisk finished, he replaced the copper orbs on their gracefully curved rods, and Morgan and Avallyn watched the portal close on the chamber housing the four books. The sudden cessation of the force field left Morgan feeling ungrounded, a feeling ameliorated by the mellifluous sound of Tamisk's voice.

Violet, blue, orange, and red, the mage said. The books were part of a rainbow like the rainbow of dragonfire. 'Twas all light, the colors of white light.

"Remember," Tamisk continued. "The chamber is timeless, a small tear in the space-time continuum. Like Dharkkum, it exists outside the bounds of physics. The books I set here in this age will be there for you in the past. You have but to fulfill your fate."

Morgan felt the weight of Scyld along his back. He knew himself to be an average man possessed of some specialized skills. Before him, Scyld had belonged to Dain Lavrans, a thoroughly unaverage man in any and all aspects, and Morgan couldn't help but wonder if a mistake had been made on the rim that day, if Dain had been the one meant to fall instead of himself.

Yet Scyld's grip had melted away within his grasp, and the sword now fit his hand better than before. Its weight was perfectly balanced, the feel of it more like an extension of his arm and will than a separate weapon.

Above them, the sun neared its zenith in the desert sky, the light streaming down in shafts of yellow and pale green through a domed ceiling formed of sheets of glass and rusted iron.

Tamisk glanced upward, and a shadow of wings passed over his face. "The time has come for me to leave," he said.

"To Magh Dun?" Avallyn asked.

"Aye. Sept riders will come for you at dusk and take you to Claerwen. I regret that there is not time for you to journey to the White

Palace. As it is, I advise you not to tarry long in the palace of bones. The forces of darkness are gathering, and our world cannot hold forever against their strength. The sooner you are to the past, the better."

"And you go south alone?" Avallyn asked.

A wry smile lifted a corner of Tamisk's mouth.

"Nay, priestess. I will have my army. The foul witch, Vishab, has left her precious book unguarded in the black fortress, thinking to keep it safe with her cauldron spells. She travels into the Waste with her master, searching for you, and even now leaves her stench upon the air of Craig Tagen. It is time for me to strike."

"What of my captain?" Morgan asked.

"The boy sleeps in innocence, not enchantment. When his weariness is gone, he will awaken."

Another shadow darted across Tamisk's face, as of a bird soaring, and then another, and another, followed swiftly by the sound of beating wings.

Morgan looked up. Crows were flocking to the tower, a great murder of them alighting on the domed roof and blocking out the sun.

"Do not falter when you face Kryscaven Crater," Tamisk warned. "Set the dragons to their task and they will crack the crystal wall. Let them deal with Dharkkum. Your task is to get the book and bring it here."

Neatly said, Morgan thought, though in his experience 'twas difficult to divorce oneself from chaos when it was running rampant all around. The fact would especially hold true with a devouring chaos like Dharkkum.

"Step lightly in Magh Dun, lord father," Avallyn said to the mage.

Tamisk's smile broadened. "Indeed, daughter, I plan to not step at all."

He turned and walked away, taking the trail that wound round the oak. As he slipped from the light into shadows, a soft mist began filtering down through the leaves and branches, and Morgan would swear he saw the mage's cloak shift and ruffle into a robe of silvery gray feathers, would swear the mage lifted his arms at his sides like a raptor's wings. Then he was gone, and as one the crows lifted off the roof and took to the desert sky.

Morgan walked partway down the trail and knelt to check the mage's tracks. Where the soft indentation of boot prints disappeared, the long-toed footprint of a bird began—three toes forward, one back, and a talon mark for each.

God save him. 'Twas magic even more strange than the sword grip melting in his hand.

He rose to his feet and found Avallyn beside him.

"Gyrfalcon," she said, kneeling and touching her fingers to the track. "We have them in the Lost Forest." She stood and gave him a quick, nervous glance. "Come along. We should tend your wounds."

"Aye," he agreed. The dragonfire had cut through his clothes and marked his skin, more like a knife than fire. The wounds had bled, but were not so deep. The sleeves of his jacket were in ribbons, though, and his shirt had fared no better.

"Tamisk has a shelter a little farther on," she said, starting down the trail. "There will be *rasca* and food, and mayhap a tunic."

He let her have the lead. The mist deepened as they walked, whorls of it rolling down the trunk of the great tree and spinning out onto the trail. She still wore her priestess robes, a straight white shift falling from her shoulders, her hooded cloak closed at her throat with her gold-and-garnet brooches. After the fires and dragon screams in the pool, and without the melodic sound of Tamisk's voice, the tower seemed strangely silent, an oasis of otherworldly tranquillity. The wind still blew, gentle gusts rising and falling on the air, setting the mist aswirl and rustling the leaves. The trail beneath their feet grew mossy, silencing their steps, and Morgan felt as if he and Avallyn were passing through a faerie realm.

"Listen," she said, stopping and holding up her hand. "Do you hear it?"

He did: the rushing of a stream, not too far ahead of them.

"Do you have any of his skill with magic?" he asked. The man was her father, though Morgan had seen no signs of familial affection. Tamisk hadn't touched her once, even knowing he would probably never see her again.

Morgan wanted to touch her. He knew how soft she was, and he wanted that softness in his arms.

"No." She shook her head, and her artless tumble of braided and twisted hair brushed across her shoulders. He wanted to reach out and gather a fistful in his hand, to draw her near . . . and kiss her. "I was raised as a priestess in the north and was not brought to the White Palace until I was half grown, too old to become a mage's apprentice, as my mother well knew." She continued walking, and Morgan moved closer to her, keeping pace.

"So you weren't coddled as a youngster?"

"Coddled?" She gave a gasp of near laughter. "No. Most assuredly not." She paused for a second, glancing at him, then asked, "Were you?"

"Oh, aye," he admitted. "Most assuredly yes. My father was a hard man of small holdings and great pride, but he was not unkind, and he was ever proud of his sons."

"You have brothers?" She stopped walking again and looked up at him, her attention fully engaged.

"I had one, an older brother, Damian."

"You must miss him terribly."

"Not as much as I miss others," Morgan admitted, and at the furrowing of her brow, offered a reluctant explanation. "There was no love lost between us once I was grown."

"And before?"

"Before that we were a family much given to hugging and bussing, especially me mum."

"Bussing?"

"Kissing," he said, and watched a soft color wash into her cheeks. She was nervous, aye, but as aware of him as he was of her.

"What happened to put you and your brother at odds?"

A fair question, he thought—a fair difficult question.

"His betrothed took a fancy to me. 'Twas as simple as that." And all he was going to say.

"Not so simple among brothers," she contradicted him.

"No."

"Did you kiss her?"

"A little," he said after a long, uncomfortable moment, hoping he wouldn't have to get any closer to a lie than that.

"Hmmm," she murmured, turning back down the trail and giving him no clue at all about what she thought of his confession.

Morgan caught up to her in two strides. "I didn't seek her out. She took me by surprise, or I might have avoided what followed." 'Twas a weak defense, but the only defense he had for the betrayal that had cost him his brother's goodwill.

"Aye." She nodded sagely. "I can imagine that she was the one seeking you."

"You can?" She could hardly have surprised him more.

"Aye. Any woman would be tempted. You're very like an Orion slave boy. Or so I thought in Racht's canal."

He'd been wrong. There was plenty of room for surprise left. Morgan didn't know whether to be offended or intrigued.

"Orion slave boys are considerably younger than I am," he corrected her.

"You were young when your brother's betrothed came to you, weren't you?"

"Sixteen . . . and easily led astray," he added for honesty's sake. "But I am not so young now, and far less easily led anywhere."

" 'Twas dark in the canal and difficult to tell your age."

"Not that dark." He laughed.

Her blush deepened, and Morgan found himself waiting expectantly for what she would say next.

"Aye, 'twas dark, but not too dark to see your face, and it took no light to feel your strange power."

"Strange power?" That sounded ominous, and not at all what he wanted her to feel with him.

The stream came into view then, with Tamisk's shelter on the other side, a bower of leafy branches with the trunk of the oak as its main wall. A great wooden chest was pushed against the tree next to a pallet on the ground. The top of the chest held a small brazier, a ewer, and a few dishes and pots, some with food. Dried herbs hung in bunches from the branches making up the bower's roof.

"At first, I thought it was the wine," she said, crossing the plank bridging the stream. Morgan followed, and when they stepped into the shelter's mossy glade, she stopped and spoke again. "Orion slave boys are known to possess powerful carnal charms."

He stood very still, letting the implication of her words sink in. The "carnal charms" of Orion slave boys were legendary. No mere catamites, they were sorcerers of sexual pleasure, trained in a secret colony somewhere in the Orion group before being sent out to be indulged in a life of ease and plenty by obscenely wealthy patrons and matrons throughout the galaxy—but only for a few years, after which they returned to their mistress on Orion and became monks.

Morgan had met one once, at a party in the Old Dominion where Ference Lieq's wife had been slumming with her prize. Even though Morgan was a lover of women, he'd recognized the young man's beauty as exceptional, and he'd recognized the nearly painful aura of sensuality surrounding him, for to look upon the slave boy was to want him. Even Morgan had felt his allure.

"Have you ever actually seen an Orion slave boy?" he asked, somewhat incredulously.

"Once, in the northern desert," she said, and his amazement was complete.

If he'd that kind of effect on her, she was an innocent indeed to have kept her hands off him.

"Not every slave returns to the Orion colony to be ordained into priesthood," she continued. "A few prefer to remain free, and thievery is not an uncommon trade for them to take up as their glamour fades."

Well, that put him in his place. "So you thought I was a rogue slave who had lost his charms?"

"Nay. For what I felt, I feared your charms were still strong."

She'd spoken softly, but Morgan heard every word.

"Avallyn . . ." He brought his hand up to cup her face. Tendrils of mist wove through her hair, twining her blond and ivory braids with ribbons of dew. Her skin shone, begging his kiss.

There had been no mistake on the rim of the weir. This was his place, here with her in this enchanted forest of Llynya's and Tamisk's making. No other man had been meant to be by her side. Not ever. 'Twas him and only him, born ten thousand years in her past.

He started to lower his mouth to hers, but she turned her face aside.

"We cannot, dread lord. I—I cannot."

"Avallyn?"

She shook her head. "I know the Red Book said we were to be as one, and I know I kissed you, but my mother forbade it, and here in the Hart the reason has become clear."

To her, mayhap, he thought, perfectly confused.

"What reason?"

"I can't think when you kiss me, to a disconcerting degree," she confessed, as if 'twas the worst consequence imaginable.

"Then all is as it should be," he assured her. "Too much thinking is the ruination of kissing."

"Aye, and kissing leads to the ruination of a priestess." She pulled away, and he reluctantly let her go.

"Avallyn, I—"

"I'm not a child, lord," she interrupted, turning her back to him and pacing the small glade. "I know about sex and mating, and the bonds of pleasure. The Ilmarryn of the Lost Forest are not shy, and I've seen what happens to priestesses who forget themselves among the fey folk." She brushed against a branch, and a leaf let go of its twig and drifted down to nest in her hair.

He watched her pace, watched another leaf follow the first, and told himself not to panic, that everything would be fine. All he had to do was say something warm and wise and gently honest about how he felt. Then she wouldn't be afraid. For 'twas fear he was hearing in her words.

"They grow wild and go to live in the canopy of the forest with their sylvan lovers," she continued, "their vows forgotten. Claerwen forgotten."

She could be his sylvan lover, Morgan thought, and for certes he'd happily live in the trees to be with her.

" 'Tis a tragedy," she said.

He thought not.

"My mother feared such an end for me, I think, and not just that I would be debauched by a drunken tech-trash thief with no lineage. Your lineage has been proven by the dragonfire, but she would not have me forget my own."

He was still a little confused, but she'd just given him a clue, one he should not have forgotten: Palinor, her death-witch mother of the northern dunes.

"Your mother has no part in this," he told her, utterly certain of at least that much. "She has no place between us. I saw as much the night you gave me Tamisk's potion." 'Twas true, no lover's lie, and she had to know it as well as he. "Whatevever power Palinor wields, 'tis not power over this."

"Nay." She stopped her pacing and faced him, and he saw that she'd been crowned by leaves, their petioles twined into her braids in a verdurous fillet. "There is no White Lady blessing for this union."

Poor chit, he thought. The very tree was giving her to him, as had her father, and still she clung to her mother's beliefs.

She was his. He had no doubts, but she still had to be won, this elfin desert-witch he loved.

Aye, and there was a startling thought. Love. He dragged a hand back through his hair. Of course he would fall in love with a hundred-and-twenty-five-year-old virgin whose mother had forbidden her to have a physical relationship with the man who was her fated destiny, even though she'd waited ten thousand years for him to show up.

"Come. Let me tend your wounds," she said, stepping toward the bower.

"If we need a blessing, we could take your father's," he suggested, following her, the voice of practicality and reason. "I think he married us back by the scrying pool. Or at least I think he married me. Mayhap you are still free to choose, but I am yours."

"I was never free to choose . . . until now," she said, the solemnity of her voice giving him his first real doubts about the eventual outcome of their byplay.

"Ah" was all he could say, at a loss again. She denied him because she finally had the courage to choose, of her own volition and with naught to do with her mother, and she did not choose him. What an odd twist of fate that would be, for her to have dragged him over half the Waste with all her talk of destiny and duty, and the minute he gave in, she changed her mind.

Aye, that would just be bloody, friggin' great—but he'd be damned if he'd let it all come to that.

Unlike some of the youngbloods at Llywelyn's court, he'd found no satisfaction in unrequited love or chivalrous adoration from afar. He'd always liked a woman warm and close, preferably wrapped around him where he and she could enjoy each other to the fullest.

Of course, that had been in the past. In the future, he'd had no such luck. The best sex he'd had in the last ten years had been when the Carillion wine had taken him back into his past to relive a particularly fine bit of swiving, like that first time with Eiryl.

Aye, he'd been there a few times, but Avallyn had taken all that away from him. He was free of the wine, thanks to her, and the price to drink again was too high, even for the pleasure of vividly remembered orgasms a mere ten thousand years old.

Sweet Christe, but he was a sad case.

She gestured for him to sit on the pallet, and after a moment's hesitation, he obliged.

"We have a great and perilous journey ahead, and I'd not have any ill will between us," she said, stopping in the act of lighting the brazier and glancing up with a questioning look. "You do understand, don't you?"

He understood she was mad, simply mad to think he could have kissed her and not want more, simply mad to think they could avoid an act of consummation. Nature simply hadn't designed him that way, and neither had Nature designed her to be satisfied with so little.

"I understand better than you," he said.

The look of relief she cast in his direction proved his point.

After unbuckling Scyld and setting aside his carbine, he took off his burned and tattered jacket. Avallyn went to draw water from the stream, while he stripped out of his shirt. Looking down at his left arm, he swore softly. The dragonfire had not been as unbridled as he'd thought. He'd been marked with the precision of a surgeon's blade, marked with runes. He turned and saw the same marks on his right arm, running from his shoulder down to his wrist.

"*Ammon, bes, ceiul,*" Avallyn murmured, kneeling beside him with the ewer of water. "The runes of refuge."

"Refuge?"

"Protection. For you . . . for us."

"Tamisk cut a spell into my skin?" God's balls, but the mage had taken a lot upon himself.

"Nay. Tamisk's magic is old, but this is far older, ancient beyond memory." She reached up and lightly touched his arm. "The runes of refuge go back to the Dark Age, when the dragons were first born. 'Tis a firespell from Ysaia's cauldron that has marked you thus."

'Twas the finishing touch to his barbaric transformation, he thought ruefully. He had a leaf imprinted on his chest, a blaze in his hair with the mark of a time-rider down his body to match, half a hand's-width of scar tissue wrapped around his torso, and now the scarification of runic incantation running the length of both his arms. He wondered who he'd really been in the past, for what he'd become in the future seemed far more aligned by cosmic purpose.

Avallyn chose some herbs from the array of dried plants hanging from the bower and put them to stew in the two pans she'd nested into the brazier's coals. More than anything, her actions reminded him of Dain. In the Hart, even with all its changes, 'twas easy to feel close to his friend, a man who had been more of a brother to him than his own. Dain had filled the tower with plants, some drying, some growing, some blooming even in winter.

If there was anyone he missed from his past, 'twas Dain Lavrans. They, too, had been bonded in blood and fire, and in sacrifice, Dain's sacrifice. One thing Morgan had been in the past was afraid. As a slave in the Holy Land, lying starved and helpless in the filth of their desert prison, his leg half smashed, the pain more than he could bear, he'd known gut-wrenching fear. A crazy fear, for he'd been as afraid of living as of dying and could not have told his own mother which he would choose, if the choice had been his. It had not. Neither had it been Dain's, yet Dain had chosen and bent the fates to his will that he and Morgan would live.

Fear had been burned out of him during the thousands of years he'd lost in the weir, fear of anything except the wormhole itself. In the future, the creed of survival had replaced fear, a view much broadened by the vision he'd seen in Tamisk's scrying pool. For ten years he'd been concerned only with his and Aja's survival. Avallyn and dragonfire made the whole world his concern—and he felt the weight of it bearing down on him.

He instinctively rose to his feet, needing to move, and rubbed the back of his neck. "How long until your infusions are ready?"

"A few minutes for the tea," she said, looking up. "A bit longer for the healing water."

He nodded in acknowledgment. "I'll be back."

"I'll come with you," she said, quickly standing. "Tamisk has set traps against intruders. You might come across one."

"No." He shook his head. "I'll be careful. I just need a few minutes."

A few minutes to find his balance, he thought, ducking out from under the bower, leaving her behind. A few minutes to think.

He walked along the stream, until he realized that what he wanted was to be in the water, not next to it. At a place where the stream widened into a pool fed by a short fall of water, he pulled off his boots, removed his lasgun, and shucked out of his pants. The stream was cool, but not icy, and when he'd waded out to where the water deepened, he dove all the way in.

Submerged, he kicked toward the waterfall and came up underneath it. Water poured over him, a steady force against the back of his head sluicing down his shoulders. 'Twas a relief, and he stood there for a long time, his feet dug into the sandy bottom, letting the stream wash him, letting the cool water numb the pain of his cuts.

He'd been wrong. He didn't need time to think. He didn't want to think. He only wanted to feel the water flowing over him and around him, to see the green of the overhanging branches and watch the leaves swirling in the eddies of the pool.

Leaning his head back, he filled his mouth with water and spit it out, then stepped out from under the falls and gave his head a shake. Water flew everywhere—but the thoughts he didn't want remained firmly in place.

Dharkkum. Christ save him, how was he to fight such a thing? He looked down at his left arm, turning it into the light. All the blood had been washed away, revealing the true delicacy of the runes. *Ammon, bes, ceiul,* she'd said. 'Twas a small price to pay, if they worked. But he wasn't willing to risk Avallyn's life on a firespell.

Avallyn. A smile curved his mouth. Sweet desert nymph, he'd felt her response to every kiss and knew exactly what it meant, even if she didn't. She had chosen him, aright. Her heart had chosen, her body had chosen.

He would journey to the past without her, but not without loving her. She was ripe for making love, and he couldn't leave her to take an un-shy Ilmarryn as her first lover—and she would. He didn't doubt it, no matter what she said. Nay, for this span of time, she was his, the Prince of Time's.

He turned his other arm into the light, watching the leaves dapple his skin with shadows. He'd been born a prince of Wales. The title had been his by rights of law, but this—his gaze drifted down the neatly incised runes, a dragons' orison—this went deeper than man's laws, deeper than the skin it had been written upon. Everything else in his life paled in comparison to the bond of duty he'd made at Tamisk's pool—everything except Avallyn. She had brought him here. He would have followed no other.

She was part of him. He'd known it when he'd first seen her in Racht. Then, he'd thought she was part of his past. Now he knew she was part of him for all time.

Kicking off again, he floated out away from the waterfall and rolled onto his back. Mist swirled through the rays of sunlight streaming down from the glassed-in roof. Stretching his arms out, he felt something hit his right hand. When he turned to look, he realized the fragility of Tamisk's magic. 'Twas more than sunlight streaming down from the top of the tower. Sand was leaking in, trickles of it falling into the pool in an intermittent golden stream.

Not even the Hart would hold forever, not even with magic. What the darkness didn't devour, the desert would bury in sand. Lowering his hand, he let the golden grains wash away. There were no fish in the stream, no minnows, just as there weren't any birds or squirrels in the oak tree, and Morgan found himself hoping the Lost Forest wasn't as barren. What use to save a forest, if it was silent?

You think me silent? A voice, low and resonant, rippled across his skin.

Morgan stilled.

Had Llynya's Oak just spoken to him? he wondered, willing to believe anything anymore.

Have you not heard the wind and the water? The sound slowed to a rumbling vibration he felt all around. *Have you not heard the leaves rustle and the branches sway?*

"Aye," he said softly, turning toward the tree.

Then listen deep, man-child, listen deep . . .

Chapter 18

Avallyn had panicked, nothing more, and now she wished she hadn't.

She stood at the edge of the bower, staring out at the thickening mist and telling herself he was safe in the Hart, that no harm would come to him in Tamisk's tower, not when he was there by Tamisk's command. Still, he'd been gone far longer than a few minutes, and besides the worry and the regret, she missed having him close. She missed him. Too much, she feared.

Aye, she chided herself, her longing for him would be the death of her common sense. Easy enough to deny their attraction when she was frightened to death he might act upon it. Not so easy when she was alone, feeling bereft, and needing him to be by her side.

Morgan ab Kynan, the Prince of Time and hers for the having, if she had the courage. He was no Ilmarryn sprite to seduce her from her duty. She knew as much. She'd watched the dragonfire run a course through his body. She'd seen the tempering of his convictions and watched them harden into steel. Her decision had been born in duty; his had been birthed in fire, and she didn't doubt whose was the stronger.

Aye, he would go back to the past to save the Lost Five, but first he had to come back to her. She'd heard no signs of trouble, but Tamisk—and his traps—were nothing if not subtle.

She glanced up through the oak's branches. Rain was coming. She smelled it in the air.

A soft sound from the west brought her head down . . . and there he was, walking out of the heavy drape of mist, his hair wet and clinging to his nape, his pants streaked with dampness, his boots and lasgun in his hands.

Relief flooded through her. She took a step toward him, then hesitated, holding herself in check.

Morgan saw the relief and uncertainty on her face, and he saw the longing she couldn't hide. 'Twas in the soft vulnerability of her expression, in the way she couldn't tear her gaze away from him.

"Is the tea ready?" he asked, stopping next to her and tossing his boots so they landed inside the bower. He leaned over and rested the lasgun against the bower wall. The nearly impossible was going to happen in a few minutes. It was going to rain in the middle of the Deseillign Waste, inside the Hart Tower of Wydehaw Castle. He felt the change in the air.

And the not nearly as impossible was going to happen even before that. She was going to kiss him.

"Aye," she said, taking a step back.

He caught her before she could take another, lifting his hand to her face and drawing her back to him.

"Good," he said, rubbing his thumb across her cheek.

She was so exquisite, her skin softer than velvet, her eyes shining silver in the falling light. Clouds were forming above them near the ceiling, blocking the fierceness of the sun.

"You should have a cupful," her words came out hesitant, unsure, " . . . every hour."

"Later." He brushed his fingertips over her lower lip, and her mouth parted. "You're beautiful," he told her, his voice husky with emotion.

God's truth, he was besotted with the fair elfin maid, with her delicately sculpted face and wild mop of silver blond hair, with her green-rimmed gray eyes and her pretty mouth, and with the brave heart that beat beneath the soft curve of her breasts.

"Morgan?"

He hushed her with a kiss, a gentle caress of her mouth before he softly bit her lower lip and then laved it with his tongue. He didn't want her unsure of anything between them. He didn't want her frightened. He just wanted her.

"Morgan." She breathed his name again, and he deepened the kiss, opening his mouth wider over hers. She moaned, a small sound of pleasure, and a heavy ache settled in his groin, hotly sweet. He really didn't need to worry about the time weir or the crystal crater waiting for him in the caverns beneath Merioneth. If he couldn't get closer to her, if he couldn't get himself buried deep between her thighs and feel her come because he was there, he'd die of frustration long before they reached Claerwen. Even the thought of her climaxing was enough to push him close to the edge, to have her body stretched taut beneath his, to hear the catch in her breath as he pushed into her and made her give it all up for him.

It had been a long, long time since he'd had a woman, but the feelings she aroused triggered all the right responses. He remembered how to kiss a woman breathless, how to kiss her until she melted, until mouths were hot and wet and a kiss itself became a consuming act of love. He remembered how to tease a maid out of her chemise and how to convince her to give him license to her secrets. In the past it had all been a gloriously sensual game where everybody won, and the only tears had been not because he'd ever taken too much, but because he hadn't come back to take more. Aye, he'd long ago learned to wield tenderness to banish uncertainty or shyness in a woman. No maid had been shy with him for long, and even the shyest maids had learned the pleasures of wantonness in his arms.

But Avallyn was no maid to be won. What was between them was no game to be played. He needed her beyond the release she could give his body. He needed their connection to be strong, strong enough to reach across ten thousand years and grant him peace after he was gone. Sex could be only one part of what bound them, because for certes they wouldn't be making love again once he dropped into the time weir. 'Twas a painful truth that tightened around his chest like an iron band.

He slowly broke their kiss and just held her, his hands wrapped around her upper arms, his head resting on hers. He held her and tried to catch his breath and somehow ease the ache of losing her.

Christe, he was certifiably insane, and if he'd thought for a moment that there was any place in the galaxy he could take her and outrun his fate, he would grab her and be gone on the first off-world transport he could find.

But there was no place to hide from what he'd seen and felt in Tamisk's pool, no place to hide from the love he felt for Avallyn, which bound him to his fate as surely as Stept Agah's blood.

"For ten years I've wondered why I was brought here," he said, his voice rough. "But it wasn't until the first time I kissed you that I began to understand. I'm here to protect you, to fight for you, to keep you from harm." He lifted his head and dragged a hand back through his hair, a rueful grin curving his lips. "God's truth, Avallyn, it seems the only reason for my existence."

Looking up at him, the taste of him still on her lips, Avallyn felt much the same, that her existence revolved around him, that his kiss was the light revealing her purpose.

"That doesn't keep me from wanting you," he went on, his brow furrowing, the wings of his eyebrows drawing together above the indigo gaze holding hers so intently, "but it can keep me from having you." A breath of yearning crept into his voice. "And I want you so very badly. I want your mouth on mine, your hands on me everywhere." He slid his hand around her waist, his voice softening to a murmur meant only for her ears. "I want to be inside you and feel you come undone all over me, princess. I want to take you someplace you've never been."

With gentle pressure, he drew her even nearer. His lashes swept down over his eyes, and he slid his nose along the side of hers, bringing their mouths closer and closer, but not touching.

"I want your kiss, Avallyn, only yours." His breath blew over her mouth. "What do you want? Tell me."

She couldn't. She didn't know the words for what she wanted, but held this close to him, his desire echoing in her own heart, she knew it was more than a kiss, more than an act of love. She slid her hand down his chest, smoothing it over his damp skin, tracing the ridge of his scar to where it crossed above his navel. The journey here had not been an easy one for him. He'd come a long, long way through incredible pain and

been washed up on a hostile shore, alone, not knowing she'd been waiting her whole life for him.

She slowly spread her hand down across his lower abdomen,
across a taut plane of hard muscle and the line of dark hair arrowing below the waistband of his pants.

His stomach tightened, and a soft sound—half sigh, half laugh—
escaped him . . . and she knew exactly what she wanted.

"I want you," she whispered, lifting herself the bare inch necessary
to touch her lips to his. He responded immediately, his arms coming
around her, pulling her against the length of his body, his mouth opening
over hers.

Morgan . . . The taste of him flooded her senses, a melange of fla-
vors unique in all the universe. He was what she wanted, all of him. She
wanted to feel him beside her, to be with him . . . *always*. This was the
promise of the Red Book.

She knew the way of it. How to bind him to her with the enchantments of desire and words of love, how to take him to the green line and
meld his consciousness with hers. She was half Ilmarryn, and if there was
a price to pay in Claerwen for her disobedience, so be it.

She slipped her hand up his chest, reveling in the warm, hard feel
of him, wondering if she dared to bind him in such a way, and wondering if she dared not, when to kiss him was to taste the heavens. 'Twas
there, the aching vastness of the weir, the course he'd charted across space
and time, a coolness in the hot wetness of his mouth. Elemental earth was
there as well, a taste of the ancient past. He was rich, the Prince of Time,
beguiling and complex. She was enthralled by the warrior fate had sent
her.

"Cariad," he whispered against her lips, bringing his hand up to
cup her breast, and her thoughts fled, chased by the thrill of his touch.

A soft groan escaped her, and she leaned in closer, sliding her
hands to his shoulders. Powerful muscles flexed beneath her palms,
bringing her in closer yet. For long, endless moments he plundered her
mouth and caressed her breasts, until she was weak with hot, sweet pleasure. *Shadana.* He was magic.

When his hand slid to the zipseam on her shift, she offered no
protest, for there was naught she wanted more in the whole world than
to fall deeper under his spell.

Morgan slipped his hand inside the opening of her dress and felt the gods smile. She was completely naked beneath her priestess robes. He smoothed his hand over soft, soft skin, warm skin, and prayed he could somehow make her first time last. His doubts were high. She was so open to his touch, and he was so very hard. He wanted to kiss her forever, everywhere, and when forever came to an end, sink himself inside her and start all over again.

With their clothes still between them, he pressed his hips against hers and ever so slowly slipped his tongue into her honeyed mouth. Heat flashed through him, drugging heat. He withdrew, opened his mouth wider, and took her again.

Like a benediction, her low groan echoed in his mouth and started a riot in his body. He rocked against her, holding her tighter, letting her feel the full length of his erection, and slid his hand down the front of her dress, opening the zipseam all the way to the juncture of her thighs, a heavenly place made even more so when he slipped his fingers between her legs. She was incredibly soft and wet—and gloriously real, no Carillion illusion. When he caressed her, her whole body responded, a tightness and trembling of her muscles, a sigh he captured with his mouth, and more of the gloriously slick moisture that told him she was pleasured by his touch, by his kiss. There was no greater lure. It brought him to his knees, literally, in a slow slide down the front of her body, desire pooling in his groin, his mouth open to taste every curve—soft breasts to fill his mouth, smooth skin to delight him, and her vulva . . . sweet mystery, a place to get lost in. He pressed his tongue to her, and her hips thrust forward on a startled gasp, her hands lacing through his hair, holding him to her.

Ah, yes, he remembered. He'd always been good at this, and never better than with his tongue guided by the earthly lust of his love for her, with the scent of her swirling around him, filling him up, more intoxicating than Carillion wine. 'Twas the fragrance of flowers, lilies and lavender, and the ever-present scent of crushed grass in a birkland glade, so green and lush.

He slipped his fingers inside her, loving the satin softness closing around him, and her knees weakened. He caught her to him with his other arm, holding her close while he continued his teasing assault on her senses and his own.

God's truth, he'd missed the taste of a woman, missed the way a woman melted into a man's mouth, missed the feverish excitement of taking a lover to the edge—where Avallyn was, so close to climax. He could take her there. She was ready, making soft sounds of need, her body pulsing, but he held her back, wanting to be with her.

He kissed her once more and rose to his feet, swinging her up into his arms. She was in perfect dishabille, her clothes undone, her skin glowing, her eyes glazed with passion. Carrying her inside the bower, he kissed her again, deeply, sweeping his tongue through her mouth and letting her taste herself on him.

Outside the rain began. No herald of thunder announced its arrival, only a slow and steady susurrus of raindrops whispering down through the leaves, shrouding them in the half-light of the clouds.

He let her slip to her feet next to the pallet and took her face in his hands. Her eyes were languid, darkened by desire to a smoky shade of gray. Her mouth was swollen, so pretty, and his for the taking. He lowered his lips to hers, loving the way she flowed toward him, the way she gave herself up, her melting acquiescence all he needed for her to be woman to his man.

Avallyn knew the spells of love, but she'd never known anything like what she felt with Morgan, the throbbing intensity of full-blown desire. She'd not known a man could burn with an inner heat she would want to wrap herself in. She'd not known there could be so much tenderness in strength—and despite all that they'd been through together, she'd not known just how much strength was in him. His body was hard and lean, the source of his grace, full of latent power, a landscape of muscle from the solid wall of his chest to the ridged plane of his abdomen. His arms were corded with muscle—yet his mouth was softness itself, so gentle in its devouring.

She smoothed her hands down over his hips to the hard curves of his thighs, and his pelvis came forward in a slow, rhythmic thrust. He slid his mouth to her neck.

"Touch me," he whispered, rubbing against her with another move of his hips.

She knew what he meant. His erection was undeniable. There was little in her way, only the zipseam of his pants. She slipped her fingers beneath his waistband and hesitated.

"I've not . . ." Her voice trailed off on a sudden bout of shyness.

"Just take me in your hand," he murmured, then licked a path to her ear and drove her a little bit crazy.

"Morgan." His name came out on a soft cry.

"Come on, Avallyn," he urged. "Take my clothes off and touch me."

She did, running her fingers down the zipseam and feeling the hard rise of him under her hand. Beneath his pants, he wore a pair of very brief underwear, a scrap of cloth covering no more than the minimum, and failing at that in his present state. When she reached the bottom of the zipseam, she pushed both articles of clothing lower on his hips . . . and he waited, tunneling his hands through her hair and kissing her brow.

A long swath of his hair brushed her face and fell across his shoulder in a silky ebony skein. The smell of him, intensely aroused and so very warm, made her mouth go dry. She could almost taste him. Putting her hands on his waist, she traced downward over the jut of his hipbones, following the indentation of muscle on either side of his stomach to his groin, then she came back up, encircling the shaft of his penis with her hand.

He thrust into her palm, groaning, and she was filled with a deep ache of longing. With a sigh, she opened her mouth on his neck, tasting him, grazing him with her teeth. He belonged inside her. She wanted to feel him there, to feel him filling her. There was power in sex, an ancient, primal power. She'd never felt the truth of it more than when she held him in her hand.

"Morgan," she murmured, stroking her hand up and down his erection in a languorous rhythm. His body tightened in response, and she licked a hot path across his skin, wanting her mouth on him everywhere, wanting his mouth everywhere on her—back down between her legs, on her breasts, on her mouth, everywhere—so afraid she wouldn't get enough of him.

His hands slid down to her shoulders, and he unclipped her cloak. The material pooled on the ground at her feet, followed by her dress. He smoothed one hand down her naked back and cupped her breast in the other, teasing her nipple with his thumb. Her breath caught on a wave of desire, and she grew still.

"Don't stop," he whispered, moving against her hand. "Don't ever stop."

She stroked him again, varying her rhythm, and when she slid her hand all the way between his legs, a shudder ran through him.

"Lie down," he said hoarsely, guiding her to the pallet and holding her hand as she sank into a pile of silky green blankets and pillows.

Morgan released her to finish stripping out of his clothes, and he watched her gaze drift down his body. She'd set him on fire with her boldness and her hot mouth, but he took his time removing his pants, letting her look her fill. He knew what he was, knew she'd seen most of him, but she'd not seen the scar running the length of his thigh, his legacy from the Holy Land and a Saracen's butchering blade. He'd been cut deep before he'd been trampled by the soldier's horse.

Yet it wasn't pity he saw in her eyes, nor was it revulsion. Nay, 'twas desire, the same pure wanting he felt when he looked at her. She was all creamy skin and gentle curves against the foresty bedclothes, graceful curves that begged a man's touch.

Settling in on the pallet, he drew a blanket over them and pulled her beneath him. Aye, he thought. This was what he'd wanted since he'd first laid eyes on her, to lie naked with her with nothing between them except skin and heat.

Gazing down at her, his phallus nested between her thighs, heavy and pulsing with need, her expression inviting, he'd never felt such love, such lust. The rain grew heavier, drenching the oak and forming rivulets of water across the forest floor, but the bower stayed dry. The wind arose, blowing in sweeping gusts around the tree.

Carefully, he pushed partway inside her, and his thought processes started shutting down in rapid succession, until there was only her and him and the place where they joined.

"Is this going to hurt you?" he murmured. He could go slow, he told himself, painstakingly slow, if it would keep her with him.

"Only if you stop." She took his face in her hands and brought his mouth down to hers. "I am elfin, Morgan. There is no barrier to be breached." Her kiss, when she gave it, was an enticement, asking him to come deeper. In truth, he could have done nothing else. He thrust into her silky softness and was lost.

Sweet Gods, she was a witch, hot and tight and so wondrously fitted to him. Buried inside her, he felt the truth of the Red Book more surely than ever before. She had been made for him. He withdrew partway and slid in again, deeper, and in response she sucked on his tongue, a delicate tugging that was nearly his undoing. He thrust again, and a verdant scent washed through him, dark and rich and unbelievably erotic, unlike anything he'd ever felt.

"Morgan, Morgan," she whispered against his lips, then blew into his right ear. A flick of her tongue followed. When she did the same to his left ear, and the verdant eroticism seeped into him through his pores, he knew Tamisk's daughter was weaving a spell. His skin was coming alive with it, bound by the green tendrils of desire she was conjuring with her delicate touches. She licked him from the middle of his chin to his mouth and lingered to kiss him, a soft, slow, thoroughly bewitching kiss. All resistance flowed out of him, resistance he hadn't even known he'd harbored, as if he'd unconsciously held a portion of himself apart. Her witchery allowed no holding back. He hungered for her, every thrust of his body making him want her more.

Aye, she would have all of him.

With devoted concentration, she marked him with her breath and her tongue, the sides of his nose, both temples, weaving her web of enchantment, her body moving with his. Lastly, she pressed her lips to the center of his brow—with amazing results.

He went utterly still above her, his awareness drifting out from her kiss to the furthest reaches of his body, an extension of the green eroticism already playing through his senses, an awareness that went far beyond their sexual joining.

She was made of stardust. So was he. The same star from whence all the magic of earth had come, and earth was magic. From the lost oceans to the deep forests of the ancient past, there was naught but magic, a thin green line of it running like a ribbon through time . . . through her . . . through him.

He'd been from one corner of the galaxy to the other in the last ten years, and he'd tried a lot of wild things before settling on Carillion wine as his intoxication of choice—but he'd never felt anything like the priestess-princess's lovespell. 'Twas a green ribbon of fire she was kindling in his body, binding him to her, making him crazy with wanting. His thrusting quickened, his phallus hot and hard and heavy, every inch of him sensitized by the feel of her around him.

"Avallyn," he groaned, a rough whisper of her name, an invocation.

She wound a trail of sweet kisses down his face to his mouth, each soft pressing of her lips against his skin telling him he was loved. 'Twas an intoxication all its own, bringing him to the cusp of climax. Sheathing himself deep with a final thrust, he felt her first contraction, and his world came apart with a fierce jolt of pleasure. He jerked against her and felt the hot rush of his seed spilling out. He came again, groaning from deep in his chest and saw the green ribbon of time unfurl across his inner horizon, beckoning. Again and her climax washed into his, taking him over the edge into ecstasy.

Avallyn saw it, too; was there with him as wave after wave of the purest sensation rolled through her body. He filled her completely, stealing her breath, taking everything she had with the magic that was Morgan alone, taking her away. Aye, beyond the reach of the stars and the passing of ages, she and the Prince of Time had been meant for each other.

His arms came around her, holding her closer as the enchantment ran its course from high passion into a deep pool of contentment, leaving her limp with satisfaction and wondrously weary. Sighing, she stretched beneath him, and a soft laugh escaped her.

"What?" he asked, his voice low and husky in her ear, his hand coming up to caress her breast.

"You were worth waiting for, my most dread lord, the whole ten thousand years."

Morgan grinned, her breathless confession making him grow hard all over again.

"Wench," he called her, pressing into her again and bringing his mouth down to bite her neck.

'Twas a sweeter loving the second time, and in the long, quiet moments that followed, Morgan was suffused with peace. Avallyn's breath was soft on his chest, her hair in silken disarray beneath his cheek. She sighed, and he pulled her closer, angling his head down to kiss her brow. She was not the death of him, but the life of him, even should he die in Kryscaven Crater. The truth was undeniable. He reached for her hand, and her fingers wrapped around his, warm and secure—and in that strange place, ten thousand years from the land of his birth, with enchantment all around, Morgan knew he'd finally come home.

Chapter 19

"Aye, and there ye be." A familiar voice brought Morgan's head around. He and Avallyn were sitting on the pallet inside the bower, sharing food and a cup of tea. She'd used *rasca* to soothe his dragonfire wounds and had found him a shirt and tunic out of Tamisk's trunk. The shirt was russet brown, embroidered with thick swirls of silver thread, with the overtunic a rich shade of forest green. They were the same cut and colors of the Magia Lord's own clothes, though larger, and Morgan couldn't help but think that having him dressed in magician's weeds had been part of Tamisk's plan.

He smiled at Aja and rose to his feet.

"You look well rested," he said. "Though damp."

Aja quirked a brow at him. "And you look well lai—"

Morgan quelled him with a glance.

"Well . . . yes . . . very well yourself," Aja finished, his grin belying every hastily substituted word. "I don't suppose you know how I ended up thirty feet off the ground, asleep in the tree?"

"Tamisk," Morgan told him.

Aja nodded, his grin giving nothing away, though his eyes darkened. "I warned you, milord, and pray you haven't suffered in my absence, for 'tis well known that a man's captain is his best protection." The boy's gaze moved over him, looking for signs of injury.

"I suffered no more than necessary," Morgan said.

When Aja saw the bandages wrapped around his wrists, the white ends showing from beneath his sleeves, the boy's grin faded. "You've been hurt." He cast a suspicious glance in Avallyn's direction.

"No more than necessary," Morgan repeated, "as seems my lot. But you are well, so I'll not complain."

His lack of complaint did little to mollify the boy, whose expression grew grim, his green eyes meeting Morgan's.

"I saw as much when I cast my bones on the Medain. This place is ripe with enchantment," Aja warned, casting another quick glance at Avallyn, "none of it benign. There is power here, Morgan, awesome power. I felt it in my dreams, a fiery wave of it rushing over me, and then something unlike anything I've ever felt before, an energy so pure, it seemed to cut right through me. I fear the harm this power has done to you is as naught to what it can and will do, if we do not leave . . . even if . . . even if we have to take the princess with us." He finished the last in a rush, the concession hard won by the look on his face—half resignation, half grimace.

"There was fire here," Morgan admitted, hiding his own grin, not overly surprised by Aja's prescience or his suspicion of Avallyn. The boy had lived in Pan-shei for ten years, long enough to know the dangers of women.

Aja nodded in agreement, though he didn't look too pleased at being right.

"And there was fierceness," Morgan continued, "but truly I am none the worse for being here, despite the wounds, and in your dream-filled sleep you have shed the burdens of the last months. You look nigh your age for the first time since Sonnpur-Dzon."

"That was the beginning of it, wasn't it, milord? The damn dragon," the boy stated flatly.

"For you, aye," Morgan said. "My path here started long ago."

"But this isn't the end of it. Riders approach even as we delay. I saw them from my perch through the west window."

Morgan turned toward Avallyn.

"Sept Seill again," she confirmed. "Tamisk said they would come at dusk."

She, too, had found clothes in Tamisk's trunk, an all-green tunic and leggings, with a dark blue undershirt embroidered with gold stars. He'd kissed her a hundred times while they'd shared their tea, and still every time he looked at her he wanted to kiss her again, to lay his mouth on her anywhere and breathe her in, to just feel the softness of her skin.

"So we are to leave this place?" Aja asked.

Morgan detected relief in the question—and well the boy should be relieved. For in the end, Aja was right. If Morgan survived the fearsome journey through the weir, and the cataclysmic breaking of the seals on Kryscaven Crater, and if by some great conjunction of skill, luck, chance, and magic he actually got back to the Hart Tower with the Indigo Book in hand, well, he duly expected that all hell would break loose before Dharkkum let itself be destroyed—and he, of course, would be smack dab in the middle of it, probably not too far from where he stood now.

'Twas a disconcerting thought.

"Aye, captain. We are away," he said.

But not for long, he thought, looking around the tower. When he returned with the book, the Hart wouldn't be an elfin glade holding a lovers' bower. Nay, the tower would be a hell pit— and, more than likely, his grave.

Time, Corvus brooded, *is at a crux. Forcesssss are coming to bear.*

He felt them all around, forces of darkness in infinite shades of black—black like Vishab's incessant howling. From where he hovered in the steel struts of his warship's great hold, he could see the black foulness of her cries. She spouted black pain every time she opened her mouth, black pain and black rage for the loss of her Yellow Book. His prisoners, the woman Ferrar and her giant, were drenched in black fear of a complete other shade, cowering in the corner where he had them chained. His captain had fainted dead away. Or perhaps she'd died a black death. Either way, she hadn't moved since his unfortunate outburst. She lay like a stone, her new epaulets grimed with black soot. The messenger from the command center had definitely died, squeezed to infinitesimal thinness by Corvus's left hand. He was no more than a wet spot on the floor, the black floor. All was black, everywhere, like the veil of shadows covering Corvus's one good eye.

It was Vishab's fault, and the fault of a fool named Tamisk who had dared to breach Magh Dun and ravage her tower.

Tamissssk. He rolled the name over in his dark mind, loathing the feel of it, loathing the being who claimed it, and loathing Vishab for keeping such a person hidden from him all these years.

Tamissssk could have saved him, *Tamissssk* and his dragons who lived in a tepid pool beneath a lost forest in a white palace by the Sand Sea.

He had enough jaw left to clench, but he dared not. Clenched jaws fed anger, and he had no more room for mistakes of any kind.

Dragonsssss, the foul witch. How could she have kept dragons from him for ten years?

Claerwen held all the power in the Waste, Vishab had told him since the day she'd found him in the sand, and his memories of his previous life had confirmed such truth. The Priestesses of the Bones ruled in Deseillign. 'Twas the White Ladies of Death, she'd sworn, that must be destroyed if he was to save himself, and he was only too glad to believe. They and they alone held the means to his salvation, the time weir he'd come through and the knowledge of Dharkkum. They were the ones deserving of his revenge, for it had been the foul desert mothers who had sent him through the time weir the first time.

He'd never thought to look for another.

Never thought.

Now Vishab's book, *his* book, had been stolen from Magh Dun, a breach of security for which many would pay, and suddenly the little dark death-witch had an enemy named Tamisk she'd never bothered to mention before. *Tamissssk* with the power to invade Magh Dun and break her cauldron spells. *Tamissssk,* a Magia Lord of the Books of Lore.

"Booksss," Corvus spat. He'd known books. He'd had his fill of books in the past, and they had not saved him. Tamisk could have all the damned books he could steal. Corvus wanted the blasted dragons. Or, rather, he had wanted them. It was too late for dragons now. They would eat him alive. Dragons and Dharkkum had been mortal enemies from

the most ancient of ages. He'd read as much in the Yellow Book—and looking down at himself, he knew he dared not get within their reach.

No, he had to go to Claerwen, back to the worms.

Ten thousand years ago he'd known Merioneth as a land of *pryf* and the time weir. He'd searched the future for it, scoured the Waste and the Sand Sea in hopes of finding its remains and an alternative weir to the cosmic whip that lighted at Claerwen—friggin' impregnable Claerwen with its friggin' impregnable priestesses. But all his searching had been for nothing. War and sand had wiped the earth clean of anything that resembled the lands he'd lived in when he'd been in the past. Rumors arose now and again of a lost forest, but what would the people of a wasteland dream about, if not a forest?

Mirage, Vishab had confessed in her despair. The White Palace was concealed by mirage and a mountain of stones, a mirage conjured by *Tamisssssk*.

Hidden well, indeed, for even in his life before he'd been banished to the past, when he'd been lord of a half-dozen planets and twice again as many moons, when Earth had been a minor refueling base on a second-class trade route outside the boundaries of his empire, even then Corvus had not known of a White Palace. If he had, he wouldn't have cared. His life then had been lived on a scale outside the imagination of any backwater Earthling. Now his life hung by a thread in the selfsame backwater. Corvus Gei, Emperor, had been reduced to Corvus Gei, Warmonger—and all because of a backwater-born princess who had caught his eye, stolen his heart, and sent him to his doom.

"*Love*." He spat another word into the darkness.

In his other life, kings and potentates across the Milky Way had been only too glad to give him gifts, be they riches or princesses. The priestesses of Claerwen had felt otherwise, hoarding their precious chit for a nameless prince to claim. A goddamn prince, when she could have had an emperor.

He'd spent years wooing her, coming back to the planet time and time again, setting up trade with the priestesses and going so far as to destroy the Warmonger of that time to free them from their enemy. He'd backed them in their treaty negotiations with the Old Dominion, helping them secure the borders of the Waste, and for all his trouble and billions of marks spent on their behalf, they had still denied him the one thing he wanted, Avallyn Le Severn.

She'd been so pure, he remembered, and so purely arrogant, so sure of herself, and he'd wanted to conquer her as he'd conquered worlds.

She'd been beautiful, too, wildly beautiful. Imperfect, yes, unlike the genetically altered wonders that came from the Psilord's vaults, and in her imperfections he'd found a grace of form unlike any he'd ever seen, a fairness he'd wanted all to himself.

She'd been ageless, nearly a hundred years old when he'd first seen her and as fresh as a rosebud pearled with morning dew. She had smelled like green grass and immortality, and he'd wanted to spend the rest of his life being close to her, loving her and being loved by her.

And now—his black, smoky fingers twitched—now he discovered that she had a father named *Tamissssk*, a mage of boundless powers, who somehow had not overly interested Vishab, whose sole goal, it seemed, was not the salvation of her master, but the meeting of her own ends, the destruction of Claerwen.

The wretched, disavowed priestess-turned-witch had underestimated the importance of a man, and for this she had paid dearly. Her book was gone, taken, she was oh-so-certain, to the White Palace where Tamisk dwelled on the shores of the Sand Sea with his dragons.

The bitch. The vile, vile bitch.

It was too late for her book, and too late for him to go to the White Palace, and too late for him to have Avallyn. She had been among the riders in Rabin-19, along with the friggin' tech-trash thief from Pan-shei. A skraelpack had tracked them to a camp in the Medain where their trail had run cold.

Yes, she had disappeared into the Waste, and there, Corvus was sure, she would stay, awaiting her friggin' nameless prince, forever out of his reach, along with the friggin' dragon statue that would never do him any good.

"*Dragonssss,*" he hissed, the shadowy remnants of his body beginning a slow spiral with the flow of his anger. *Dragonssss.*

He'd been deceived. Cheated. Destroyed.

Vishab wailed, drawing his unfortunate attention.

He could put her out of her misery. The price would not be so high.

He glanced at his prisoners, his spiral picking up speed, undulating in the cavernous understructure of the hold, and he saw their fear turn to terror. He could take them as well, except ... except the giant would require effort, too much effort. Vishab was no more than a wisp's worth of destruction. The giant would take a full measure of smoke, and the time-rider, for all her slightness, had a clarity of will that would take great exertion to subsume.

No. He dipped down from the ceiling, reaching for Vishab on the floor. He would claim only the dark witch for now. Then he'd turn his warship toward the great bone walls of Claerwen and the priestesses who would finally pay for the destruction they had wrought on his life.

He would show the White Ladies death as they had never imagined it could be.

Chapter 20

The bone walls of Claerwen rose out of the sand, soaring hundreds of feet into the air, like the prow on a ship of death, a great, buttressed mass of mortar and the skeletal remains of the millions upon millions who had died in the wars of the Trelawney Rebellion. As they approached, Morgan could see the infamous skull towers, round edifices encrusted with sun-bleached skulls, empty eye sockets facing outward to the Waste, looking across the gaping canyon at Claerwen's base, silent witnesses to what had been.

The Sept Seill riders had taken Morgan, Avallyn, and Aja to their sept on masutes, where Tamisk's rover had been waiting. From there, they'd headed north, a two-day journey made hazardous by the battles raging the length of Deseillign.

"There were so many dead after the Wars," Avallyn murmured by Morgan's side.

Aye, he could see how many had died. 'Twas unbelievable. The walls looked to be made up of a whole world's popula-tion—and in truth, they very nearly were. The Old Dominion was all that remained of the once great cities of Earth, with only pockets of civi-lization scattered elsewhere on the planet.

"At the time of the rebellion," Avallyn said, "eleven hundred years ago, Claerwen was no more than a small abbey, well out of the main fighting. Afterward, when the Trelawneys had won, the priestesses took it upon themselves to sanctify the dead. The task proved overwhelming. There was no burial ground big enough even for just the thousands of their own district, so they started aboveground burials, packing the bones in mortar to keep the Rift dogs from dragging them away. Word got out about the holy women and the bones, and soon whole towns were bring-ing their dead to Claerwen. The survivors of a family or tribe would gather the bones of their loved ones and bring them. City-states sent their bones in by land barge. Whole districts brought bones in by caravan. For a hundred years, it was the holiest of pilgrimages, to take the bones of the dead to Claerwen and have them blessed and laid to rest by the priest-esses, the Priestesses of the Bones, the White Ladies of Death."

Another misconception of his laid to rest, Morgan thought. To him, and to many in the Old Dominion and Pan-shei, the priestesses were scavengers, scouring the dunes looking for bones, especially the bones of men, even if they had to speed death along to get what they wanted.

But no one who had ever seen the walls could have been so misled. The bones of Claerwen had been made by weapons of mass destruction on a grand scale, not by women riding the Waste on masutes, looking for carrion.

The rover banked to the left, following the western rim of the canyon, heading toward the temple complex, an expanse of buildings numbering in the hundreds. On the eastern rim, the Warmonger's army was spread out like a black plague, the battle well engaged. The priest-esses had been forewarned of Avallyn's arrival, and directions had been given for the rover to dock in one of the ports carved out of the canyon's walls.

As the port came into view, Morgan saw a huge stone platform just beyond it, a white disk jutting out of the canyon's face. A series of small buildings were clustered along its cliff side. The half hanging out over the abyss was clear of everything save two stone towers crowned with dragon heads. A trickle of cold dread rolled down his spine, and Morgan knew that, like Sonnpur-Dzon, Claerwen was indeed a place of time worms.

From a window in the west wing of the cloisters, Avallyn saw Morgan, Aja, and the Sept Seill riders enter the courtyard below. The men had been quarantined upon their arrival, but she had insisted that Morgan be brought to her quarters after the briefest possible detention, reminding the attending priestesses that he was the Prince of Time and should be treated accordingly, as should his escort.

He was so beautiful—her hand clenched into a fist at her side—and he was hers. She had waited as the Red Book had decreed. She'd not given herself to any other, but she'd given herself to him, and she would not be denied.

"A cripple," the woman beside her said with disapproval, watching Morgan's limping stride as he crossed the walkways leading to Severn Hall. "Just as Dray reported."

Fighting back a retort, Avallyn glanced at her mother and was caught like a snared rabbit by the older woman's sharply discerning gaze.

"A wine junkie as well?" Palinor demanded.

"Nay," Avallyn told her. "Tamisk's potion freed him from the Carillion addiction."

"And the price?"

There was always a price.

"Steep enough. He saw his fate."

Palinor said naught, dismissing Morgan's grim future with the ease of years of practice. She glanced back out the window, an expression of resigned disgust drawing her features tight.

"Even with Dray's warning, I had somehow expected more in a prince. Yet I fear the thief proved to be man enough for you."

Avallyn's fist tightened even more. Her fingernails dug into her palm.

She hadn't tried to hide anything from her mother, knowing the uselessness of such an attempt, but neither had she said or done anything to reveal what had happened in the Hart. Still, her mother knew. Morgan had marked her as his, and no priestess of Palinor's skill would have missed the signs.

"Tamisk set you up," her mother continued, "and you fell into his trap. Though what he hopes to gain by your debauchery, I don't know, unless it's humiliation for me."

"I have not been debauched," Avallyn said.

Her mother looked to her and named her a fool with a dismissive glance. Behind them, a melodic tone chimed at the far end of the hall, announcing the sept riders' arrival.

"Call it what you will, you have ruined yourself and ruined my plans for you."

"Plans?" A frisson of unease skittered down Avallyn's spine. "What plans?"

"You didn't have to stay in the past. You could have returned." Palinor swept away from the window and signaled for one of her acolytes to answer the call. "*Fata Ranc Le* or nay, the priestesses have chosen not to make covenant with the mad thief. If he is meant to be sacrificed to Dharkkum, so be it. We have not accepted him as your consort. You could have returned through the weir and taken your rightful place as a High Priestess in Claerwen."

Return to the future without Morgan? A chill ran through her. To be separated from him by ten thousand years of cold and empty space?

"Tamisk says the weir will be destabilized if we are successful. There is no coming back."

"Tamisk is no weir master," Palinor said, rejecting the idea out of hand. "In this, you would be wiser to trust the High Priestess."

Avallyn blanched, worried that she could be brought back against her will. Her mother was not without power. She didn't have Tamisk's magic, but she had the High Priestesses behind her, and they ruled through casting the fates of people's lives. They didn't change what was so much as they changed what would be, going so far—she'd once heard—as to use their most arcane powers to write desired fates in the Red Book. People's lives were the priestesses' work, and ten thousand years wasn't far enough away to keep them from meddling.

"And what would the High Priestess have of me now?" she asked.

"Now?" Palinor let out a grieved sigh. "Now you have ruined yourself with a tech-trash prince from Pan-shei. You could still return, but it would not be as a ruling priestess. Worse, though—"

The scraping open of the doors at the end of the hall captured Avallyn's attention, and she heard no more of what her mother said, her gaze riveted by the entrance of the men.

The riders still wore their desert robes, and Aja his Pan-shei garb.

The Prince of Time had been dressed in white. He stopped in front of her and went down on bended knee.

"Milady," he said, his head bowed, the fall of his dark hair with its white blaze hiding his face from her. As one, the sept riders knelt behind him, a courtesy they'd not bothered to perform during their dash across the Waste.

Behind her, she heard her mother tsk. A quick glance proved Palinor drawing herself up taller and tightening her cloak around herself, and suddenly Avallyn understood the source of much of her mother's disapproval. 'Twas far more basic than Morgan being a crippled tech-trash thief from Pan-shei. He was a man, and her daughter, the most prized priestess in the purely female stronghold of Claerwen, had allied herself with him, with the opposition. After one hundred and twenty-five years of obedience, her child had broken free of her bonds—truly, though, only to be bound to another: Morgan.

"Dread lord." She called him by his most rightful title, extending her hand. Beneath his clothes, he'd been marked with the runes of the dragon-maker's firespell. Beneath his skin beat a heart of valor. He was cunning, and fast, and skilled at keeping himself alive, a fact proven with every breath he took. Ten years of thievery in the far-flung quarters of the Old Dominion were nine and a half longer than all but the very best survived.

Taking her hand in his, he kissed her fingers. His mouth was soft and partly open, suffusing her skin with warmth—and she knew he'd fared no better than she with their half-day separation.

Outside, the battle still raged. The Bridge of Knells had fallen, and the north wall was under attack, but the priestesses had only begun to prepare for the coming of the time worms, and Avallyn would spend what time there was with him. The battle outside was not hers to fight, not on this day.

Without releasing her hand, he rose to his feet, his gaze meeting hers with a fierce ardor ameliorated only by the gentleness of his touch.

"Are you well?" he asked, and Avallyn knew 'twas no simple question.

"Aye," she answered. "With you by my side, I am well."

Relief softened his gaze, and he shifted his attention to her mother.

"Lady Palinor." He addressed her with a short bow. "I believe this is yours." He loosed the leather bag at his belt and offered it with an open hand.

Palinor gestured for the nearest acolyte to come forward and take the bag. The girl did, and at the priestess's next command, she loosened the ties. When she'd finished with the knot, the softly cuffed leather fell back and revealed the dragon statue in all its golden glory.

"*Ddrei Goch,*" Palinor breathed, reaching out to take hold of the statue, obviously surprised.

She turned the dragon in her hand, letting the sunlight that streamed through the window glance off its gleaming reddish gold curves.

" 'Tis indeed Claerwen's," Palinor said after a thorough examination of the statue. "Taken from us months past and, after many months more, resurfacing in Sonnpur-Dzon Monastery." She lifted a mocking gaze to Morgan's face. "We thank you for its return . . . prince." The word fell like lead from her mouth.

'Twas no more gracious an acknowledgment than Avallyn would have expected from Palinor.

An easy smile curved Morgan's mouth. " 'Tis a small price to pay for all I've taken that I cannot, and will not, return," he said, meeting her mother's eyes with his unflinching gaze, and holding it until a rose-shaded hint of color washed into the older woman's face.

"Prince," Palinor said in a less haughty tone, lowering her eyes with the slightest bow of her head. Her hands tightened on the statue as she shifted her attention to Avallyn. For a moment, it looked as if she would say more, but then she signaled for her acolytes and, with another brief bow, swept from the hall.

Morgan dismissed the sept riders and Aja with a glance. The riders obeyed without question, Aja after a moment's hesitation, leaving only the two of them and a dozen servants in the hall.

Avallyn felt her heart beating in her chest. He took her hand again and lifted it to his lips for a fervent kiss and a taste of her skin.

"I *must* be alone with you," he murmured. "Where are your quarters?"

"These are my quarters," she told him. "All of Severn Hall."

Drawing her closer, he glanced at the high timbered ceilings and the white stone walls, carved columns, and vaulted arches.

"It's very nice, milady," he assured her with a smile, "but does it have a bedroom? Preferably one not crawling with servants?"

"Aye." A blush blossomed on her cheeks, and his smile broadened.

" 'Tis my fondest wish, *cariad,* to make you blush like that all over. Take me to your private chamber."

With his hand in hers, she led the way to a timbered staircase that curved upward to an intricately carved wooden balcony, the whole of it overlooking the hall. The door at the top was open, until they crossed the threshold, whereupon Morgan closed it behind them, threw the lock, and took her into his arms.

His mouth came down on her hers, sweetly insistent, teasing her lips with soft breaths and gentle bites, while his body pressed fully against her, urging her back against the door and letting her feel the hard ridge of his arousal. The heat and weight of him sent a wave of longing crashing through her. She opened her mouth wider beneath his, and he deepened the kiss, the sweetness dissipating into a devouring need.

She arched against him, wanting to be closer, loving the taste of him, letting it suffuse her senses and swirl through her on the twining tendrils of his past. He'd been kissed before, thousands of times. Ancient impressions of his pleasure seeped into her, heightening her own arousal, which she gave back to heighten his.

"*Gods,*" he said on a sharply indrawn breath, breaking their kiss. "You're doing something again. I can feel it."

"Women have loved kissing you." The words were whispered across his skin.

"A few," he admitted, running his hands down and around her hips and pulling her tighter against him.

"They have loved touching you . . . everywhere."

Aye, he'd have to agree with that, but truly she was light-years ahead of him. He didn't want to think beyond the one woman in his arms and how good she felt.

"Are you deep-scenting me again?" he asked, concerned enough to ask, but truly too distracted to care overly much.

"Nay, just skimming the surface of your kiss, tracing your pleasures back to their source and stealing them for myself."

"Ahh," he murmured. She was welcome to the pleasures of his past, all of them, for they paled in comparison to the pleasures of his present. He bunched her white priestess gown up around her waist and slid his hands beneath it. A low groan escaped him. "You're naked again."

"Aye," she said, and laid a damp path of kisses from his chin to his ear, her teeth grazing his jaw. In a matching move, she slid her hand down the front of his pants and slowly, inexorably set him on fire.

His breathing grew rougher. One-handed, he released the buckle on his belt, letting it clatter to the floor as he tore open the zipseam of his fly. She found him with her hand and made her palm a hot, silken-skinned sheath for him to pump into, but even that delight could not assuage his greater need to bury himself so deep inside her he was lost.

"Wrap your legs around me," he ground out, lifting her higher on the door and fitting himself to the slick, magical place between her legs. He held himself there, only pushed partway inside, and let her set the pace. She went so agonizingly slowly, he had to grit his teeth to keep from pushing into her harder, faster.

"Morgan," she sighed, when he was hardly more than halfway inside. Her head fell back, exposing the long, elegant line of her throat, every part of her body telling him what she wanted, what she needed. Her hands gripped his shoulders. Her mouth was open, her breath coming in short gasps.

Women were the loveliest, most exquisitely sensitive creatures God ever put on the earth, and Morgan was most exquisitely in tune with the one on the verge of coming in his arms. Though he was surprised with how little of him she'd taken, he wanted nothing more than to give her exactly what she needed. He slowly ground his hips against hers, giving her the gentle, sweet loving she was primed to take, and he watched her face, taking note when her lashes fluttered, when her teeth bit down on her lower lip.

A moan was dragged up from deep in her chest, and he began the same moves again . . . and again . . . and again, until she was whimpering and he was sizzling with gut-wrenching need.

Despite the release he craved, he let her take her time and only as much of him as she wanted. His reward was worth the strain. When she came, she came so sweetly, her soft cry echoing in his ears, a rosy blush flashing across her skin, and all those wondrously rippling contractions cascading down his shaft, making him harder than granite.

When she would have gone bonelessly limp in his arms, he thrust into her deeper, keeping her back against the door and her weight on him, letting her know there was more, that there was someplace else he wanted to take her. Her gasp this time was more of surprise than pleasure, and mayhap a bordering edge of discomfort, but he knew enough not to hurt her, and he knew how to take her where he wanted to go.

He began with long, even strokes, feeling her lush softness envelop him on every thrust. He kept his mouth and hands on her, moving over her, breathing her in and kissing her every place his lips touched. 'Twas a madness of the most wondrous kind, the sweet fire she ignited in his loins. He pumped into her again and again, until he was mindless, his body running on pure instinct and need, her soft cries urging him on. When he felt the first tense pressure of his orgasm, he locked his mouth over hers and probed her deeply with his tongue, mimicking the carnal rhythm he set with his hips, pushing her higher with each thrust, and pushing himself closer to the edge. She tightened around him and went wild in his arms, bucking against him, her low groan giving him the fiercest satisfaction.

Holding her in the vise of his arms, he plunged into her, forcing her one step higher, then another, claiming her with every pulsing second of her release, until he could take no more and came in his own fierce hot rush, pouring himself inside her, giving her everything he had. By the time he finished, he was shaking. His mind was cloudy with the erotic haze of the aftermath, making it impossible to think. All he could do was kiss her face and whisper her name, over and over.

It took a tremendous amount of effort to make it to her green bower of a bed, but when they'd collapsed together onto it and cocooned themselves amidst her blankets and pillows, Morgan felt the results were worth the price. They were warm and safe. He was wearily sated down to the depths of his soul, and she was in his arms.

The bed itself fascinated him, partly because it was hers, partly because of how it had been made. 'Twas oak carved with runic inscriptions and plants of every kind. Sheathed leaves of grass twined upward from clusters of flowers cut into the bed's feet. Pinecone finials graced its high posts, which were in turn draped with gossamer lengths of sheer green silk embroidered with leaves, each one different. 'Twas a bed fit for a half-faerie princess, and the thief who loved her.

Chapter 21

"And here is where the mark of *Ammon* lies, one of the runes of refuge," Avallyn said, putting her finger on a three-dimensional map laid out in the anteroom of Severn Hall. The map was a good five feet square, built to scale, and an exact depiction of Wales as Morgan had known it. Beside Morgan, Aja leaned closer to get a better look.

"In Dragon's Mouth," he said, looking down at her upturned face, intrigued. "The runes have actual places of refuge?" He might need refuge in the past. In fact, he could nigh well guarantee it.

"Aye," she said. "*Bes* is much farther into the deep dark, past the gates of time and the Magia Wall, in a small cavern northeast of the cave where Stept Agah was born." Her finger moved across the map. "It's a crystal cavern. Here." Her finger stopped on an area of land surrounded on three sides by Mor Sarff, the Serpent Sea.

The words "deep dark" had an ominous sound to them, more so because Morgan had a difficult time imagining being someplace even deeper and darker than where he'd already been. The caverns down through the Canolbarth and past Lanbarrdein into the *pryf* nest had seemed endless, and yet according to her map, they were only the beginning.

"And *Ceiul*?"

"Closer to Kryscaven Crater." Her finger moved again, crossing the Serpent Sea and stopping at a small cavern northwest of the much larger crater marked by a chunk of amethyst—just as in his dream.

"There are no trails into Kryscaven," he pointed out.

"In each of the rune caverns, there is a marker, and on each marker a lock for which dreamstone crystals are the key. We will unlock the path to Kryscaven Crater with crystal, as we will unlock Nemeton's celestial sphere with the orbs."

"More blood?" Morgan asked, disturbed by the prospect.

"Nay." She shook her head. "Not for the path into Kryscaven. The crystal rods will suffice and are plentiful in the past. Every Quicken-tree Liosalfar warrior has a dreamstone crystal dagger, and crystal by its nature is geometrically consistent. If there are Liosalfar to help us place the keys, all the better. If not, I know the way to each rune marker."

Which wasn't going to do him much good.

"Is there a smaller map, a cartographic chart?" he asked. Even if he was going to take her, he'd still want a map. Planning for every contingency had saved him more than once.

"The priestesses will have one in our weir kit."

Ferrar had a weir kit. Morgan had seen it many times. It always hung from a pouch on her belt: a small stash of chrystaalt and a juice-jacked carbo-bar with enough calories to feed her and Jons for a week. The third component was the encrypted star chart of the galaxy tattooed down Jons's back, from the base of his skull to his heels. Despite Jons's size, to Morgan it had never seemed like quite enough to go off traversing time and space with, but then he'd managed with far less.

"How do you know we'll end up in the right place at the right time?" he asked.

"You left a trail. Once we're in the wormhole, we'll catch it and follow it down."

What could be simpler? he thought, hiding a pained grin. They would just drop down the equivalent of a cosmic cyclone and find the trail he'd left. The only problem was that he didn't remember leaving any trail, or seeing any the last time he'd been swallowed by a worm.

"What makes you so sure we'll find this trail?" He didn't like being skeptical of her meager plan, but he'd put more effort into mapping a crosstown route from Pan-shei to the Southern Quarter.

"Every cell in your body is fine-tuned to the path you left the first time you came through the weir. You are the guide, Morgan."

So they were back to his cells.

"Milord? Milady?" One of Claerwen's acolytes paused in the doorway leading into the anteroom. No more than sixteen years old, she had plump curves, a sweet smile, and her eye on his captain, if Morgan wasn't mistaking the sideways glances he'd seen passing between the two of them all day.

Mayhap 'twas time for Morgan to have a talk with the boy. Not about the facts of life—Aja was well familiar with those—but priestesses were a different breed, and for certes naught but trouble and frustration when considering what the boy's expression said he had in mind.

"Yes, Sachi?" Avallyn addressed the girl.

"The High Priestess will see you in her quarters now, milady," Sachi said with a short bow. "The preparations on the weir platform are nearing completion."

And so it begins, Morgan thought.

The Hall of the High Priestess of Claerwen was a towering edifice of architectural femora. Millions of leg bones had been packed into the mortar of the walls. Thousands more had been cemented together to form the twisting pillars flanking the dais and spiraling up over four stories to a ribbed vault. Desert sunlight fell into the great chamber from the hall's hundred Gothic windows.

Morgan felt as if he were trapped inside some giant's bleached skeleton. Everything in the hall was bone white, except for the faces of the fifty or so priestesses waiting for them in formation on the raised dais.

All but one, an ancient crone standing in front of a bone throne, wore white battle uniforms and carried lasguns. The old one stood apart from the rest and wore yellow, a richly embroidered gown of purest saffron. A ragged group of wild boys stood to the priestesses' right. A small cadre of Night Watchers in black robes stood on the left. All of them knelt when Avallyn stepped up on the dais, all except the old woman.

"Daughter," the High Priestess said, extending her gnarled, age-spotted hand for Avallyn's kiss. Her face, like Tamisk's, was tattooed on one side with blue swirls and runes. Unlike Tamisk's tattoo, the High Priestess's was nearly lost in the thin folds of her wrinkles. She was wiry, the bones showing beneath the ancient sack of her skin. Her eyes were a piercing, all-seeing, glacial blue. Even without the identifying robes, Morgan would have known her for what she was—queen of the death-witches.

"Mother," Avallyn replied, kneeling and pressing her lips to the woman's ring.

The crone shifted her gaze to Morgan in the barest acknowledgment of his existence, yet he felt her icy glance like a touch, a rather unpleasant touch.

"The prince?" she asked, returning her attention to Avallyn.

"Aye, Mother."

"From Stept Agah's line," she said, and Morgan realized he'd just been deep-scented again. Tamisk could learn a thing or two from the old woman.

"Aye."

"The *Fata Ranc Le* did not tell all, then."

"Not all, Mother."

"Rhayne." The High Priestess uttered the name with obvious dissatisfaction. "She would ever have her surprises. Or do you think she has forgotten what she once knew?"

"Nothing is forgotten in Claerwen," Avallyn replied.

"No," the High Priestess confirmed. "But we cannot remember what Ysaia never wrote down, or what her shape-shifting selves have never bothered to tell us. And who is this?" Her gaze moved to Aja, and the boy's eyes widened, his eyebrows rising nigh into the top of his forehead; Morgan knew he'd just had his first taste of deep-scenting.

Morgan started to answer her question, but she waved him off, obviously having found out all she needed.

"Where is the dragon from Sonnpur-Dzon?" she asked.

"With Palinor," Morgan said, not particularly caring for the tone of the conversation or her imperious manner. He'd met his share of haughty women, but the crone had an edge to her he didn't quite trust. He decided to ask a few questions of his own. He was, after all, the Prince of Time, and like every other woman in the room, the High Priestess of Claerwen had waited her whole life for him. He tried not to let the fact go to his head, certain she'd have that very head on a pike if it so suited her, Prince of Time or nay. "What's in it that's worth destroying half the Waste for?"

"The Warmonger's salvation, or so he believed up until Pan-shei," she replied. "He thought the statue would lead him to real dragons, but 'tis too late for Ddrei Goch and Ddrei Glas to save him."

Morgan understood the last, too well. "The dragons will eat him. They'll eat his darkness, and after what we saw in Pan-shei, darkness is the most of him now."

"Exactly," the High Priestess said, giving him a longer, more discerning look.

"So why is he still here, knocking on your door?" Knocking was a deliberate understatement. An hour earlier the report had come that Corvus had shifted his troops to the east wall and Whitethorn Bridge, doing his best to gouge out an entrance into the temple complex. Cannon blasts could be heard on three sides of Claerwen, their echoes reverberating even into the innermost sanctum of the hall.

"A chance," she said. "Either he can destroy us, his hated enemies—and himself in the bargain, for he will not survive in any form of a man—or he can try to return through the weir to a place before Dharkkum took hold of him."

"And which do you think he'll choose?" Morgan had never met the Warmonger, only heard the stories and dealt with the trader and a few minions. All he'd ever gotten from them was an appreciation for their fear of Magh Dun's master. They had loathed him even as they'd been terrified of him—all that "left hand" business.

Well, Corvus Gei had more than a dangerous left hand to terrify his minions with now.

"His mind has grown too dark to penetrate," the priestess answered. "It has become an abyss filled with evil blackness."

Considering the ease with which she'd just penetrated his mind, Morgan figured Corvus's must be a tar pit to have thwarted the High Priestess of Claerwen.

The old woman made a simple gesture, and the entire ranks of priestesses, wild boys, and Night Watchers rose to their feet.

"Your escort," she said. "It is time. The East Gate has been breached and the north wall is soon to follow. We've sealed off as much of the temple grounds as we can, but Corvus Gei is unlike any Warmonger who has come before him. No mere despot, he has been touched by the enemy, Dharkkum. Naas should never have sent him back to us, but then, mayhap we should never have sent him to her time."

" 'Twas the Council's decision," Avallyn said.

"Aye, and because of it, all of time is in a tangle."

"Mother?"

The old woman turned toward the windows framing a view of the canyon and the deepening shadows of sunset. "Corvus is growing more powerful by the minute. I can feel it. Dharkkum has always been alive and twisting in the past, but now we have it in the present as well, and there are no laws between a naked singularity and its spawn. Absolutely none. I fear the whole universe may turn itself inside out, or that as the Warmonger gets stronger, the years in between then and now will begin to disappear, one by one. He is dangerous, very dangerous, the situation full of uncertainty . . ." Her voice trailed off, her gaze slowly coming back to Morgan. "And Fate has sent us no more than a man to fight the enemy."

In the presence of the High Priestess, a woman who looked old enough and tough enough to have packed all the bones into the walls herself, Morgan realized his own doubts were as naught. No matter how long she'd waited for the Prince of Time, she didn't think he had a chance in hell of succeeding in his task.

And as for its being time, he wasn't ready. 'Twas a damnable turn of events, but true. He simply wasn't ready, not to face the worms, and not to leave Aja and Avallyn.

With a sweep of her robes, the old death-witch started across the dais, for certes not caring if he was ready or not. Avallyn followed by her side, and he and Aja followed Avallyn.

"Are you still of a piece?" he asked the boy.

Aja flashed him a quick grin. "She stripped me down, Morgan," he said. "Had me stark naked in her mind all the way down to my innards. Best trick I ever saw. Do you think she'd teach me how to do it?"

"No." Morgan tousled the boy's hair, glad for his light mood. "But Sachi might."

The thought of Sachi captured the boy's interest, and his grin turned mischievous. "Aye, she might at that."

Ahead of them, the High Priestess tilted her head toward Avallyn.

"If Corvus Gei had not been so relentless in his pursuit of you, dear daughter, perhaps we would not have turned against him," the crone murmured in a startling and unwelcome aside Morgan wasn't sure he was meant to hear. "At the time, we thought the price he demanded for his help was too high, but now we wonder if losing you might not have been the better bargain after all."

Between one step and the next, Morgan had put the Magia Blade to the death-witch's throat and pulled Avallyn behind him. Over fifty lasguns were drawn and cocked in response, no doubt all pointing at him, but he didn't take his eyes off the old woman. Every muscle in his body was on alert, strung tight as a cocked bow, every instinct telling him the woman's threat was no idle musing. She would throw Avallyn to the wolf before she let Claerwen fall.

"She's mine," he said succinctly, from between gritted teeth; blood would be drawn before that fact changed. Give Avallyn to the Warmonger? Not while he lived.

And after he left her? What then? he wondered. Was she truly only safe with him, no matter the danger they faced?

The High Priestess held his gaze, her unconcern with the sword at her throat rivaling Tamisk's utter indifference. Her eyes, though, were unlike the elf mage's. Colder than a north wind, her gaze bore into him, pushing at him, probing his psyche in a manner she didn't bother to hide. Her presence was an icy river in his veins, coursing beneath his skin— and growing colder, threatening to freeze him from the inside out.

"*Bitch,*" he called her, and knew that here was the power of the Waste, beating in the depths of a wizened heart, ruthlessly focused on a single goal. Claerwen stood its ground in a desolate landscape of bones and desert, tempered by harsh storms and harsher duty, and ruled by a High Priestess whose every breath was law.

"You're weak," she said, "and full of fear."

The icy river she'd made of his blood finished its circuit and began pumping back toward his heart, sure to kill him when it reached its destination. Still, he did not move, or so much as blink. He didn't dare, not if he valued his life.

"I could crush you," she said, with negligent surety, as if he wasn't worth the effort of his destruction. "And if I so choose, Avallyn will go to the Warmonger to appease his black soul."

"No," he said, pressing the edge of his blade deeper into her papery skin, but to no avail. There was no cut, no blood, nothing to force her to withdraw. He was so cold, as cold as he'd been in the wormhole. Soon he wouldn't be able to move.

"She was all he ever wanted from the very beginning," the old woman taunted him. "Corvus assassinated the previous Warmonger to safeguard Claerwen for Avallyn's sake, brought the man's bones in himself and set them into the north wall. 'Twould soothe him mightily to finally have her for himself. Mayhap his desire would be enough to turn him back into a man and make him forsake the darkness."

"*No.*" Morgan ground out the word in a cloud of frozen vapor, pressing his sword edge deeper, and still not making a cut.

"You are helpless to stop me," she said, her thin lips curling in disgust, "as you will be helpless against Dharkkum."

She was wrong, and he'd friggin' had enough. He was the Prince of Time. He'd survived the weir, ten friggin' years of the future, and Tamisk's melting of Scyld's grip. He had to have some advantage he could use against the crone to keep her from freezing him solid.

Ysaia's firespell, cut into his skin with the dragons' fire. Sweet Christ, it had to be worth something.

"*Ddrei Goch.*" He invoked the red dragon's name, filling his mind with an image of the beast. The words left his mouth in another cloud of vaporous cold, but he felt a spark of heat in his left arm.

The High Priestess's gaze narrowed.

"*Ddrei Glas.*" He called the green dragon, and the runes on his right arm lit with the fire of their making.

God save him, he thought, stunned by the sensation of warmth traveling down his arms. Was this how magic was made, then? Were sorcerers no more than men rebirthed in pain and blood and fire?

The heat flooded through him, down into his hands where they held the sword, and a flame kindled to life in the heart of the Magia Blade's dreamstone grip.

"Tamisk was generous, indeed," the old woman said, a shade of fierceness retreating from her eyes. "Perhaps you will be of some use after all."

Slowly, the last of the cold left him, replaced by the warmth of the dreamstone. The High Priestess offered no apology, made no concession, and Morgan demanded none. His point had been made, but so had hers. She would sacrifice anyone, if she deemed it for the common good.

He looked to Avallyn, knowing his plan had gone awry. He couldn't leave her with such a threat hanging over her head—not unless he took the Warmonger with him.

Bloody hell. His gaze dropped to the sword. 'Twas a magnificent blade, possessed of a power he could actually feel, but he was still doomed.

"Light the fires in the towers," the High Priestess commanded her troops. "Sound the Dragon Hearts to call the time worms. The Prince of Time has come and needs the way opened into the past."

What he needed was a way out, if one had ever existed. He thought not. All his roads of all his years had led here. He had only to feel the heat of the runes subsiding on his arms to know the truth of it. He had only to look at Avallyn to know he would change nothing.

But *Sweet Jesu,* ten thousand years wrapped in the Warmonger's black hold, only to face an even greater darkness when he reached the past? He'd long ago figured he was destined for a rueful end, but his imagination had failed him completely in light of the truth.

Corvus recognized the sound before its first resonant vibration echoed to its end against the canyon walls—*the Dragon Heartssss.* Claerwen was calling the worms.

His pulse quickened.

"Vishab." He spat the name and laughed. What did he need the witch for? He'd come farther on his own than he'd ever managed with her guidance. He'd breached the Bridge of Knells and the East Gate and was nearly at the inner walls of Claerwen—and the worms were coming. His days of being doomed were nearly at an end. The whole future could run itself straight to hell. He was going back to the past, where he'd been whole.

"Captain!" he yelled.

A squat, rotund man dressed in mail from head to toe hurried to the fore. Corvus didn't recognize him, but the man was wearing the soot-grimed epaulets the last captain had been wearing when she'd collapsed on the floor. Apparently, this man had taken up the gauntlet of power.

"My lord?" The fat man went down on one knee—a nice touch.

"Call your *sssoldiers* and the *sssskraelpack* we left on the bridge. Get the *prisssssoners.* We're going into Claerwen, to the *towersss* in the canyon where the *firesss*—Wait!" He held up his hand, his left hand, and the blood drained from the captain's face.

Corvus paid him no mind. The fool would soon enough realize he hadn't been killed on the spot.

"Do you hear it?" he asked, cocking a wispy ear toward the sound. The Dragon Hearts had been rung again, as they would be all night long until the worms came.

He remembered. He remembered it all so clearly—the beating of the bronze gongs, the heat of the fires as they'd roared up through the towers to make the dragons breathe smoke and flames, the smell of chrystaalt. He remembered the chains they'd hung on his body, the manacles they'd clapped around his wrists and ankles, and how they'd staked him out on that windblown platform to meet his fate. He remembered the sand blowing all around, scouring his skin. He remembered Avallyn walking away, and he remembered fear.

He would not be afraid this time. This time he was going down the worm's gullet by choice.

It was not too late.

He could still be saved.

Chapter 22

Morgan kept a firm grip on Avallyn as they made their way through the corridors and levels of Claerwen, though for her reassurance or his he could hardly tell anymore. His mood had grown unbearably grim with the realization of how close he was to his terrible end.

The priestesses had held the way open to the Dragon Hearts, though not without paying a price. Corvus's troops had launched a fresh assault even since they'd left the hall, detonating a sonic blast inside the East Gate and proving the High Priestess right. He was coming into the heart of the temple, tearing down the walls to get at something, either Avallyn, the weir, or his chance for annihilation.

Light shone through an arch leading into a courtyard, cutting a swath through the shadows in the corridor. Two of the Night Watchers ran ahead for reconnaissance, their soft boots silent on the stone floor.

"Refectory courtyard clear," the report came back.

They passed through the arch five abreast and were halfway across the courtyard when a skraelpack broke through a gate on the north side. Soldiers and priestesses alike peeled off into battle formation, with a core of soldiers surrounding the High Priestess, Avallyn, and Morgan. Aja was too quick to get caught in their net, his lasgun already drawn and firing as the ranks closed behind him.

"*Har maukte har! Har! Har!*" The skraelpack rushed into the courtyard, weapons firing.

Morgan pushed his way out of the cordon that was whisking the High Priestess and Avallyn to safety, and went after the boy. Skraelings poured through the gate, lunging beasts slavering at their mouths. A priestess and a wild boy went down in front of him, strafed by lasgun fire. Morgan swung his own lasgun up and fired even as he pulled his carbine over his shoulder. One-handed, he locked in a charge and blasted a skraeling as the beastman fell on the downed priestess. 'Twas a skraeling's greatest weakness in battle, its need to eat.

He looked for Aja and saw the boy moving fast through the courtyard, catching the sides of the walls and lofting himself off, cutting down skraelings right and left.

A lascannon mortar was launched over the north wall of the courtyard, catching the light in a blinding flash of silver before it detonated on the far side of the refectory. The dining area's walls exploded into the courtyard, catching the pack of skraelings and blowing them to bits. Screams were heard from every quarter, the high-pitched squeals of skraelings dying in the rubble, and the cries of Claerwen's soldier-priestesses fighting through the sudden destruction. Dust roiled up, choking the air and making visibility nil.

Friggin' Corvus had murdered his own troops to breach the courtyard.

"Aja!" Morgan yelled over the chaos. "Captain!"

A fresh tumble of stones and bones came crashing down ahead of him. He leapt to the top of the heap and tried to see across the destruction. Skraelings were the boy's bailiwick, but Morgan feared that this time Aja's speed had done him more harm than good.

"Aja!" he yelled again, jumping down on the other side of the heap.

To Morgan's left, a crushed skraeling lay half buried under a rubble pile, his finger locked on the trigger of his lasgun, sending short blasts at the base of a nearby wall. Chips and shards were flying out of the stone like shrapnel, with the blasts ricocheting into the adjoining cloisters.

Morgan swore and ducked, swinging his carbine around and leveling it at the skraeling's hand in one move. A single shot silenced the beast's gun.

"Aja!" he shouted.

"Here, prince," a priestess called out.

Morgan saw a hand waving through the cloud of dust and ran to where the woman knelt by a pile of stones. Next to her was a rumpled pile of boy and clothes crowned with a thatch of red hair. Sweet gods. He fell to his knees by the boy. Aja's leg was trapped beneath the debris.

He put a hand to the boy's neck and sent up a prayer of thanks when he felt a pulse.

"Get help," he said.

The priestess pointed. "They're already here."

Two Sha-shakrieg had come up behind him and were carefully but quickly removing the mix of bones and rock that had taken Aja down, making sure not to dislodge a fresh avalanche of rubble. The courtyard had been destroyed by the lascannon mortar. A count of priestess dead was being taken at the same time as the wounded were being checked and transported, the whole process carried out with a quickness and efficiency that reminded Morgan that the Priestesses of the Bones had been fighting Warmongers for centuries. They were a religious order order honed for war.

The Sha-shakrieg removed the last of the stones, and Morgan heard a faint groan from the boy.

"Shh, captain." He kept his hand on Aja's chest and looked down the boy's body. His leg was broken, the tibia at an odd angle. He was scraped up fairly badly, but nothing too deep, and he hadn't taken any lasgun hits. His pulse was steady, though Morgan wished 'twas stronger.

"Skraelings?" Aja whispered, and Morgan took hold of his hand.

"All dead," he assured the boy. "Claerwen made a clean sweep with this one, and you're in luck—the place is crawling with medics." He didn't tell him all the medics were White Ladies of Death.

He raised his head, looking for Avallyn. The soldiers had been moving her and the High Priestess back into the corridor at a dead run, the old crone carried by a Night Watcher. They must have made it.

A movement from inside the refectory caught his eye, a dead wild boy being dragged across the floor by a hairy, clawed fist reaching out from behind what was left of the dining area's south wall.

"Friggin' skraelings," Morgan muttered, coming to his feet but staying in a crouch. Body low, he ran across the intervening space. Heat shimmered off the courtyard's stones. Dust filled the air.

The wild boy had nearly disappeared behind the wall when Morgan reached it. He pressed his back against the stones and set his carbine on automatic. Then he took a deep breath and stepped around the wall, firing.

There were three skraelings at the picnic, none of them quick enough to save themselves. He finished them off and pulled the wild boy out from under the biggest one's hairy fist, leaving him for the priestesses to pick up.

Back by Aja's side, Avallyn and a pair of White Ladies had come with a stretcher, and after a cursory examination, the Ladies gave the boy an injection and told Morgan he could be moved.

"He's lucky," the woman with the hypodermic said. "No internal injuries and young enough that his leg will heal. Take him to the B wing in the hospital."

Their instructions given, they went on to the next wounded soldier, signaling for another stretcher.

"B wing isn't far and wasn't hit," Avallyn said somewhat breathlessly, kneeling down and helping him lift Aja onto the stretcher. The boy moaned louder.

"You were safe?" he asked.

"Aye. The Mother and I were kept in the corridor until the dust started to settle."

"Good."

"Not so good," she disagreed, slanting him a brief glance. "I should have been with you. And the way to the weir platform has been blocked. The Night Watchers will find another route. But for now we need to get everybody out of here, before Corvus decides to launch another blast."

"Aye." He pushed the hover control on the stretcher's frame, while Avallyn snapped a strap over the boy to hold him on.

With a whoosh, the stretcher rose into the air.

"Take him," he told her. "I'll help here and meet you there."

Avallyn nodded and headed off across the courtyard, pushing

Aja's stretcher in front of her, guiding it through the people and the litter from the blast. As he watched her go, Morgan became aware of a deep, resonant sound that the battle had briefly obliterated. The Dragon Hearts were still being rung, and every knell found an echo in his veins.

He had to go, no matter his fears.

Half an hour later he made it to the hospital. Aja was well in hand, his leg set in a cooling gelcast, the lovely Sachi by his side, but Avallyn was nowhere to be seen.

"Have you seen the princess?" he asked the acolyte.

Soft brown eyes looked up at him. "She was here until I took over. There are so many wounded."

Aye. Morgan looked around. B wing had more than a hundred beds and all of them were filled, with cots set up in between them.

He scanned the hospital wing again, searching for Avallyn. What caught his attention was two people in desert robes making their way through the ward with a half-dozen blue-robed priestesses following in their wake. They stayed no more than a few seconds by each bed, but there was a noticeable difference in each area they left, as if the two were bestowing peace with each touch they gave.

Oddly, Morgan felt a spark of recognition, though from such a distance, it was hard to tell why. He'd met a few desert walkers in his time, but none who would have business in Claerwen.

The man moved with Tamisk's grace, but he was too tall, his shoulders too wide, for him to be the mage. No, Morgan thought, the familiarity came from something else. The man's hair was long, pulled back and tied at his nape, hanging in a loosely twisted skein down his back. 'Twas a deep, rich brown, an earth color, but half the sept riders Morgan had met wore their hair long.

The woman's hair was white, not the white of old age, but a gleaming, lustrous white, like pearls. She wore it in a thick braid that fell past her shoulders. Most strangely, she had a patch over her right eye, a sickle of silver cloth that looked like a crescent moon gracing the space between her cheek and brow.

The woman gestured for one of the priestesses to come near and spoke into her ear. To Morgan's surprise, when the priestess glanced up, she looked directly at him. When the woman was finished speaking, the priestess nodded and walked off.

A low groan from the bed brought Morgan's attention back to

Aja. He smoothed a swath of hair off the boy's brow; his skin was warm, but not hot, his eyes closed. His clothes had been removed, and to Morgan's consternation the boy looked a bit thin beneath his blanket. He held himself responsible. Over the last few months, they'd spent too much time in bars and hellholes like Racht Square, and not enough time eating decent meals.

"He's strong, milord, and will recover," Sachi said.

Morgan looked up at the girl, noticing again why she'd so quickly caught Aja's eye. Her hair was a rich dark brown and fluffed into loose curls that framed an uncommonly pretty face, all rosy cheeks and sweetly molded features. She wore white priestess robes, the shift hanging to the floor, draping across the full curves of her breasts and hips. Aja had always preferred a well-rounded lass, and Sachi was sensually rounded, enough so to have easily whetted the boy's appetite—a fact bound to get him in trouble.

"Your captain has the lineage of Sept Rush in the north," the acolyte said, laying her hand on Aja's chest. "I remember when the Sept was destroyed by a skraelpack running contraband out of Leag II. Our search party didn't find any survivors, and all feared the line was lost. Your captain's appearance has brought great joy to the White Ladies."

Aja would love that, Morgan thought wryly, imagining all the poking and prodding that would go along with being the last genetic link to a desert tribe. Lineage was Claerwen's work, compiling all the lineages of Earth. The better to manipulate them—so Avallyn had told him.

"I think he's gifted with second sight," Morgan said, giving the girl another bit of information. He would as soon Aja was kept in Claerwen and out of trouble, providing the temple complex held. If he could get to the past and destroy Dharkkum, he was bound to improve the priestesses' chances of survival.

"Many in Sept Rush were," Sachi said. "Where did you come across him?"

"He was with me when I reached Pan-shei ten years ago."

"He could have been no more than a child then, when you and he came out of the desert," she murmured, smoothing her hand down to Aja's waist and back up to cup his jaw.

Morgan wondered if he was imagining the boy relaxing deeper into the bed, or if the girl had a healer's touch.

"What makes you think we came out of the desert?" he asked.

Her gaze strayed to the stripe in his hair before returning to Aja.

"All time-riders come out of the desert, usually within a hundred-mile radius of either Claerwen, Pushranjure in the Southern Kingdom, or Sonnpur-Dzon in the Dhaun Himal. In the old days, when the worms were earthbound, all time-riders came through an earthbound weir. Now ..." She shrugged. "There's no telling for sure where the worms will strike, especially if our chrystaalt supplies are low and the miners and black marketeers have hoarded theirs. Chrystaalt will always draw a worm."

"So how do you know when a time-rider has landed?"

"Storms," she said. "The worms always bring great sandstorms."

Morgan remembered a storm, a killing storm of sand and dust that had near choked the life out of him—and the next thing he remembered had been walking into Pan-shei with Aja.

Sachi turned and pulled another blanket from a cupboard in the wall. As she tucked it around Aja, its silky green folds molding to the boy's body, Morgan remembered where he'd seen such cloth before. Tamisk's pallet had been covered in the same blankets, but long before Morgan had known the mage's magic, he'd seen the cloth on the Quicken-tree of Merioneth.

"Is it silk?" he asked, fingering an edge. 'Twas amazingly soft.

"*Pryf* silk," Sachi told him. "The dragons stopped breeding long before I was born, but some silk remains in the old nest beneath the White Palace, much of it still green."

"What of worms in Claerwen? Don't you have them here?"

"They broke free of their weir over a thousand years past and now snake across the sky. 'Tis not down you'll go this time, prince, but up."

Well, hell, and wasn't that a damned discomfiting image, he thought, wishing he hadn't asked. At least going down, a person could be assured they were still on Earth. Going up? Hell, that could be anywhere in the parsec.

He shifted his gaze to the ward, wondering where Avallyn was, feeling more and more certain that the time for leaving had come. Once again his attention was captured by the two desert walkers and their cadre of priestesses.

Aye, they were definitely familiar, he thought, his brow furrowing.

The man turned then, and Morgan saw the stripe in his hair. *Time-riders.* His pulse quickened.

Bed by bed, they drew closer, talking to the wounded, and with every step, Morgan's sense of familiarity grew—especially about the man.

At one of the cots, the man looked up and caught Morgan's gaze, and something tightened in Morgan's chest. The desert walker could have been Dain Lavrans . . . could have been, but wasn't. The similarities were painfully clear, the long line of his jaw, the dark-winged arch of his eyebrows, the wry smile that should have belonged to Dain, and could have belonged only to one of his descendants.

A flurry of activity near the east doors drew everyone's attention and heralded the High Priestess's entrance into the ward. The old crone strode forth through the beds, obviously summoned, her face flushed, her robes still dusty from the courtyard debacle. Avallyn was with her, and when both women reached the pair of desert walkers, they knelt on the floor.

No mere time-riders, then, Morgan thought, watching the exchange. He was the Prince of Time and the High Priestess hadn't knelt to him.

"Who are they?" he asked, knowing every eye in the place was on the pair.

" 'Tis Rhayne," Sachi murmured. "White Bitch of the Dangoes and her consort, Kael Lavrans."

"Lavrans?" Morgan asked, stunned.

"Aye, milord. His powers are said to put even Tamisk's to shame."

A considerable feat, Morgan thought, but then what else for the dragon-maker, Ysaia, than an equally powerful mage. Dain would be pleased to know his line had held so true.

As if hearing her ancient name, the woman lifted her gaze from the kneeling priestess and princess and looked to him. With a lift of her hand, she commanded him to come forth.

Morgan wasn't sure if getting that close to her was in his best interest, but there was no gainsaying the witch-mage. He felt conspicuous as hell crossing the ward with everyone watching.

"Time is short for you," Rhayne said in a rich, honeyed voice when he reached her. 'Twas a sweet and slow-flowing voice, with a soothing depth, as if though time was short for him, all of time were hers. 'Twas a voice made for enchantments.

Her face was artfully lean, her skin luminous in stark contrast to the drabness of her clothes. She looked to have traveled a thousand miles across the Waste, though considering the blaze in her consort's hair, they'd probably come much farther than that.

"Milady," he said, bending his knee in an act of obeisance.

She stopped him halfway to the floor and raised him up, her touch sending a deep awareness of her through him. *Rhayne,* he thought. *Blessed, wild Rhayne.*

"Do you not remember me, old friend?" The voice and her words lured him into meeting her gaze. Her left eye was blue, a strange, infinite landscape of unnerving depth, like the heavens themselves. Colors floated across her iris in a mesmerizing dance of varying hues, the subtlest shift-shape he'd yet seen, and indeed, looking upon her, he felt a bit entranced.

"No one could forget you," he said honestly.

"Then look again, and do not be fooled by my current form."

Her words triggered a memory, but not of her. 'Twas Mychael ab Arawn he thought of, and the red dragon, and how the two had become one. And he remembered Tamisk and the gyrfalcon. And when he looked at her again, he remembered the Hart Tower and the sleek albino levrier Dain had kept.

"Numa." The word was a whisper, as was Rhayne's smile of satisfaction.

'Twas Numa, come to him across ten thousand years—but not the hound. Numa the hound had died on the sands of the Serpent Sea, fighting in battle. 'Twas Ysaia, she whose cauldron had conjured the firespell emblazoned on his skin.

"Aye, you know me for what I am—and for what I once was."

He lowered his gaze, filled with the memory of how he'd last seen her, dying on a dark shore, her gleaming white coat stained with blood, the gaping wound where her right eye had been. He'd had little time to notice her and even less to give comfort.

"My apologies, lady," he said, his voice hoarse.

"No regrets, Morgan. I lived as a hound and died as a hound, and because I died, Ceridwen lived and gave me Kael to share the burden of the turning wheel, an avatar kissed by the worms in his mother's womb."

Morgan's head came up. Ceridwen's son? And Dain's?

"Morgan," the man said, acknowledging his startled glance with an enigmatic smile.

No far-flung descendent, but Dain's own son. Morgan had to restrain his impulse to embrace the man.

"You're very like your father," he said after taking a steadying breath.

"No, not very," Kael said, his smile broadening. As Morgan looked at him, he realized Kael's words were no reproof, only the truth. Where Rhayne's eyes reflected the heavens by day, Kael's were the starry nights, windows on the doorways between the past and the future. Both the man and the woman were timeless in a way Tamisk had yet to master, and in a manner Dain could not have imagined—until, of course, his son had been born.

Sweet Jesu. Dain must have had at least a few sleepless nights with the boy. Avatar, Rhayne had said, and when Morgan looked in his eyes, he believed Kael might actually be a god made flesh.

"I gave you a boy, Morgan," Rhayne said, bringing his attention back to her. "A red-haired boy from Sept Rush. My first gift."

"Sept Rush was destroyed ten years ago, lady," the High Priestess said, coming to her feet. She'd obviously had enough of bowing and scraping and being ignored.

"The sept, but not the boy," the witch-mage replied. "I would have known if the boy had died."

"He's been wounded," Morgan told her.

"All the more reason to take me to him. Now." 'Twas a command, not a request, and with a sweep of her hand, she bade him lead the way.

Aja remembered her. There was no forgetting the White Lady of Light. No forgetting the day she had chosen him as companion to the ragged man who had walked into Sept Rush from out of the desert. There had been a storm. A worm storm, his mother had called it. Dust and sand had blown across the Waste, forming a wall hundreds of feet high and blocking out the sun. Behind the face of the wall, a dancing tunnel of wind and sand had bucked and rolled, twisting through the dunes and leaving destruction in its wake.

Destruction and Morgan ab Kynan.

The lady had come soon after his arrival, within a matter of days. Long enough for Aja's mother, Ahzur, to have healed some of the man's hurts. Long enough for him to have finally eaten and held his food down. The septs were always at war with the Warmonger. Even as a child Aja was used to battle and warriors who had reached their end, and he'd never seen anyone who looked so terrible survive. The man's eyes had been sunk into his head, his hair frayed like a wildman's. He'd been caked in blood, yet he'd had no open wounds, only the scrapes and scratches that Ahzur had covered with salve and bound with soft cotton. He'd been delirious, raving, his skin cold to the touch and pale as ice, except along the wicked scar that ran diagonally across his torso. There his skin had been bruised black, blue, and a sickly purple spreading into yellow and green, great splotches of color that bespoke of a trauma Ahzur and Aja's father, the Sept Lord Miekle, had whispered about long after they thought the children had fallen asleep.

Then the lady had come, and of all the people in the sept, she had chosen him, Aja, to bind to the man with sacred vows. Now the man and the lady were before him again, and Aja's greatest fear was that they'd come to undo those vows, that the time had come for Morgan to be taken from him.

"Shhh," the lady hushed him when he would have spoken and sat by his side. She was not beautiful like Sachi, but always there was the light that shone from within her, in her glowing white hair and luminous skin.

Aja shifted his gaze to his lord, who stood behind her, and he felt the edge of his fear sharpen. Morgan's face was grim. Morgan who, despite his delirium, had saved him when the sept and everyone he'd loved had been destroyed. All had been chaos in the caves, skraelings running everywhere, murdering and devouring. It had been Morgan who had cut the arm off the skraeling that had snatched him from his bed. Morgan who had stood in the doorway with his bloody sword, barely able to stay on his feet, and killed the next three beastmen who had tried to make a battle ration out of a small boy. Only Morgan who had still been alive with him when it had all been over and the Warmonger's troops had withdrawn.

Aja had found his mother's body, what was left of it, and with trembling hands, his whole being wracked with gut-wrenching nausea, he'd forced himself beyond his shock and horror and picked her finger bones out of the sand. With the utmost care, he'd packed them into his yellow wallet—his talisman forever. When he'd finished, Morgan had taken his hand and a dead sept rider's lasgun and led them out of the dark cave and into the desert. The two of them had wandered for months, the madman and an orphaned boy, before the lights of Pan-shei had drawn them out of the Waste.

Those months were as lost to Aja as they were to Morgan. All he ever remembered from that time was how cold the nights had been and how Morgan had held him, sharing his warmth and yet so silent, his night blue eyes starkly wild; and how he'd prayed that the man wouldn't go completely mad or die and leave him alone.

"I never meant for you to be parted," the White Lady said, her hand smoothing the hair off his brow. Her touch was soothingly cool. "But this wound you've taken will keep you abed for much longer than we have to give. Morgan must go, boy, and you cannot go with him."

She'd known his fear, and she'd spared him nothing.

Aja shot Morgan a wild look.

"You went through the weir wounded. I saw you. You were still covered in blood when you came to the sept." 'Twas an accusation as well as a plea. Morgan couldn't leave him, and for certes not for such a flimsy reason as a broken leg. They'd been through far worse and always pulled through—together.

Morgan leaned over the bed and took the boy's hand in his. 'Twas not easy, what he had to say, especially in light of Rhayne's declaration. She'd meant for Aja to go with him into the hellhole of Kryscaven Crater. Was everyone he loved meant to be as doomed as himself?

The panic in Aja's voice didn't make it easy either. His captain had never panicked, not in any of the hundreds of places where they'd pulled off jobs with their lives hanging in the balance.

"You know as well as I that the wormhole isn't a place either of us wants to be, but I *must* go, and soon, very soon," he said to the boy. With his free hand, he pushed up his opposite sleeve, revealing the runes. "I've seen the dragons, Aja. These are their marks, and they give me no choice. I have been sworn to a duty as binding as the oath you swore to me."

The words damn near stuck in his throat, but he choked them out, wondering if it was destiny that had set him on this path, or if was it something far less noble. In the Hart, he'd believed in the fate he'd seen. In Claerwen, that belief was crumbling around him, leaving him little purchase—except for the friggin' Dragon Hearts. They called to him every time they rang, called to his blood.

"Morgan . . ." the boy began, trying to rise, pushing himself up with his elbow.

The effort proved too much, and he gasped with pain. Morgan caught him around the shoulders before he could fall backward, and gently laid him on the bed.

" 'Tis no good, Aja." Holding his anger in check, he brushed the boy's cheek with his thumb and felt all his misdeeds come home to roost in the softness of Aja's skin. The boy didn't even have a beard, and Morgan had made him into one of the most accomplished thieves on Earth. Aja's name was well known in the Old Dominion and in the Lunar colonies, and even as far out as Europa.

Too well known.

"You'll be staying here," he said, as much to reassure himself as anyone. "Chein has a place for you with the riders of Sept Seill when you've recovered, if you want to leave Claerwen, or you can while away your days here with Sachi." He forced a smile. "No hardship, I think."

The boy didn't blush as he'd hoped, only stared up at him, his hair matted with blood on one side, the rest of it sticking straight up, his face seeming to collapse with the descending weight of his sadness.

Morgan's jaw tightened. He was a beautiful boy, lightly freckled across his upturned nose, his eyebrows the same deep russet color as his hair, his eyes the green of summer trees. He was beautiful, and strong, his mind as facile as any Morgan had ever known—and for most of his life, he'd been Morgan's to love.

He gentled his grip on the boy's hand, realizing he was holding him too hard. "There is only one promise I can make you, Aja—that I will never forget you. Never."

"Take me with you, Morgan." The boy held to him tight, asking the impossible.

Morgan bent his head and pressed a kiss to Aja's brow, his other hand coming up to cup the boy's face. He held him for a moment, but didn't trust himself to hold him a moment more. With one last kiss, he lifted his head and met the boy's gaze. Then he rose and walked away, knowing there was no going back.

Avallyn fell into step beside him, along with the others.

"We've brought the *Treo Veill Le,* the Green Book of Trees, to set into the Hart," Rhayne said, her pace easily matching his as he strode down the ward.

He didn't reply until he'd pushed through the B wing's doors and was out of sight of the boy, and the only thing that kept him from grabbing Rhayne and shaking her godlike attitude out of her was his sure knowledge of Kael's response: He'd strike Morgan dead on the spot.

"Why me?" he demanded, coming to a stop when the doors closed. "I'm not indispensable here. You, and Tamisk, and Kael—hell, even the High Priestess—know more about what's going on here than I do, so why me? And why Avallyn?"

Rhayne halted when he did, thoroughly unperturbed by the anger he feared would consume him, if he let it all out.

"Your blood chose you, not I, just as Avallyn's blood chose her. If you would know who chose the blood, for Avallyn 'twas Nemeton and the bargain he made to release us from Dharkkum."

"And me?" he asked. "Who chose my blood, if not Ysaia who made the blade and cut her firespell into my skin? If not you, Rhayne, who?"

He'd as much as called her a liar, no doubt a tricky, uncertain business when dealing with beings nearly as old as Earth, shape-shifting mages with the heavens in their eyes.

"Though not nearly as mortal as you, Morgan, I am no god," she said, her voice so rich and sweet—and so damnably reasonable—'twas difficult not to believe every word she said. "I made a cauldron in the Dark Age, hoping to save this planet from destruction, and from the cauldron came the dragons to save us from Dharkkum, and the blade to save us from the dragons. From the Starlight-born came the aethelings whose hands fit the blade—including you, Morgan. If you would have more answer than that, 'tis to the stars you'll have to go."

He'd been there once, thank you, with a mouth full of blood and his body near hewn in two.

Friggin' mages.

He turned and started walking again, his strides long and determined. He didn't like what she'd said. He didn't like it at all, but every single damn friggin' cell in his body told him it was the truth—or as much as he was going to get without retiring to a mountaintop and spending the rest of his life contemplating his soul.

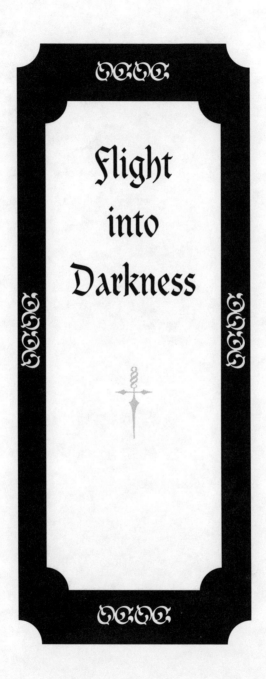

Flight into Darkness

Chapter 23

While they'd been in the wards, the Warmonger's army had breached Claerwen's north wall. The last part to fall was the bell tower. The reverberations of the building's collapse and the raucous clanging of the falling bell rippled through the whole temple complex—but even that did not mute the Dragon Hearts. Each sounding of the gongs followed the last in perfect rhythm, urging Morgan on toward the weir. The soldiers of Claerwen had opened a new route to the weir platform, and as Morgan and Avallyn hurried along after them, Morgan wondered who would reach the platform first, themselves or Corvus.

The time worms were coming at last. His awareness of their impending arrival skittered across his skin in little flashes of heat. His chest was starting to feel tight, and still he strode onward, toward the platform jutting out over the canyon's abyss, no gaping hole as he'd known the wormhole before, but a massive stone disc set into the canyon wall, the greatest part of it hanging in midair.

Rhayne, Kael, and the High Priestess were behind him and Aval-lyn. They ascended the last level to the platform and were met with chaos, as priestesses and laity alike hastily erected defenses. The First Guard were pushing through from the Bridge of Knells to the weir—and Corvus was with them. His presence behind the far gallery of buildings was unmistakable.

Morgan looked to the High Priestess, and the glance she returned confirmed his cognizance. The dark lord of Magh Dun was close, within the temple and moving toward his goal.

The platform was a hundred yards in diameter, its white stone lightly veined in shades of lavender and pearl gray. A starburst of sapphire gemstone outlined with a band of gold had been inset between the Dragon Hearts, the top of it nearly covered with concentric piles of chrystaalt, a world's fortune of it. That sight more than anything sent home a very prosaic fact for Morgan: Tamisk, Palinor, all the people of the White Palace, Sha-shakrieg and Ilmarryn alike, and all the death-witch priestesses of the Waste were spending a bloody fortune to send him back in time. A billion marks' worth of universal salt was laid out on the platform, and the worms would take it all, every grain.

Dozens of white-clad priestesses were filing between the Dragon Hearts, their steps carefully skirting the midnight blue star inlay, each of them taking the striking hammers and hitting the gongs in turn, each adding a small stream of chrystaalt to the platform as they passed. Their chant rose and fell with the rising of the wind through the canyon, a humming undercurrent to the sounds of war gathering strength in the halls of Claerwen.

On either side of the gongs, the towers were alight with shooting flames, great gushing projections of fire escaping through the gaping jaws and golden teeth of the bone-and-stone dragons. Above them, the sky had grown dark, a great vault of night. Clouds were rolling in all along the horizon, encircling the canyon walls and obliterating the stars. Naught but a pale orb of light remained of the moon.

'Twas a night for fierce and dangerous magic, for mysteries to be revealed. Perhaps a night for death.

Morgan tightened his hold on Avallyn and pulled her aside from the stream of soldiers taking their places behind the defensive walls, ready for the Warmonger's final attack. He'd run out of time.

"You are like breath to me," he said, and still the words were inadequate to describe the way she made him feel.

"And you for me, Morgan," she answered, her face shining bright in the light of the dragon flames.

"I'm not ready for what happens next," he confessed.

"I'm frightened too," she said, and he could see the truth of it in her eyes. "But we are here, and we have each other. We have only to wait for the time worms to come."

"No," he said. "We're not going to have each other."

All expression drained from her face, leaving it curiously flat-looking. "What do you mean?"

"You're not going. I'm taking the Warmonger in your place, if I have to grab him around what's left of his throat and drag him into the worm myself. The High Priestess will not sacrifice you to Corvus."

A spark of life lit her eyes, but he couldn't tell if it was relief or something else.

"No, she won't," Avallyn agreed, her voice tight. "Because I would never allow myself to be sacrificed. What I choose as duty is mine by right of birth, the chance to go through the weir with you. A choice, Morgan, not a sacrifice."

Not relief, then, but the argument he expected.

"I'm making a different choice for you," he said bluntly, and that was the end of it.

"The choice is not yours to make, prince." Her eyes shone with a gray fierceness. "Do you not yet understand? Even if I could leave you, I wouldn't. You are mine. We are destined to die together, Morgan. Whether tonight or in a time long past is up to the gods to decide. Until they do, I will fight by your side." No compromise was offered.

Above the eastern rim of the canyon, a striated tracing of chain lightning caught his eye, flashing behind the clouds and making them glow. He stopped breathing for the space of a heartbeat and saw Avallyn glance toward the sky.

The worms.

Panic seeped into his veins. *Kyrie eleison*.

He forced himself to take a breath.

"You have a life here," he said, "something I can't guarantee in the past." 'Twas the truth, a simple enough fact to understand, but she failed to grasp it.

"I am always safer with you, no matter who or what we face. It has been written, Morgan. There is naught you or I can do to change what is known to be. Come." Her expression softened and she pulled him forward, toward the Dragon Hearts. "If you want, we can talk about this again in ten thousand years. For now, time awaits."

Her hand in his trembled. She'd seen the lightning as well as he, but to her there was no choice. As her next breath would come, so would the worms, and she would go with him, leaving this world and all she knew for another: his world.

Wales. Dare he hope that it would still be there, whole and waiting for him, all the meadows and fells and the snow-capped peaks of Yr Wyddfa?

The High Priestess signaled to two of the Sha-shakrieg Night Watchers. Rhayne and Kael had slipped to the back, letting Claerwen's crone have her day.

The chain lightning flashed again, the circle of it reaching out to the north and south, the farthest bolts stretching toward each other on the western horizon, wreathing the temple with their fiery grace. Morgan felt the heat of it race along his skin.

Avallyn met his gaze, her face pale.

He scanned the sky above them. The clouds were piling in thick and heavy, one atop another and obscuring the last hint of moonlight. There was naught left in the heavens except the dark surging masses of air and vapor and the bolts of lightning that streaked through them.

Morgan remembered lightning from the weir beneath Carn Merioneth, crackling and sizzling, the blue-white flash of it consuming him. *Christe eleison.*

Battering rams could be heard pounding against the eastern doors. If Corvus wanted the weir, he didn't dare use sonic blasts or any other explosion near the platform.

"The time has come," the High Priestess said, motioning them all forward.

Avallyn's hand was still in his, and Morgan knew it would stay there for the next ten thousand years. He was not letting go of her, not for an instant.

The High Priestess led the way to the middle of the platform. A priestess there handed her a golden chalice. Dragons were chased into the metal, one with emerald eyes, the other with ruby—Ddrei Glas and Ddrei Goch. Fire of topaz and diamonds rolled out of their mouths. Their bellies were softly lustrous with pearls. Chrysolite, jacinth, amber, and sapphire gems sparkled along the rim, banded below by a row of amethyst.

As soon as Morgan and Avallyn reached the star inlay, the crone held the chalice out for him to drink.

He swallowed a portion of the briny liquid, knowing immediately what it was, and the ancient priestess gave the chalice to Avallyn. The golden cup went back and forth twice more before 'twas drained of the chrystaalt potion. Palinor stepped forward to take the chalice away.

"Take care, daughter," she said, her hands encompassing Avallyn's on the golden cup. Her voice was steady, her gaze even more so.

"Aye, Mother."

Leaning forward, Palinor pressed a kiss to her daughter's cheek and whispered into her ear, "Return if you can, bringing your thief if you must."

Morgan doubted if anyone else had heard Palinor over the chanting, but he had heard the priestess's words and took them as a sort of blessing—even knowing he was probably being overly optimistic.

The High Priestess removed a small packet from the depths of her robes. The weir kit, Morgan supposed, and not much more than the promised map, judging by its size and thinness. It certainly wasn't big enough to be holding a juice-jacked carbo-bar. She gave the kit to Avallyn.

"Welcome, children of Arianrod, daughter of Don, Mother Goddess of us all, called Danu, Dana of the light, Domnu of darkness, she who has the earth as her womb and the sun as her heart," the High Priestess intoned. "She whose tides pull with the moon, whose limbs spread wide to hold the stars. We are all children of the one who came before. Listen, children, to your mother."

"*Domnu, Domnu, Domnu,*" the priestesses chanted, their voices rising and falling in song. "*A matria patro leandra, eso a prifarym, Dommmm-nu.*"

Morgan had heard the words before, deep in the caves of the Canolbarth, by the scrying pool. Then, as now, they were used to call the worms. Now, as then, he didn't doubt that they would do the job.

A fearsome roll of thunder rumbled overhead, accompanied by a crackling bolt of forked lightning. It seared a path across the sky and hit the canyon wall, sending shards of stone flying and a thousand fingers of fire skittering over the face of the rock. His pulse leapt.

"You are the Prince of Time," the High Priestess solemnly reminded him. "Take your place."

He turned to Avallyn. "Are you sure?" he asked her one more

time. "Corvus is going to break through any minute. I can still take him in your place."

She shook her head, though her eyes were wide and frightened.

So it was written, so it would be, he thought, resigned to her choice and trying not to feel too damn grateful.

"Then remember I love you, and that you are safer with me than anywhere else in the galaxy."

At her nod, he pressed a soft kiss to her lips and led her through the piles of chrystaalt to the center of the star. The gemstone flickered beneath their feet, the firelight striking off its crystalline structure, revealing it to its depths. To Morgan's discomfiture, the gemstone ran all the way through the platform, making it seem as if they were standing over a dark hole open to the fathomless canyon, and looking disconcertingly like the wormhole he'd fallen into the last time he'd taken this trip.

The priestesses quickened the rhythm of their chant and their pace, their white robes flowing against each other like wings, swirling, ever swirling. The High Priestess approached them once more, a dragon statue in each hand, one a reddish gold, the one he'd stolen what seemed like a lifetime ago from Sonnpur-Dzon, the other paler with a bluish sheen. The crackle of lightning drowned out most of her words as she lifted the statues toward their respective towers, but Morgan heard something about begging the worms to accept the priestesses' offering.

A quick grin curved his mouth. She was working too hard. It didn't take nearly the effort the women were putting into the ceremony to get a worm to swallow you.

Show up.

Get swallowed.

'Twas as simple as that.

He looked again to the sky. The clouds were tumbling over each other, piling up in dark billows. It wouldn't be long now.

Avallyn stood with Morgan in the middle of the star, amidst a fortune in chrystaalt, and awaited her destiny. She'd imagined this moment a thousand times in her hundred and twenty-five years. She'd studied all aspects of the weir. She knew precisely when the worms would come. She knew that one of them, the largest and strongest, would be the conduit through which they passed.

She had not imagined Morgan ab Kynan as her prince. She'd not known enough of men to have imagined one she would love so fully with all her heart. She'd not imagined being frightened. It had always been the glorious adventure promised by the Red Book. Fear, she'd thought, wouldn't take hold of her until she faced Dharkkum.

She'd been wrong in that. Here she was, still in Claerwen, and the only thing holding her up was Morgan, his one arm around her, their other hands entwined and held close between their breasts. He was frightened, too, but he wasn't trembling like she was.

With a spoken command, the High Priestess set the Sha-shakrieg weavers to work, spinning a chrysalis for Avallyn and Morgan. They used golden *pryf* silk, the rarest kind, from the time worms themselves. One by one, the threads were thrown, each with a word of power first recited in the ancient, star-wrought desert of Deseillign: *bh'ismi'llah . . . ahl'el-ard . . . salema, hamdy, khothra.*

The threads did not touch Morgan and Avallyn, but circled in lazy, twisting spirals from their heads to their feet, intertwining, passing one through the other, shining like thin ropes of pure light.

Four lightning bolts hit the canyon walls in quick succession, creating a deafening crack of sound. For a moment afterward, all was quiet on the platform except for the chanting of the priestesses.

It wouldn't be long now.

Avallyn looked up to the dark sky and saw the clouds begin to roll back. They turned in upon themselves, tumbling backward, opening a hole into deep space. Stars shown in the opening, a dark sea of tranquil eternity lit with spots of light, the whole of it floating in the midst of the lightning's ring of chaos.

"Morgan." She bade him look up and see the path they would follow.

"Aye," he said, and she heard the soft confidence in his voice.

The threads spun and spun, around and around, drawing the two of them closer and closer together and farther and farther from the world. One of the stars above grew bigger, and brighter, and more golden with each passing breath.

A great crash of stone and timbers and the cries of a battle fully engaged announced the Warmonger's entrance onto the platform, but it seemed to be happening in another age. Avallyn looked once as the sound of her name ricocheted off the canyon walls in a raspy, anguished scream, and saw legions of soldiers and skraelings pouring out of a great rent in the eastern gallery. She saw the giant, Jons, and Ferrar break through the Warmonger's lines to the safety of the priestesses' wall—and she saw Corvus Gei, whirling and running in a strange forward motion toward her and Morgan, leaving a trail of destruction in his wake, his body half obscured by a veil of dark, twisting smoke, his mouth a gaping maw of pure blackness screaming her name.

He was too late . . . *late . . . late . . .*

Her gaze drifted back to the center of her world—Morgan. His eyes were as dark as the sky and filled with as many stars. Smiling, he lowered his mouth to hers, and she parted her lips to receive his kiss. Aye, he was the Prince of Time, and they were on their way to the stars.

In a blinding flash of golden light, they were gone.

In the year 1208 A.D., in Wydehaw Castle in South Wales, Mychael ab Arawn woke at his wife's startled gasp, instantly alert, his hand on the dagger he kept by the bed. Moonlight poured in through the window, pouring a milky river of light across the floor. He saw nothing, sensed nothing, and in truth it would take an exceedingly brave man or a totally deranged fool to attempt thievery or mayhem in the Hart Tower, especially with the lord in residence. Everyone knew the power wielded by the mages of the Hart and the Druid Door.

"Llynya?" He turned to the woman by his side. Wide eyes stared up at him, unreadable in the darkness, but he felt her fear, could almost hear the pounding of her heart.

"Oh, Mychael." She covered her face with her hands and rolled closer to him.

"What is it, love? Tell me." He helped her to a sitting position and drew her securely into his embrace. She'd made a man of him a long time ago, and he knew the comfort she would take from the warmth of his body, from his strength and the solid beating of his heart.

"Morgan." The name was a pained sigh, breathed against his chest. Morgan.

There was only one, Morgan ab Kynan, his cousin. Morgan had been lost in the weir ten years ago, during the battle for Balor. He'd been under Llynya's protection when Caradoc's blade had delivered its final blow, and the connection she shared with Morgan had caused her to suffer his fall through time—hours, sometimes days, when she, too, had felt the land and the sky slip away from her, moments when she'd found no purchase on earth, but had been suspended in awful limbo.

"You can feel him falling again?" He kept his voice calm, though he wanted to curse. Morgan was the one pain he couldn't keep from her.

In all his studies, he had yet to discover what tied his wife to the Thief of Cardiff, what could have bound them in such a manner; and even though he'd long thought the ordeal behind them, he had searched for an answer. Now, more than ever, he wished he'd found one.

"Aye, but . . ." She took a deep breath, hesitating, as if unsure of what she felt. "But it's not so terrible this time. It startled me when I first felt it, but he's not afraid, Mychael. I think . . . I think he's coming home."

"It's been ten years," he said doubtfully, even as he prayed it was true. 'Twould help solve the mystery, to have his cousin right at hand. And Llynya's grief aside, Morgan had always been more of an adventurer than a scholar of esoteric sciences. Time travel could not have suited him overly well. For certes he'd had none of the necessary preparation when he'd fallen into the weir.

He glanced down and found Llynya giving him a look of wifely exasperation. 'Twas the weir they were talking about, a wormhole that snaked across time and space as if both were naught. Ten years or ten hundred years were the same in the weir. Her expression, though, did much to ease his fears for her. She couldn't be too frightened, if she was capable of exasperation.

"We should be there when he comes through," she said, her voice strengthening with conviction. "We should be there to meet him."

He brushed a long, silky lock of dark hair behind her faerie-like ear, dislodging half a dozen leaves with the gesture. Living with Llynya meant living with leaves, green leaves freshly budded in the spring, golden leaves to see her through autumn and the long winter. They all found a place in her hair, adorning her beauty with their own.

She was right, of course. If Morgan was coming through the weir, they should—and would—be there, and Madron. Aye, the druid woman should be at the gates of time for the arrival of any traveler. With Llynya not in danger, Mychael was able to feel the wonder of her news. Morgan was coming home. For ten years, he'd been somewhere on the other side of time, and he would have stories to tell.

"We'll leave for Carn Merioneth at first light," he said, allowing his gaze to drift to the curve of his wife's bare breast. He'd seen many wondrous sights in the weir, and had learned of magic and miracles in Nemeton's Hart Tower, but nothing compared to Llynya. She was so lovely by moonlight . . . by sunlight . . . in the deepest dark of night. After ten years, the smell and taste of her was part of him, his favorite part.

He glanced at the foot of the Hart's great bed, to the two tow-headed children sprawled in deepest slumber amidst their blankets, his and Llynya's five-year-old twins, Bran and Rhiannon. Two Merioneth hounds slept next to them, white levriers stretched out against the footboard. One tabby kitten lay in a curled-up pile next to Bran.

He'd never thought to have so much, to have his life be so full. He'd never thought to have love, the kind of love Llynya showered on him and the children. He'd never thought to have fair-haired babes to crawl into his lap and give him sticky sweet kisses. Yet through the grace of God he'd been given his deepest heart's desire, and every day he offered his thanks from his most pagan heart to the most Christian God he'd loved and followed in his youth.

Aye, the prayers of childhood were still the path he took into the mysteries, and his love for Llynya was the path he took into his humanity. Given his dragonish proclivities, 'twas no small need he had of her.

"Can you sleep now?" he asked, knowing she'd been tired of late.

In answer, she stretched against him, lifting her mouth to his.

"Aye," she whispered against his lips. "If you'll love me, I'll slip back into dreams."

He answered with a kiss, bearing her back onto the bed. Loving her was a dream, otherworldly with the magic of her touch, the dream he'd slipped into the first time he'd ever kissed a woman—her. The dream had deepened and grown richer with every passing day of the last ten years, a dream that would blossom again with the new child she carried. 'Twas a girl, she'd told him, and this child, she thought, would have the ears of her Yr Is-ddwfn mother.

Chapter 24

Morgan awoke to the sound of water being poured, the smell of woodsmoke, and the certainty that Avallyn was still in his arms. Assured of her presence, he promptly drifted back into sleep, dreaming again of the weir—*an endless passageway through time, a cosmic serpent over a million miles long with the marks of its own teeth in its tail, its entrails entwined, circling, ever circling, ever spiraling, and a thousand thousand time worms snaking across the universe and beyond, to places even his dreams weren't allowed to go. The chrystaalt flowed into his cells, purifying every one, making them shine with the bioluminescence of the golden worm that carried them through the vortex. All was peace, and peace, and peace, and light.*

"We almost had him," Llynya said to Moira, the Quicken-tree healer with her in the south tower. "I thought for certes he would stay with us a bit longer the next time he woke, he and his lady." She looked to the woman sleeping by Morgan's side, marveling at her countenance and her wild hair. She'd had a map on her when she'd come through the weir, and it named her Avallyn Le Severn, Priestess of the Bones and the Princess of the White Palace.

Llynya knew the name. A man named Corvus Gei had once called Llynya "Avallyn" in a brambled glade in Riverwood, the forest outside Carn Merioneth's walls. He had not seemed pleased to think Avallyn was in the woods with him. Madron, the Arch Druidess of Merioneth, and Naas, an ancient Quicken-tree seer, had sent Corvus down the wormhole after he'd revealed himself to be a felon from the future. Now it seemed that deed had come home to roost.

"She's one of yours and Mychael's, without doubt," Moira said. "I only wonder from how far down the family tree."

"The resemblance is amazing," Llynya murmured, smoothing the woman's golden hair back off her face. She could have been Llynya's twin sister, if she had one, which she didn't. Without doubt she was Morgan's lover. Even in sleep, they breathed as one, curved toward each other, touching. Llynya often found them with their hands entwined.

"Yr Is-ddwfn blood runs true. Just look at her ears," Moira said. "She's an aetheling, like you, definitely of royal blood, definitely Starlight-born. I think the thief went a very long way to find her."

"I do too," Llynya murmured, taking the girl's hand in her own. "I do too."

She adjusted the blankets back on the pair, leaving the golden net of silk threads closest to their bodies. *En chrysalli,* Moira had said, but with silk from the time worms themselves. Llynya remembered when the Liosalfar warrior, Nia, had been bound *en chrysalli* and taken by the Sha-shakrieg to Deseillign. Nia had survived her dreadful descent into the deep dark, but it had taken her many years to recover.

As she tucked the blankets around Morgan, Llynya's fingers grazed his chest and the sign of the leaf marked on his skin. She knew every leaf she'd ever been given, and Morgan's was one of hers, or rather it had been. He must have taken it from her before he'd fallen into the weir. 'Twas what had bound them, Mychael believed. 'Twas what had saved him, Moira believed, being well versed in the sustaining powers of plants. For certes something had saved him. He'd had no chrystaalt before starting his journey across time, and the wounds he'd suffered had been mortal. The scars on his body defied survival, yet he had survived. In truth, Llynya thought she'd paid the smaller price of his fall, and if the rowan leaf had kept the magic of his life force alive, then she had not failed in her duty. In the end, she had guarded him well.

"*Pwr wa ladth. Pwr-rrr wa ladth,*" she sang to the two, hoping to bring them out of their sleep. Run deep. Run deep.

"*Fai quall a'lommm-arian.*" Wind through leaf, and stem, and root.

"*Es sho-leee-i par es cant.*" Flow like a river into the earth.

"*Pwr-rrr wa ladth.*" Run deep.

When next Morgan woke, 'twas to the crackling sound of a fire and the smell of food, something warm and savory.

He knew where he was. He knew exactly where he was: Carn Merioneth, Wales. He couldn't have missed this place in a million years, let alone a mere ten thousand. He could hear the sea and smell it, a briny tang in the air.

Beside him, Avallyn smelled green and warm. The firelight glimmered along her skin, turning it a rosy hue. He pressed a kiss to her brow, and she let out a soft sigh, shifting in her sleep to get closer to him.

A smile graced his mouth. She was safe. They'd made it.

Thus reassured, he let his gaze wander around the room.

The walls were curved and made of stone, definitely one of Carn Merioneth's towers. 'Twas night, and no lights shone through the narrow window or the open door.

In the past, he'd never known much history beyond his lineage. In the future, he'd been bombarded with it. Every comstation was a database of the world's comings and goings since before the emergence of life from the primordial ooze. There wasn't a comstation in the room, nor were there any lamps or power-source mechanics of any kind. They'd definitely gone back far enough to predate electricity, and Morgan had a feeling they'd gone back a good deal further.

With a slight turn of his head, he shifted his gaze to the fire. A man sat next to the hearth, dressed in a dark tunic with a dark cloak wrapped loosely around his shoulders. He had one booted foot resting on a stool, his knee bent. The other leg was drawn up on the chair, his elbow resting on his knee. 'Twas a position of limber gracefulness, but not of disregard. There was a watchfulness about the man as he stared into the fire, an aura of energy carefully leashed. His hair was pulled back and tied at his nape, golden blond hair shot through with silver and strands of white and one broad band of brightest copper. The blaze was braided in five pieces, a *fif* braid.

Morgan recognized him immediately. He was the image of his sister in masculine form, and he'd grown into a man since the last time Morgan had seen him. No boy bound by an oblate's vows, but a man rebirthed in fire. Morgan had watched the deed in Tamisk's pool.

"Mychael," he said, and the man turned. Pale gray eyes met his from across the room, steady and grave.

"You've awakened." Mychael rose to his feet, unfolding himself from the chair with a sorcerer's grace.

He strode across the tower room, moving with a subtle ease Morgan did not mistake for relaxation. A sense of alert awareness radiated off the tall figure.

"No, don't get up, not yet," he said when Morgan would have sat. "Let me attend to you first."

Mychael's examination was efficient, yet thorough, leaving little of Morgan unprodded.

"You still had traces of chrystaalt in your mouth when you arrived, and this netting wrapped around you." Mychael fingered the golden *pryf* silk. "You're both in fair trim, your humors remarkably balanced."

"How long ago did we come out of the weir?" Morgan asked, sitting up and accepting the tunic, shirt, and chausses Mychael offered. Only the slightest trace of dizziness affected him. Overall, he felt stronger than when he'd left Claerwen. For certes he was better rested. Those last days in the future had been hard won.

"Last night," Mychael answered. "We brought you up from the caves before dawn, and you've slept the day."

Morgan swore and looked over his shoulder at Avallyn, resting so peacefully in the lavender-scented bed. They'd lost a whole day.

"Can we wake her? Or do we have to wait for her to come around on her own?" he asked, turning back to Mychael. "When we left the future, people were dying. Their only hope lies in what we can do here, in this time. We dare not delay—"

"—In your journey to Kryscaven Crater." Mychael finished the sentence, withdrawing the weir kit from a pouch on his belt. "According to this, the Princess Avallyn is the key to your success."

"The map?" Morgan asked.

"And more." Mychael handed it over. "The runes of refuge are upon it, aye, and their purpose, and a plea for dragons." He didn't seem at all pleased about the last.

"Your old enemy has near destroyed the world," Morgan explained. "I've come back to vanquish Dharkkum and exile it from Earth. To that end, I need your help."

"I can't be Ddrei Goch for you, Morgan, no matter what is at stake." His expression turned grim.

"I saw you do it. I saw the last battle in a scrying pool in the future."

"To make the transformation again would destroy us both," Mychael said, "the red dragon and me. 'Twas exceedingly unpleasant the first time. A second time would be catastrophic and leave you one dragon short for your task, odds that would ensure your defeat."

"The first time was monstrous." A woman's voice broke into their conversation.

Morgan looked up and was washed through with a sense of déjà vu. 'Twas Llynya, the elfin maid of so many of his dreams, but a sprite no more. She'd matured, dignity having taken the place of exuberance. A calmer beauty suffused a face once lit by a fiery spirit. She was not so thin, so implike, but had blossomed into the full loveliness of womanhood. Seeing her again, he was struck once more by her and Avallyn's resemblance, but his heart knew the difference even more than his eyes. He'd been born for the desert maid.

"A second time is impossible," Llynya finished, walking farther into the room. Her clothes were elegant, a tunic and chausses as always, but of a material unlike any Morgan had seen before. All green and silver, it shimmered like rain sheeting down around her body. Her hair was full of leaves, the fresh green leaves of spring. They twined through her ebony braids in a verdant garland, with nary a twig in sight.

"You've lost your sticks," he said, coming to his feet, as did Mychael.

"Even sprites grow up, dear Morgan, and if you saw the battle, you saw much of that deed. Before that, it was losing you into the weir that aged me so." She glanced toward his chest, and he immediately understood. He'd lived with the mark too long to be unaware of it.

"I meant no harm."

"And little enough was done," she assured him. "Moira says the leaf was your sustenance and salvation. One small bit of green to nurture you through all the frozen years you spent in the weir. 'Twas a small price for me to pay to save the life of Stept Agah's heir."

"You knew?" Morgan asked, surprised.

"No." She shook her head, and leaves fluttered to the floor. "Not until you came back through the weir with the Magia Blade strapped to your back. Madron says it is *druaight,* an enchanted thing, and it has not been seen since Stept Agah wielded it himself. The Blade will have to do for you, Morgan, for 'tis true what Mychael says. He cannot become the red dragon again."

"Yet you will have my help," Mychael promised, "and of any and all in Carn Merioneth."

"Ahh," Llynya murmured, brushing past the two of them, her gaze on the bed. "Your princess stirs, Morgan. Mychael, will you send for Madron and Moira? I would be here myself when Princess Avallyn awakes."

She moved to the bed and rested her palm on Avallyn's brow, bending low to bestow a kiss.

"Can you hear me, Avallyn?" Llynya said softly. " 'Tis time to come nigh. Morgan awaits and all of the carn."

Avallyn heard her name and Morgan's, and she knew the lovely voice was right. 'Twas time to awake. The sleep had been long, an eternity turning in upon itself, over and over again, until this moment, when she should awake.

Yet there was peace to be had in the golden sleep of the time worms, and 'twas hard to let it go.

"Avallyn," another voice called to her, a voice she knew well, and there was no denying that voice, not Morgan's. They had shared the wondrous, lush sleep through time. Where he was, that was where she would be—and Morgan was in the land of the awakened.

As quickly as that, she opened her eyes, sleep having lost its appeal if Morgan was not there to share it.

Her first sight amazed her, for 'twas herself looking down at her—except her hair was lustrously dark, unmanageably long, and filled with leaves, all kinds of leaves in all shades of green, from soft grayish greens to greens so deep they appeared nearly blue. Her clothes were shimmering in hues of silver and green, like the depths of a fast-running, moss-filled stream, ethereally beautiful. The eyes that gazed down at her were the color of ancient forests, and Avallyn knew she was in the presence of an earth magic mage, a green woman.

"I am Llynya," the woman said, and Avallyn thought that she'd already known, before the woman had spoke.

"Llynya of the Oak and of Yr Is-ddfwn," Avallyn said. "Your name and Mychael ab Arawn's are forever engraved on the doors of the Court of the Ilmarryn. I am from your line."

Laughter rippled up and out of the lovely elf, laughter like tumbling water. "Oh, aye, fair child. Thou art mine, of that there is no doubt. But the time has come to wake—for you've slept the day away, and Morgan says there are no days, or even any hours to waste. The path is open to the deep dark, and if you would save the world you left behind, it is there you must go posthaste."

Aye, Avallyn thought, turning to Morgan. 'Twas to the deep dark they must go, and quickly. The urgency of the task pulsed through her awakened veins, and when she looked at Morgan, she saw the same need in his gaze. To the deep dark they must go . . . and quickly.

Deep in the earth beneath Carn Merioneth, past the Canolbarth and Llanbardein, past the *pryf* nest and beyond the shores of Mor Sarff, in a little-known cavern, a thin wisp of dark smoke wafted out of a forgotten wormhole, one of the small holes the worms had made when the great weir had been sealed. All the others had been subsumed back into the great weir when it had been opened, but one time worm had missed the call, and that worm had continued to burrow and swirl and keep its path open.

The smoke curled in upon itself and awoke to a strange, disconcerted consciousness. It had a form . . . somewhere.

Tugging and pulling, it finally managed to drag almost half a face and two-thirds of a hand out of the little yellow weir.

It was enough. It would have to be enough. The rest of him was all smoke—which wasn't right. He'd made the journey to redeem himself, to redeem the body the smoke was stealing from him.

And something else was wrong, terribly wrong. He smelled dragons.

By the powers of darkness, how could that be? How could he have been delivered into the hands of his enemies? He'd run himself into the ground to catch that last friggin' worm as it had lighted upon the rich pile of chrystaalt.

Why? he wondered, his attention distracted by a more intriguing thought.

To redeem his body, yes, but there had been another, even more compelling reason that played along the edge of his memory. If he'd stayed, he could have given himself over to the darkness and annihilated his most hated enemies, all of them, every last bloodless priestess, except for . . . except for . . .

The thought trailed off, incomplete, leaving him with only a nagging sense of its importance.

He glanced around with his eye, and his half-mouth curled in distaste. He'd been delivered into a hole, and there were dragons about. He could smell their sulfurous breath and their wet-serpent odor.

He needed to regroup, literally pull himself together and make his plans. He'd arrived in the past. It was time for him to begin undoing what had been done to him. For that he needed a safe place, which most certainly wasn't where he was, bound by dragons on one side and by . . . something else on the other.

A powerful something else. He sensed the swirling force of it, heard it calling to him through the deep earth, through miles of rock and dirt, calling to his dark, twisting self.

Of a sudden, he knew what it was: the friggin' crud that had birthed him. Now the vile filth wanted the rest of him, wanted his cheek, the last bit of his brow, his one good eye, and his hand—which, for all that it wasn't quite whole, still worked. He still had a thumb, by God. He was still of the higher order.

He had to escape.

Whirling around, he looked for a way out and found two openings in the rock. One led to water—and dragons, he feared. The other had a fresher scent and led to the north.

He took the northern route. Once on the surface he would find a place of power in which to hide himself and make his plans. He'd always been drawn to power, and power had always been drawn to him. He had always ruled and bent minions to his superior will. They would bend again.

Yes. Once on the surface, he would find a place of incredible power. It was there. Places of power were always there, waiting to be ruled by a strong hand—and, by God, he still had one.

Chapter 25

They traveled by Daur ship through the dark canyon of the Serpent Sea, their prow lit with dreamstone and the lanterns that hung from the yardarm. On a lonely shore where the sea turned inland, two Quicken-tree disembarked for *Bes,* the second rune of refuge. The healer Moira and a young Liosalfar named Pwyll were to make their way to the damson crystal shaft north of Crai Force, the cave where Stept Agah had been born, and where ten years earlier Mychael had seen a marker in the shifting shadows of the crystalline wall. The markers at each rune were the key to opening the hidden way to Kryscaven Crater.

Shortly after setting sail again, the sea began to churn, the chop rising with the wind blowing in from the west. Morgan stood at the rail and watched as great houndfish leaped close to the ship, cutting through schools of silver sandsmelt. Other fish could be seen farther out and all of them were racing deeper into Mor Sarff, pushed by the waves building behind them.

"The dragons will feed well today," Mychael said, coming to stand by his side.

Dragons, Morgan thought, looking back toward the ship's wake and balancing himself as the next wave broke aft. Of course, dragons. Naught could keep the beasts from the coming fight, and naught could save the houndfish and smelt they were herding toward the final shore.

As they sailed by the Dangoes, the captain ordered more lanterns lit, for 'twas here that Elixir, Dain's black hound, known as Conladrian among the elves, had last been seen. But no hound was there that day.

No ice music rang out from the frozen caverns, either. The melodies, he'd been told, drove men mad and sent them to their deaths. No icy fingers crawled forth to pluck at the living, thank the gods, but the smell of the frozen dead seeped out of the cavern, even, Avallyn said, as it did in her time. So cold, the rot suspended in time.

In silence, they floated by the huge pillars of blue-green ice and cliffs thick with the frozen wash of waves. Even without the music, Morgan felt the eeriness of the place. 'Twas where Rhayne had passed so many years in transition, frozen in her tomb as the White Bitch. 'Twas not a place for the living to stay overlong.

The Daur captain dropped anchor close to the opposite shore and had the company ferried to a narrow shingle beach. Besides Morgan, Avallyn, and Mychael, three more had come along: Madron, the druidess witch he'd known in Wroneu Wood near Wydehaw Castle, and two Liosalfar warriors, Trig, a captain, and Math. Llynya had been left behind, not so much because of her condition, but because if the worst came to pass in Kryscaven, the Quicken-tree would still have a leader. Of course, if the absolute worst came to pass, there wouldn't be any Quicken-tree to lead, or anyplace to lead them, a possibility Morgan couldn't completely shake off and ignore.

The cliff face of the Magia Wall rose from the beach, streaked with great, sweeping scorch marks. Inside their blackened borders, the rock was stained in a rainbow arc of color. Other flash marks lower down were edged in vermilion.

"Vermilion is the color of Ailfinn's magic," Mychael said, walking over and placing his hand on the lower burns. "The Lost Five had all been together in Rastaban, and she brought them to Kryscaven Crater by this route. The other marks"—he pointed up at a large scorch—"were made by Ddrei Goch. You'll see Ddrei Glas's marks farther into the tunnel that leads to *Ceiul*."

Their destination, Morgan thought, the last rune of refuge, where Trig and Math would stay and wait for them.

In the Dragon's Mouth, by the first rune of refuge, *Ammon,* an old woman named Naas and another Liosalfar called Nia were waiting.

Naas was the most ancient living creature Morgan had ever seen. She surpassed even the High Priestess of Claerwen in age. He couldn't begin to guess how many years Naas had walked the planet, but certainly enough to have come by a fierce sweetgrass habit. She chewed a variety called *kel* and was never without a thick wad tucked into her cheek. Besides chewing, spitting, and chanting at all hours, her most important task was to bring down the great wall of Carn Merioneth and return the land to its pristine state. Neither Morgan nor Avallyn had the heart to tell the old white-eyed woman that the Ilmarryn had dug it all up and rebuilt it as best they could, but Avallyn had spared her nothing in the telling of Corvus Gei's future and the destruction he had wrought upon his return there.

"Nothing is without purpose, child. The past is always clearer than the future," had been Naas's gravel-voiced reply, before she'd gone off to tend the coals in her brazier.

Standing in the small company on the beach, Morgan looked up at the cliff and the marks blasted all along its face. He remembered the battle in Tamisk's pool, the fierceness of the beasts, the raging fire of their breath, and he had to wonder at the price of success, if the six of them had a chance in hell.

Trig, the Liosalfar captain, was wondering as well. He remembered all too clearly the last time he'd stepped upon this nether shore. After the battle with Dharkkum, he and his soldiers had searched the caves for days, looking for Mychael and Llynya, and for Rhuddlan and his company, fearful they would find naught, and even more fearful they would find something unbelievably monstrous.

They'd all seen the druid boy shape-shift on the beach of the gates of time, had seen him devoured by Ddrei Goch's flames and transformed into the beast. In all his many years, including the Thousand Years War and the Wars of Enchantment, Trig had never seen a stranger deed.

Hundreds upon hundreds of Light-elves had died in the caverns beneath Carn Merioneth during the Dharkkum battle, leaving the Kings Wood and Red Leaf tribes decimated. Half the Daur had been killed, with the Quicken-tree, Wydden, and Ebiurrane faring little better.

So much had been lost, and now these two, Morgan ab Kynan and

Avallyn Le Severn, had come from the future and said they must relive the annihilation.

Trig doubted if they could—yet he'd come with them to do his part. He was a warrior by nature as well as fact. In all his long life he'd fought when the time had come to fight, and always he'd fought by the elf king's side, Rhuddlan of the Quicken-tree, until Rhuddlan had been lost.

But the man Morgan said he and Avallyn had seen him, seen the elf king in the scrying pool of a mage in the future, and because they'd seen him, they'd traveled through time to save the Lost Five and Ailfinn's book.

'Twas always a damned book, Trig thought. They'd been naught but trouble in all the wars, and the cause of many, if not most, of those wars. The books were power to those who held them. Seven Books of Lore they were, but Trig had long ago begun calling them the Seven Books of War. Nemeton himself had struggled to find and hold on to the books. Now Morgan and Avallyn said the books were to be their salvation from Dharkkum, from ever having to deal with the darkness again. Nemeton's bargain, the princess had called it, and Trig had certainly lived long enough to recognize the powerful Arch Druid's fine hand in their undertaking.

He looked up at the cliffs and the marks burned into the stone. 'Twas here they'd found Mychael and Llynya ten years ago, on this very beach. The boy no longer a dragon, but back in his own form. Both of them scorched and beaten, their clothes in shreds.

A year after the battle, Mychael had come to Trig and, finally, the whole tale of those dark days when they'd fought so fiercely had been told. Mychael had spoken of dragons, of what 'twas like to feel the beast's heart beating as his own, to feel flames churn into being in his gut and have them sear a path out his throat; the sensation of flight, lifting off with the strength of great leathery wings—and the fury, the never-ending fury of a dragon's battle-force rage.

And he'd told Trig what had happened to his king, how Ailfinn had led her company into Kryscaven Crater and called for Dharkkum, how the darkness had followed her and the dragons had pursued. The Prydion Mage had sealed herself and four others inside the crater with the enemy, an eternal living death their reward for leashing Dharkkum.

The memories had been hard-won, Mychael had said, dragging

up visions that he'd seen through dragon eyes. Llynya had made it no farther than the beach, where she'd collapsed, so she'd not seen the sealing of the crater. Mychael wished he'd never remembered, for 'twas a haunting vision. There had been fear, stark, raving fear on the faces of men he knew to be among the world's most courageous.

They'd deserved better, Trig had thought, his jaw locked in anger by the time Mychael had finished. Rhuddlan, and Wei, and the Welshman, Owain, even the damned Sha-shakrieg, Varga of the Iron Dunes, had deserved better.

So Trig had come with Morgan to free the four, and the friggin' mage be damned. Mages were ne'er but trouble, as were their damned books. Always, they sacrificed good fighters for a common good only they could see with their damned scrying and divinations.

"How long until the dragons come?" he heard Avallyn ask Madron.

"Soon enough," the druidess replied. "Naas has called them, and with the Magia Blade, Morgan will set them to their task."

Their task. Trig grunted. Their task was daunting: to break the seal and hold Dharkkum at bay, while freeing lost souls and retrieving the *Elhion Bhaas Le*.

'Twould then be up to Morgan and Avallyn to finish with the damned book—or for Dharkkum to finish with them all.

The trail to *Ceiul* led them deeper and deeper into the earth along a twisting path through stone tunnels scored and melted by the dragons' fiery breath. Trig and Math were to stay in the rune cavern and not enter Kryscaven. For himself, Morgan didn't see a whole hell of a lot of difference between being at ground zero and being a cavern away. Everyone was in danger.

They ate on the march, sharing gourds of catkins' dew and seedcakes laced with lavender, Llynya's recipe especially concocted to lighten the weight of traveling through the deep dark. Once he got used to the never-ending darkness again, to having their way lit only by dreamstone, Morgan didn't find the journey too different from the time he'd spent in the Light Caves and the upper caverns. Trig, Mychael, and Math had all been beyond the Magia Wall before, and were hardened to the darkness. Avallyn, for certes, had been in far less hospitable environments. 'Twas only Madron who worried Morgan. For all her knowledge of earth and magic, the druid woman had never been so deep, and her anxiety was palpable.

Proving her unsteadiness, Madron stumbled on a smooth section of the trail. With a quick move, Morgan was able to catch her before she fell.

"Thank you," she murmured, straightening herself back up. She was still a beautiful woman, her auburn hair neatly coiled at her nape, her eyes as green as any Quicken-tree's. She had a daughter, he remembered, a mute lass named Edmee. Dain had told him that Rhuddlan was the girl's father—which for Morgan explained why the woman was so determined to make the march. Mychael had revealed an even more compelling reason for the druidess to ignore her fears. She was Nemeton's daughter.

Somehow, that news had heartened him. Not that the daughter appeared to have the depth of powers Nemeton had wielded, but because Morgan thought it fitting that someone close to the ancient, time-traveling mage would bear witness to the fulfillment of the bargain he'd made. That Madron was a blood relative only made her presence more fitting in Morgan's mind.

"I remember your daughter from Wydehaw and during the battle for Balor. I pray she's well," he said. The conversation was only slightly idle. He did hope for Edmee's well-being, and he hoped to manage a bit more well-being for Edmee's mother by distracting her from the dark all around them.

"Aye. She married an Ebiurrane pony-master, Tabor Shortshanks, and lives in the north. They have three babes and another on the way."

It all sounded good to Morgan. He looked ahead to where Avallyn strode along with the grizzled Quicken-tree captain, Trig. If he and Avallyn lived long enough to have children, Morgan would count himself blessed indeed.

Trig was another one he remembered from the battle for Balor. He'd been Rhuddlan's captain and was still captain of the Liosalfar, though he and Mychael seemed to share the authority of leadership.

"Four children should keep her out of trouble," he replied to Madron, then instantly regretted the words, realizing what he'd said.

The curious look the druidess gave him proved he'd been imprudent, for the kind of trouble Edmee had been wont to get into with Dain Lavrans was not the kind a girl shared with her mother.

"*Ceiul* ahead," Mychael called back from the front of their line, saving Morgan from any explanation.

Avallyn knew where the rune marker was, the information being far more accessible in the future than it had been in the past, and she led them to it without any hesitation or wandering.

'Twas there, standing in front of the long, rectangular marker, that Morgan felt the full weight of the feat they must achieve. Succeed or perish was their creed, and looking around the cavern, Morgan couldn't help but feel that they were too few to manage success.

Trig stood by, ready to slide the crystal hilt of his dreamstone dagger into the top of the notches keyed into the marker by the long-ago Prydion Magi. Madron had pulled four pouches from her belt and was lighting a sanctifying fire to bless them and act as a beacon, though retreat was an unlikely occurrence, being as good as death.

No, once they started forth, there would be no turning back.

Math had taken his place by Trig, a guardian of *Ceiul*. Avallyn knew her place was with Morgan, and she stayed close, her dagger drawn and ready.

Mychael was the most enigmatic of them all, his face giving away nothing. It had been ten years since he'd been the dragon, and though he'd had dealings with them since, not since the last battle with Dharkkum had they been seen in war.

Morgan pulled the Magia Blade up out of its scabbard and hoped to hell he was ready, for the time had come. He nodded to Trig, and the Quicken-tree captain slipped his dagger's hilt into the marker's lock.

Naught happened at first, and Morgan wondered if Naas and Moira had failed to secure the other two runes. Then the dreamstone hilt lit with a flash of pure blue light. Like a laser, the light cut across the cavern to the far wall, and the dagger began to move, sliding down through the notches one small increment at a time. Each move was exaggerated on the opposite wall, carving lines two feet high. The first rune revealed was *Ammon*.

No one doubted that the way to Kryscaven would be opened when the dagger reached the bottom of the marker: only the manner of the revelation and what awaited them on the other side was unknown. All six had weapons at the ready. Dreamstone blades were kept warm and glowing in both steady and unsteady hands.

The light from the marker dagger blazed in a single tight beam, incising the remaining two runes on the cavern's far wall, scoring them into the rock. Sparks flew in every direction, smoke wafted off the burning stone, until the three runes were complete. Then the light went out and the noise stopped—and within seconds, the whole wall sloughed away into a pile on the floor, almost more mirage than earth and stone.

Clouds of dust and ash billowed into the air, yet behind the pile, off in the distance, Kryscaven Crater could be seen, its amethystine wall soaring up into the shadowy darkness of an immense, domed chamber.

"Prydion magic," Mychael said, drawing a leaf-bladed sword from the sheath on his belt. He nodded toward Kryscaven. "We'd best get there before Ddrei Goch and Ddrei Glas, or there'll be nothing left when we do. Even with your Magia sword, Morgan, you'll find them untamed beasts."

"Aye," Madron said. "Mychael is right. All will go better if we are in place before the dragons come." She turned to Trig. "Don't let the fire go out, Captain. We'll need it to find our way back."

"Ye know I'll be here," the Quicken-tree man replied, his face set with grim determination.

"Step lightly," Math said, wishing them an elfin Godspeed, his face no less grim.

Aye, and they'd need Godspeed to outlive Dharkkum, Morgan thought. At his signal the four set off by the light of their dreamstone daggers.

Chapter 26

Passing beneath the broken wall, they entered the domed chamber, its roof so high above them, it was lost in darkness. Morgan felt dwarfed by the towering hugeness of the cavern. 'Twas a mile from where they stood to the amethystine crystal wall that held their enemy and the purpose of their quest, the Lost Five and the Indigo Book.

The floor was littered with a fortune in broken crystals and opalescent veins of gemstone. They made their way carefully around the larger chunks of amethyst, Mychael in the lead. Morgan brought up the rear and tried not to worry overmuch about the dragons soon to catch up with them. He had the Magia Blade and a good idea of how to wield it to control the beasts. No one had taught him or told him. 'Twas something he *knew,* something he felt in the energy skittering along the runes marked on his skin, something he understood better with every pulse of his blood. Stept Agah had wielded the blade, and Stept Agah's blood was his, and as the ancient Douvan king had brought the creatures to heel, so would Morgan.

They walked on in a silence broken only by the crunch of crystal shards beneath their feet. The air in the vaulted chamber was remarkably fresh, not sea-tainted like the air in *Ceiul,* making Morgan think there might be an opening somewhere above them. If there was, he wondered how far away it was and how difficult it would be to access. Having more than one way out could only help.

About a hundred yards from the crater, he noticed something strange about the crystal seal over it. He said nothing, but his gut started tying itself into a knot. The others all stopped within the next few steps, and he knew they'd seen it as well: something moving behind the deep purple seal. Something big and dark, like a giant, writhing shadow.

"Dharkkum," Madron whispered, and the knot in Morgan's gut tightened.

He'd seen it on the comstation in Rabin-19, and he'd seen it racing toward him and Avallyn on the weir platform in Claerwen, admittedly with parts of the Warmonger still attached, and both times the sight had filled him with cold dread. But this . . . this pulsing, bulging, gargantuan tornado of destruction was beyond any plan they'd devised. That the amethyst seal held it at all was a miracle only a fool would tamper with.

And he was the friggin' fool. He ground out a curse between his teeth and thought that life lived as a drunken sot in Racht Square had not been completely devoid of pleasures. He'd had plenty with the wine, and if eventually he would have died from indulging in the Carillion concoction, well, the operative word was "eventually." As it stood, he gave himself about another half hour to live.

"This is insane," he said, loud enough to make sure everyone heard him. He wanted his stand made clear.

"It is written" was Madron's reply, her voice sounding stronger, as if in this most dangerous of places, she had finally found her purpose in braving the deep dark.

God's balls. They had a naked singularity off the cusp of a black hole from some far-flung star system, the weirdest mess of "no-laws physics" in the universe staring them in the face, and a pair of dragons— *dragons!*—coming up behind them ready to eat their lunch, and all Morgan had to control this circus with was a sword that had already damn near killed him.

He wanted Aja, and as desperately as he wanted the boy, he was twice as thankful Aja wasn't with him. He could die knowing he'd at least spared the boy this, and then he remembered where he'd left him and knew he hadn't spared Aja anything. Chances were that Claerwen hadn't survived the day he and Avallyn had spent sleeping off their journey in Carn Merioneth.

As for himself, he was trapped in a great hole in the earth with a druidess, a dragon-shape-shifter, and a faerie woman so beautiful and so much a part of his heart, he knew he couldn't be anyplace except by her side. He'd come a hell of a long way for a man who'd once warded himself against magic.

He swore again, a foul word that didn't begin to encompass his frustration.

Then, to make matters worse, the floor trembled beneath him. The dragons were upon them.

A quick glance proved that the others felt the shaking of the floor too, and all four of them had the same reaction—to break into a dead run. No one wanted to be caught in the middle of the chamber with fire-breathing dragons about.

Avallyn was at the crystal wall in seconds. *Tlas buen,* Madron had called her unusual quickness, elfin speed. Aja, Morgan remembered, was even faster.

Avallyn looked back from the wall and yelled, "Hurry!"

The darkness inside writhed, drawing her attention. In the next second, her hands went flat against the wall, her body stiffening. She'd seen the Lost Five, Morgan thought. Ten years in the grip of devouring darkness couldn't have left any of them in anything other than gruesome condition.

Behind him, Madron was gasping, and he could imagine how long it had been since the druidess had run for her life. Pivoting, he went back and grabbed her arm. Mychael must have had the same thought, for he'd backtracked as well, and between the two of them, they practically lifted Madron off the ground as they raced for the wall.

When they reached Avallyn and looked beyond the seal to the crater, Morgan was startled to see that the Lost Five were all whole, appearing frozen in time and no worse the wear for being trapped with the devouring scrouge of Earth. Their features were clear, their stances unyielding: Ailfinn, Rhuddlan, Wei, Varga, and Owain, all of them standing close to a stone ring alive with rainbow-colored flames.

"The fire still burns," Madron whispered breathlessly.

And the book was there, Morgan confirmed with grim satisfaction, held in Ailfinn's hands, just waiting for some stupid bastard with no sense of self-preservation to steal it out from under Dharkkum's nose.

He couldn't believe that bastard was him. Self-preservation had been his and Aja's holiest religion, and by God, they'd done well by it.

"Rhuddlan?" the druidess asked, looking deeper.

"They're all there, all five," Morgan assured her. "We'll—"

A trembling in the walls stopped him. Chunks of rock shook loose from up above them and tumbled down in a deadly rain, sending them flat against the wall for meager cover. The floor quaked beneath their feet, and all of them stumbled, trying to keep their footing. Far on the other side, for a moment, Morgan could still see the glow of the fire Trig and Math were tending. Then a blast of smoke and flames sweeping out of the tunnel from the Serpent Sea obliterated everything in *Ceiul* from view. The floor shook again, vibrating with the repercussion of something huge striding across it. Another cloud of smoke sparked through with fire was belched into the cavern and out into the giant domed chamber.

"*Sticks,*" Avallyn breathed, and Morgan agreed—friggin' sticks.

These were the dragons from Tamisk's pool, beasts in full blood and filled with fury, cauldron forces conjured for war. More flames backed by a ferocious roar poured into the chamber.

He tightened his grip on the Magia Blade, and the sky blue crystal lit with a violet flash at its core. Heat raced up his arm, the heat of power, raw and urgent.

An enraged shriek followed the roar—Ddrei Glas—and more smoke billowed into the chamber, smoke laced with greenish blue flames. Behind the veil of smoke came the dragons, Ddrei Goch's incarnadine hide flashing like the flames of hell, his scales sheened with seawater, Ddrei Glas a rippling Leviathan, her leathery green wings spread wide and ready to take to the air.

They roared again, and the fearsome flames licked at the crater's seal. Closer and closer they came, steam rising from their bodies to mix with the billowing smoke, the heat of their breath threatening to fry him where he stood. Their claws scraped and scrabbled over the boulders of broken crystal, the razor-sharp edges as naught to their inch-thick scales.

Once inside the dome, Ddrei Goch lifted his wings with a screech. Rivers of seawater ran off his forelimbs, draining onto the floor with the force of a cresting wave. It broke against the wall at their backs, soaking them all.

God's beasts, Morgan thought.

The dragons of Merioneth were likely to kill them long before they noticed Dharkkum. Destruction was their nature no less than it was their enemy's.

But they could be bent to his will, and he dare not wait any longer to force them to their knees.

"Ddreigiau!" he shouted above their cries, holding the Magia Blade high, determined to rule. To not rule meant death. *"Gorchmynnaf ichi ddyfod!"* Dragons, I bid you come.

He strode forth, distancing himself from the others in case Welsh was not the language of dragons.

It was.

Two great, scaled heads swung low in a deadly sweep, and two pairs of luminous yellow eyes locked onto him, singling him out from the others and making the hairs rise all along the nape of his neck. Flames shot forth from their mouths as step by step they moved closer, crushing crystal beneath their bony feet and scraping sparks off the floor with their claws.

Morgan felt Avallyn come behind him and lay her hand on the small of his back.

"Croesawaf," she whispered—welcome—and Ddrei Glas lifted her head and screeched, shooting more flames toward the unseen top of the vaulted dome.

Ddrei Goch lowered his head even more, the graceful rise of his neck arcing downward, his rigid crest throwing a shadow across half his face. He snorted, blowing smoke through his nostrils, and pinned Morgan with his shadowed golden eye. Deep orange streaks marked his iris, adding to the richness of the color. A pale lemon yellow hue spread outward from his black pupil, adding another layer of light, but in no way lessening the wildness of the gaze. The beast was primal, basely fierce, a fact forgotten at one's peril.

Morgan felt his scrutiny like the deep-scent presence of a Claerwen priestess, skilled, searching, and distinctly unnerving.

The red dragon's gaze narrowed, his knobby, scaled lid lowering to an intent angle, and Morgan's instincts went on full alert. The bastard thing was considering whether or not to fry him.

"No," he said softly, firmly, and brought the Magia Blade down on Ddrei Goch's bewhiskered snout. He pressed the sword into the dragon's skin, deliberately drawing blood. A small stream of it ran down the beast's scaled hide, shimmering in rainbow hues. The golden eye did not shift so much as an inch, yet there was a shift in the creature's awareness, a subtle flash of knowing that was echoed in the runes that marked his own skin. Ddrei Goch knew who he was, and like any wild beast, balked at being brought to heel. A master was easy enough to destroy, especially such a small master. One step of the red dragon's foot would crush him, one fiery breath or one whip of his long, serpentine tail would kill him.

"No," Morgan repeated.

Smoke issued forth from the beast on his next breath, and Morgan lifted the blade.

Released, Ddrei Goch jerked his head up with frightening speed and roared, a sound of pure dragonish fury.

Morgan held his ground, and his sword, and prayed he held the upper hand.

Ddrei Glas followed suit with a piercing cry, the cacophony from both beasts ricocheting off the chamber's walls and loosening more stones. Great wings were lifted and brought down with driving force, and a rushing wind pushed Morgan back toward the wall.

"Ddreigiau!" He lifted the Magia Blade with both hands tightly wrapped around the hilt. He squeezed with all his strength and light burst forth from the thick crystal rod, a sharp-edged flash with a heart of violet racing along the edge of the blade and streaking through the air to strike the crystal wall. Sparks and shards showered out from the collision.

With the first crack in the wall, the deed was done; their doom was sealed. A wisp of Dharkkum leaked out, the thinnest trailing of death spiraling upward. Another chip of crystal fell out of the wall below the wisp and the thin trail grew thicker, spiraled faster.

Ddrei Glas picked up the scent first and with an enraged scream took off after the black spiral, beating her wings against the clouds of dragon smoke and taking to the air. Ddrei Goch retaliated with a fierce blast of flame aimed at releasing more of his enemy—and thus the battle was truly engaged.

A maelstrom was born inside the domed chamber, fueled by wind and fire and the seawater whipped up from the floor. Mychael had been there once before, with dragons all around and Dharkkum corrupting the very air.

Crystal melted from the wall, flowing into pools that quickly cooled. Steam boiled up from the floor, making the chamber unbearably hot. Sweat poured down Morgan's body as dragonfire limned the crater and singed his clothes. They were all burned by stray sparks of dragonfire. The rainbow flames scored and melted crystal, scorched their boots and tunics, and left paths of burning heat on their skin. The wind grew stronger and hotter, filling up with the dragon's smoke. It beat at them and tore their clothes, and Morgan realized they were completely, amazingly outmatched. Chunks of crystal were picked up by the wind and smashed into the walls.

Avallyn let out a cry as a shard caught her in the thigh, slicing through her chausses to the skin beneath. Blood poured out of the wound.

They'd made a terrible mistake, Morgan thought, his deathlike grip on the Magia Blade welding his hands to the hilt. The four of them wouldn't survive the next five minutes, let alone accomplish what they'd set out to do. The Red Book of Doom had been wrong. No one should have opened the seal on Kryscaven Crater.

A great *boom!* sounded above them, and rocks showered down. *Boom!* The sound came again. *Boom!*

Dharkkum was pouring out of the hole in the wall, screaming past them not a hundred yards distant, a twisting, whirling mass of light-eating darkness. He'd called it mindless, and it was, but Morgan could only think that it had fought the dragons too many times not to know where its greatest threat lay. Ten years was as nothing, less than a nanosecond, compared to the eternity of the naked singularity from NGC 2300. To Dharkkum, this was the same fight it had fought when Mychael was the dragon, and it was chasing its enemy up to the vault.

Boom! Fire flashed and Morgan saw Ddrei Goch crash into the top of the dome. *Boom!* Tremors ran down the wall and quaked through the floor. A crack opened at their feet and snaked through the stone, snapping the floor into disjointed pieces. They were all rocked off balance. Madron slipped into the abyss with an anguished cry, and only Mychael's quick action saved her. He grabbed her arm as she went over the side and helped her scrabble back to safety.

Morgan was tossed off his feet by a sudden upheaval and sent crashing into the floor. *Sweet Gods!* Pain held him paralyzed, his leg near wrenched from its socket, his friggin' lame leg.

"Morgan!" Avallyn's cry brought him around.

A wisp of darkness had broken free of the mass, halting in the wind-driven maelstrom, one separate thread of stillness hovering in the air before them.

Fear stole Morgan's breath and got him to his feet, his sword in hand.

He pushed Avallyn aside and lashed out with the light of his sword, knowing all the death he and she would ever need was in that one hovering thread of smoke. The power of the blade surged through him, racing up the runes on his arms and freshening with every beat of his heart, uniting them as one. The thread, for all its thinness, had surprising strength, yet was no match for the Magia Blade. The two met with a clash and sizzle, and the thread was no more.

Hundreds more rose up out of the mass to take its place. One after the other, he cut them down, he and the sword moving as a single protective force, the crystal in the hilt blazing. Mychael, Madron, and Avallyn fought by his side, catching any misses with their dreamstone daggers. The four of them battled in deadly rhythm, slashing away at the threads that would have them.

As more of Dharkkum escaped the inner crater, more of Ailfinn's fire shone through, burning a rainbow path into the heart of Kryscaven. When it reached the broken seal, Mychael and Madron rushed into the breach.

"*Khardeeeen!*" Mychael cried, running toward the Lost Five, his sword at the ready. "*Asmen taline!*"

"*Khardeen!*" Avallyn echoed, following the two.

Morgan brought up the rear. Once past the amethyst wall, the brunt of the battle was behind them, with all of Dharkkum focused on the dragons in the cavern, rather than on the frail mortals in the crater.

Racing toward the fire, Morgan barely registered Rhuddlan, Owain, Wei, or Varga. They were no more than a blur in his peripheral vision, for 'twas Ailfinn who totally dominated the arena.

Dharkkum still flowed by, a river of darkness bound for the dragons, but she was radiant, her cloud of white hair shining and floating in an aureole about her head, her emerald eyes no less bright for having been in darkness for so many years.

"You!" She pointed a thin hand at Avallyn. "Do what must be done!"

Avallyn reached the fire, and the Prydion mage thrust the *Elhion Bhaas Le* into her hands.

"By the powers of light and darkness," Ailfinn intoned, her eyes growing fierce. "By the blood of the dragons and the breath of the worms, do not delay! *Ddrei Glas, gorchmynnaf ichi ddyfod!*"

Boom! Boom! Again a great crashing resounded in the chamber, with boulders the size of cottages falling from the dome. The cracks in the floor widened all around. The whole place was crumbling, breaking up.

The green dragon flew down into the crater, her eyes wild, streams of smoke drifting from between her jaws. She opened her mouth and screamed, her wings flapping, torn from her duty by a strong hand.

"Go!" Ailfinn shouted above the whirlwind, and Ddrei Glas took a step toward Avallyn.

Morgan leapt onto the dragon's back and reached a hand down for Avallyn, damned if he'd give the creature a chance to leave him behind. Avallyn no sooner made it to the beast's wing than Morgan felt a shift in the wind.

"To the Hart!" the mage shouted, her words already seeming to come from a long distance as everything began to blur around them.

He felt Ddrei Glas lift off, could feel the strength of her beating wings. He pulled Avallyn closer, securing her in front of him. Churning currents of smoke and fire and steam surrounded them with disorientating abandon, yet he knew they were flying up, and up, and up. White fire streaked past them to open the way, coming from Ddrei Goch, who flew on their left flank. To their right were the fathomless depths of Dharkkum, and above them was the night sky, showing through the gaping crack wrought in the dome by the beasts and the darkness.

Faster and faster Ddrei Glas flew, hurtling toward the field of stars beyond the open dome. They had no sooner breached the opening, when all sense of motion ceased. Between one wing beat and the next they were floating in silence . . . floating through time and space on the dragon's back.

Great Mother of all the time worms who had ever swirled in a weir, she was not without time-craft herself, especially when set to the task by a Prydion mage.

The full moon shone down on them from above, limning the dragon's wings and lighting a path through the darkness, and coursing ever so infinitesimally through the night. Time was on hold as the dragon flew. Leaping ten thousand years seemed crude in comparison to the delicacy required of such a brief passage. The stars reeled overhead and Wales slipped by below, both heaven and earth aligning them on the path from Carn Merioneth to Wydehaw Castle and the Hart Tower of the once mighty Nemeton.

Chapter 27

The spell was broken with a dragon's scream and a flapping of wings over the confluence of the rivers Wye and Llynfl. They'd reached the Hart in the midst of a storm. Thunder rolled, rain pelted down, and the protected, floating sensation gave way to the feel of powerful muscles working in flight, and wet, cold air rushing over them. Below, the lightning-lit walls and towers of Wydehaw Castle soared into view between breaks in the clouds.

Ddrei Glas let out a flaming screech to match the storm, her great, leathery wings catching an updraft and lifting them higher and higher, until she banked into a turn and began to descend at a frightful rate of speed.

Avallyn felt the effort it took for Morgan to hold on to the dragon, felt the muscles in his arms turn rockhard with the strain. She could hardly hold herself on to him and Ddrei Glas's back. But the worst was over. They'd escaped Kryscaven with the book. All that was left for them was to put it in place.

Ddrei Glas leveled off in her approach, and Avallyn looked down at herself, at the streaks of her own blood darkening her overtunic, at blistered skin and tattered cloth. During their traverse of Wales, she'd felt as if they'd been suspended in a comforting dark sea of the night sky, surrounded by an ocean of stars. That feeling had disappeared and all her hurts had returned. She'd been wrenched and pummeled in the crater, and now ached down to the marrow of her bones.

Ddrei Goch and Dharkkum had been left behind, but she feared not for long. The book she held in her arms was the key. They had to get it into the Hart, and into Nemeton's sphere, or all of those they'd left behind in Kryscaven would be destroyed, and mayhap all of those they'd left behind in Claerwen as well.

Lightning flashed again, a great bolt of it close by the castle walls. To the west, a tree went up in flames, a burning torch against the night-darkened land. Ddrei Glas slid down between the clouds and landed on the roof of the tower with another bloodcurdling screech.

Sweet Mother, she'd wake the dead.

Avallyn slid down and dropped onto the Hart's roof. Morgan dismounted behind her.

She heard his gasp and turned to help.

"Nay," he said, waving her off. "It will hold."

Ddrei Glas was no sooner free of their weight than she took off into the sky again, circling upward into the dark clouds of rain.

Morgan took Avallyn's hand, and after a quick glance around to orient himself, started off at a limping run. On either side of them were other towers, the castle's bulwarks against invasion, and as at Carn Merioneth, the forest was everywhere around the castle, wild and far-reaching, the nearest sand being far to the south on the shores of the Bristol Channel.

A sharp pain lanced up his leg with every stride he took, but he dared not stop. Kryscaven Crater had been collapsing in upon itself when they had left, and there was still Aja in the future, with the bone walls of Claerwen under attack by the Warmonger.

He remembered the Hart well, and he remembered the eyrie had been his least favorite room, even less favored than the sulfurous alchemy chamber on the ground floor. A premonition, perhaps? he wondered.

He found the trapdoor leading down from the roof, and they descended on well-worn stairs. 'Twas dreadfully dark inside the tower, and cloyingly close. Not what he'd expected in the elf maid's abode, but 'twas also a place of deep magic, and magic, Morgan had learned, always left a trace of itself behind.

Great changes had taken place in the tower since Dain Lavrans had held it. Llynya's oak had already pushed up through the eyrie's floor, and if 'twas possible, the place was full of even more apparatuses and paraphernalia.

Most importantly, Nemeton's armillary sphere was right where it was supposed to be, still holding its place in the middle of the tower.

Relief flooded through him.

"Thank the gods," Avallyn murmured beside him.

In answer, he squeezed her hand. Victory was so very close.

He went straight to the dreamstone-encrusted sphere and began searching through the rods for the eight stars of Draco. Avallyn did the same, both of them working by the glow of her dreamstone dagger. Its light caught on the pedestal's dreamstones, warming them to a luminous hue, and soon the area around the sphere was bathed in soft blue light. The rest of the eyrie remained cloaked in black shadows, the high curves of the ceiling seeming to defy the light.

Outside, the storm was building in force, with more and more lightning flashing across the sky, followed by deep, rolling thunder. 'Twas the kind of storm that struck terror in weak hearts and sent even the brave for cover—and it was coming from the north, where the caverns beneath Carn Merioneth were being torn asunder.

"*Llagor, Rastaban.*" He found and released the first orb, the eye of the dragon, and the sphere began to hum.

"*Llagor, Etamin.*" Avallyn found the second star.

The orbs had been made by Nemeton to float in the air, a floating key set to align subtle meridians and a broad band of particle waves. Tamisk had taught Morgan and Avallyn how to find the spiraling current of air that circled 'round the sphere and to set the orbs upon it.

"*Llagor, Grumium,*" Avallyn whispered, releasing the third star orb.

Morgan reached for the fourth.

"*Llagor, Rakis,*" he intoned, and the energy coming from the sphere rocketed to a higher plane, setting his hair on end. He'd expected the increase, but was still taken by surprise by its intensity. The pedestal's dreamstones brightened, drawing energy from the sphere.

He glanced at Avallyn. She was looking back, her eyes wide, her hair streaming out from her head like a charged halo.

"More potent," she shouted above the humming noise.

"Aye," he agreed, wondering what they could expect when the eighth orb was released. Her expression told him she was wondering the same thing, wondering and worrying.

He set himself back to the task of finding the remaining orbs, so focused on that, it was another moment before he realized the darkness in the tower was deepening despite the increase in dreamstone light, and that the cloying closeness of the place had taken on a wicked smell.

Corvus watched the pretty, pretty pair work their petty magic, and his mind seethed. He'd found his place of power. It had drawn him like a magnet the night he'd risen from the earth. All had been dark, except for one brilliant beacon of light in the south, a beacon he'd been too basely crude to find the last time he'd been in the past. In his new, highly refined state of existence, he'd seen the place for what it was, what it had always been—Nemeton's stronghold, the lost mage who had first traveled through time and returned with the tales of the cosmos, the man who had last written in the *Prydion Cal Le,* the Blue Book of the Magi.

The tower had been good to Corvus, restoring him somewhat, giving him a bit more form. He could count the fingers on his right hand again, and his vision had cleared out of his right eye. He had more of a right leg and could feel a pulse beating in the side of his neck. He had at last found his salvation. It was here in Nemeton's place, where the very stones were bathed in the redemptive force of the mage's power.

He'd been saved. Saved by his own cunning and quickness.

And what were they about down there with their little copper balls, setting them all afloat in the air? he wondered. And what would be the best way to kill them? he wondered even more—though whether to do it now or later was taking on equal importance. They'd released something in the armillary sphere, some kind of energy he felt flowing through him. To feel anything was a novelty; to feel a corporeal sense of power was grimly satisfying. Perhaps the pretty pair could hasten his salvation.

Best to let them finish then, he advised himself, wondering if it was a heartbeat he was beginning to hear in his chest.

He knew who they were. His memory had returned crystal clear, and with his memory all his hate had returned—and the painful horror of his disbelief when he'd seen Avallyn, *his* Avallyn, Princess of the White Palace and Priestess of the Bones, the most exalted and precious White Lady of Death from the northern dunes, when he'd seen her standing on the weir platform in Claerwen, seen her gaze *lovingly* at the man who would take her away, a time-rider with a white blaze streaking through his hair.

And not just any time-rider. He felt himself twist tighter into the crevices between stone and mortar at the very top of the tower wall. Not just any time-rider, but the tech-trash thief from Pan-shei.

She could have had an emperor, and she'd chosen a drunken thief, a ragged bastard who ran with a motley crew of other tech-trash renegades, a madman who had dared to steal from the Warmonger of the Waste.

For all these sins the man would die the most agonizing death Corvus could contrive, and the most agonizing death he could contrive included letting the thief watch Avallyn die first. To that end, he stirred himself from the wall.

She was still so beautiful. It was almost a pity to destroy her.

"*Avallynnnn.*" He breathed her name into the room with all the evil intent of his deepest longings.

Morgan froze at the sound, the last copper orb lifting off his fingertips. They were not alone in the tower.

"*Avallynnnn.*" The voice came again, nearer, the horror of it overriding even the fierce force crackling to sudden life off Nemeton's celestial sphere.

Morgan felt on fire with the sphere's energy, his skin crawling with it, yet he drew the Magia Blade and held it tight. He just wished he had a lasgun and a blast cannon—and a dragon. Only one person, if person he could be named, could call to her with such depravity: Corvus Gei. The Warmonger had been quick enough after all in Claerwen, and now he had them well and truly trapped. Even if they could make it out one of the doors, they dare not leave, not until the Indigo Book was set in place.

Avallyn backed closer to him, her dagger drawn, the book held tightly against her chest.

"Corvus," she shouted close to his ear, and there was fear in her voice.

"Aye." Morgan searched the room.

A drift of man of shadow tore away from the tower wall, and he countered with the blade, slicing through air and nothing else.

"You *fffool*." A black wisp snaked down from the ceiling and snagged his ankle. With a twist and jerk, he was slammed into the floor. "Do you think you can fight me?"

The breath knocked out of him, Morgan struggled to his feet, grateful he still had two. He knew what Corvus could do with his smoky darkness, and he could only wonder why the Warmonger hadn't taken part of him.

"Corvus!" he yelled over the growing noise of the storm and the sphere. "You have no place here. Be gone!"

"No *placcce?*" the Warmonger hissed. "You are the trespasser here, thief. This is *my* place."

The shadowy man shifted again, like a curtain rippling in the wind, and Morgan instinctively lashed out, the sword's cutting edge sliding through more nothing.

"*Fffool* indeed, if you think you can cut me with a steel edge." Another black tendril escaped from the wall and snapped like a whip across the room, catching Morgan in the chest, cutting through his tunic and slamming him back against the jagged pedestal.

Pain exploded in his head, and with a grunt, he fell in a heap at the base of the sphere. Lights danced behind his closed eyelids. His skull felt cracked, and there was definitely something warm and wet running down the back of his neck.

"Corvus!" he heard Avallyn cry through the haze of his agony, and he feared she'd be dead or worse before he could raise himself up.

"No," he croaked, forcing his eyes open to a narrow slit and seeing her standing in front of him, still whole. Her hair writhed like golden snakes around her head. Light from the sphere's dreamstones limned her body. Her shoulders were squared, her feet set apart, the dreamstone dagger balanced in her hand with a knife-fighter's skill. The crystal haft radiated pure light, green with a violet core.

The bastard was right, he thought, trying to focus on the light. He couldn't fight Corvus with steel. There wasn't enough of him to take a blade. Just as in Kryscaven, it took light to defeat darkness. Only the white light of the seven books could defeat Dharkkum and its spawn, the fiendish half-creature Corvus had become.

He had to get the chamber opened. Where were those friggin' orbs?

He looked up through Llynya's tree and almost passed out as pain stabbed up into his head, but the orbs were there, lazily circling the sphere, wandering on their spiral path as if they had all eternity to align themselves, deflecting subatomic particles and God knew what else. Tamisk had been condescendingly vague about the quantum physics of the whole friggin' operation, which hadn't bothered Morgan at all. He'd learned to be as good a lasgun technician as any tech-trash runner in Pan-shei, and he knew enough electronics to get himself killed in a second or less. But when mechanics crossed the line into physics, he was out of his league, and in the Hart he knew Nemeton had gone one step further, just as Tamisk had, and physics had crossed the line into metaphysics and magical conjurations.

Whatever the orbs had to do first, he just wished like hell they'd hurry up and do it and make their friggin' ring.

The shape of a man coalesced in the shadows curving off the tower's wall and glided toward Avallyn, or rather half the shape of a man, with a half a ghastly smile on his half face. The rest of him was shadow and smoke, an undulating darkness without true form.

"*Avvvallyn,*" Corvus crooned. There was threat in his tone, unde-niable threat, but also a thin thread of hope, and 'twas the hope that made Morgan's blood run cold.

Corvus wanted her, not just for vengeance, but in all the ways a man wanted a woman. Morgan had seen a lot of strange things in a lot of strange places, but nothing that churned his gut with more sick rage than what the Warmonger had just revealed.

He tightened his grip on the Magia Blade, squeezing the crystal haft, forgoing steel for light, and a flash burst from between his fingers with a cracking whine. The light skimmed the edge of the Warmonger's shadow, with most going awry and hitting a table next to the wall, shat-tering glass vessels and scorching wood.

Corvus reacted instantly, throwing another smoky thread around Morgan and jerking it. Morgan gasped as his body was pulled into the air, then released to crash back onto the floor. The Magia Blade flew out of his hand.

"A good trick, thief, but tricks will not save you," Corvus sneered, his voice clearer, less sibilant, his form becoming more distinct. "Did you really think you could take her from me?"

Morgan had not. He'd never once considered the Lord of Magh Dun as a rival, but as long as Corvus was talking, he wasn't attacking, so Morgan lied.

"Yes." The word came out a weak gasp. Wrapping his arm

around his chest, he tried to sit up. "You had your chance a long time ago." Blood flowed over his hand, warm and sticky where he held himself together.

He had to get his sword.

Morgan heard two of the orbs click into place overhead, starting the ring that would open the portal into the chamber.

The Warmonger laughed, a curiously empty sound—and Morgan realized 'twas because Corvus had no chest to hold the breath necessary for rich laughter. His next realization proved the last one to be fleeting. Even as he watched, Corvus's chest and hip were materializing out of the shadows, faintly at first, then with more substance, giving the man a whole right side, from the top of his dark-haired head to his booted foot.

"And it seems I'll have a second chance. Thanks to you and Nemeton's strange contraption." Corvus laughed again, the sound richer than before. He moved closer to the sphere. "Look."

Sweet Jesu. The energy from the armillary sphere was restoring shape to the Warmonger's left foot and part of his leg.

"Yes, it seems I'll have my chance, whereas you will have none."

Morgan glanced desperately around for the Magia Blade and saw where it had landed next to the tower wall, too far away for him to reach. He pushed himself to his feet, though every muscle rebelled at the pain, and took two steps before Corvus stopped him with a single gesture of his blackly ephemeral left hand, sending a thread of smoke snaking around his throat.

Morgan fell back to the floor, clutching at the strangling tendril. There was nothing to grasp, only the power of it tightening around his neck. He choked, praying that whatever purpose kept Corvus from disintegrating him would hold.

"Stop!" Corvus commanded when Avallyn would have raced to his side. "Stop, or I'll kill him."

As if he wasn't already killing him, Morgan thought, feeling faint. Above him, two more orbs clicked into place, but not nearly quick enough.

"What do you want for his release, Corvus?" Avallyn demanded.

"More." The half-smile came again. "More of this power you have conjured with the copper balls and the armillary sphere. It suits me, can't you see? My body is re-forming."

"Release him, then, for he is the Prince of Time, and the sphere is his, passed down to him from Nemeton," she said, her knife still held for a quick offense.

"You know of Nemeton?" There was a hint of surprise in the Warmonger's question.

The pressure lightened a bare degree, and Morgan dragged a deep breath into his lungs.

"Aye," she said, "and of the sphere."

No wind blew inside the tower, but the shadowy half of Corvus rippled and folded in upon itself, making a column of darkness next to its human half.

"Then give me more."

"And when you are whole?" she asked. "What then, Warmonger?"

"Then you shall be mine for all eternity," Corvus said as if 'twas a perfectly reasonable—nay, the perfectly desirable—end to it all.

Morgan thought not. Strengthened by a fresh influx of fear, he lunged for the Magia Blade, pushing himself up and diving across the floor. He rolled once and came up with the sword in his hands, blasting with light the smoky tendril that held him at the same time as he swung the cutting edge of the blade in a death stroke. If Corvus would have a body, then he would pay the price.

The blow landed true, eliciting an enraged howl from the Warmonger, for the sword had made him even less of a man than he'd been.

Corvus and his darkness retreated in the same terrifying manner as Morgan had seen Dharkkum do in Tamisk's pool: The creature imploded, drawing in on itself with whiplash speed; behind, on the floor, it had left its right arm, the fingers stretching out to grasp Avallyn's boot.

Morgan blasted the arm again with the Magia Blade's light.

Another enraged howl tore through the Hart.

"My aaarrrrmmmm," Corvus cried. *"My aaa-rrrrmmmm!"*

Morgan whirled on his feet, hearing the creature swing around the sphere to come at them from the other side. The speed and force of his motion created havoc in the Hart, whipping up everything that wasn't nailed down and flinging it into the air.

A rat was snatched up off the floor by a fistful of darkness, its body stretched thinner and thinner by the seething force of Corvus's ethereally black left hand.

"Deathhh-witch, see your fate." The rat was thrown aside with virulent force.

Morgan parried Corvus's next attack with the Magia Blade's light, his one edge against the darkness. Again and again the Warmonger came at them, striving to reach Avallyn, the whirlwind of his movements dragging Mychael's work table across the floor. Vials and jars were sucked up into Corvus's storm, smashing into walls and sending cutting shards slicing through the air.

Almost subconsciously, Morgan heard and felt more of the orbs coming together . . . *click* . . . *click* . . . *click.*

A wooden bench careened off the sphere, shattering a chunk of dreamstone. The tower had become a perilous place.

"Deathhh-witch," Corvus moaned, his rage twisting the words into black knots. *"I will haaaavve you."*

Morgan ducked the creature's next blow and rolled back onto his feet, crouched and ready. He looked for Avallyn, and his heart stopped. She'd been laid low, her body outstretched on the floor, her lifeblood running freely from a long gash on her head. Broken glass and the pieces of Mychael's alembic lay all around her. The Indigo Book was by her side, her fingers curled around it, holding it tight.

She was still alive.

The runes on his arms lit with the fires of his own towering fury, and like the dragons who would eat Dharkkum, he roared, a fearsome sound that echoed round and round the tower, telling the Warmonger he had met his doom.

Blinded with rage, Morgan went on the attack, his sword arm becoming one with the Magia Blade, his blood harkening back to a long-ago age, when Stept Agah had ruled and fought beyond death to claim the victory that had to be won.

He was an animal, his anger a primal driving force that knew no bounds of humanity. He was the Warmonger's death, and he was the death of Dharkkum.

Both ends of the blade were his to wield with killing force, the light to cut shadows, the steel to cut flesh—and cut he did, hacking Corvus's body to pieces even as it formed with the sphere's energy.

The Warmonger's maddened screams echoed throughout the eyrie, swearing retribution for every lost pound of flesh.

The storm outside was no less than the one inside. Booming peals of thunder shook the tower. Lightning ripped across the sky.

The last orb clicked into place, and the ring began to spin, opening the portal onto eternity.

"Avallyn!" Morgan cried. Her blood was everywhere, all down her face, all over the floor—and in one small vial inside the portal. He could see it and the crystal tunnel where it had to be placed.

He was the Prince of Time, her protector, the one man who could keep her alive, and he was failing.

"Avallyn!"

She didn't move.

The ring of orbs spun and spun. The portal awaited.

With another great roar, he doubled his efforts, beating Corvus back, deeper and deeper into the tower, his sword singing the Warmonger's death song.

He had only one chance to save her, one chance to save them all, Mychael and Aja, Llynya and Jons and Ferrar, Owain and Madron, all of them in this world and the world to be. One chance—and he took it.

With a final slashing strike and blasting stream of light, he laid Corvus low and ran for the sphere. Faster than he'd ever been, he grabbed the vial and shoved it home. The window of light opened, revealing the spinning chamber within.

There was no time to wait for the chamber to coast to a stop, a design flaw Morgan would have loved to take up with Nemeton. What in the hell had the mage been thinking? That Dharkkum would wait while his friggin' contraption ran down?

Instead, Morgan scooped the Indigo Book off the floor and took his chances, especially since he could see smoky threads of darkness snaking across the floor toward him. He waited a nanosecond, then two, and dared wait no more. Guided by faith and fate, he thrust the book inside the chamber.

A blinding flash of the purest white light burst into being, searing the inside of the tower and blasting beyond the walls. It had no texture and made no sound. Morgan couldn't smell it. The light was simply there, filling every atom of the Hart, and then it was gone, and so was Corvus—and so was Avallyn.

Stunned, Morgan could only stand there, his chest heaving, his mind refusing to believe what he saw.

She couldn't be gone.

She couldn't be.

Yet the place where she'd lain was empty.

The books glittered in front of him, all lined up in the radiant gradations of a rainbow, Seven Books of Lore sparkling and twinkling, every one of them shot through with luminous light. 'Twas like having all the gemstones in all the world polished and piled up to catch the sun's brightest rays—and all Morgan could see was death.

Her death.

He dropped to his knees, his body unable to bear the shock or hold the sorrow.

Avallyn. He couldn't breathe.

What had happened? Had one of Corvus's smoky threads reached her in the split second before he'd shoved the book home?

He tried to draw a breath, but his chest hurt so badly, he thought death had come for him as well. The pain doubled him over, but he didn't look away from the books. He would never look away from the books.

Time, he told himself. *There has to be a way.*

He'd been lost in time, floated through time, nearly died and been healed in time. His life had been restored in time.

He could pull the books out, rip them out of Nemeton's chamber, but would that stop time? Or reverse it?

Does Corvus have her? Will Corvus have her for all eternity, when she should have been mine?

A racking groan tore loose from his throat, a harsh sound utterly inhuman in its agony.

"*Avallyn!*" Her name was wrenched out of him, from the bottom of his soul.

He was going to die. The pain building inside him was ripping him apart. He would have died in her place, should have died in her place.

Where is she?

The NGC 2300 cluster of galaxies was Dharkkum's home, and Morgan was staring at the map that told how to get there—the books and the path of light they'd laid—if he only knew how to read it. He didn't know what happened to people who were sucked into a black hole. He knew the theories and had seen the awful thinning of their corporeal bodies, but the universe was full of unexpected things, and none more unexpected or more tenacious than life.

Anguished, he rose to his feet, forcing himself to stand. If he could help her at all, it wouldn't be on his knees. He needed a mage, one who could chart the courses of the stars and send him through time with the precision of a Lyran mark-tracker's nose.

Prince of Time? He'd be a friggin' Psilord of Time before he was through searching for her.

A noise at the top of the stairs had him spinning around, the Magia Blade again at the ready, its gridelin edge gleaming.

The noise came again, sounding almost human, and Morgan felt a flash of hope so intense, he had to shake it off before he could move.

He strode across the room, his heart pounding in his chest.

"Morr—"

He heard her voice and ran, taking the stairs two and three at a time. He found her huddled on the landing, her face deathly pale, her clothes in shreds. She was cut and bleeding, but she was alive.

He knelt and gathered her close, his pulse racing, his hands moving over her to prove she was real.

A deep sigh shuddered through her, and she turned deeper into his arms. Her hand grasped his shirt and tunic.

"He couldn't hold me," she said, her voice a weak rasp. "He had me, and when the light took him, he didn't have the power to hold me. There wasn't enough of him left to hold on to me."

Relief so pure it hurt stole the last of his strength, and he had to lean back against the wall to support himself while he cradled her in his arms. But he knew—with every beat of his heart he knew—that he was Stept Agah's son, rune-marked and dragon-tempered, and if the need was nigh, even now he could rise and slaughter Corvus all over again.

Chapter 28

Soren D'Arbois, the Baron of Wydehaw, stood on the threshold of the Hart Tower's Druid Door, quaking ever so slightly yet determined to see his way through, even if he had to tear the blasted door out with his teeth. There had been dragons in the night, dragons and a terrible storm. Trees had been pulled out by their roots in the woods. The River Wye had risen beyond its banks in a great wave and flooded half the demesne. Fish were flopping in his bailey.

His concern, though, what had sent him scurrying out from under his bed at the first light of dawn, was the Lady Llynya. She was with child again, and he'd not have her harmed. She and Mychael had left for Carn Merioneth over a fortnight past, but 'twasn't unusual for them to return without fanfare in the middle of the night.

And dragons. *God's balls.* If there were going to be dragons about, Soren wanted his *sorcier* home where he belonged. Even dragons, he was sure, would not discomfit Mychael ab Arawn. The man was a rock of self-assuredness, a rather aesthetic and sorcerish sort of rock, but solid to the core. Lord Mychael knew what he was about in the world, and probably—Soren crossed himself—in the Other World as well.

With a muttered prayer, Soren lifted his hand and knocked on the door, a weak sound, even to his own ears.

He couldn't swear to seeing a dragon himself, but half the night watch had seen *something,* and the closest description the seneschal had been able to get out of them had led Soren to think of dragons.

Soren was about to knock again, when a commotion outside drew his attention to the bailey. Stepping down two stairs, he looked out the arrow loop and his interest piqued. A man had ridden up on a horse, a white horse dappled in palest gray with a flowing white mane, a magnificent animal, the only more magnificent animal in the bailey being its rider. Llynya had introduced him once as Lord Shay of Liosalfar, but Soren had his doubts about the lord part. He'd never heard of a holding on either side of the March called Liosalfar.

He watched the man dismount in a single, fluid act of grace. Shay of Liosalfar was beautiful, aright, enough so to make dairymaids swoon and a man think twice—but only think. Soren's wilder days were behind him.

He turned back to the door, and soon enough heard the young man bounding up the stairs.

"Milord," Shay said, breathless, acknowledging him with a brief bow of his head, though his gaze strayed to the door.

Soren couldn't help but be grateful for his interest. Liosalfar was probably overrun with dragons, and he was more than willing to let experience lead the day.

"Lord Shay," he grumbled, hesitating less than usual over the title, though the man never seemed to notice. Llynya adored him, and Soren had oft wondered if that was more a part of his pique than he was comfortable admitting.

"May I?" Shay gestured at the door. He had green eyes the color of the forest at dawn, and dark, silky hair, and a face of artfully contrived perfection. He would have been pretty if he'd had even the faintest trace of effeminacy about him. He did not.

More's the pity, Soren thought.

"Proceed," he said, taking a few careful steps back.

The door was locked. The Druid Door was always locked, but Mychael had obviously taught Shay the key, for the young man did not hesitate in moving his hands over the metal rods set in zodiacal patterns in the panels.

In minutes they were in, with Soren deferring once again and letting Shay take the lead. The man seemed to know exactly where he was going. He crossed the northern solar in five running strides and went straight to another door, pushing it open and bounding up the stairs. Soren waited a bit before following, not wanting to walk into a dragon's gaping jaws, in case there was one lying in wait.

When he finally did dig up the courage to enter the eyrie, he found the place in shambles, all of Lord Mychael's alchemy apparatuses busted and tossed every which direction, burn marks scorched onto tables and even the walls. The Lady Llynya's oak tree seemed to be of a piece, but the rest of the eyrie was destroyed, except for a strange rock-and-rod contraption in the center of the room.

Soren avoided it. Something about it set him on edge.

Picking his way around the tower, he found more burn marks and broken glass, and one oddly long, thin dead rat. He heard voices, more than one, but not Llynya's, nor Mychael's, and so kept to a cautious rate. He wasn't yet so far from the door as to preclude escape.

Finally, there was nothing for it but to approach the group coming into view around the branches of Llynya's tree. A woman was speaking with Shay, and—*God's teeth*—she was wearing chausses and a tunic. Soren could see the whole shape of her thigh. She was lovely, with strangely short blond hair, ears like Llynya's, which Soren was always too polite to notice, and the face of an angel. If his heart hadn't already belonged to his wife, he would have lost it on the spot.

His gaze shifted to the man who had one arm around the angel, and his heart dipped into his stomach before lodging firmly in his throat. Here was a man he knew, and knew to be dead: a prince of Wales named Morgan ab Kynan, a minor prince to be sure—a minor dead prince who'd been great friends with Soren's previous *sorcier*, Dain Lavrans.

More than ever, Soren wished Mychael and Llynya were at home. If Wydehaw was going to be overrun with dragons and the risen dead, he was going to need more magic on his side.

"Er . . . uh . . . Lord Morgan," he mumbled in greeting, keeping his distance and trying to look as if he weren't. What with all the goings-on, a person couldn't be too careful, especially a lord whose responsibilities were quite nearly boundless. Aye, for the sake of every soul in Wydehaw, Soren would keep his distance.

Morgan looked up, confusion furrowing his brow, but only for a moment before a wide grin lit up his face.

"D'Arbois," he said. "Baron, 'tis good indeed to see you."

"And you," Soren lied as politeness dictated. In truth, the man looked like hell. He was bleeding and scraped up, and though he may have forgotten, he and Soren were enemies. Morgan ab Kynan was one of the rebellious Welsh. He had once stolen an earl of the realm from his bed inside Cardiff Castle and, by God, had held him hostage until a bit of Welsh land had been returned to its former owners. The stunt had earned the minor prince the sobriquet of "The Thief of Cardiff," and thus he'd been known throughout the March. None of the Marcher barons had forgotten that trick of his in Cardiff, and Soren could probably get a pretty penny for his head.

Morgan didn't miss the sudden gleam of avarice lighting the baron's eyes. The absurdity of it nearly unhinged him. He let out a short laugh, then another, and if laughing hadn't hurt so badly, shaking parts of him that were better left unshook, he might have dissolved into a full fit of it.

Sweet Christ. He'd just saved the whole friggin' world, and the Baron of Wydehaw wanted to turn him over to the king for a few gold marks.

"Shay," he said, ignoring the baron and looking to the Quickentree man. "Can you take us home?"

"Aye, Morgan, you and your lady."

Under Shay's subtle coaching, Soren came around enough to get them a cart. Then, on a seeming whim, he added blankets and wine, and before they left he returned with two kitchen maids laden with eight loaves of bread, two roasted chickens, a ham, a bushel basket of apples, and a round of cheese. At the last, catching them at the gate, he brought a velvet cloak for Avallyn, making it hard for Morgan to think too poorly of him.

Shay guided them home to Carn Merioneth through the mountains and valleys of Morgan's greatest longings. The air in Wales was fresher than anything the future had offered, cleaner and brighter, and it went to his head like wine.

With easy charm and a quick laugh, Shay regaled them with stories and songs, Soren's good food, and better company. Morgan spent a portion of each day fearing Avallyn was half infatuated with the younger man, and he spent each night loving her and making her his own.

Messengers were sent every day from Mychael, assuring them of no need for haste. All had survived in Kryscaven Crater, most none the worse for wear, even if not yet completely healed. Owain swore he wouldn't feel right until he saw Morgan. For Rhuddlan, the tonic he needed was Yr Is-ddwfn, and he and Madron were going to make the journey together. An old love that had never died was being given a second chance.

Trig and Math had taken a beating in *Ceiul,* having been washed up and dragged out to sea by the tumultuous entrance of Ddrei Goch and Ddrei Glas. Trig's biggest fear had been that the fire Madron had sanctified had gone out, and he'd spent a rough hour fighting his way back into the cavern—an act of bravery to be sung about for years—to stand on a shelf of rock with his dreamstone held high, so that there would be at least one light lit for the last rune of refuge. Naas and Nia had fared better in *Ammon.*

"Tell 'em barely a ripple wasn't felt in the Dragon's Mouth," Naas had informed Mychael's messenger. Nia had begged to differ, describing a wave forty feet high and a trembling of the entire cavern.

Moira and Pwyll had struggled a bit more in *Bes,* with the repercussions from the battle in Kryscaven near shaking the walls down around them. One thing everyone agreed on was the sudden end of the battle. One moment all had been in chaos, the whole world beginning to tremble—despite Naas's assertion—and then it had stopped, and it was over, for all time, forever. Not since the Age of Wonders had there been such peace on the land.

On the fifth day of their journey, the walls of Carn Merioneth rose before them. Dain and Ceridwen would be there, Shay had said. They'd already been on their way from Thule when Mychael had sent Shay after them. He'd caught them in southern Scotland. 'Twas how he'd been able to reach the Hart so quickly.

All of Carn Merioneth came out to greet them as they rode up to the castle. The portcullis had been strewn with early spring flowers. Garlands of greenery hung down either side of the gate. 'Twas like coming home and riding into paradise at the same time, with the Quicken-tree all around and songs in the air. A hearth fire had been set beneath a huge cauldron in the bailey, with mounds of food being prepared for the night's celebration, when Rhuddlan and Madron would bless the earth and all her people.

For Morgan, there was but one face he wanted to see, and with Avallyn by his side, he walked through the crowds searching for a man of easy grace and languid manner, who—long before Tamisk—had shown him the power of magic and the depths of selfless love.

They found him by the stables, watching Rhuddlan's mares run in the green grass with their new foals. Ceridwen and Kael were with him. The horses were either pure white or dappled gray. Many had braided manes and tails, for the Quicken-tree were ever ones to knot and braid and twist and do their best to tie the world together, and the children were ever ones to practice the art of brambling on any handy beast.

Ceridwen's mass of white-gold hair hung to her waist in rippling curls and tiny braids. Kael glanced over his shoulder as they approached, and Morgan could have sworn he saw a familiar awareness in the depths of the young boy's eyes, but his attention was more drawn to the boy's father. Dain's hand was on the boy's shoulder, a strong hand that more than once had pulled Morgan out of harm's way. His head came up as Morgan approached from the back, and then Morgan spoke his name.

"Dain."

His friend hesitated for a moment, then turned, all the years of practiced grace giving even his smallest movement a fluid ease. The intensity of his gaze had not lessened with the passage of time, and Morgan felt it move over him like a touch, cataloguing parts, checking for missing pieces and marks of pain, and finding at least one—the time-rider blaze in his hair that spoke of countless years and strange lands, a blaze that matched the one in Dain's hair.

His smile, when it came, was oh, so familiar, both wry and welcoming, and still so much older than his years.

"Morgan." He strode forward, his arms held wide, and in the embrace of Lavrans's friendship, Morgan knew he'd finally come back to where he'd started so many thousands of years ago.

Chapter 29

A light summer rain drifted down through the trees as Avallyn and Morgan made their way along a wooded track east of Wydehaw Castle. Wroneu Wood was in full bloom, with sweet woodruff scenting the air and ferns unfurled. When they reached the river, Morgan took her hand and led her along a narrow trail that wound behind the cascade of a thundering waterfall. Mist shot through with sunlight gathered in the spray, forming clouds of water and light.

On the other side of the falls, set deep in the heart of the woods, was the Quicken-tree camp of Deri, home of the mother oak, the object of Morgan's quest. A limestone cliff protected the camp on the west. To the north and east, the Quicken-tree had woven a tangle out of shrubs and bracken called The Bramble. The south was guarded by the river, leaving the water track as the only entrance.

'Twas a quiet place, especially in the heat of

midafternoon. Morgan and Avallyn had traveled south from Carn Meri-oneth after the summer solstice, and at Morgan's request, Llynya had given them directions to Deri.

" 'Tis a fair and beautiful place you've brought me, Morgan," Avallyn said.

"For you are a fair and beautiful woman." He stopped and leaned down for a kiss. After a moment of gently pressed lips, he opened his mouth wider and asked for more.

He always wanted more, and she always responded with a warmth that utterly enchanted him. Or mayhap ensorcelled was a truer word. When they kissed, he forgot all else in the world. His life became the feel of her lips, the taste of her mouth, the press of her body against his.

'Twas the simplest thing in the world to kiss her, and together they filled their lives with simple things, the ephemeral scent of violets, the taste of honeycakes, sunrises to greet the day, and nights of love to soothe the soul.

He lifted his head when the kiss ended and smoothed his fingers over her cheek. Her gaze held his as his hand tunneled into the silky length of her hair. A few leaves fell out, but she had extras to spare.

"Shall we spend the night?" he offered. "I have blankets and food in the pack."

"Aye," she said, a smile curving her mouth. She never grew tired of spending time with him in the forests of Wales. The wild forests, she called them, differentiating them from the Lost Forest of the Waste. From Riverwood to Wroneu, they had explored them all and would soon be traveling with Dain and Ceridwen to their home, journeying through the truly wild woods of the far north.

She could hardly wait. Morgan was more inclined to stay put until after their babe was born, but she'd convinced him otherwise.

They entered the glade, and Morgan shrugged out of his pack. A moment's worth of rummaging around was all it took for him to find the small packet he wanted.

The mother oak in Deri was five times the size of Llynya's Oak in the Hart. A small tribe could have lived in its branches. Its roots rose up out of the ground a good three feet in every direction. 'Twas the tree for which the term "mighty oak" had been coined.

In Tamisk's Hart, Morgan had listened to Llynya's tree, listened to the story of the mother oak of Deri, and of its own planting and all the years of its growing before the sands had come and buried it unto its death. 'Twas the history of the world from a very long view, a long enough view to have granted him some peace. For that tree, he'd brought with him through time a handful of acorns. For himself, he'd vowed to see them planted in Deri.

They ate supper around a small fire, and when the moon had risen, they lay down on their pile of blankets, holding each other and gazing at the stars. Avallyn knew many of the stars by name, whereas Morgan tended only to remember the major signposts in the galaxy and the bigger attractions in the Milky Way.

They'd come so far. He was content, more content than he'd ever been or ever hoped to be in his life . . . and yet, looking at all the millions of stars and knowing they weren't truly out of reach, well, it made for a bit of wanderlust.

"Do you think we'll ever go back?" Avallyn asked, snuggling closer to his warmth.

"Do you want to?"

"It's so beautiful here," she said, sounding ambivalent, "but I know there's so much more out there."

He did, too, and he couldn't quite get it out of his mind, just how much more was out there in the vastness of space.

"Well, if we could get the weir to work . . ." His voice trailed off.

"Mychael and Madron think the worms are already back in sync, moving through the continuum."

"And we'd need chrystaalt. I'm never going back through without chrystaalt." The difference between his first passage and his second had been amazing.

"Aye, we'd need chrystaalt," she agreed.

"And a way of figuring out how to get where we wanted to go, if we wanted to go anyplace other than Claerwen," he continued.

"Didn't you ever talk to Ferrar?" Avallyn asked. "From what you've told me, she and Jons went pretty much at will."

"Aye, they did, but for all those years in the future, saving mayhap my last two days, the weir was my least favorite topic of conversation." In fact, at the time, wild horses couldn't have dragged him into a wormhole, not for all the gold in the Middle Kingdom.

"I wonder where they are now. Probably not in Claerwen."

Morgan tended to agree. He couldn't imagine Ferrar spending too much time with the High Priestess without grabbing Jons and leaping into time.

"They're probably having the greatest adventure," Avallyn said, and Morgan thought he detected a switch in her voice from ambivalence to longing. Her next words proved it. "If we went, mayhap to the slave boy colony on Orion, we could have an adventure too."

That got his attention.

He rolled over on his side to better see her face and the little grin teasing her mouth.

"You've got all the slave boy you need, wench," he growled, leaning down to gently gnaw on her neck.

She giggled, and he relented. Pregnancy had made her delightfully ticklish. He kissed her mouth and pulled her back into his arms, settling deeper with her into the blankets to watch the night sky.

Saturn and Jupiter were in Aries, shining bright. Mars had already set, and Venus would not be seen again until next month. Above them, a shooting star arced across the vault of the heavens, a meteor trailing a glittering cloud of celestial dust. They watched until it disappeared against the ink black darkness of deep space.

"I made a wish for us," Avallyn whispered into the silence.

Morgan turned and pressed a kiss to her mouth.

"So did I," he said, and then he kissed her again.

Epilogue

"No offense, Ferrar, but that's the crikiest crap I ever tasted." Aja screwed his face up in disgust and handed her back the cup.

"Hush, Aja," Ferrar admonished him. "If it wasn't for you, we wouldn't be out here, freezing our fannies off and praying for worms."

Aja had to agree about the fanny part. It was friggin' cold on Claerwen's weir platform, but it wasn't all his fault that they'd gotten locked out of the temple. Ferrar had been at loggerheads with the High Priestess since she'd arrived at the great pile of bones. What had happened with Sachi in the cloisters had been next to naught. Aja had hardly kissed her and had certainly not had time to do anything else. He was quick, but he wasn't that quick. Nor did he want to be where kissing was concerned, a fact he'd tried to explain to the High Priestess, but the more he'd talked, the less she'd liked, until she'd practically exploded on him.

He'd been pretty fast at that point and ended up on the weir platform, exactly where he'd wanted to be, with Jons and Ferrar right behind him.

The temple complex was still pretty much intact, but there were rumors out in the Waste that some of the priestesses were more than a little upset by the damage the Warmonger had done to the north and east walls. They especially missed their bell tower, and the word in the dunes was that they were out for more bones to rebuild—anybody's bones.

After meeting the High Priestess, Aja didn't doubt it for a minute. Morgan had been lucky to get out of the place alive, and he had gotten out alive. Ferrar and Jons had seen the worms take him.

Of course, with Vishab dead and the Warmonger gone, bones were going to be at a premium. If Aja had been going to stay, which he wasn't, he'd be going into the bone business.

"Ferrar," Jons said, directing her attention to the sky.

Aja glanced up with her and saw clouds rolling in, lots of clouds.

"Here," she said, handing Jons the refilled cup.

He drank the stuff down like it was water, and it most definitely was not water. Ferrar had put chrystaalt in it to prepare them for the time worms.

As a concept, getting swallowed by a time worm left Aja feeling a little queasy. As a means to an end, though, he was willing to put up with queasiness.

He noticed Ferrar drank her share with the same ease as Jons. Mayhap it just took some getting used to. Next, Ferrar broke a juice-jacked carbo-bar—cherries and shampberries, Aja's favorite—into three pieces. He chewed up the portion she offered and watched the sky. The clouds had gotten darker, and he thought he saw lightning in the distance.

He took another bite, keeping his gaze to the east. Definitely lightning, he thought, seeing a big bolt of it light the clouds. The wind was picking up, chilling him a bit, and he wondered if it was going to be warm in thirteenth-century Wales.

Ferrar watched the boy, smiling. He was a handful, and a rare talent, but for all his talent he hadn't noticed the subtle shift in time that made the world they were in now different from the world they had been in just a moment past. Tufts of vegetation grew in the crevices of the cliff wall, sea campion and vetch. Above them, she could just make out the tops of the trees in Claerwen's apple orchard. 'Twas a place of orchards, the temples of bones shaded by their leafy crowns. Below them, a river ran through the canyon, washing toward the sea.

Jons had noticed the shift in time. He'd been with her too long not to notice.

It wasn't that the Waste was no longer a desert, or that an ocean now beat upon its eastern shore where before there had been none. For the people of Earth in the 6,247th year of the Trelawney Rebellion, the ocean had never disappeared, the desert had never existed. The wars had still happened, for war was a human endeavor. But the scourge of Dharkkum had been defeated in an age now long past, and the damage it had inflicted on Earth had never happened.

But Ferrar knew the difference. Every Prydion Psilord of Time would have felt the shift in the time-space continuum caused by Morgan ab Kynan's victory in the past.

Somewhere in space and time, Nemeton would have felt it too. "Sanctuary" he'd been called since the dawn of the Dark Age, and a sanctuary he had proven to be for all the children of the forested planet called Earth.